RANDOM HOUSE
LARGE PRINT

Pop
Goes the
Weasel

A NOVEL BY

JAMES
PATTERSON

RANDOM HOUSE
LARGE PRINT

A Division of Random House, Inc.
Published in Association with Warner Books
New York 2000

Copyright © 1999 by James Patterson
*First Large Print paperback edition
published October 2000*

All rights reserved under International and
Pan-American Copyright Conventions.
Published in the United States of America
by Random House Large Print
in association with Warner Books, New York
and simultaneously in Canada by
Random House of Canada Limited, Toronto.
Distributed by Random House, Inc., New York

Library of Congress Cataloging-in-Publication Data
Patterson, James 1947–
Pop goes the weasel / James Patterson.
p.   cm.
ISBN 0-375-72793-0
1. Large type books.   I. Title
{PS3566.A822P66   1999b}
813'.54—dc21   99-28491
CIP

Random House Web Address:
www.randomlargeprint.com

Printed in the United States of America

2 4 6 8 10 9 7 5 3 1

This Large Print Edition published in
accord with the standards of N.A.V.H.

This is for Suzie and Jack,
and for the millions of Alex Cross readers
who so frequently ask,
Can't you write faster?

Prologue

GEOFFREY SHAFER, dashingly outfitted in a single-breasted blue blazer, white shirt, striped tie, and narrow gray trousers from H. Huntsman & Sons, walked out of his town house at seven-thirty in the morning and climbed into a black Jaguar XJ12.

He backed the Jag slowly out of the driveway, then stepped on the accelerator. The sleek sports car rocketed up to fifty before it reached the stop sign at Connecticut Avenue, in the posh Kalorama section of Washington, D.C.

When Shafer reached the busy intersection, he didn't stop. He floored the accelerator, picking up more speed.

He was doing sixty-five and ached to crash the Jag into the stately fieldstone wall bordering the avenue. He aimed the Jag closer to the wall. He could see the head-on collision, visualize it, feel it all over.

At the last possible second, he tried to avoid the deadly crash. He spun the wheel hard to the left. The sports car fishtailed all the way across the avenue, tires screeching and burning, the smell of rubber thick in the air.

The Jag skidded to a stop, headed the wrong way on the street, the windshield issuing its glossy black stare at a barrage of early oncoming traffic.

Shafer stepped on the accelerator again and headed forward *against* the oncoming traffic. Every car and truck began to honk loud, sustained blasts.

Shafer didn't even try to catch his breath or bearings. He sped along the avenue, gaining speed. He zoomed across Rock Creek Bridge and made a left, then another left onto Rock Creek Parkway.

A tiny scream of pain escaped from his lips. It was involuntary, coming swiftly and unexpectedly. A moment of fear, weakness.

He floored the gas pedal again, and the engine roared. He was doing seventy, then pressing to eighty. He zigged and zagged around slower-moving sedans, sport-utility vehicles, a soot-covered A&P delivery truck.

Only a few honked now. Other drivers on the parkway were terrified, scared out of their minds.

He exited the Rock Creek Parkway at fifty miles an hour, then he gunned it again.

P Street was even more crowded at that hour than the parkway had been. Washington was just waking up and setting off to work. He could still *see* that inviting stone wall on Connecticut. He shouldn't have stopped. He began searching for another rock-solid object, looking for something to hit very hard.

He was doing eighty miles an hour as he approached Dupont Circle. He shot forward like a ground rocket. Two lines of traffic were backed up at a red light. No way out of this one, he thought. Nowhere to go left or right.

He didn't want to rear-end a dozen cars! That was no way to end this—end his life—by smashing into a commonplace Chevy Caprice, a Honda Accord, a delivery truck.

He swerved violently to the left and veered into the lanes of traffic coming east, coming right at him. He could see the panicked, disbelieving faces behind the dusty, grime-smeared windshields. The horns started to blast, a high-pitched symphony of fear.

He ran the next light and just barely squeezed between an oncoming Jeep and a concrete-mixer truck.

He sped down M Street, then onto Pennsylvania Avenue, and headed toward Washington Circle. The George Washington University Medical Center was up ahead—a perfect ending?

The Metro patrol car appeared out of nowhere, its siren-bullhorn screaming in protest, its rotating beacon glittering, signaling for him to pull over. Shafer slowed down and pulled to the curb.

The cop hurried to Shafer's car, his hand on his holster. He looked frightened and unsure.

"Get out of the car, sir," the cop said in a commanding voice. "Get out of the car right now."

Shafer suddenly felt calm and relaxed. There was no tension left in his body.

"All right. All right. I'm getting out. No problem."

"You know how fast you were going?" the cop asked in an agitated voice, his face flushed a bright red. Shafer noticed that the cop's hand was still on his gun.

Shafer pursed his lips, thought about his answer. "Well—I'd say about thirty, Officer," he finally said. "Maybe a little over the speed limit."

Then he took out an I.D. card and handed it over. "But you can't do anything about it. I'm with the British Embassy. I have *diplomatic immunity*."

THAT NIGHT, as he was driving home from work, Geoffrey Shafer started to feel that he was losing control again. He was beginning to frighten himself. His whole life had begun to revolve around a fantasy game he played called the Four Horsemen. In the game, he was the player called Death. The game was everything to him, the only part of his life with real meaning.

He sped across town from the British Embassy, all the way to the Petworth district of Northwest. He knew he shouldn't be there, a white man in a spiffy Jaguar. He couldn't help himself, though, any more than he could that morning.

He stopped the car just before he got to Petworth. Shafer took out his laptop and typed a message to the other players, the Horsemen.

Friends,
Death is on the loose in Washington. The game is on.

He started the Jag again and rode a few more blocks to Petworth. The usual outrageously provocative hookers were already parading up and down Varnum and Webster streets. A song called "Nice and Slow" was playing from a vibrating blue BMW. Ronnie McCall's sweet voice blended into the early evening.

The girls waved to him and showed their large, flat, pert, or flabby breasts. Several wore colorful bustiers with matching hot pants and shiny silver or red platform shoes with pointy heels.

He slowed to a stop beside a small black girl who looked to be around sixteen and had an unusually pretty face. Her legs were long and slender for such a petite body. She wore too much makeup for his taste. Still, she was hard to resist, so why should he?

"Nice car. Jaguar. I like it a lot," she cooed, then smiled and made a sexy little *o* with her lipsticked mouth. "You're cute, too, mistah."

He smiled back at her. "Jump in, then. Let's go for a test ride. See if it's true love or just infatuation." He glanced around the street quickly. None of the other girls were working this corner.

"A hundred for full-service, sweetie?" she asked as she wiggled her tight little butt inside the Jag. Her perfume smelled like eau de bubble gum, and she seemed to have bathed in it.

"As I said, get into the car. A hundred dollars is petty cash for me."

He knew he shouldn't be picking her up in the Jaguar, but he took her for a joy ride anyway. He couldn't help himself now.

He brought the girl to a small, wooded park in a part of Washington called Shaw. He parked in a thicket of fir trees that hid the car from sight. He looked at the prostitute, and she was even smaller and younger than he had thought.

"How old are you?" he asked.

"How old you want me to be?" she said, and smiled. "Sweetie, I need the money first. You know how it works."

"Yes. But do you?" he asked.

He reached into his pocket and pulled out a switchblade knife. He had it at her throat in an instant.

"Don't hurt me," she whispered. "Just be cool."

"Get out of the car. Slowly. Don't you dare scream. *You* be cool."

Shafer got out with her, staying close, the knife still pressed to the hollow of her throat.

"It's all just a game, darling," he explained. "My name is Death. You're a very lucky girl. I'm the best player of all."

As if to prove it, he stabbed her for the first time.

Book One

THE JANE DOE MURDERS

THINGS WERE going pretty well that day. I was driving a bright-orange school bus through Southeast on a blistering-hot morning in late July, and I was whistling a little Al Green as I drove. I was in the process of picking up sixteen boys from their houses and also two foster homes. Door-to-door bus service. Hard to beat.

Just one week earlier I had returned from Boston and the Mr. Smith murder case. Mr. Smith and a deranged killer named Gary Soneji had both been involved in that one. I needed a rest, and I'd taken the morning off to do something I'd been looking forward to for a change.

My partner, John Sampson, and a twelve-year-old named Errol Mignault sat behind me on the bus. John was wearing Wayfarer shades, black jeans, and a black T-shirt that read ALLIANCE OF CONCERNED MEN. SEND DONATIONS TODAY. He is six-nine, a very solid two hundred fifty pounds. We've been friends since we were ten, when I first moved to D.C.

He, Errol, and I were talking about the boxer

Sugar Ray Robinson, almost shouting over the bus's blustery, occasionally misfiring engine. Sampson had his huge arm lightly draped over Errol's shoulders. Proper physical contact is encouraged when dealing with these boys.

Finally, we picked up the last little guy on our list, an eight-year-old who lived in Benning Terrace, a tough project known to some of us as Simple City.

As we left the project, an ugly smear of graffiti told visitors everything they needed to know about the neighborhood. It read YOU ARE NOW LEAVING THE WAR ZONE, AND YOU LIVED TO TELL ABOUT IT.

We were taking the boys out to Lorton Prison in Virginia. They would be visiting their fathers for the afternoon. They were all young, between eight and thirteen. The Alliance transports forty to fifty kids each week to see their fathers and mothers in different prisons. The goal is a lofty one: to bring the crime rate in Washington down by a third.

I'd been out to the prison more times than I cared to remember. I knew the warden at Lorton pretty well. A few years back I'd spent a lifetime there, interviewing Gary Soneji.

Warden Marion Campbell had set up a large room on Level One where the boys met with their fathers. It was a powerful scene, even more emotional than I'd expected. The Alliance spends time training the fathers who want to participate in the program. There are four steps: how to show love;

accept fault and responsibility; attain parent-and-child harmony; discover new beginnings.

Ironically, the boys were all trying to look and act tougher than they actually were. I heard one boy say, "You weren't in my life before, why should I listen to you now?" But the fathers were trying to show a softer side.

Sampson and I hadn't made the run to Lorton before. It was our first time, but I was already sure I'd do it again. There was so much raw emotion and hope in the room, so much potential for something good and decent. Even if some of it would never be realized, it showed that an effort was being made, and something positive could come from it.

What struck me most was the bond that still existed between some of the fathers and their young sons. I thought about my own boy, Damon, and how lucky we were. The thing about most of the prisoners in Lorton was that they knew what they had done was wrong; they just didn't know how to stop doing it.

For most of the hour and a half, I just walked around and listened. I was occasionally needed as a psychologist, and I did the best I could on short notice. At one little group, I heard a father say, "Please tell your mother I love her and I miss her like crazy." Then both the prisoner and his son broke into tears and hugged each other fiercely.

Sampson came up to me after we'd been in the prison for an hour or so. He was grinning broadly.

His smile, when it comes, is a killer. "Man, I love this. Do-gooder shit is the best."

"Yeah, I'm hooked myself. I'll drive the big orange bus again."

"Think it'll help? Fathers and sons meeting like this?" he asked me.

I looked around the room. "I think today, right now, this is a success for these men and their sons. That's good enough."

Sampson nodded. "The old one-day-at-a-time approach. Works for me, too. I am *flying,* Alex."

So was I, so was I. I'm a sucker for this kind of stuff.

As I drove the young boys home that afternoon, I could see by their faces that they'd had positive experiences with their fathers. The boys weren't nearly as noisy and rambunctious on the way back to D.C. They weren't trying to be so tough. They were just acting like kids.

Almost every one of the boys thanked Sampson and me as he got off the big orange bus. It wasn't necessary. It sure was a lot better than chasing after homicidal maniacs.

The last boy we dropped off was the eight-year-old from Benning Terrace. He hugged both John and me, and then he started to cry. "I miss my dad," he said before running home.

Chapter 2

THAT NIGHT, Sampson and I were on duty in Southeast. We're senior homicide detectives, and I'm also liaison between the FBI and the D.C. police. We got a call at about half past midnight telling us to go to the area of Washington called Shaw. There'd been a bad homicide.

A lone Metro squad car was at the murder scene, and the neighborhood psychos had turned out in pretty fair numbers.

It looked like a bizarre block party in the middle of hell. Fires were blazing nearby, throwing off sparks in two trash barrels, which made no sense, given the sweltering heat of the night.

The victim was a young woman, probably between fourteen and her late teens, according to the radio report.

She wasn't hard to find. Her nude, mutilated body had been discarded in a clump of briar bushes in a small park less than ten yards off a paved pathway.

As Sampson and I approached the body, a boy

shouted at us from the other side of the crime tape: "Yo, yo, she just some street whore!"

I stopped and looked at him. He reminded me of the boys we'd just transported to Lorton Prison. "Dime-a-dozen bitch. Ain't worth your time, or mine, *Dee-fectives*," he went on with his disturbing rap.

I walked up to the young wisecracker. "How do you know that? You seen her around?"

The boy backed off. But then he grinned, showing off a gold star on one of his front teeth. "She ain't got no clothes on, an' she layin' on her back. Somebody stick her good. Sure sound like a whore to me."

Sampson eyed the youth, who looked to be around fourteen but might have been even younger. "You know who she is?"

"Hell *no!*" The boy pretended to be insulted. "Don't know no whores, man."

The boy finally swaggered off, looking back at us once or twice and shaking his head. Sampson and I walked on and joined two uniformed cops standing by the body. They were obviously waiting for reinforcements. Apparently, we were it.

"You call Emergency Services?" I asked the uniforms.

"Thirty-five minutes ago and counting," said the older-looking of the two. He was probably in his late twenties, sporting an attempted mustache and trying to look as if he were experienced at scenes like this one.

"That figures." I shook my head. "You find any I.D. anywhere around here?"

"No I.D. We looked around in the bushes. Nothing but the body," said the younger one. "And the body's seen better days." He was perspiring badly and looked a little sick.

I put on latex gloves and bent down over the corpse. She did appear to be in her mid- to late teens. The girl's throat had been slit from ear to ear. Her face was badly slashed. So were the soles of her feet, which seemed odd. She'd been stabbed a dozen or more times in her chest and stomach. I pushed open her legs.

I saw something that made me sick. A metal handle was barely visible between her legs. I was almost sure it was a knife and that it had been driven all the way into her vagina.

Sampson crouched and looked at me. "What are you thinking, Alex? Another one?"

I shook my head, shrugged my shoulders. "Maybe, but she's an addict, John. Tracks on her arms and legs. Probably behind her knees, under her arms. Our boy doesn't usually go after addicts. He practices safe sex. The murder's brutal, though. That fits the style. You see the metal handle?"

Sampson nodded. He didn't miss much. "Clothes," he said. "Where the hell did they go to? We need to find the clothes."

"Somebody in the neighborhood probably stripped them off her already," said the young uniform. There was a lot of disturbance around the body. Several footprints in the dirt. "That's how it goes around here. Nobody seems to care."

"We're here," I said to him. "*We* care. We're here for all the Jane Does."

Chapter 3

GEOFFREY SHAFER was so happy he almost couldn't hide it from his family. He had to keep from laughing out loud as he kissed his wife, Lucy, on the cheek. He caught a whiff of her Chanel No. 5 perfume, then tasted the brittle dryness of her lips as he kissed her again.

They were standing around like statues in the elegant galley hall of the large Georgian house in Kalorama. The children had been summoned to say good-bye to him.

His wife, the former Lucy Rhys-Cousins, was ash-blond, her sparkling green eyes even brighter than the Bulgari and Spark jewelry that she always wore. Slender, still a beauty of sorts at thirty-seven, Lucy had attended Newnham College at Cambridge for two years before they were married. She read useless poetry and literary novels, and spent most of her free time at equally pointless lunches, shopping with her expatriate girlfriends, going to polo matches, or sailing. Occasionally, Shafer sailed with her. He'd been a very good sailor once upon a time.

Lucy had been considered a prize catch, and he supposed that she still would be, for some men. Well, they could have her skinny, bony ass and all the passionless sex they could stomach.

Shafer hoisted up four-year-old twins Tricia and Erica, one in each arm. Two mirror images of their mother. He'd have sold the twins for the price of a postage stamp. He hugged the girls and laughed like the good papa he always pretended to be.

Then he formally shook twelve-year-old Robert's hand. The debate being waged in the house was over whether Robert should be sent back to England for boarding school, perhaps to Winchester, where his grandfather had gone. Shafer gave his son a crisp military salute. Once upon a time, Colonel Geoffrey Shafer had been a soldier. Only Robert seemed to remember that part of his father's life now.

"I'm only going away to London for a few days, and this is *work*, not a holiday. I'm not planning to spend my nights at the Athenaeum or anything like that," he told his family. He was smiling jovially, the way they expected him to be.

"Try to have some fun while you're away, Dad. Have some laughs. God knows, you deserve it," Robert said, talking in the lower-octave man-to-man's voice that he seemed to be adopting lately.

"Bye, Daddy! Bye, Daddy," the twins chorused shrilly, making Shafer want to throw them against the walls.

"Bye, Erica-san. Bye, Tricia-san."

"Remember Orc's Nest," Robert said with sudden urgency. "*Dragon* and *The Duelist*." Orc's Nest was a store that sold role-playing books and gaming equipment. It was located on Earlham, just off Cambridge Circus in London. *Dragon* and *The Duelist* were currently the two hot-shit British magazines covering role-playing games.

Unfortunately for Robert, Shafer wasn't actually going to London. He had a much better plan for the weekend. He was going to play his fantasy game right here in Washington.

Chapter 4

HE SPED due east, rather than toward Washington's Dulles Airport, feeling as if a tremendously burdensome weight had been lifted. God, he hated his perfect English family, and even more, their claustrophobic life here in America.

Shafer's own family back in England had been "perfect" as well. He had two older brothers, and they'd both been excellent students, model youths. His father had been a military attaché, and the family had traveled around the globe until he was twelve, when they'd returned to England and settled in Guildford, about half an hour outside London. Once there, Shafer began to expand on the schoolboy mischief he'd practiced since he was eight. The center of Guildford contained several historic buildings, and he set out to gleefully deface all of them. He began with the Abbot's Hospital, where his grandmother was dying. He painted obscenities on the walls. Then he moved on to Guildford Castle, Guildhall, the Royal Grammar School, and Guildford Cathedral. He scrawled more obscene words, and splashed large penises in bright colors. He had no idea why he took such joy in ruining beautiful things, but he did. He loved it—and he especially loved not getting caught.

Shafer was eventually sent to school at Rugly, where the pranks continued. Then he attended St. John's College, where he concentrated on philosophy, Japanese, and shagging as many good-looking women as he possibly could. All his friends were mystified when he went into the army at twenty-one. His language skills were excellent, and he was posted to Asia, which was where the mischief rose to a new level and where he began to play the *game of games*.

He stopped at a 7-Eleven in Washington Heights for coffee—three coffees, actually. Black, with four sugars in each. He drank most of one of the cups on his way to the counter.

The Indian cashier gave him a cheeky, suspicious look, and he laughed in the bearded wanker's face.

"Do you really think I'd steal a bloody seventy-five-cent cup of coffee? You pathetic jerkoff. You pitiful wog."

He threw his money on the counter and left before he killed the clerk with his bare hands, which he could do easily enough.

From the 7-Eleven he drove into the Northeast part of Washington, a middle-class section called Eckington. He began to recognize the streets when he was west of Gallaudet University. Most of the structures were two-storied apartments with vinyl siding, either redbrick or a hideous Easter-egg blue that always made him wince.

He stopped in front of one of the redbrick garden apartments on Uhland Terrace, near Second Street. This one had an attached garage. A previous tenant had adorned the brick facade with two white concrete cats.

"Hello, pussies," Shafer said. He felt relieved to be here. He was "cycling up"—that is, getting high, manic. He loved this feeling, couldn't get enough of it. It was time to play the game.

Chapter 5

A RUSTED and taped-up purple and blue taxi was parked inside the two-car garage. Shafer had been using it for about four months. The taxi gave him anonymity, made him almost invisible anywhere he chose to go in D.C. He called it his "Nightmare Machine."

He wedged the Jaguar beside the taxicab, then he jogged upstairs. Once inside the apartment, he switched on the air-conditioning. He drank another sugar-laced coffee.

Then he took his pills, like a good boy. Thorazine and Librium. Benadryl, Xanax, Vicodin. He'd been using the drugs in various combinations for years. It was mostly a trial-and-error process, but he'd learned his lessons well. *Feeling better, Geoffrey? Yes, much better, thank you.*

He tried to read today's *Washington Post*, then an old copy of *Private Eye* magazine, and finally a catalog from DeMask, a rubber and leather fetish wholesaler in Amsterdam, the world's largest. He did two hundred push-ups, then a few hundred sit-ups, impatiently waiting for darkness to fall over Washington.

At quarter to ten, Shafer began to get ready for a big night on the town. He went into the small, barren bathroom, which smelled of cheap cleanser. He stood before the mirror.

He liked what he saw. Very much so. Thick and wavy blond hair that he would never lose. A charismatic, electric smile. Startling blue eyes that had a cinematic quality. Excellent physical shape for a man of forty-four.

He went to work, starting with brown contact lenses. He'd done this so many times, he could almost do it blindfolded. It was a part of his trade-craft. He applied blackface to his face, neck, hands, wrists; thick padding to make his neck seem broader than it was; a dark watch cap to cover every last strand of hair.

He stared hard at himself—and saw a rather convincing-looking black man, especially if the light wasn't too strong. Not bad, not bad at all. It was a good disguise for a night on the town, *especially* if the town was Washington.

So let the games begin. The Four Horsemen.

At ten twenty-five, he went down to the garage again. He carefully circled around the Jaguar and walked to the purple and blue taxicab. He had already begun to lose himself in delicious fantasy.

Shafer reached into his pants pocket and pulled out three unusual-looking dice. They were twenty-sided, the kind used in most fantasy games, or RPGs. They had numerals on them rather than dots.

He held the dice in his left hand, rolling them over and over.

There were explicit rules to the Four Horsemen; everything was supposed to depend on the dice roll. The idea was to come up with an outrageous fantasy, a mindblower. The four players around the world were competing. There had never been a game like this—nothing even came close.

Shafer had already prepared an adventure for himself, but there were alternatives for every event. Much depended on the dice.

That was the main point—anything could happen.

He got into the taxi, started it up. Good Lord, was he ready for this!

Chapter 6

HE HAD a gorgeous plan mapped out. He would pick up only those few passengers—"fares"—who caught his eye, fired up his imagination to the limit. He wasn't in a hurry. He had all night; he had all weekend. He was on a busman's holiday.

His route had been laid out beforehand. First, he drove to the fashionable Adams-Morgan neighborhood. He watched the busy sidewalks, which seemed one long syncopated rhythm of movement. Bar-grazers slouching toward hipness. It seemed that every other restaurant in Adams-Morgan called itself a café. Driving slowly and checking the glittery sights, he passed Café Picasso, Café Lautrec, La Fourchette Café, Bukom Café, Café Dalbol, Montego Café, Sheba Café.

Around eleven-thirty, on Columbia Road, he slowed the taxicab. His heart began to thump. Something very good was shaping up ahead.

A handsome-looking couple was leaving the popular Chief Ike's Mambo Room. A man and a woman, Hispanic, probably in their late twenties. Sensual beyond belief.

He rolled the dice across the front seat: six, five, four—a total of fifteen. A high count.

Danger! That made sense. A couple was always tricky and risky.

Shafer waited for them to cross the pavement, moving away from the restaurant canopy. *They came right toward him.* How accommodating. He touched the handle of the magnum that he kept under the front seat. He was ready for anything.

As they started to climb into the taxi, he changed his mind. He could do that!

Shafer saw that neither of them was as attractive as he'd thought. The man's cheeks and forehead were slightly mottled; the pomade in his black hair was too thick and greasy. The woman was a few pounds heavier than he liked, plumper than she'd looked from a distance in the flattering streetlights.

"Off duty," he said, and sped away. Both of them gave him the finger.

Shafer laughed out loud. "You're in luck tonight! Fools! Luckiest night of your lives, and you don't even know it."

The incomparable thrill of the fantasy had completely taken hold of him. He'd had total power over the couple. He had control of life and death.

"Death *be* proud," he whispered.

He stopped for more coffee at a Starbucks on Rhode Island Avenue. Nothing like it. He purchased three black coffees and heaped six sugars in each.

An hour later, he was in Southeast. He hadn't stopped for another fare. The streets were crowded to the max with pedestrians. There weren't enough taxis, not even gypsies in this part of Washington.

He regretted having let the Hispanic couple get away. He'd begun to romanticize them in his mind, to visualize them as they'd looked in the streetlight. Remembrance of things past, right? He thought of Proust's monumental opening line: *"For a long time I used to go to bed early."* And so had Shafer—until he discovered the game of games.

Then he saw her—a perfect brown goddess standing right there before him, as if someone had just given him a wonderful present. She was walking by herself, about a block from E Street, moving fast, purposefully. He was instantly high again.

He loved the way she moved, the swivel of her long legs, the exactness of her carriage.

As he came up behind her, she began looking around, checking the street. Looking for a taxi? Could it be? Did she want him?

She had on a light cream suit, a purple silk shirt, high heels. She looked too classy and adult to be going to a club. She appeared to be in control of herself.

He quickly rolled the twenty-sided dice again and held his breath. Counted the numerals. His heart leaped. This was what the Horsemen was all about.

She was waving her hand at him, signaling. *"Taxi!"* she called. "Taxi! Are you free?"

He guided the taxi over to the curb, and she took three quick, delicate steps toward him. She was wearing shimmery, silken high heels that were just delightful. She was much prettier up close. She was a nine and a half out of ten.

The cab door swung open and blocked his view of her for a second.

Then he saw that she was carrying flowers, and wondered why. Something special tonight? Well, that was certainly true. The flowers were for her own funeral.

"Oh, thank you so much for stopping." She spoke breathlessly as she settled into the taxi. He could tell that she was letting herself relax and feel safe. Her voice was soothing, sweet, down-to-earth and real.

"At your service." Shafer turned and smiled at her. "By the way, I'm Death. You're my fantasy for this weekend."

Chapter 7

MONDAY MORNINGS I usually work the soup kitchen at St. Anthony's in Southeast, where I've been a volunteer for the past half-dozen years. I do the seven-to-nine shift, three days a week.

That morning I felt restless and uneasy. I was still getting over the Mr. Smith case, which had taken me all over the East Coast and to Europe. Maybe I needed a real vacation, a holiday far away from Washington.

I watched the usual lineup of men, women, and children who had no money for food. It was about five deep and went up Twelfth Street to the second corner. It seemed such a pity, so unfair that so many folks still go hungry in Washington, or get fed only once a day.

I had started helping out at the kitchen years before on account of my wife, Maria. She was doing casework as a social worker at St. Anthony's when we first met. Maria was the uncrowned princess of St. Anthony's; everybody loved her, and she loved me. She had been shot, murdered in a drive-by incident not far from the soup kitchen.

We'd been married four years and had two small children. The case has never been solved, and that still tortures me. Maybe that's what drives me to solve every case I can, no matter how bad the odds.

At St. Anthony's soup kitchen, I help make sure nobody gets too riled up or causes undue trouble during meals. I'm six-three, around two hundred pounds, and built for peacekeeping, if and when it's necessary. I can usually ward off trouble with a few quiet words and nonthreatening gestures. Most of these people are here to eat, though, not fight or cause trouble.

I also dish out peanut butter and jelly to anyone who wants seconds or even thirds of the stuff. Jimmy Moore, the Irish American who runs the soup kitchen with much love and just the right amount of discipline, has always believed in the healing power of p.b. and j. Some of the regulars at the kitchen call me "Peanut Butter Man." They've been doing it for years.

"You don't look so good today," said a short ample woman who's been coming to the kitchen for the past year or two. I know her name is Laura, and that she was born in Detroit and has two grown sons. She used to work as a housekeeper on M Street in Georgetown, but the family felt she'd gotten too old for the job and let her go with only a couple weeks' severance and warm words of appreciation.

"You deserve better. You deserve *me*," Laura said, and laughed mischievously. "What do you say?"

"Laura, you're too kind with your compliments," I said, serving up her usual extra dish. "Anyway, you've met Christine. You know I'm already spoken for."

Laura giggled as she hugged herself with both arms. She had a fine, healthy laugh, even under the circumstances. "A young girl has to dream, you know. Nice to see you, as always."

"Same to you, Laura. As always, nice to see you. Enjoy the meal."

"Oh, I do. You can *see* I do."

As I said my cheery hellos and dished out heaped portions of peanut butter, I allowed myself to think about Christine. Laura was probably right; maybe I didn't look so good today. I probably hadn't looked too terrific for a few days.

I remembered a night about two weeks back. I had just finished working a multiple-homicide case in Boston. Christine and I stood on the porch in front of her house out in Mitchellville. I was trying to live my life differently, but it's hard to change. I had a saying I really liked: HEART LEADS HEAD.

I could smell the flowers in the night air, roses and impatiens growing in profusion. I could also smell Gardenia Passion, a favorite perfume that Christine was wearing that night.

She and I had known each other for a year and a half. We'd met during a murder investigation that had ended with the death of her husband. Eventually we began to go out. I was thinking that it had all been leading to this moment on the porch. At least it had in my mind.

I had never seen Christine when she didn't look good to me and make me feel lightheaded. She's tall, almost five-ten, and that's nice. She had a smile that could probably light up half the country. That night, she was wearing tight, faded jeans and a white T-shirt knotted around her waist. Her feet were bare, and her nails were dabbed with red polish. Her beautiful brown eyes were shining.

I reached out and took her into my arms, and suddenly everything seemed right with the world. I forgot all about the terrible case I'd just finished; I forgot about the particularly vicious killer known as Mr. Smith.

I cupped her sweet, kind face gently in my hands. I like to think that nothing scares me anymore, and many things don't, but I guess the more good things you have in your life, the easier it is to experience fear. Christine felt so precious to me—so maybe I was scared.

Heart leads head.

It isn't the way most men act, but I was learning.

"I love you more than I've ever loved anything in my life, Christine. You help me see and feel things in new ways. I love your smile, your way with people—especially kids—your kindness. I love to hold you like this. I love you more than I could say if I stood here and talked for the rest of the night. I love you so much. Will you marry me, Christine?"

She didn't answer right away. I felt her pull back, just a little, and my heart caught. I looked into her eyes, and what I saw was pain and uncertainty. It nearly broke my heart.

"Oh, Alex, Alex," she whispered, and looked as if she might cry. "I can't give you an answer. You just came back from Boston. You were on another horrible, horrible murder case. I can't take that. Your life was in danger again. That terrible madman was in your house. He threatened your family. You can't deny any of that."

I couldn't. It had been a terrifying experience, and I had nearly died. "I won't deny anything you said. But I do love you. I can't deny that, either. I'll quit the police force if that's what it takes."

"No." A softness came into her eyes. She shook her head back and forth. "That would be all wrong. For both of us."

We held each other on the porch, and I knew we were in trouble. I didn't know how to resolve it. I had no idea. Maybe if I left the force, became a full-time therapist again, led a more normal life for Christine and the kids. But could I do that? Could I really quit?

"Ask me again," she whispered. "Ask me again, sometime."

Chapter 8

CHRISTINE AND I had dated since that night, and it just felt right, easy, comfortable, and romantic. It always was that way between us. Still, I wondered if our problem could be fixed. Could she be happy with a homicide detective? Could I stop being one? I didn't know.

I was brought out of my reverie about Christine by the high-pitched, stuttering wail of a siren out on Twelfth Street, just turning off E. I winced when I saw Sampson's black Nissan pull up in front of St. Anthony's.

He turned off the siren on his rooftop but then beeped the car horn, sat on it. I knew he was here for me, probably to take me somewhere I didn't want to go. The horn continued to blare.

"It's your friend John Sampson," Jimmy Moore called out. "You hear him, Alex?"

"I know who it is," I called back to Jimmy. "I'm hoping he goes away."

"Sure doesn't sound like it."

I finally walked outside, crossing through the soup-kitchen line and receiving a few jokey jeers.

People I had known for a long time accused me of working half a day, or said that if I didn't like the job, could they have it.

"What's up?" I called to Sampson before I got all the way out to his black sports car.

Sampson's side window came sliding down. I leaned inside the car. "You forget? It's my day off," I reminded him.

"It's Nina Childs," Sampson said in the low, soft voice he used only when he was angry or very serious. He was trying to deaden his facial muscles, to look tough, not emotional, but it wasn't working real well. "Nina's dead, Alex."

I shivered involuntarily. I opened the car door and got in. I didn't even go back to the kitchen to tell Jimmy Moore I was leaving. Sampson jerked the car away from the curbside fast. The siren came on again, but now I almost welcomed the mournful wail. It numbed me.

"What do you know so far?" I asked as we rushed along the intensely bleak streets of Southeast, then crossed the slate-gray Anacostia River.

"She was dumped in a row house, Eighteenth and Garnesville. Jerome Thurman is out there with her. Says she's probably been there since the weekend. Some needle pusher found the body. No clothes or I.D., Alex," Sampson said.

I looked over at him. "So how did they know it was Nina?"

"Uniform guy on the scene recognized her. Knew her from the hospital. Everybody knew Nina."

I shut my eyes, but I saw Nina Childs's face and I opened them again. She had been the eleven-to-seven charge nurse in the E.R. unit at St. Anthony's Hospital, where once I'd run like a tornado, with a dying little boy in my arms. Sampson and I had worked with Nina more times than I could remember. Sampson had also dated Nina for over a year, but then they'd broken it off. She'd married a neighborhood man who worked for the city. They had two kids, two little babies, and Nina had seemed so happy the last time I saw her.

I couldn't believe she was lying dead in a tenement cellar on the wrong side of the Anacostia. She had been abandoned, like one of the Jane Does.

Chapter 9

NINA CHILDS'S body had been found in a battered row house in one of the city's most impoverished, destroyed, and dismaying neighborhoods. There was only one patrol car on the scene, and a single rusted and dented EMS van; homicides in Southeast don't attract much attention. A dog was barking somewhere, and it was the only sound on the desolate street.

Sampson and I had to walk past an open-air drug mart on the corner of Eighteenth Street. Mostly young males, but a few children and two women were also gathered there defiantly. The drug marts are everywhere in this part of Southeast. The neighborhood youth activity is the crack trade.

"Daily body pickup, Officers?" said one of the young men. He was wearing black trousers with black suspenders, no shirt, socks, or shoes. He had a prison-yard physique and tattoos everywhere.

"Come to take out the trash?" an older man cackled from behind an unruly patch of salt-and-pepper beard. "Take that muhfuckin' barkin'-all-night dog while you here. Make yourselves useful," he added.

Sampson and I ignored them and continued walking across Eighteenth, then into the boarded-up, three-storied row house straight ahead. A black and white boxer leaned out of a third-floor window, like a lifetime resident, and wouldn't stop barking. Otherwise the building appeared deserted.

The front door had been jimmied a hundred times, so it just swung open for us. The building smelled of fire, garbage, water damage. There was a gaping hole in the ceiling from a burst steam pipe. It was so wrong for Nina to have ended up in this sad, abominable place.

For over a year I had been unofficially investigating unsolved murders in Southeast, many of them Jane Does. My count was well over a hundred, but no one else in the department was willing to agree to that number, or anything close to it. Several of the murdered women were drug abusers or prostitutes. But not Nina.

We carefully descended a circular stairwell that had a shaky, well-worn wooden railing that neither of us would touch. I could see flashlights shining up ahead, and I already had my Maglite turned on.

Nina was deep in the basement of the abandoned building. At least somebody had bothered to tape off the perimeter to protect the crime scene.

I saw Nina's body—and I had to look away.

It wasn't just that she was dead; it was how she'd been killed. I tried to put my mind and eyes somewhere else until I regained some composure.

Jerome Thurman was there with the EMS team. So was a single patrol officer, probably the one who had identified Nina. No M.E. was present. It wasn't unusual for a medical examiner not to show up for homicides in Southeast.

There were dead flowers on the floor near the body. I focused on the flowers, still not able to look at Nina again. It didn't fit with the other Jane Does, but the killer didn't have a strict pattern. That was one of the problems I was having. It might mean that his fantasy was still evolving—and that he hadn't finished making up his gruesome story yet.

I noted shreds of foil and cellophane wrappers lying everywhere on the floor. Rats are attracted to shiny things and often bring them back to their nests. Thick cobwebs weaved from one end of the basement to the other.

I had to look at Nina again. I needed to look closely.

"I'm Detective Alex Cross. Let me take a look at her, please," I finally said to the EMS team, a man and a woman in their twenties. "I'll just be a couple of minutes, then I'll get out of your way."

"The other detectives already released the body," the male EMS worker said. He was rail-thin, with long dirty-blond hair. He didn't bother to look up at me. "Let us finish our job and get the hell out of this cesspool. Whole area is highly infectious—smells like shit."

"Just back away," Sampson barked. "Get up, before I pull your skinny ass up."

The EMS techie cursed, but he stood and backed away from Nina's body. I moved in close, tried to concentrate and be professional, tried to remember specific details I had gathered about the previous Jane Does in Southeast. I was looking for some connection. I wondered if a single predator could possibly be killing so many people. If that was the case, then this would be one of the most savage killing sprees ever.

I took a deep breath and then I knelt over Nina. The rats had been at her, I could see, but the killer had done much worse damage.

It looked to me as if Nina had been beaten to death, with punches and possibly kicks. She might have been struck a hundred times or more. I had rarely seen anyone given this much punishment. Why did it have to happen? She was only thirty-one years old, a mother of two, kind, talented, dedicated to her work at St. Anthony's.

There was a sudden noise, like a rifleshot, in the building. It reverberated right through the basement walls. The EMS workers jumped.

The rest of us laughed nervously. I knew exactly what the sound was.

"Just rattraps," I said to the EMS team. "Get used to it."

Chapter 10

I WAS at the homicide scene for a little over two hours, much longer than I wanted to be there, and I hated every second. I couldn't fix a set pattern for the Jane Doe killings, and Nina Childs's murder didn't help. Why had he struck her so many times and so savagely? What were the flowers doing there? Could this be the work of the same killer?

The way I usually operate at a crime scene is to let the homicide investigation take on an almost aerial view. Everything emanates from the body.

Sampson and I walked the entire crime scene, from the basement to each floor and on up to the roof. Then we walked the neighborhood. Nobody had seen anything unusual, which didn't surprise either of us.

Now came the really bad part. Sampson and I drove from the woeful tenement to Nina's apartment in the Brookland section of Washington, east of Catholic University. I knew I was being sucked in again, but there was nothing I could do about it.

It was a sweltering-hot day, and the sun hammered Washington without mercy. We were both silent and withdrawn during the ride. What we had to do was the worst thing about our job— telling a family about the death of a loved one. I didn't know how I could do it this time.

Nina's building was a well-kept brownbrick apartment house on Monroe Street. Miniature yellow roses were blooming out front in bright-green window boxes. It didn't look as if anything bad should happen to someone who lived here. Everything about the place was so bright and hopeful, just as Nina had been.

I was becoming more and more disturbed and upset about the brutal and obscene murder, and about the fact that it probably wouldn't get a decent investigation from the department, at least not officially. Nana Mama would chalk it up to her conspiracy theories about the white overlords and their "criminal disinterest" in the people of Southeast. She had often told me that she felt morally superior to white people, that she would never, ever treat them the way they treated the black people of Washington.

"Nina's sister, Marie, takes care of the kids," Sampson said as we rode down Monroe. "She's a nice girl. Had a drug problem one time, beat it. Nina helped her. The whole family is close-knit. A lot like yours. This is going to be real bad, Alex."

I turned to him. Not surprisingly, he was taking Nina's death even harder than I was. It's unusual for him to show his emotions, though. "I can do it,

John. You stay here in the car. I'll go up and talk to the family."

Sampson shook his head and sighed loudly. "Doesn't work that way, sugar."

He snugged the Nissan up to the curb, and we both climbed out. He didn't stop me from coming along to the apartment, so I knew he wanted me there with him. He was right. This was going to be bad.

The Childs apartment took up the first and second floors. The front door was slightly ornate, aluminum. Nina's husband was already at the door. He had on the proletariat uniform of the D.C. Housing Authority, where he worked: mud-stained work boots, blue trousers, a shirt marked DCHA. One of the babies snuggled in his arms, a beautiful girl who looked at me and smiled and cooed.

"Could we come inside for a moment?" Sampson asked.

"It's Nina," the husband said, and started to break down right there in the doorway.

"I'm sorry, William," I spoke softly. "You're right. She's gone. She was found this morning."

William Childs started to sob loudly. He was a powerful-looking workingman, but that didn't matter. He held his bewildered little girl to his chest and tried to control the crying, but he couldn't.

"Oh, God, no. Oh, Nina, Nina baby. How could somebody kill her? How could anybody do that? Oh, Nina, Nina, Nina."

A young, pretty woman came up behind him. She had to be Nina's sister, Marie. She took the baby from her sister's husband, and the little girl began to scream, as if she knew what had happened. I had seen so many families, so many good people, who had lost loved ones on these merciless streets. I knew it would never completely stop, but I felt it ought to get better. It never did.

The sister motioned for us to come inside, and I noticed a hall table on which there were two pocketbooks, as if Nina were still about. The apartment was comfortable looking and neat, with light bamboo and white-cushioned furniture. The whir of a window air conditioner was constant. A Lladro porcelain figure of a nurse stood on an end table.

I was still sorting through details of the homicide scene, trying to connect the murder to the other Jane Does. We learned that Nina had attended a health-care charity dinner on Saturday night. William had been working overtime. The family called the police late Saturday night. Two detectives had shown up, but no one had been able to find Nina until now.

Then I was holding the baby while Nina's sister took the chill off a bottle of formula. It was such a sad and poignant moment, knowing this poor little girl would never see her mother again, never know how truly special her mother had been. It reminded me of my own kids and their mother, and of Christine, who was afraid I would die during some murder investigation like this one.

The older little girl came up to me while I was holding her baby sister. She was two or three at the most. "I got a new hairstyle," she said proudly and did a half-turn to show me.

"You did? It's beautiful. Who did those braids for you?"

"My mommy," said the girl.

It was an hour later when Sampson and I finally left the house. We drove away in silence and despair, the same way we'd come. After a couple of blocks, Sampson pulled over in front of a ramshackle neighborhood bodega covered with beer and soda posters.

He gave a deep sigh, put his hands to his face, and then cried. I'd never ever seen John like this before, not in all the years we'd been friends, not even when we were just boys. I reached out and laid a hand on his shoulder, and he didn't move away. Then he told me something he hadn't shared before.

"I loved her, Alex, but I let her get away. I never told her how I felt. We have to get this son of a bitch."

Chapter 11

I SENSED I was at the start of another homicide mess. I didn't want it, but I couldn't stop the horror. I had to try to do something about the Jane Does. I couldn't just stand by and do nothing.

Although I was assigned to the Seventh District as a senior detective, my job as liaison with the FBI gave me some extra status and also the freedom to occasionally work without too much supervision or interference. My mind was running free, and I'd already made some associations between Nina's murder and at least some of the unsolved killings. First, there had been no identification on the victims at each crime scene. Second, the bodies had frequently been dumped in buildings where they might not be found quickly. Third, not a single witness had seen anyone who might be a suspect. The most we ever got was that there had been traffic, or people out on the street, where one of the bodies had been found. That told me that the killer knew how to blend in, and that he possibly was a black man.

Around six that night, I finally headed home.

This was supposed to be my day off. I had things to do there, and I was trying to balance the demands of job and homelife as best I could. I put on a happy face and headed inside the house.

Damon, Jannie, and Nana were singing "Sit Down, You're Rockin' de Boat" in the kitchen. The show tune was music to my ears and other essential parts of my anatomy. The kids looked happy as could be. There is a lot to be said for the innocence of childhood.

I heard Nana say, "How about 'I Can Tell the World'?" Then the three of them launched into one of the most beautiful spirituals I know. Damon's voice seemed particularly strong to me. I hadn't really noticed that before.

"I feel like I just walked into a story by Louisa May Alcott," I said, laughing for the first time that long day.

"I take that as a *high* compliment," Nana said. She was somewhere between her late seventies and early eighties now, but not telling—and also not showing—her age.

"Who's Louise Maise Alcott?" Jannie said, and made a lemon-sucking face. She is a healthy little skeptic, though almost never a cynic. In that way, she takes after both her father and her grandmother.

"Look it up tonight, little one. Fifty cents in your pocket for the correct answer," I told her.

"You're on." Jannie grinned. "You can pay me right now if you like."

"Me, too?" Damon asked.

"Of course. You can look up Jane Austen," I said to him. "Now what's with the heavenly harmonizing? I like it very much, by the way. I just want to know what the special occasion is."

"We're just singing while we prepare dinner," Nana said, and stuck up her nose and twinkled her eyes. "You play jazz and the blues on the piano, don't you? We harmonize like angels sometimes. No special reason necessary. Good for the soul, and the soul food, I suppose. Can't hurt."

"Well, don't stop singing on my account," I said, but they had already stopped. Too bad. Something was going on; I'd figured out that much. A musical mystery to be solved in my own house.

"We still on for boxing after dinner?" I asked cautiously. I was feeling a little vulnerable because I didn't want them to turn me down for the boxing lesson that has become a ritual.

"Of course," Damon said, and frowned like I must be out of my mind to even ask such a question.

"Of course. Pshaw. Why wouldn't we be?" Jannie said, and brushed off my silly question with a wave of her hand. "How's Ms. Johnson?" she asked then. "You two talk today?"

"I still want to know what the singing was all about?" I answered Jannie with a question of my own.

"You have valuable information. Well, so do I. Tit for tat," she said. "How do you like that?"

A little later, I decided to call Christine at home. Lately it had seemed more like the way it had been between us before I got involved with the Mr. Smith case. We talked for a while, and then I asked her to go out on Friday.

"Of course. I'd like that, Alex. What should I wear?" she asked.

I hesitated. "Well, I always like what you choose—but wear something special."

She didn't ask why.

Chapter 12

AFTER ONE of Nana's roast-chicken dinners with baked sweet potatoes and homemade bread, I took the kids downstairs for their weekly boxing lesson. Following the Tuesday night fight with the kids, I glanced at my watch and saw that it was already a little past nine.

The doorbell rang a moment later. I set down a terrific book called *The Color of Water* and pushed myself up from my chair in the family room.

"I'll get it. It's probably for me," I called out.

"Maybe it's Christine. You never know," Jannie teased, then darted away into the kitchen. Both of the kids adored Christine, in spite of the fact that she was the principal at their school.

I knew exactly who was out on the porch. I had been expecting four homicide detectives from the First District—Jerome Thurman, Rakeem Powell, Shawn Moore, and Sampson.

Three of the detectives were standing out on the porch. Rosie the cat and I let them inside. Sampson arrived about five minutes later, and we all gathered in the backyard. What we were doing at the house wasn't illegal, but it wouldn't make us a lot of friends in high places in the police department.

We sat on lawn chairs, and I set out beer and low-fat pretzels that two-hundred-seventy-pound Jerome scoffed at. "Beer and low-fat pretzels. Give me a *break,* Alex. You lost your mind? Hey, you having an affair with my wife? You must have got this bad idea from Claudette."

"I bought these especially for you, big man. I'm trying to give your heart a break," I told him, and the others guffawed loudly. We all pick on Jerome.

The five of us had been getting together informally for a couple of weeks. We were beginning to work on the Jane Does, as we called them. Homicide had no official investigation going on; it wasn't trying to link the murders to a serial killer. I'd tried to start one and been turned down by Chief Pittman. He claimed that I hadn't discovered a pattern linking any of the murders, and besides that, he didn't have any extra detectives for duty in Southeast.

"I suppose you've all heard about Nina Childs by now?" Sampson asked the other detectives. All of them had known Nina, and of course Jerome had been at the murder scene with us.

"The good die young." Rakeem Powell frowned severely and shook his head. Rakeem is smart and tough and could go all the way in the department. "Least they do in Southeast." His eyes went cold and hard.

I told them what I knew, especially that Nina had been found with no I.D. I mentioned everything else I had noticed at the tenement crime scene. I also took the occasion to talk some more about the rash of unsolved murders in Southeast. I went over the devastating stats I had compiled, mostly in my free time.

"Statistic like that in Georgetown or the Capitol district, people in this city be enraged. Going ballistic. Be *Washington Post* headlines every day. The president himself be involved. Money no object. National tragedy!" Jerome Thurman railed on and waved his arms around like signal flags.

"Well, we are here to do something about it," I said in a calmer voice. "Money *is* no object with us. Neither is time. Let me tell you what I feel about this killer," I continued. "I think I know a few things about him."

"How'd you come up with the profile?" Shawn Moore asked. "How can you stand thinking about these kinky bastards as much as you do?"

I shrugged. "It's what I do best. I've analyzed all the Jane Does," I said. "It took me weeks working on my own. Just me and the kinky bastard."

"Plus, he studies rodent droppings," said Sampson. "I saw him bagging the little turds. That's his real secret."

I grinned and told them what I had so far. "I think one male is responsible for at least some of the killings. Maybe as many as a dozen murders. I

don't think he's a brilliant killer, like Gary Soneji
or Mr. Smith, but he's clever enough not to be
caught. He's organized, reasonably careful. I don't
think we'll find he has any prior record. He probably has a decent job. Maybe even a family. My
FBI friends at Quantico agree with that.

"He's almost definitely caught up in an escalating fantasy cycle. I think he's into his fantasies
big-time. Maybe he's in the process of becoming
someone or something new. He might be forming
a new personality for himself. He isn't finished
with the killing, not by any means.

"I'll make some educated guesses. He hates his
old self, though the people closest to him probably
don't realize it. He might be ready to abandon his
family, job, any friends he has. At one time he
probably had very strong feelings and beliefs about
something—law and order, religion, the government—but not anymore. He kills in different
ways; there's no set formula. He knows a lot about
killing people. He's used different kinds of
weapons. He may have traveled overseas. Or
maybe he's spent time in Asia. I think it's very
possible he's a black man. He's killed several times
in Southeast—no one's noticed him."

"Fuck me," Jerome Thurman said to that. "Any
good news, Alex?"

"One thing, and this is a long shot. But it feels
right to me. I think he might be suicidal. It fits
the profile I'm working on. He's living danger-

ously, taking a lot of chances. He might just blow himself up."

"Pop goes the weasel," Sampson said.

That was how we came to name the killer: the Weasel.

Chapter 13

GEOFFREY SHAFER looked forward to playing the Four Horsemen every Thursday night from nine until about one in the morning.

The fantasy game was everything to him. There were three other master players around the world. The players were the Rider on the White Horse, Conqueror; the Rider on the Red Horse, War; the Rider on the Black Horse, Famine; and himself, the Rider on the Pale Horse, Death.

Lucy and the children knew they were forbidden to disturb him for any reason once he locked himself into the library on the second floor. On one wall was his collection of ceremonial daggers, nearly all of them purchased in Hong Kong and Bangkok. Also on the wall was the rowing oar from the year his college team had won the "Bumps." Shafer nearly always won the games he played.

He had been using the Internet to communicate with the other players for years, long before the rest of the world caught on. Conqueror played from the town of Dorking, in Surrey, outside

London; Famine traveled back and forth between Bangkok, Sydney, Melbourne, and Manila; and War usually played out of Jamaica, where he had a large estate on the sea. They had been playing Horsemen for seven years.

Rather than becoming repetitive, the fantasy game had expanded itself. It had grown every year, becoming something new and even more challenging. The object was to create the most delicious and unusual fantasy or adventure. Violence was almost always part of the game, but not necessarily murder. Shafer had been the first to claim that his stories weren't fantasies at all, that he lived them in the real world. Now the others would do so as well from time to time. Whether they really lived their fantasies, Shafer couldn't tell. The object was to create the evening's most startling fantasy, to get a rise out of the other players.

At nine o'clock his time, Shafer was on his laptop. So were the others. It was rare for one of them to miss a session, but if he did, he left lengthy messages and sometimes drawings or even photographs of supposed lovers or victims. Films were occasionally used, and the other players then had to decide whether the scenes were stage-acted or cinema verité.

Shafer couldn't imagine missing a chapter of the game himself. Death was by far the most interesting character, the most powerful and original. He had missed important social and embassy affairs just to be available for Thursday nights. He had played when he had pneumonia, and once when he'd had a painful double-hernia operation the day before.

The Four Horsemen was unique in so many ways, but most important was the fact that there was no single gamemaster to outline and control the action of the game. Each of the players had complete autonomy to write and visualize his own story, as long as he played by the roll of the dice and remained inside the parameters of the character.

In effect, in Horsemen there were four game-masters. There was no other fantasy game like it. It was as gruesome and shocking as the partici-pants' imaginations and their skills at presentation brought them.

Conqueror, Famine, and War had all signed on. Shafer began to type.

Death has triumphed again in Washington. Let me tell you the details, then I'll listen to the glorious stories, the imaginative power, of Conqueror, Famine, and War. I live for this, as I know all of you do as well.

This weekend, I drove my fantastic taxi, the "Nightmare Machine," once again. . . . Listen to this. I came upon several choice and delectable victims, but I rejected them as unworthy. Then I found my Queen, and she reminded me of our days in Bangkok and

Manila. Who could ever forget the blood lust of the boxing arena? I held a mock kickboxing match. Gentlemen, I beat her with my hands and feet. I am sending pictures.

Chapter 14

SOMETHING WAS up, and I didn't think I'd like it very much. I arrived at the Seventh District Police Station just before seven-thirty the following morning. I'd been summoned by the powers-that-be to the station, and it was a tough deal. I'd worked until two in the morning trying to get a lead on Nina Childs's murder.

I had a feeling that the day was starting out wrong. I was tense and more uptight than I usually let myself become. I didn't like this early-morning command appearance one bit.

I shook my head, frowned, tried to roll the kinks out of my neck. Finally, I gritted my teeth tightly before opening the mahogany door. Chief of Detectives George Pittman was lying in wait in his office, which in fact consists of three connecting offices, including a conference room.

The Jefe, as he's called by his many "admirers," had on a boxy gray business suit, an overstarched white shirt, and a silver necktie. His gray-and-white-streaked hair was slicked back. He looked like a banker, and in some ways he is one. As he never tires of saying, he is working with a fixed budget and is always mindful of manpower costs, overtime costs, caseload costs. Apparently, he is an efficient manager, which is why the police commissioner overlooks the fact that he's a bully, bigot, racist, and careerist.

Up on his wall were three large, important-looking pushpin maps. The first showed two consecutive months of rapes, homicides, and assaults in Washington. The second map did the same for residential and commercial burglaries. The third map showed auto thefts. The maps and the *Post* said that crime was down in D.C., but not where I live.

"Do you know why you're here, why I wanted to see you?" Pittman asked point-blank. No socializing or small talk from The Jefe, no niceties. "Of course you do, Dr. Cross. You're a psychologist. You're supposed to know how the human mind works. I keep forgetting that."

Be cool, be careful, I told myself. I did the thing Chief Pittman least expected: I smiled, then said softly, "No, I really *don't* know. I got a call from your assistant. So I'm here."

Pittman smiled back, as if I'd made a pretty good joke. Then he suddenly raised his voice, and his face and neck turned bright red; his nostrils flared, exposing the bristly hairs in his nose.

One of his hands was clenched into a tight fist, while the other was stretched open. His fingers were as rigid as the pencils sticking up from the leather cup on his desk.

"You're not fooling anybody, Cross, least of all me. I'm fully fucking aware that you're investigating homicides in Southeast that you aren't assigned to—the so-called Jane Does. You're doing this against my explicit orders. Some of those cases have been closed for over a year. *I won't have it*—I won't tolerate your insubordination, your condescending attitude. I know what you're trying to pull. Embarrass the department, specifically embarrass me, curry fucking favor with the mayor, making yourself some kind of folk hero in Southeast in the process."

I hated Pittman's tone and what he was saying, but I learned one trick a long time ago, and it is probably the most important thing to know about politics inside any organization. It's so simple, but it's the key to every petty kingdom, every fiefdom. Knowledge truly is power, it's everything; if you don't have any, pretend you do.

So I told Chief Pittman nothing. I didn't contradict him; I didn't admit to a thing. I did nothing. Me and Mahatma Gandhi.

I let him think that maybe I was investigating old cases in Southeast—but I didn't admit to it. I also let him think that maybe I had some powerful connections with Mayor Monroe and God only knows who else in the City on the Hill. I let him think that maybe I was after his job, or that I might have—God forbid—even loftier aspirations.

"I'm working the homicides assigned to me.

Check with the captain. I'm doing my best to close as many cases as I can."

Pittman nodded curtly—*one* nod. His face was still heart-attack red. "All right, I want you to close *this* case, and I want you to close it fast. A tourist was robbed and gunned down on M Street last night," he said. "A well-respected German doctor from Munich. It's front fucking page in today's *Post*. Not to mention the *International Herald Tribune*, and every newspaper in Germany, of course. I want you on *that* murder case, and I want it solved pronto."

"This doctor, he's a white man?" I asked, keeping my expression neutral.

"I told you, he's German."

"I already have a number of open cases in Southeast," I said to Pittman. "A nurse was murdered over the weekend."

He didn't want to hear it. He shook his head—*one* shake. "And now you have an important case in Georgetown. Solve it, Cross. You're to work on nothing else. That's a direct order . . . from The Jefe."

Chapter 15

AS SOON as Cross walked out of Chief Pittman's inner office, a senior homicide detective named Patsy Hampton slipped in through a side door that led to the attached conference room. Detective Hampton had been instructed by Pittman to listen in on everything, to evaluate the situation from a street cop's perspective, to advise and to counsel.

Hampton didn't like the job, but those were her orders from Pittman. She didn't like Pittman, either. He was wound so tight that if you stuck coal up his ass, in a couple of weeks you'd have a diamond. He was mean and petty and vengeful.

"You see what I'm dealing with here? Cross knows how to push all my buttons. In the beginning he would lose his temper. Now he just ignores what I say."

"I heard everything," Hampton said. "He's slick, all right." She was going to agree with Chief Pittman, no matter what he said.

Patsy Hampton was an attractive woman, with sandy blond hair cut short, and the most piercing blue eyes this side of Stockholm. She was thirty-one years old, and on a very fast track in the department. At twenty-six, she'd been the youngest homicide detective in Washington. Now she had much loftier goals in mind.

"You're selling yourself short, though. You got to him. I know you did." She told Pittman what he wanted to hear. "He just internalizes it pretty well."

"You're sure he's meeting with those other detectives?" Pittman asked her.

"They've met three times that I know of, always at Cross's house on Fifth Street. I suspect there have been other times. I heard about it through a friend of Detective Thurman."

"But they don't meet while any of them is on duty?"

"No, not to my knowledge. They're careful. They meet on their own time."

Pittman scowled and shook his head. "That's too goddamn bad. It makes it harder to prove anything really damaging."

"From what I've heard, they believe the department is holding back resources that could clear a number of unsolved homicides in Southeast and parts of Northeast. Most of the murders involve black and Hispanic women."

Pittman tensed his jaw and looked away from Hampton. "The numbers that Cross uses are complete bullshit," he said angrily. "They're dogshit. It's all political with him. How much financial

resource can we put against the murders of drug
addicts and prostitutes in Southeast? It's criminals
murdering other criminals. You know how it goes
in those black neighborhoods."

Hampton nodded again, still agreeing when she
saw the chance. She was afraid she'd lost him, said
the wrong thing by speaking the truth. "They
think that at least some of the victims were innocent women from their neighborhoods. That E.R.
nurse who was killed over the weekend, she was a
friend of Cross and Detective John Sampson. Cross
thinks a killer could be loose in Southeast, preying
on women."

"A serial killer in the ghetto? Give me a break.
We've never had one there. They're rare in any
inner city. Why now? Why here? Because Cross
wants to find one, that's why."

"Cross and the others would counter that by
saying we've never seriously tried to catch this
squirrel."

Pittman's small eyes suddenly burned into
her skull. "Do you agree with that horseshit,
Detective?"

"No, sir. I don't necessarily agree or disagree. I
know for a fact that the department doesn't have
enough resources anywhere in the city, with the
possible exception of Capitol Hill. Now *that's*
political, and it's an outrage."

Pittman smiled at her answer. The chief knew
she was playing him a little, but he liked her anyway. He liked just being in a room with Patsy

Hampton. She was such a doll, such a cutie. "What do you know about Cross, Patsy?"

She sensed that the chief had vented enough. Now he wanted their talk to be more informal. She was certain that he liked her, had a crush on her, but he was too uptight to ever act on his desires, thank God.

"I know Cross has been on the force for just over eight years. He's currently the liaison between the department and the FBI, works with the Violent Criminal Apprehension Program. He's a profiler with a good reputation, from what I hear. Has a Ph.D. in psych from Johns Hopkins. Private practice for three years before he came to us. Widower, two kids, plays the blues on the piano at his house. That enough background? What more do you want to know? I've done my homework. You know me," Hampton said, and finally smiled.

Pittman was smiling now, too. He had small teeth with spaces between them, and always made her think of Eastern European refugees, or maybe Russian gangsters.

Detective Hampton smiled, though. She knew he liked it when she played along with him—as long as he thought she respected him.

"Any other worthwhile observations at this point?" he asked.

You're such a soft, flabby dick, Patsy Hampton wanted to say, but she just shook her head. "He has some charm. He's well connected in political circles. I can see why you're concerned about him."

"You think Cross is charming?"

"I told you, he's slick. He *is.* People say he looks like the young Muhammad Ali. I think he likes to play the part sometimes: dance like a butterfly, sting like a bee." She laughed again—and so did he.

"We're going to nail Cross," Pittman said. "We'll send him flying back to private practice. Wait and see. You're going to help get it done. You get things done. Right, Detective Hampton? You see the bigger picture. That's what I like about you."

She smiled again. "That's what I like about me, too."

Chapter 16

THE BRITISH Embassy is a plain, Federal-style building located at 3100 Massachusetts Avenue. Its immediate neighbors are the vice president's house and the Observatory. The ambassador's residence is a stately Georgian building with tall, flowing white columns; the Chancery is the actual office building.

Geoffrey Shafer sat behind his small mahogany desk at the embassy and stared out onto Massachusetts Avenue. The embassy staff currently counted 415 people—soon to be cut to 414, he was thinking to himself. The staff included defense experts, foreign-policy specialists, trade, public affairs, clerks, and secretaries.

Although the United States and Britain have an agreement not to spy on each other, Geoffrey Shafer was nonetheless a spy. He was one of eleven men and women from the Security Service, formerly known as MI6, who worked at the embassy in Washington. These eleven in turn ran agents attached to the consulates general in Atlanta,

Boston, Chicago, Houston, Los Angeles, New York, and San Francisco.

He was feeling restless as hell today, getting up from his desk frequently, pacing back and forth across the carpet that covered the creaking parquet floors. He made phone calls he didn't need to make, tried to get some work done, thought about how much he despised his job and the everyday details of life.

He was supposed to be working on a truly silly communiqué about the government's absurd ongoing commitment to human rights. The foreign secretary had rather bombastically proclaimed that Britain would support the international condemnation of regimes that violate human rights; support international bodies involved in the cause; and denounce human-rights abuses, *blah, blah, blah*, ad nauseam.

He glanced through a few of the computer games he enjoyed when he was uptight like this—Riven, MechCommander, Unreal, TOCA, Ultimate Soccer Manager. None of them appealed to him right now; nothing did.

He was starting to crash, and he knew the feeling. *I'm going down, and there is only one certain way to stop it: play the Four Horsemen.*

To make matters worse, it was raining and woefully gray-skied outside. The city of Washington, and also the surrounding countryside, looked forlorn and depressing. It sucked. Christ, he was in a bad mood, even for him.

He continued to stare east across Massachusetts Avenue, looking into the trees bordering a park dedicated to the pacifist bullshit artist Kahlil Gibran. He tried to daydream, mostly about fucking various attractive women currently working at the embassy.

He had called his psychiatrist, Boo Cassady, at her home-office, but she was about to start a session and couldn't talk for long. They agreed to meet after work: a nasty quickie at her place before he went home to face Lucy and the sniveling brood.

He didn't dare play Horsemen again tonight. It was too soon after the nurse. But God Almighty, he *wanted* to play. He wished he could take somebody out in some very imaginative way, right there inside the embassy.

He did have one excellent thing to do today— saving it until now—three in the afternoon. He had used the dice already, played a bit of Horsemen, just to help him make a personnel decision.

He had called Sarah Middleton just before lunch and told her they needed to have a chat and could she stop by his office, say at three?

Sarah was obviously tense on the phone and told him she could do it earlier, anytime, at his convenience. "Not busy, then, nothing much to do today?" Shafer asked. Three o'clock would be fine, she answered hastily.

His secretary, the bestial Betty formerly from Belgravia, buzzed him promptly at three. At least he'd finally gotten through to her about punctuality.

Shafer let her buzz him several times, then picked up the phone abruptly, as if she'd interrupted him at something vital to security.

"What is it, Ms. Thomas? I'm extremely busy with this communiqué for the secretary."

"I'm sorry to disturb you, Mr. Shafer, but Ms. Middleton is here. You have a three-o'clock appointment with her, I understand."

"*Hmmm.* Do I? Yes, you're right. Can you ask Sarah to wait? I'll need a few more minutes. I'll buzz when I'm ready to see her."

Shafer smiled contentedly and picked up a copy of *The Red Coat,* the embassy's employee newsletter. He knew Betty hated it when he used Ms. Middleton's Christian name: Sarah.

He fantasized about Sarah for the next few moments. He'd wanted to have a go at Mzzz Middleton from their first interview, but he was too careful for that. God, he hated the bitch. This was going to be such fun.

Schafer watched the rain hammer down on the traffic crossing Massachusetts Avenue for another ten minutes. Finally he snatched up the phone. He couldn't wait a minute longer. "I'll see her now. Send Sarah in."

He fingered his twenty-sided dice. This could be fun, actually. *Terror at the office.*

Chapter 17

THE LOVELY Sarah Middleton entered his office and managed a cordial look, almost a smile. He felt like a boa constrictor eyeing a mouse.

She had naturally curly red hair, a moderately pretty face, a superior figure. Today she wore a very short suit, a red V-necked silk blouse, black stockings. It was obvious to Shafer that she was out to catch a husband in Washington.

Shafer's pulse was beating hard. He was aroused by her, always had been. He thought about taking her, and very much liked that phrase. She didn't look as nervous and unsure of herself as she had recently, so that probably meant she was really scared and trying not to show it. He tried his best to think like Sarah. That made it more fun, though he found it a real challenge to be as squir-relly and insecure as she would surely be.

"We certainly needed the rain," Sarah said, and then cringed before the sentence was even finished.

"Sarah, please sit down," he said. He was trying to keep a straight business face. "Personally, I loathe the rain. It's one of the many reasons I've never been stationed in London."

He sighed theatrically behind the rigid tent he'd made with his fingers. He wondered if Sarah noticed the length of his fingers and if she ever thought about how large he was elsewhere. He would bet anything that she did. It was how people's minds worked, though women like Sarah would never admit to it.

She cleared her throat, then put her hands on her knees. The knuckles of her fingers were white. Christ, he was enjoying her obvious discomfort. She looked ready to jump out of her skin. How about out of her tight little skirt and blouse?

He began to stretch the fingers on his right hand, playing his part as dominator to the hilt. "Sarah, I think I have some bad news—quite unfortunate, really, but can't be avoided."

She sat nervously forward in her chair. She really was nicely built up top. He was getting hard now. "What is it, Mr. Shafer? What do you mean? You *think* you have bad news? You do or you don't?"

"We have to let you go. *I* have to let you go. Budget cuts, I'm afraid," he said. "I know you must find this immensely unfair, and unexpected as well. Particularly when you moved halfway across the world from Australia to take this job, and you've been living in Washington for less than six months. Suddenly, the ax falls."

He could tell she was actually fighting back

tears. Her lips were trembling. Obviously, she never expected this. She had no idea. She was a reasonably smart and controlled woman, but she couldn't help herself now.

Excellent. He had succeeded in breaking her down. He wished he had a movie camera this minute to record the look on her face and play it back countless times in private.

He saw the very instant that she lost it, and treasured it. He watched her eyes moisten, saw the large tears roll over her cheeks, streaking her working-girl makeup.

He felt the power, and it was as good as he'd hoped it would be. A small insignificant game, certainly, but a delicious one. He loved being able to instill such shock and pain.

"Poor Sarah. Poor, poor dear," he murmured.

Then Shafer did the cruelest, most unforgivable thing. Also the most outrageous and dangerous. He got up from his desk and came around to comfort her. He stood behind her, pressing himself against her shoulders. He knew it was the last thing she wanted, to be touched by him, to feel that he was aroused.

She stiffened and pulled away from him as if he were on fire. "Bastard," she said, between clenched teeth. "You are a consummate prick!"

Sarah left his office, shaking and in tears, running in that stumbling way women often do in heels. Shafer loved it. The sadistic pleasure, not only of hurting someone but of destroying this innocent woman. He memorized the stunning image for all time. He would play it back, over and over.

Yes, he was a prick. Consummate indeed.

Chapter 18

ROSIE THE cat was perched on the windowsill, watching me dress for my date with Christine. I envied the simplicity of her life: *Love to eat those mousies, mousies what I love to eat.*

I finally headed downstairs. I was taking the night off from work, and I was more nervous, distracted, and fidgety than I had been in a long time. Nana and the kids knew something was up, but they didn't know what, and it was driving my three favorite busybodies crazy.

"Daddy, tell me what's going on, *please?*" Jannie clasped her hands in prayer and begged.

"I told you no, and no is no. Not even if you get down on your bony little knees," I said, and smiled. "I have a date tonight. It's just a date. That's all you need to know, young lady."

"Is it with Christine?" Jannie asked. "At least you can tell me *that* much."

"*That's* for me to know," I said as I knotted my tie in the mirror beside the stairs. "And *you not* to find out, my overinquisitive girlfriend."

"You're wearing your fancy blue-striped suit,

your fancy dancing shoes, that fancy tie you like. You're *so* fancy."

"Do I look good?" I turned and asked my personal clothier. "For my date?"

"You look beautiful, Daddy." My girl beamed, and I knew I could believe her. Her eyes were shiny little mirrors that always told the truth. "You know you do. You know you're handsome as sin."

"That's my girl," I said, and laughed again. *Handsome as sin.* She got that one from Nana, no doubt.

Damon mimicked his sister. "You look beautiful, Daddy. What a little brownnoser. What do you want from Daddy, Jannie?"

"Do I look good?" I turned to Damon.

He rolled his eyes. "You look all right. How come you're all duded up? You can tell me. Man to man. What's the big deal?"

"Answer the poor children!" Nana finally said.

I looked her way and offered up a wide grin. "Don't use the 'poor children' to try to get your gossip quotient for the day. Well, I'm off," I announced. "I'll be home before sunrise. *Moo-ha-ha-ha.*" I did my favorite monster imitation, and all three of them rolled their eyes.

It was a minute or so before eight, and as I stepped onto the porch, a black Lincoln Town Car pulled up in front of the house. It was right on time, and I didn't want to be late.

"A limousine?" Jannie gasped, and nearly

swooned on the front porch. "You're going out in a *limousine?*"

"Alex Cross!" Nana said. "What *is* going on?"

I practically danced down the steps. I got into the waiting car, shut the door, told the driver to go. I waved out the back window and stuck out my tongue as the car smoothly pulled away from our house.

Chapter 19

MY LAST image was of the three of them—Jannie, Damon, and Nana—all mugging and sticking out their tongues at me. We do have some fabulously good times together, I was thinking as the car headed over to Prince Georges County, where I had once confronted a homicidal twelve-year-old during the halcyon days of the Jack and Jill killers, and where Christine Johnson lived.

I had my mantra all set for tonight: *Heart leads head.* I needed to believe that was so.

"A private car? A limousine?" Christine exclaimed when I picked her up at her house in Mitchellville.

She looked as stunningly beautiful as I've ever seen her, and that's saying a lot. She wore a long, sleeveless black shift, black satin pumps with straps, and had a floral brocade jacket draped over her arm. The heels made her a little over six feet tall. God, how I loved this woman, everything about her.

We walked to the car and got inside.

"You haven't told me where we're going

tonight, Alex. Just that it was fancy. Someplace special."

"Ah, but I've told our driver," I said. I tapped the partition window, and the Town Car moved off into the summer night. Alex the mysterious.

I held Christine's hands as we drove along on the John Hanson Highway, back toward Washington. Her face tilted toward mine, and I kissed her in the cozy darkness. I loved the sweetness of her mouth, her lips, the softness and smoothness of her skin. She was wearing a new perfume that I didn't recognize, and I liked that, too. I kissed the hollow of her throat, then her cheeks, her eyes, her hair. I would have been happy to do just this for the rest of the night.

"It is unbelievably romantic," she finally said. "It *is* special. You are something else . . . *sugar.*"

We cuddled and hugged all the way into Washington. We talked, but I don't remember the subject. I could feel her breasts rising and falling against me. I was surprised when we arrived at the intersection of Massachusetts and Wisconsin avenues. We were getting close to the surprise.

True to her word, Christine hadn't asked any more questions. Not until the car eased up in front of Washington National Cathedral, and the driver got out and held the door open for us.

"The National Cathedral?" she said. "We're going in here?"

I nodded and stared up at the stunning Gothic masterpiece that I'd admired since I was a boy. The cathedral crowns over fifty acres of lawns and woods and is Washington's highest point, even higher than the Washington Monument. If I remembered correctly, it was the second-largest church in the United States, and possibly the prettiest.

I led the way, and Christine followed me inside. She held my hand lightly. We entered the northwest corner of the nave, which extends nearly a tenth of a mile to the massive altar.

Everything felt special and very beautiful, spiritual, just right. We walked up to a pew under the amazing Space Window at midnave. Everywhere I looked there were priceless stained-glass windows, over two hundred in all.

The light inside was exquisite; I felt blessed. There was a kaleidoscope of changing colors on the walls: reds, warm yellows, cool blues.

"Beautiful, isn't it?" I whispered. "Timeless, sublime, all that good Gothic stuff Henry Adams used to write about."

"Oh, Alex, I think it's the prettiest spot in Washington. The Space Window, the Children's Chapel—I've always loved it here. I told you that, didn't I?" she asked.

"You might have mentioned it once," I said. "Or maybe I just knew it."

We continued walking until we entered the Children's Chapel. It is small, beautiful, and wonderfully intimate. We stood under a stained-glass window that depicts the story of Samuel and David as children.

I turned and looked at Christine, and my heart was beating so loud I was sure she could hear it. Her eyes were sparkling like jewels in the flickering candlelight. The black dress shimmered and seemed to flow over her body.

I knelt on one knee and looked up at her.

"I've loved you since the first time I saw you at the Sojourner Truth School," I whispered, so that only she could hear me. "Except that when I saw you the first time, I had no way of knowing how incredibly special you are on the inside. How wise, how good. I didn't know that I could feel the way I do—whole and complete—whenever I'm with you. I would do anything for you. Or just to be with you for one more moment."

I stopped for the briefest pause and took a deep breath. She held my eyes, didn't pull away.

"I love you so much, and I always will. Will you marry me, Christine?"

She continued to look into my eyes, and I saw such warmth and love, but also humility, which is always a part of who Christine is. It was almost as if she couldn't imagine my loving her.

"Yes, I will. Oh, Alex, I shouldn't have waited until tonight. But this is so perfect, so special, I'm almost glad I did. Yes, I will be your wife."

I took out an antique engagement ring and gently slid it onto Christine's finger. The ring had been my mother's, and I'd kept it since she died, when I was nine. The exact history of the ring was unclear, except that it went back at least four generations in the Cross family and was my one and only heirloom.

We kissed in the glorious Children's Chapel of the National Cathedral, and it was the best moment of my life, never to be forgotten, never to be diminished in any way.

Yes, I will be your wife.

Chapter 20

TEN DAYS had passed without another fantasy murder, but now a powerful mood swing had taken hold of Geoffrey Shafer, and he let himself go with the flow.

He was flying high as a kite—hyper, manic, bipolar, whatever the doctors wanted to call his condition. He'd already taken Ativan, Librium, Valium, and Depakote, but the drugs seemed only to fuel his jets.

That night at around six he pulled the black Jaguar out of the lot on the north side of the embassy, passing by the larger-than-life Winston Churchill statue with its stubby right hand raised in V for Victory, its left hand holding his trademark cigar.

Eric Clapton played guitar loudly on the car's CD. He turned up the volume higher, slapping his hands hard on the steering wheel, feeling the rhythm, the beat, the primal urge.

Shafer turned onto Massachusetts Avenue and then stopped at a Starbucks. He hurried in and fixed up three coffees his way. Black as his heart, with six sugars. *Mmm, hmmm.* As usual, he had nearly finished the first before he got to the cash register.

Once he was inside the cockpit of his Jag again, he sipped a second cup at a more leisurely pace. He downed some Benadryl and Nascan. Couldn't hurt; might help. He took out the twenty-sided game dice. He had to play tonight.

Anything twelve or higher would dispatch him directly to Boo Cassady's place for a kinky quickie before he went home to the dreaded family. A seven to eleven was total disaster—straight home to Lucy and the kids. Three, four, five, or six meant he could go to the hideaway for an unscheduled night of high adventure.

"Come three, four, five. Come, baby, come! I need this tonight. Need a fix! I need it!"

He shook the dice for what must have been thirty seconds. He made the suspense last, drew it out. Finally, he released the dice onto the gray-leather car seat. He watched the roll closely.

Jesus, he'd thrown a four! Defied the odds! His brain was on fire. He could play tonight. The dice had spoken; fate had spoken.

He excitedly punched a number on his cell phone. *"Lucy,"* he said, and he was smiling already.

"Glad I caught you at home, darling. . . . Yes, you guessed it, first try. We're completely swamped here again. Can you believe it? I certainly can't. They think they own me, and I suppose they're half right. It's the drug-trafficking rubbish again. I'll be home when I can. Don't wait up, though. Love to the kids. Kisses to everybody. Me, too, darling. I love you, too. You're the best, the most understanding wife alive."

Very well played, Shafer thought as he breathed a sigh of relief. Excellent performance, considering the drugs he'd taken. Shafer disconnected from his wife, whose family money, unfortunately, paid for the town house, the holidays away, even the Jag, and her fashionable Range Rover, of course.

He punched another number on the cell phone.

"Dr. Cassady." He heard her voice almost immediately. She *knew* it was him. He usually called from the car on his way over to see her. They liked to get each other hot and bothered on the phone. Telephone sex as foreplay.

"They've done it to me again," Shafer whined miserably into the phone, but he was smiling again, loving his flair for the overdramatic.

A short silence, then, "You mean they did it to *us,* don't you? There's *no way* you can get away? It's only a bloody job, and one that you detest, Geoff."

"You know I would if I possibly could. I do hate it here, *loathe* every moment. And it's even worse at home, Boo. Jesus, you of all people know that."

He imagined the tight little frown and Boo's pursing her lips. "You sound high, Geoffrey. Are you, dear? Take your pills today?"

"Don't be horrible. Of course I've taken my medications. I *am* rushed. I *am* high. On the ceiling, as a matter of fact. I'm calling between blasted staff meetings. Oh hell, I miss you, Boo. I want to be inside you, deep inside. I want to do your pussy, your ass, your throat. I'm thinking about it right now. Christ, I'm as hard as a rock here in my government-issue office. Have to beat it down with a stick. *Cane* it. That's how we British handle such things."

She laughed, and he almost changed his mind about standing her up. "Go back to work. I'll be at home, if you finish early," she said. "I could use a little finishing myself."

"I love you, Boo. You're so kind to me."

"I am, and I could probably get into a little can-ing, too."

He hung up and drove to the hideaway in Eckington. He parked the Jag next to the purple and blue taxi in the garage. He bounded upstairs to change for the game. God, he loved this, his secret life, his nights away from everything and everyone he *loathed.*

He was taking too many chances now, but he didn't care.

Chapter 21

SHAFER WAS totally pumped up for a night on the town. The Four Horsemen was on. Anything could happen tonight. Yet he found that he was introspective and pensive. He could flip from manic to depressive in the blink of an eye.

He watched himself as if he were an observer in a dream. He had been an English intelligence agent, but now that the Cold War had ended, there was little use for his talents. It was only the influence of Lucy's father that had kept him in his job. Duncan Cousins had been a general in the army and now was chairman of a packaged-goods conglomerate specializing in the sale of detergents, soaps, and drugstore perfumes. He liked to call Shafer "the Colonel," rubbing in his "rise to mediocrity." The General also loved to talk about the glowing successes of Shafer's two brothers, both of whom had made millions in business.

Shafer shifted his thoughts back to the present. He was doing that a lot lately, fading in and out like a radio with a bad connection. He took a settling breath, then pulled the taxi out of the garage. Moments later, he turned onto Rhode Island Avenue. It was beginning to rain again, a light mist that made the passing traffic lights blurry and impressionistic.

Shafer drifted over to the curb and stopped for a tall, slender black man. He looked like a drug dealer, something Shafer had no use for. Maybe he would just shoot the bastard, then dump the body. That felt good enough for tonight's action. A sleazebag dope dealer whom nobody would miss.

"Airport," the man announced haughtily as he climbed inside the taxi. The inconsiderate bastard shook off rainwater onto the seat. Then he shut the creaking car door behind him and was on his cell phone immediately.

Shafer wasn't going to the airport, and neither was his first passenger of the night. He listened in on the phone call. The man's voice was affected, surprisingly cultured.

"I think I'll just make the nine o'clock, Leonard. It's Delta *on* the hour, right? I picked up a cab, thank the Lord Jesus. Most of them won't stop anywhere near where my poor Moms lives in Northeast. Then along comes this purple and blue absolute wreck of a gypsy cab, and merciful God, it stops for me."

Christ, he'd been identified. Shafer silently cursed his bad luck. That was the way of the game, though: incredible highs and vicious lows. He would have to take this asshole all the way out to National Airport. If he disappeared, it would be connected to a purple and blue cab, an "absolute wreck of a gypsy cab."

Shafer stepped on the accelerator and sped out toward National. The airport was backed up, even at nine in the evening. He cursed under his breath. The rain was heavy and punctuated by rolling thunder and spits of lightning.

He tried to control his building anger, his darkening mood. It took nearly forty minutes to get to the bloody terminal and drop off the passenger. By that time he'd settled back into another fantasy, had another huge mood swing. He was cycling *up* again.

Maybe he should have gone to see Dr. Cassady, after all. He needed more pills, especially Lithium. This was like a carnival ride tonight—up and down, up and down. He wanted to push things as far as he could. He also felt crazed. He was definitely losing control.

Anything could happen when he got like this. That was the thing. He pulled into the queue of taxis waiting to get a fare back to D.C.

As he got closer to the front of the line, there was more thunder. Lightning crackled high above the airport. He could see the prospective victims huddled under a dripping canopy. Flights were undoubtedly being postponed and canceled. He savored the cheap-seat melodrama, the suspense. The victim du jour could be anyone, from a corporate executive to a harried secretary, or maybe even a whole family back from a vacation to Disney World.

But not once did he look directly at the queue of potential victims as he inched closer and closer. He was almost there. Just two more taxis in front of him. He could see the queue out of the corner of his eye. Finally, he had to snatch a quick peek.

It was a tall male.

He peeked again, couldn't help himself.

A white male, a businessman, stepped off the curb and was climbing inside the taxi. He was cursing to himself, pissed off about the rain.

Shafer looked the man over. He was American, late thirties, full of himself. Investment analyst, maybe, or banker—something like that.

"We can *go*—whenever you're in the mood," the man snapped at him.

"Sorry, sir," Shafer said, and smiled obsequiously into the rearview mirror.

He dropped the dice on the front seat: *six!* His heart began to hammer.

Six meant *immediate action.* But he was still inside National Airport. There was a heavy lineup of traffic and cops, bright lights glittering everywhere. It was too dangerous, even for him.

The dice had spoken. He had no choice. The game was *on* right now.

A sea of red rear lights glowed at him. Cars were everywhere. How could he do this here? Shafer began to perspire heavily.

But he had to do it. That was the point of the game. He had to do it now. Had to murder this asshole right here at the airport.

He swerved into the nearest parking area. This was not good. He sped down a narrow lane. Another bolt of lightning flashed overhead; it seemed to underscore the madness and chaos of the moment.

"Where the *hell* are you going?" the businessman shouted at him. He slammed his palm into the back of the seat. "This isn't the way out, you ass!"

Shafer glared at the business creep in his rearview mirror. He hated him for calling him an ass. The bastard also reminded him of his brothers.

"I'm not going anywhere," he yelled back. "But *you're* going straight to hell!"

The businessman blubbered, "What did you say to me? What did you just say?"

Shafer fired his Smith & Wesson nine-millimeter and hoped no one would hear it above the thunder and honking horns.

He was soaking wet with perspiration, and he was afraid his black face would run and smear. He was expecting to be stopped at any moment. Waiting for policemen to surround the taxi. Bright-red blood was splattered all over the backseat and window. The businessman was slumped in the corner as if he were asleep. Shafer couldn't see where the bloody bullet had exited the taxi.

He made it out of National before he went completely mad. He drove carefully to Benning Heights in Southeast. He couldn't risk being stopped for speeding. But he was out of his head, not sure he was doing the right thing.

He stopped on a side street, checked out the

body, stripped it. He decided to dump the corpse out in the open. He was trying his best not to be predictable.

Then he sped away from the crime scene and headed home.

He'd left no identification on the victim. Nothing but the body.

Just a little surprise—a *John* Doe.

Chapter 22

I GOT home from Christine's house at two-thirty in the morning feeling exhilarated, the happiest I'd been in years. I thought about waking Nana and the kids to tell them the news. I wanted to see the surprised looks on their faces. I wished that I had brought Christine home with me, so we could celebrate together.

The phone rang moments after I stepped inside the house. *Oh no,* I thought, *not tonight. Nothing good comes from phone calls at two-thirty* A.M.

I picked up in the living room and heard Sampson's voice on the line. "Sugar?" he whispered.

"Leave me alone," I said. "Try again in the morning. I'm closed for the night."

"No you're not, Alex. Not tonight. Get over to Alabama Avenue, about three blocks east of Dupont Park. A man was found there naked and dead, in the gutter. The guy is white, and there's no I.D. on him."

First thing in the morning, I would tell Nana and the kids about Christine and me. I had to go. The murder scene was a ten-minute ride across the

Anacostia River. Sampson was waiting for me on a street corner. So was the John Doe.

And a lively, mean-spirited crowd. A naked white body dumped in this neighborhood had prompted lots of curiosity, almost like seeing a deer walking down Alabama Avenue.

"Casper the Friendly Ghost been *offed*." A heckler contributed his twenty-five cents as Sampson and I stooped down under the yellow plastic crime-scene tape. In the background were rows of dilapidated brick buildings that almost seemed to scream out the names of the lost, the forgotten, the never-had-a-chance.

Stagnant water often pools on the street corners here since the storm drains are hardly ever inspected. I knelt over the twisted, naked body that was partly immersed in the cesspool. There would be no tire marks left at the watery scene. I wondered if the killer had thought of that.

I was making mental notes. No need to write them down; I'd remember everything. The man had manicured fingernails and toenails. No calluses showed on either his hands or his feet. He had no bruises or distinct disfiguring marks, other than the cruel gunshot wound that had blown away the left side of his face.

The body was deeply suntanned, except where he'd worn swim trunks. A thin, pale ring ran around his left index finger, where he'd probably worn a wedding band, which was missing.

And there was no I.D.—just like the Jane Does.

Death was clearly the result of the single, devastating gunshot to the head. Alabama Avenue was the primary scene—where the body was found—but I suspected a secondary homicide scene, where the victim was actually murdered.

"What do you think?" Sampson crouched down close beside me. His knees cracked loudly. "Sonofabitch killer is pissed off about something."

"Really bizarre that he wound up here in Benning Heights. I don't know if he's connected to the Jane Does. But if he is, the killer wanted us to find this one in a hurry. Bodies around here usually get dumped in Fort Dupont Park. He's getting stranger and stranger. And you're right, he's very angry with the world."

My mind was rapidly filling with crime-scene notes, plus the usual stream of homicide-detective questions. Why leave the body in a street gutter? Why not in an abandoned building? Why in Benning Heights? Was the killer black? That still made the most sense to me, but a very low percentage of pattern killers are black.

The sergeant from the Crime Scene Unit came strolling up to Sampson and me. "What do you want from us, Detective?"

I looked back at the naked white body. "Videotape it, photograph it, sketch it," I told him.

"And take some of the trash in the gutter and sidewalk?"

"Take everything. Even if it's soaking wet."

The sergeant frowned. "Everything? All this wet trash? Why?"

Alabama Avenue is hilly, and I could see the Capitol Building brightly illuminated in the distance. It looked like a faraway celestial body, maybe heaven. It got me thinking about the *haves* in Washington, and the *have-nots*.

"Just take everything. It's how I work," I said.

Chapter 23

DETECTIVE PATSY Hampton arrived at the chilling homicide scene around 2:15. The Jefe's assistant had called her apartment about an unusual murder in Benning Heights that might relate to the Jane Does. This one was different in some ways, but there were too many similarities for her to ignore.

She watched Alex Cross work the crime scene. She was impressed that he'd come out at this early hour. She was curious about him, had been for a long time. Hampton knew Cross by reputation and had followed a couple of his cases. She had even worked a few weeks on the tragic kidnapping of Maggie Rose Dunne and Michael Goldberg.

So far, she had mixed feelings about Cross. He was personable enough, and more than good-looking. Cross was a tall, strongly put-together man. She felt that he received undeserved special treatment because he was a forensic psychologist. She'd done her homework on Cross.

Hampton understood that she had been assigned to show Cross up, to win, to knock him down a peg. She knew it would be a tough competition, but she also knew that she was the one to do it; she never failed at anything.

She'd already done her own examination of the crime scene. She had stayed on at the scene only because Cross and Sampson had unexpectedly shown up.

She continued to study Cross, watched him walk the homicide scene several times. He was physically imposing, and so was his partner, who had to be at least six-nine. Cross was six-three and weighed maybe two hundred. He appeared younger than his age, which was forty-one. He seemed to be respected by the assisting patrolmen, even by the EMS personnel. He shook a few hands, patted shoulders, occasionally shared a smile with someone working the crime scene.

Hampton figured that was part of his act, though. Everybody had one these days, especially in Washington. Cross's was obviously his charisma and charm.

Hell, she had an act herself. Hers was to appear nonthreatening and "feminine," then perform contrary to the expectations of the males on the force. She usually caught them off guard. As she'd risen in the department, the men had learned that she could be tough. Surprise, surprise. She worked longer hours than anyone else; she was a hell of a lot tougher than the men; and she never socialized with other cops.

But she made one big mistake. She broke into a

homicide suspect's car without a warrant, and was caught by another detective, a jealous older male. That was how Pittman got his hooks into her, and now he wouldn't let go.

At around a quarter to three, she walked to her forest-green Explorer, noting that it needed a wash. She already had a few ideas about the dead man in the street. There was no doubt in her mind that she would beat Cross.

Book Two

DEATH RIDES A PALE HORSE

GEORGE BAYER was Famine among the Four Horsemen. He'd been playing the fantasy game for seven years, and he loved it. At least he had until recently, when Geoffrey Shafer started to go out of control.

Famine was physically unimpressive at around five-eight, a hundred ninety pounds. He was paunchy, balding, wore wire-rim glasses, but he also knew that his appearance was deceiving, and he'd made a living off those who underestimated him. People like Geoffrey Shafer.

He had reread a forty-page dossier on Shafer during his long plane ride from Asia to Washington. The dossier told him everything about Shafer, and also about the character he played, Death. At Dulles Airport he rented a dark-blue Ford sedan, under a false name. He was still detached and introspective during his thirty-minute drive into the city.

But he was also anxious: he was nervous for all of the Horsemen, but especially for himself. He was the one who would have to confront Shafer, and he was worried that Shafer might be going mad, that he might blow up in all of their faces.

George Bayer had been an M man—MI6—and he'd known Shafer in the service. He had come to Washington to check out Shafer firsthand. It was suspected by the other players that Geoffrey might have gone over the edge, that he was no longer playing by the rules and was a grave danger to them all. Since Bayer had once been stationed in Washington, and knew the town, he was the one to go there.

Bayer didn't want to be seen at the British Embassy on Massachusetts Avenue, but he had spoken to a few friends who he knew would keep silent about having been contacted. The news about Shafer was as bad as he'd suspected. He was seeing women outside his marriage, and he wasn't being discreet. There was a psychologist who was also a sex therapist, and he had been observed going over to her place several times a week, often during working hours. It was rumored that he was drinking heavily and possibly taking drugs. Bayer suspected the latter. He and Shafer had been friends and they had done their share of drugs while posted in the Philippines and Thailand. Of course, they were younger and more foolish then—or at least that was true of Bayer.

The D.C. police had recently put in a complaint to the embassy about a reckless-driving incident. Shafer might have been high at the time. His current assignments at the embassy were minimal, and he would have been dismissed, or sent back to England, if it weren't for his wife's father, General Duncan Cousins. What a terrible mess Shafer had made of his life.

But that's not the worst of it, is it, Geoffrey? George Bayer was thinking as he drove into the Northeast section of Washington known as Eckington Place. *There's more, isn't there, dear boy? It's much worse than the embassy thinks. It's probably the biggest scandal in the long history of the Security Service, and you're right at the heart of it. But of course, so am I.*

Bayer locked the doors of his car as he pulled up to a traffic light. The area looked highly suspicious to him, like so much of Washington these days. What a sad, totally insane country America had become. What a perfect refuge for Shafer.

Famine took in the sights on the mean streets as he continued through the decidedly lower-class neighborhood. There was nothing to compare with this in London. Row upon row of two-storied redbrick garden apartments, many of them in dreadful disrepair. Not so much urban decay as urban apathy.

He saw Shafer's lair up ahead and pulled over to the curb. He knew the exact location of the hide-away from the elaborate fantasy tales Shafer had spun for his fellow players. He knew the address. Now he needed to know one more thing: were the murders that Geoffrey claimed he'd committed fantasies, or were they real? Was he actually a cold-blooded killer, operating here in Washington?

Bayer walked to the garage door. It took him only a moment to pick the lock and let himself in.

He had heard so much about the "Nightmare Machine," the purple and blue taxi that Shafer used for the murders. He was looking at it. The taxi was as real as he was. Now he knew the truth. George Bayer shook his head. Shafer had killed all of those people. This was no longer a game.

Chapter 25

BAYER TRUDGED upstairs to the hideaway apartment. His arms and legs felt heavy, and he had a slight pain in his chest. His vision was tunneled. He pulled down the dusty blinds and began to look around.

Shafer had boastfully described the garage and taxi several times during the game. He had flaunted the existence of the hideaway and sworn to the other players that it was real and not just some fantasy in a role-playing game. Geoffrey had openly dared them to see it for themselves, and that was why Bayer was in Washington.

Well, Geoffrey, the hideaway is real, he agreed. *You are a stone-cold killer. You weren't bluffing, were you?*

At ten o'clock that night Bayer took Shafer's taxi out. The keys were there, almost as a dare. Was it? He figured he had a night to experience exactly what Shafer had experienced. According to Geoffrey, half the fun of the game was foreplay—checking out the possibilities, seeing the whole game board before you made a move.

From ten o'clock until half past eleven, Bayer explored the streets of D.C., but he didn't pick up a fare. He kept his off-duty sign on. *What a game,* Bayer kept thinking as he drove. *Is this how Geoffrey does it? Is this how he feels when he's prowling the city?*

He was pulled out of his daydream by an old tramp with a crushed hat who wheeled a cart filled with cans and other recyclables right in front of him. He didn't seem to care whether he got run over or not, but Bayer braked hard. That made him think of Shafer. The line between life and death had faded to nothing for Geoffrey, hadn't it?

Bayer cautiously moved on. He drove past a church. The service was over, and a crowd of people was leaving.

He stopped the cab for an attractive black woman in a blue dress and matching high heels. He needed to see what this must be like for Shafer, for Death. He couldn't resist.

"Thank you so much," the woman said as she slid into the rear of his taxi. She seemed so proper and respectable. He checked her furtively in the mirror. She didn't have much to offer up top. Pretty enough face, though. Long brown legs encased in sheer stockings. He tried to imagine what Shafer might do now, but he couldn't.

Shafer had boasted that he was killing people in the poorer sections of Washington, since nobody cared about them anyway. Bayer suspected he was telling the truth. He knew things about Shafer from when they were in Thailand and the Philippines. He knew Shafer's deepest, darkest secrets.

Bayer drove the attractive and well-spoken black woman to her apartment and was amused when she gave him a sixty-cent tip for the four-dollar ride. Fifteen percent to the penny. He took the money and thanked her graciously.

"An English cabdriver," she said. "That's unusual. Have a nice evening."

He continued to drive until past two in the morning. He drank in the sights, played the dizzying game. And then he had to stop again. Two young girls were hailing for a taxi on the corner. The area was called Shaw, and Howard University was very close according to several signs.

The girls were slender, delectable in stacked heels and shiny clothes that glowed in the dark. One of them wore a microskirt, and he could see the tops of black or navy thigh-highs as he stopped to pick them up. *They must be hookers—Shafer's favorite prey,* Bayer thought to himself.

The second prostitute was even prettier and sexier than the first. She wore white stacked bath sandals, side-striped white athletic pants, a teeny tank top in blue camouflage.

"Where are we going?" Bayer asked as they scampered over to the taxi.

The girl in the microskirt did the talking.

"*We're* going to Princeton Place. That's Petworth, darlin'. Then *you're* going away," she said. She tossed her head back and issued a taunting laugh. Bayer snickered to himself. He was beginning to get into this now.

The girls climbed in, and Bayer couldn't resist checking them out in the mirror. The foxy one in the microskirt caught him looking. He felt like a schoolboy, found it intoxicating, didn't avert his eyes from hers.

She casually flipped him the finger. He didn't stop looking. Couldn't. *So this was how it felt to Shafer. This was the game of games.*

He couldn't take his eyes off the girls. His heart was pounding. Microskirt wore a tightly fitted ribbed tank top. Her long fingernails were air-brushed in kiwi and mango colors. She had a pager on her belt. Probably a gun in her handbag.

The other girl smiled shyly in his direction. She seemed more innocent. Was she? A necklace that read BABY GIRL dangled between her young breasts.

If they were going to Petworth, they had to be hooking. They were certainly young and foxy; sixteen, seventeen years old. Bayer could see himself having sex with the girls, and the image was beginning to overpower his imagination. He knew he ought to be careful. This could get completely out of hand. He was playing Shafer's game, wasn't he? And he liked it very much.

"I have a proposition for you," he said to Microskirt.

"All right, darlin'," she said. "Be one hundred for the half. Plus our ride to Petworth. That's my proposition for you."

Chapter 26

SHAFER LIKED to know when any of the other players traveled, especially if they came to Washington. He had gone to a lot of trouble to hack his way into their computers to keep track of them. Famine had recently bought plane tickets, and now he was here in D.C. Why?

It wasn't hard to follow George Bayer once he got to town. Shafer was still reasonably good at it; he'd had plenty of practice in tracking and surveillance during his years in the Service.

He was disappointed that Famine had decided to "intersect" with his fantasy. Intersection happened occasionally in the game, but it was rare. Both players were supposed to agree beforehand. Famine was clearly breaking the rules. What did he know, or think he knew?

Then Bayer genuinely surprised him. Not only did he visit Shafer's hideaway, but he actually took the taxi for a ride. What the hell was he doing?

At a little past two in the morning, Shafer watched the gypsy cab pick up two young girls in Shaw. Was Bayer copycatting? Was he setting some kind of trap for Shafer? Or was it something else altogether?

Bayer took the girls to S Street, which wasn't far from the pickup point. He followed the girls up the darkened stairs of an aging brownstone, and then they all disappeared inside.

He had a blue anorak thrown over his right arm and Shafer suspected that a pistol was under the coat. Christ! He'd taken two of them. He could have been seen by anyone on the street. The cab could have been spotted.

Shafer parked on the street. He waited and watched. He didn't like being in this part of Shaw, especially without his disguise, and driving the Jaguar. There were some old crumbling brownstones and a couple of boarded-up, graffiti-covered shacks on the street. No one was outside.

He saw a light blink on the top floor and figured that was where Bayer had taken the two girls. Probably their flat.

He watched the brownstone from two until close to four. He couldn't take his eyes away. While he waited, he imagined dozens of scenarios that might have brought Famine here. He wondered if the others were in Washington, too. Or was Famine acting alone? Was he playing the Four Horsemen right now?

Shafer waited and waited for Bayer to come out of the brownstone. But he didn't come down, and Shafer grew more impatient and worried and angry. He fidgeted. His breathing became labored.

He had lurid, paranoid fantasies about what Bayer might have done up there. Had he killed the two girls? Taken their identification? Was this a trap? He thought so. What else could it be?

Still no George Bayer.

Shafer couldn't stand it any longer. He climbed out of the Jaguar. He stood on the street and stared up at the windows of the flat. He wondered if he, too, was being watched. He sensed a trap, wondered if he should flee.

Christ, where the hell is Bayer? What game is Famine playing? Was there a back way out of the building? If so, why had he left the taxi as evidence? Evidence! Damn him!

But then he saw Bayer finally leave the building. He quickly crossed S Street, got into the cab, and drove away.

Shafer decided to go upstairs. He jogged over to the building and found the wooden front door unlocked. He hurried up the steep, winding stairs. He had a flashlight in one hand, and turned it on. His semiautomatic was in the other.

Shafer made his way to the fourth floor. He immediately knew which of the two flats was the one. A poster for Mary J. Blige's *What's the 411?* album was on the splintered and scarred door to his right. The girls lived here.

He turned the handle and carefully pushed the door open. He pointed his gun inside, ready.

One of the young girls came out of the bathroom wearing a fluffy black towel on her head, nothing else. She was a hot number with pert little titties. Christ, Famine must have paid for it. What a fool! What a wanker!

"Who the hell are you? What are you doing in here?" the girl shouted angrily.

"I'm Death," he grinned, then announced, "I'm here for you and your pretty friend."

Chapter 27

I HAD gotten home from the John Doe murder scene at a little past three-thirty in the morning. I went to bed but set my alarm for six-thirty. I managed to get myself up before the kids went off to school.

"Somebody was out very, very, very late last night." Jannie started her teasing before I had made it all the way downstairs and into the kitchen. I continued down and found her and Damon in the breakfast nook with Nana.

"Somebody sure *looks* like he had a late night," Nana said from her customary catbird's seat.

"Somebody's cruising for a bruising," I said to quiet them. "Now, there's something important I need to tell you before you head out to school."

"Watch our manners. Always pay attention in class, even if the teacher's boring. Lead with our left if it ever comes to a fight in the schoolyard," Jannie offered with a wink.

I rolled my eyes. "What I was going to say," I said, "is that you should be especially nice to Mrs. Johnson today. You see, last night Christine said that she'd marry me. I guess that means she's marrying all of us."

At that point, everything became hugging and loud celebrating in the kitchen. The kids got chocolate milk and bacon grease all over me. I'd never seen Nana happier. And I felt exactly the same. Probably even better than they did.

I eventually made it to work that morning. I had made some progress on the John Doe homicide, and early on Tuesday morning, I learned that the man whose body had been dumped on Alabama Avenue was a thirty-four-year-old research analyst named Franklin Odenkirk. He worked at the Library of Congress for the Congressional Research Service.

We didn't release the news to the press, but I did inform Chief Pittman's office as soon as I knew. Pittman would find out anyway.

Once I had a name for the victim, information came quickly, and as it usually is, it was sad. Odenkirk was married and had three small children. He had taken a late flight back from New York, where he'd given a talk at the Rockefeller Institute. The plane landed on time, and he deboarded at National around ten. What happened to him after that was a mystery.

For the remainder of the week, I was busy with the murder case. I visited the Library of Congress and went to the newest structure, the James Madison Building, on Independence Avenue. I talked to nearly a dozen of Frank Odenkirk's coworkers.

They were courteous and cooperative, and I was told repeatedly that Odenkirk, while haughty at times, was generally well liked. He wasn't known to use drugs or drink to excess; wasn't known to gamble, either. He was faithful to his wife. He hadn't been involved in a serious argument at the office for as long as he'd been there.

He was with the Education and Public Welfare Division and spent long days in the spectacular Main Reading Room. There was no apparent motive for his murder, which was what I had feared. The killing roughly paralleled the Jane Does so far, but of course the chief of detectives didn't want to hear that. There *was* no Jane Doe killer, according to him. Why? Because he didn't want to shift dozens of detectives to Southeast and begin an extensive investigation on the basis of my instincts and gut feelings. I had heard Pittman joke that Southeast wasn't part of *his city.*

Before I left the Madison Building, I was compelled to stop and see the Main Reading Room once again. It was newly renovated, and I hadn't been there since the work had been done.

I sat at a reader's table and stared up at the amazing dome high over my head. Around the room were stained-glass representations of the seals of forty-eight states, along with bronze statues of famous figures, including Michelangelo, Plato, Shakespeare, Edward Gibbon, and Homer. I could imagine poor Frank Odenkirk doing his work here, and it bothered me. Why had he been killed? Had it been the Weasel?

The death was a terrible shock to everyone who had worked with him, and a couple of Odenkirk's coworkers broke down while talking to me about his murder.

I wasn't looking forward to interviewing Mrs. Odenkirk, but I drove out 295 and 210 to Forest Heights late on Friday afternoon. Chris Odenkirk was home with her mother, and also her husband's parents, who had flown in from Briarcliff Manor in Westchester County, New York. They told me the same story as the people at the Library of Congress. No one in the family knew of anyone who might want to harm Frank. He was a loving father, a supportive husband, a thoughtful son and son-in-law.

At the Odenkirk home, I learned that the deceased had been wearing a green seersucker suit when he left home, that his business meeting in New York had run over, and that he had been nearly two hours late getting to La Guardia Airport. He generally took a cab home from the airport in Washington because so many flights arrived late.

Even before I went to the house in Forest Heights, I had two detectives sent out to the airport. They showed around pictures of Odenkirk, interviewed airline personnel, shopworkers, porters, taxi dispatchers, and cabdrivers.

Around six I went over to the medical examiner's office to hear the results of the autopsy. All the photos and sketches from the crime scene were laid out. The autopsy had run about two and a half hours. Every cavity of Frank Odenkirk's body had been swabbed and scraped, and his brain had been removed.

I talked to the medical examiner while she finished up with Odenkirk at about six-thirty. Her name was Angelina Torres, and I'd known her for years. The two of us had started in our jobs at about the same time. Angelina was a tick under five feet and probably weighed around ninety pounds soaking wet.

"Long day, Alex?" she asked. "You look used and abused."

"Long one for you, too, Angelina. You look good, though. Short, but good."

She nodded, grinned, then stretched her small slight arms up over her head. She let out a low groan that approximated the way I felt, too.

"Any surprises for me?" I asked, after allowing her to stretch in peace and moan her little heart out.

I hadn't expected anything, but she had some news. "One surprise," Angelina said. "He was sodomized after he died. Someone had sex with him, Alex. Our killer seems to swing both ways."

Chapter 28

ON THE drive home that evening, I needed a break from the murder case. I thought about Christine, and that was much better, easier on the frontal lobe. I even switched off my beeper. I didn't want any distractions for ten or fifteen minutes.

Even though she hadn't talked about it recently, she still felt my job was too dangerous. The trouble was, she was absolutely right. I sometimes worried about leaving Damon and Jannie alone in the world, and now Christine as well. As I drove along the familiar streets of Southeast near Fifth, I considered whether I could actually leave police work. I'd been thinking about going into private practice and working as a psychologist, but I hadn't done anything to make it happen. It probably meant that I didn't really want to do it.

Nana was sitting on the front porch when I arrived home at around seven-thirty. She looked peeved, an expression of hers that I know all too well. She can still make me feel like I'm nine or ten years old and she's the one with all the answers.

"Where are the kids?" I called out as soon as I

opened the car door and climbed out. A fractured Batman and Robin kite was still up in a tree in the yard, and I was annoyed at myself for not getting it down a couple of weeks ago.

"I shackled them to the sink, and they're doing the dishes," Nana said.

"Sorry about missing dinner," I told her.

"Tell that to your children," Nana said, frowning up a storm. She's about as subtle as a hurricane. "You better tell them right now. Your friend Sampson called a little earlier. So did your compatriot Jerome Thurman. There's been more murders, Alex. I used the *plural* noun, just in case you didn't notice. Sampson is waiting for you at the so-called crime scene. Two bodies over in Shaw, near Howard University, of all places. Two more young black girls are dead. It won't stop, will it? It never stops in Southeast."

No, it never does.

Chapter 29

THE HOMICIDE scene was an old crumbling brownstone in a bad section of S Street in Shaw. A lot of college kids and also some young professionals live in the up-and-down, mostly middle-class neighborhood. Lately, prostitution has become a problem there. According to Sampson, the two dead girls were both prostitutes who occasionally worked in the neighborhood but mostly turned tricks over in Petworth.

A single squad car and an EMS truck were parked at the homicide scene. A uniformed patrolman was posted on the front stoop, and he seemed intent on keeping intruders out. He was young, baby-faced, with smooth, butterscotch skin. I didn't know him, so I flashed my detective's shield.

"Detective Cross." He grunted. I sensed that he'd heard of me.

"What do we have so far?" I asked before I went inside to trudge up four steep flights. "What do you hear, Officer?"

"Two girls dead upstairs. Both pros, apparently. One of them lived in the building. Murders were called in anonymously. Maybe a neighbor, maybe the pimp. They're sixteen, seventeen, maybe younger. Too bad. They didn't deserve this."

I nodded, took a deep breath, and then quickly climbed up the steep, winding, creaking stairs to the fourth floor. Prostitutes make for difficult police investigations, and I wondered if the Weasel knew that. On average, a hooker out of Petworth might turn a dozen or more tricks a night, and that's a lot of forensic evidence just on her body.

The door to apartment 4A was wide open, and I could see inside. It was an efficiency, with one large room, kitchenette, bath. A fluffy white area rug lay between two daybeds. A lava lamp was undulating green blobs next to several dildos.

Sampson was crouched on the far side of one daybed. He looked like an NBA power forward searching the floor for a missing contact lens.

I walked into a small, untidy room that smelled of incense, peach-blossom fragrance, greasy food. A bright red and yellow McDonald's container of fries was open on the couch.

Dirty clothes covered the chairs: bike shorts, short-shorts, Karl Kani urban clothes. At least a dozen bottles of nail polish and remover, a couple of nail files, and cotton balls lay on the floor. There was a heavy, cloying smell of fruity perfume in the room.

I went around the bed to look at the victims. Two very young women, both naked from the waist down. The Weasel had been here—I could feel it.

The girls were lying one on top of the other,

looking like lovers. They looked as if they were having sex on the floor.

One girl wore a blue tank top, the other black lingerie. They both still wore "slides," stacked bath sandals that are popular nowadays. Most of the Jane Does had been left naked, but unlike many of the others, these two would be fairly easy for us to identify.

"No actual I.D. on either girl," Sampson said, without looking up from his work.

"One of them rents the apartment, though," I told him.

He nodded. "Probably pays cash. She's in a cash business."

Sampson was wearing latex rubber gloves, and was bent down close to the two women.

"The killer wore gloves," Sampson said, still without looking up at me. "Don't seem to be fingerprints anywhere. That's what the techie says. First look-through. They both were shot, Alex. Single shot to the forehead."

I was still looking around the room, collecting information, letting the details of the murder scene flow over me. I noticed an array of hair products: Soft Sheen, Care Free Curl, styling gel, several wigs. On top of one of the wigs was a green army garrison cap with stripes, commonly called a cunt cap among military personnel because it's said to be effective for picking up women, especially in the South. There was also a pager.

The girls were young and pretty. They had

skinny little legs, small, bony feet, silver toe rings that looked like they'd come from the same shop. Their discarded clothes amounted to insignificant little bundles on the bloodied hardwood floor.

In one corner of the small room, there were vestiges of brief childhoods: a Lotto game, a stuffed blue bear that was threadbare and looked about as old as the girls themselves, a Barbie doll, a Ouija board.

"Take a good look, Alex. It gets weirder and weirder. Our Weasel is starting to freak out."

I sighed and bent down to see what Sampson had discovered. The smaller, and perhaps the younger, of the two girls was lying on top. The girl underneath was on her back. Her glazed brown eyes stared straight up at a broken light fixture in the ceiling, as if she had seen something terrible up there.

The girl on top had been positioned with her face—actually, her mouth—tilted down into the other girl's crotch.

"Killer played real cute games with them after they were dead," Sampson said. "Move the one on top a little. Lift her head, Alex. You see it?"

I saw it. A completely new m.o. for the Jane Does, at least the ones I knew about. The phrase "stuck on each other" ran through my mind. I wondered if that was the killer's "message." The girl on top was connected to the one underneath—by her tongue.

Sampson sighed and said, "I think her tongue is stapled inside the other girl. I'm pretty sure that's it, Alex. The Weasel stapled them together."

I looked at the two girls and shook my head. "I don't think so. A staple, even a surgical one, would come apart on the tongue's surface. . . . Krazy Glue adhesive would work, though."

Chapter 30

THE KILLER was working faster, so I had to do the same. The two dead girls didn't remain Jane Does for very long. I had their names before the ten-o'clock news that night. I ignored the explicit orders of the chief of detectives and continued to work on the investigation.

Early the next morning, Sampson and I met at Stamford, the high school that Tori Glover and Marion Cardinal had attended. The murdered girls were seventeen and fourteen years old.

The memory of the homicide scene had left me with a queasy, sick feeling that wouldn't go away. I kept thinking, *Christine is right. Get out of this, do something else. It's time.*

The principal at Stamford was a small, frail-looking, red-haired woman named Robin Schwartz. Her resource officer, Nathan Kemp, had gotten together some students who knew the victims, and had set aside a couple of classrooms for Sampson, Jerome Thurman, and me to use for interviews. Jerome would work in one room, Sampson and I in the other.

Summer school was still in session, and Stamford was busy as a mall on a Saturday. We passed the cafeteria on the way to the classrooms, and it was packed, even at ten-thirty. No empty seats anywhere. The room reeked of French fries, the same greasy smell that had been in the girl's apartment.

A few kids were making noise, but they were mostly well behaved. The music of Wu Tang and Jodeci leaked from earphones. The school seemed to be well run and orderly. Between classes a few boys and girls embraced tenderly, with loosely locked pinkies and the gentlest brushes of cheeks.

"These were not bad girls," Nathan Kemp told us as we walked. "I think you'll hear that from the other students. Tori dropped out last semester, but her homelife was the main reason. Marion was an honor student at Stamford. I'm telling you, guys, these were not bad girls."

Sampson, Thurman, and I spent the rest of the afternoon with the kids. We learned that Tori and Marion were popular, all right. They were loyal to their friends, funny, usually fun to be around. Marion was described as "blazing," which meant she was great. Tori was "buggin' sometimes," which meant she could be a little crazy. Most of the kids hadn't known that the girls were tricking in Petworth, but Tori Glover was said to always have money.

One particular interview would stick in my mind for a while. Evita Cardinal was a senior at Stamford, and also a cousin of Marion's. She wore white athletic pants and a purple stretchy top. Her blackrimmed, yellow-tinted sunglasses were propped on top of her head.

She started to cry her eyes out as soon as she sat down across the desk from me.

"I'm real sorry about Marion," I said, and I was. "We just want to catch whoever did this terrible thing. Detective Sampson and I both live nearby in Southeast. My kids go to the Sojourner Truth School."

The girl looked at me. Her eyes were red-rimmed and wary. "You won't catch nobody," she finally said. It was the prevailing attitude in the neighborhood, and it happened to be mostly true. Sampson and I weren't even supposed to be here. I had told my secretary I was out working the murder of Frank Odenkirk. A few other detectives were covering for us.

"How long have Tori and Marion been working in Petworth? Do you know any other girls from school who work over there?"

Evita shook her head. "*Tori* was the one working the street in Petworth. Not Marion. My cousin was a good person. They both were. Marion was my little doggie," Evita said, and the tears came flowing again.

"Marion *was* there with Tori." I told her what I knew to be the truth. "We talked to people who saw her on Princeton Place that night."

The cousin glared at me. "You don't know what

you're talkin' about, Mister Detective. You're *wrong*. You ain't got the straight."

"I'm listening to you, Evita. That's why I'm here."

"Marion wasn't there to sell her body or like that. She was just afraid for Tori. She went to *protect* Tori. She never did nothin' bad for money, and I know that for a fact."

The girl started to sob again. "My cousin was a good person, my best girlfriend. She was tryin' to just protect Tori and she got herself killed for it. The police won't do nothin'. You never come back here again after today. Never happen. You don't care about us. We're nothin' to nobody," Evita Cardinal said, and that seemed to say it all.

Chapter 31

WE'RE NOTHIN' to nobody. It was a horrifying and absolutely true statement, and it was at the deepest roots of the Jane Doe investigation, the search for the Weasel. It pretty well summed up George Pittman's cynical philosophy about the inner city. It was also the reason I was feeling tired and numb to the bone by six-thirty that night. I believed that the Jane Doe murders were escalating.

On the other hand, I hadn't seen nearly enough of my own kids for the last few days, so I decided I'd better head home. On the way, I thought about Christine and calmed down immediately. Since the time I was a young boy, I've been having a recurring daydream. I'm standing alone on a cold, barren planet. It's scary, but more than anything, it's lonely and unsettling. Then a woman comes up to me. We begin to hold hands, to embrace, and then everything is all right. That woman was Christine, and I had no idea how she had gotten out of my dreams and into the real world.

Nana, Damon, and Jannie were just leaving the

house when I pulled up into the driveway. *What's this?* I wondered.

Wherever they were going, everybody was dolled up and looking especially nice. Nana and Jannie wore their best dresses, and Damon had on a blue suit, white shirt, and tie. Damon almost never wears what he calls his "monkey" or "funeral" suit.

"Where's everybody going?" I said as I climbed out of the old Porsche. "What's going on? You all aren't moving out on me?"

"It's nothing," Damon said, strangely evasive, eyes darting all over the front yard.

"Damon's in the Washington Boys Choir at school!" Jannie proudly blurted out. "He didn't want you to know until he made it for sure. Well, he made it. Damon's a *chorister* now."

Her brother swatted her on the arm. Not hard, but enough to show he wasn't pleased with Jannie for telling his secret.

"Hey!" Jannie said, and put up her dukes like the little semipro boxer that she is becoming under my watchful eye.

"Hey, hey!" I said, and moved in like a big-time referee, like that guy Mills Lane who does the big pro fights. "No prizefighting outside the ring. You know the rules of the fight game. Now what's this about a choir?"

"Damon tried out for the Boys Choir, and he was selected," Nana said, and beamed gloriously as she looked over at Damon. "He did it all by himself."

"You sing, too?" I said, and beamed at him as well. "My, my, my."

"He could be in Boyz Two Men, Daddy. Boyz Two Boyz, maybe. He's smoo-ooth and silky. His voice is pure."

"Is that so, Sister Soul?" I said to my baby girl.

"Zatso," Jannie continued to prattle as she patted Damon on the back. I could tell she was incredibly proud of him. She was his biggest fan, even if he didn't realize it yet. Someday he would.

Damon couldn't hold back a big smile, then he shrugged it off. "No big thing. I sing all right."

"*Thousands* of other boys tried out," Jannie said. "It *is* a big thing, biggest in your small life, brother."

"Hundreds," Damon corrected her. "Only hundreds of kids tried out. I guess I just got lucky."

"*Hundreds* of *thousands!*" Jannie gushed, and scooted away before he swatted her like the little gnat she can be sometimes. "And you were *born* lucky."

"Can I come to the practice?" I asked. "I'll be good. I'll be quiet. I won't embarrass anybody too much."

"If you can spare the time." Nana threw a neat jab. She sure doesn't need any boxing lessons from me. "Your busy work schedule and all. If you can spare the time, come along with us."

"Sure, Dad," said Damon, finally.

So I came along.

Chapter 32

I HAPPILY walked the six short blocks to the Sojourner Truth School with Nana and the kids. I wasn't dressed up. They were in their finery, but it didn't matter. There was suddenly a bounce in my step. I took Nana's arm, and she smiled as I tucked her hand into the crook of my arm.

"Now that's better. Seems like old times," I exclaimed.

"You're such a shameless charmer sometimes," Nana said, and laughed out loud. "Ever since you were a little boy like Damon. You certainly can be one when you want to."

"You helped make me what I am, old woman," I confided to her.

"Proud of it, too. And I'm *so* proud of Damon."

We arrived at the Sojourner Truth School and went directly to the small auditorium in back. I wondered if Christine might be there, but she wasn't anywhere to be seen. Then I wondered if she already knew that Damon had made the Boys Choir, if he had told her first. I kind of liked the thought that he might have told her. I wanted them to be close. I knew that Damon and Jannie needed a mother, not just a father and a great-grandmother.

"We're not too good yet," Damon informed me before he left to join the other boys. His face clearly showed the fear and anxiety of possibly being embarrassed. "This is just our second practice. Mr. Dayne says we're horrid as a tubful of castor oil. He's tough as nails, Dad. He makes you stand for an hour straight without moving."

"Mr. Dayne's tougher than you, Daddy, tougher than Mrs. Johnson," Jannie said, and grinned wickedly. "Tough as *nails*."

I had heard that Nathaniel Dayne was a demanding maestro—nicknamed the "Great Dayne"—and that his choirs were among the finest in the country and that most of the boys were said to profit immensely from the dedicated training and discipline. He was already organizing the boys up on the stage. He was a very broad man of below-average height. I guessed he carried about two hundred fifty pounds on his five-seven frame. He wore a black suit with a black shirt buttoned at the collar, no tie. He started the boys off with a few playful verses of "Three Blind Mice" that didn't sound half bad.

"I'm really happy for Damon. He looks so proud up there," I whispered to Nana and Jannie. "He is a handsome devil, too."

"Mr. Dayne is starting a girls choir in the fall,"

Jannie loud-whispered in my ear. "You watch. I mean, you *listen*. I'll make it."

"Go for it, girl," Nana said, and gave Jannie a hug. She is very good at encouraging others.

Dayne suddenly called out loudly, "Ugh. I hear a *swoop*. I don't want any swoops here, gentlemen. I want clean diction and pure pitch. I want silver and silk. I do not want *swoops*."

Out of the corner of my eye, I suddenly saw Christine in the hallway. She was watching Dayne and the boys, but then she looked my way. Her face was principal-serious for just a moment. Then she smiled and winked.

I walked over to see her. Be still my heart.

"That's my boy," I said with mock pride as I came up to her. She was dressed in a soft gray pantsuit with a coral-pink blouse. God, I loved seeing her now, being with her, hanging out, doing nothing—the works.

Christine smiled. Actually, she laughed a little at me. "He does everything so damn well." She didn't hold back, no matter what. "I was hoping you might be here, Alex," she whispered. "I was just this very minute missing you like crazy. You know that feeling?"

"Yes, that feeling and I are well acquainted."

We held hands as the choir practiced Bach's "Jesu, Joy of Man's Desiring." Everything felt so right, and it was hard to get used to.

"Sometimes ... I still have this dream about

George being shot and dying," she said as we were standing there. Christine's husband had been murdered in her home, and she had seen him die. It was one of the big reasons she was hesitant about being with me: the fear that I might die in the line of duty, and also the fear that I could bring terror and violence into the house.

"I remember everything about the afternoon I heard Maria was shot. It eases with time, but it never goes away."

Christine knew that. She had figured out the answers to most of her questions, but she liked to talk things through. We were both that way.

"And yet I continue to work here in Southeast. I come to the inner city every day. I could choose a nice school in Maryland or Virginia," she said.

I nodded. "Yes, Christine, you do choose to work here."

"And so do you."

"And so do I."

She held my hand a little tighter. "I guess we were made for each other," she said. "Why fight it."

Chapter 33

EARLY THE next morning I was back in the write-up room at the Seventh District Station, working the John Doe homicide. I was the first one in there.

Apparently no one had noticed Frank Odenkirk as he was leaving the airport. His clothing still hadn't been recovered. The M.E. reported that he had definitely been sodomized after he was killed. As I had suspected, there was no semen. The killer had used a condom. Just as with the Jane Does.

The police commissioner was involved in the Odenkirk case and was putting added pressure on the department. It was making everyone angry and a little crazy. Chief Pittman was riding his detectives hard, but the only case he seemed interested in was the Odenkirk killing, especially since a suspect had been arrested in the German tourist murder.

At around eleven that morning, Rakeem Powell stopped by my desk. He bent low and whispered, "Might have something interesting, Alex. Downstairs in the jail, if you've got a minute. Could be a first break on those two murdered girls in Shaw."

The jail was down a set of steep concrete stairs, just past a tight warren of small interrogation rooms, a holding room, and a booking room. All over the ceiling and walls, prisoners had scratched their street names or used black ink from finger-printing to write the names. This was incredibly dumb of them, since it gave us information for our files.

It's purposely kept dark down in the jail. Each cell is six by five feet, with a metal bed and a com-bination water fountain/ toilet. Sneakers had been tossed in the hallways outside several of the cells. It's what experienced prisoners do who won't take the laces out of their sneaks. Laces aren't allowed in the jail for safety reasons.

A small-time drug runner and petty thief named Alfred "Sneak" Streek was seated like the Fresh Prince of D.C. in one of the holding cells. The street punk looked up at me as I entered his cell. A slicky-sick smirk crossed his face.

Sneak was sporting wraparound sunglasses, dusty dreadlocks, and a bright-green and yellow crocheted hat. His white T-shirt had a drawing of Haile Selassie's face and read HEAD HUNTER. RASTAFARIAN.

"You from the D.A.'s office? I *don't think so.* No dealee, no talkee, my man," he said to me. "So get lost."

Rakeem ignored him as he spoke to me. "Sneak claims to have some useful information about the Glover and Cardinal homicides. He would like us to extend him some courtesy in return for what he claims to know. He's jammed up on a charge that he may have broken into an apartment in Shaw. He was caught coming out of a bedroom window with a Sony TV in his arms. Imagine that. Not very Sneaky of him."

"I didn't rob no ticky-tacky apartment. I don't even *watch* TV, my man. And I don't see no assistant district attorney present with the *au-tho-rity* to make a deal."

"Take off your sunglasses," I said to him.

He wouldn't look at me, so I took them off for him. As one well-known street saying goes, his eyes were like tombstones. I could tell at a glance that Sneak wasn't just running drugs anymore; he was using.

I stood across from Sneak in the jail cell and stared him down. He was probably in his early twenties, angry, cynical, lost in space and time. "If you didn't rob the apartment, then why would you be interested in seeing a lawyer from the district attorney's office? That doesn't make too much sense to me, Alfred. Now here's what I'll do for you, and it's a one-time offer, so listen carefully. If I walk out of here, I *don't* come back."

Sneak half-listened to what I was saying.

"If you give us information that directly helps solve the murders of those two young girls, *then* we will help you on the robbery charge. I'll go to the mat myself. If you don't give up the information, then I'm going to leave you in here with Detective

Powell and Detective Thurman. You won't get this generous, one-time offer again. That's another promise, and as these detectives know, I always keep my word."

Sneak still didn't say anything. A glaze was coming over his eyes. He tried to stare *me* down, but I'm usually better at it than the average TV booster.

I finally shrugged a look at Rakeem Powell and Jerome Thurman. "Okay, fine. Gentlemen, we need to know what he knows about those murdered girls in Shaw. He gets nothing from us when you're finished with him. It's possible that he's involved with the homicides himself. He could even be our killer, and we need to solve this thing fast. You treat him that way until we know differently."

I started to leave when suddenly Sneak spoke.

"Back Door, man. He hang at Downing Park. He, Back Door, maybe see who done those girls. That's how he say it at the park. Say he saw the killer. So how you gonna help me?"

I walked out of the cell. "I told you the deal, Alfred. We solve the case, your information helps, I'll help you."

Chapter 34

MAYBE WE were close to something. Two Metro cruisers and two unmarked sedans pulled up to the fenced-in entrance of tiny Downing playground in Shaw. Rakeem Powell and Sampson came with me to visit with Joe "Back Door" Booker, a well-known neighborhood menace.

I knew Back Door by sight and spotted him right away. He was short, no more than five-seven, goateed, and so good with a basketball that he sometimes played in work boots just to show off. He had on dusty orange construction boots today. Also a faded black nylon jacket and black nylon pants that accordioned at the ankles.

A full-court basketball game was in progress, a fast, high-level game somewhere between college and pro in terms of athletic ability. The court couldn't have been more basic—black macadam, faded white lines, metal backboards, and rims with chain nets.

Players from two or three other teams sat around waiting their turn to play winners. Nylon shorts and pants and the Nike swoosh were everywhere.

The court was surrounded by four walls of heavy wire fencing and was known as the cage. Everybody looked up as we arrived, Booker included.

"We got next!" Sampson called out.

The players on and off the court exchanged looks, and a couple of them grinned at Sampson's one-liner. They knew who we were. The steady *thump, thump, thump* of the game ball hadn't stopped.

Back Door was on the court. It wasn't unusual for his team to hold winners for an entire afternoon. He had been in and out of reformatories and prisons since he was fourteen, but he could play ball. He was taunting another player who was on the court in gray suit pants and high-tops, his chest bare. "You suck," said Back Door. "Take those church pants off. I play you in baseball, tennis, bowling, *any* game—you suck. Stop suckin'."

Rakeem Powell blew the silver referee's whistle he always carries. Rakeem works as a soccer ref in his spare time. The whistle is unorthodox, but it gets attention in noisy places. The game stopped.

The three of us walked up to Booker, who was standing near the foul circle in front of one basket. Sampson and I towered over him, but so did most of the players. It didn't matter; he was still the best ballplayer out there. He could probably beat Sampson and me if we played him two on one.

"Awhh, leave the brother alone. He didn't do nothin'," one of the other, taller men complained in a deep voice. He had prison-style tattoos all over his back and arms. "He was here playin' ball, man."

"Door been here *all day,*" said somebody else. "Door been here for days. Hasn't lost *a game* in days!"

Several of the young men laughed at the playground humor. Sampson turned to the biggest man on the court. "Shut the hell up. Stop dribbling that rock, too. Two young sisters been murdered. That's why we're here. This is no game with us."

The dribbler shut up and picked up the game ball. The yard became strangely quiet. We could hear a jump rope striking the sidewalk in a fast rhythm. Three little girls playing just outside the cage were singsonging, *"Little Miss Pinky dressed in blue, died last night at half past two."* It was a jump-rope rhyme, and sadly true around here.

I put my arm around Booker's shoulder and walked him away from his friends.

Sampson continued to do the talking. "Booker, this is going to be so fast and easy you and your friends will be laughing your asses off about it before we're back in our cars."

"Yeah, uh-huh," said Joseph Booker, trying to be cool in the extreme heat of Sampson's and my glare.

"I'm serious as a heart attack, little man. You saw something that can help us with the murder of Tori Glover and Marion Cardinal. Simple as that. You talk, and we walk right back out of here."

Booker glared up at Sampson as if he were staring down the sun. "I didn't see shit. Like Luki say, I been here for days. I never lose to these sorry chumps."

I held up my hand, palm out, inches from his squashed moonpie face.

"I'm on a stopwatch here, Booker, so please don't interrupt my flow. I promise you, two minutes and we're out of here. Now here's what's in it for you. One, we go away, and you gentlemen finish your game. Two, detectives Powell and Sampson will owe you one. Three, a hundred dollars now for your time and trouble.

"The clock is ticking," I said. "*Tick, tick, tick.* Easy money."

He finally nodded and held out his hand. "I seen those two girls get picked up. Around two, three in the mornin' on E Street. I *didn't* see no driver, nobody's face or nothin'. Too dark, man. But he was driving a cab. Look like purple and blue gypsy. Somethin' like that. Girls get into the back of the cab, drive off."

"Is that it?" I asked him. "I don't want to have to come back here later. Break up your game again."

Booker considered what I'd said, then spoke again. "Cabdriver a white man. Seen his arm stickin' out the side window. Ain't no white boys drivin' the night shift in Shaw, least none I seen."

I nodded, waited a bit, then smiled at the other players. "Gentlemen, as you were. Play ball."

Thump, thump, thump.

Swish.

Booker could really play ball.

Chapter 35

THE NEW pieces of information gave us something to run with. We'd done an incredible amount of thankless street work, and something had finally paid off. We had the color of the gypsy cab that had picked up the girls around the time of the murders. The fact that the driver was white was the best lead we had so far.

Sampson and I drove to my house rather than back to the station. It would be easier to work on the new leads from Fifth Street. It took me about five minutes to come up with more information from a contact at the Taxi Commission. No fleets operating in D.C. currently had purple and blue cabs. That probably meant the car was an illegal gypsy, as Booker had said. I learned that a company called Vanity Cabs had once used purple and blue cars, but Vanity had been out of business since '95. The Taxi Commission rep said that half a dozen or so of the old cars might still be on the street. Originally the fleet had been fifteen cars, which wasn't that many even if all of them were still around, which was highly doubtful.

Sampson called all the cab companies that regularly did business in Southeast, especially around Shaw. According to their records, there were only three white drivers who had been on duty that night.

We were working in the kitchen. Sampson was on the phone and I was using the computer. Nana had fixed fresh coffee and also set out fruit and half a pecan pie.

Rakeem Powell called the house at around 4:15. I picked up. "Alex, Pittman's watchdog is sniffing around here something fierce. Fred Cook wants to know what you and Sampson are working on this afternoon. Jerome told him the Odenkirk murder."

I nodded and said, "If the murders in Southeast are connected in any way, that's the truth."

"One more thing," Rakeem said before he let me go. "I checked with Motor Vehicles. Might be something good for us. A purple gypsy got a summons for running a stop sign around one in the morning over in Eckington, near the university, Second Street. Maybe that's where our boy lives."

I clapped my hands and congratulated Rakeem. Our long hours working the Jane Doe cases were finally beginning to pay off.

Maybe we were about to catch the Weasel.

Chapter 36

HE HAD been much more careful lately. The visit to Washington by George Bayer—Famine— had been a warning, a shot over his head, and Shafer had taken it seriously. The other players could be as dangerous as he was. It was *they* who had taught *him* how to kill, not the other way round. Famine, Conqueror, and War were not to be underestimated, especially if he wanted to win the game.

The day after Famine's visit, the others had informed him that Bayer had come to Washington, that he was being watched. He supposed that was his *second* warning. His activity had frightened them, and now they were retaliating. It was all part of the game.

After work that night, he headed to the hide-away in Eckington. He spotted what looked like a half-dozen or so policemen canvassing the street.

He immediately suspected the other Horsemen. They had turned him in, after all. Or were they playing a mind game with him? What were the cops doing here?

He parked the Jaguar several blocks away, then headed toward the hideaway and garage on foot. He had to check this out. He had on a pinstriped suit, city shirt, and tie. He knew he looked respectable enough. He carried a leather briefcase and definitely looked like a businessman coming home late.

Two African-American policemen were doing door-to-door questioning on Uhland Terrace. This wasn't good—the police were less than five blocks from the hideaway.

Why were they here? His brain was reeling, adrenaline rushing through his nervous system like a flash flood. Maybe this had nothing to do with him, but he couldn't be too careful. He definitely suspected the other players, especially George Bayer. *But why?* Was this the way they planned to end the game, by bringing him down?

When the two policemen up ahead disappeared down a side street off Uhland, Shafer decided to stop at one of the brownstones where they'd been asking questions. It was a small risk, but he needed to know what was happening. A couple of old men were seated on the stoop. An ancient radio played an Orioles baseball game.

"They ask you about some kind of trouble in the neighborhood?" Shafer asked the men in as casual a tone as he could manage. "They stopped me up the block."

One of the men just stared at him, terminally

pissed off, but the other one nodded and spoke up. "Sure did, mister. Lookin' for a cab, purple and blue gypsy. Connected to some killings, they say. Though I don't recall seeing any purple ones lately. Used to be a cab company called Vanity. You remember, Earle? They had the purple people-eaters."

"That was some years ago," the other man said, nodding. "They went belly up."

"I guess they were Metro police. Never showed me any I.D., though," Shafer said, and shrugged. He was being careful to speak with an American accent, which he was good at imitating.

"Detectives Cross and Sampson," the more talkative of the two men volunteered their names. "Detective Cross showed me his badge. It was the real deal."

"Oh, I'm sure it was," Shafer said, and saluted the two old men. "Good to see the police in the neighborhood, actually."

"You got that right."

"Have a nice night."

"Yeah, you, too."

Shafer circled back to his car and drove to the embassy. He went straight to his office, where he felt safe and protected. He calmed himself, then turned on his computer and did a thorough search on D.C. detectives named Cross and Sampson. He found more than he had hoped for, especially on Detective Cross.

He thought about how the new developments might change the game. Then he sent out a message to the other Horsemen. He told them about Cross and Sampson, adding that the detectives had decided to "play the game." So naturally, he had plans for them, too.

Chapter 37

ZACHARY SCOTT Taylor is a thorough, analytical, and very hard-nosed reporter on the *Washington Post.* I respect the hell out of him. His relentless cynicism and skepticism are a little too much for me to take on a daily basis; otherwise, we might be even closer friends. But we have a good relationship, and I trust him more than I do most journalists.

I met him that night at the Irish Times, on F Street, near Union Station. The restaurant-bar is in an anachronistic, stand-alone brick building surrounded by modern office structures. Zachary called it "a dumpy little toilet of a bar, a perfect place for us to meet."

In the time-honored tradition of Washington, I have occasionally been one of his "trusted sources," and I was about to tell him something important. I hoped he would agree, and would convince his editors at the *Post* about the story.

"How're Master Damon and Ms. Jannie?" Zachary asked as he sat across from me in a darkened corner, under an old photo of a stern-looking man in a black top hat. Zachary is tall, gaunt, and thin, and resembles the man in the old photo a little bit. He always talks too fast, so that the words all run into one another: *How'reMasterDamonandMs.Jannie?* There was just a hint of Virginia softening his accent.

The waitress eventually came over to our table. He ordered black coffee and I had the same.

"Two coffees?" she asked, to make sure she'd heard us right.

"Two of your very *finest* coffees," Zachary said.

"This isn't Starbucks, y'know," she said.

I smiled at the waitress's brio, then at what Zachary had said—his first words to me. I'd probably mentioned my kids' names to him once, but he had an encyclopedic memory for all kinds of disparate information.

"You should go get yourself a couple of kids, Zachary," I told him, smiling broadly.

He glanced up at an ancient whirring ceiling fan that looked as if it might suddenly spin out of the ceiling. It seemed a nice metaphor for modern life in America, an aging infrastructure threatening to spin out of control.

"Don't have a wife yet, Alex. Still looking for the right woman," said Zachary.

"Well, okay then, get yourself a wife first, then get a couple of kids. Might take the edge off your neuroses."

The waitress placed steaming cups of black coffee in front of us. "Will that be *all*?" she said. She shook her head, then left us.

"Maybe I don't want the edge taken off my rather stunning neurotic behavior. Maybe I believe that's what makes me such a damn fine reporter, and without it my work would be pedestrian shit, and then I'd be nothing in the eyes of Don Graham and company."

I sipped the day- or two-day-old coffee. "Except that if you had a couple of kids, you could never be nothing."

Zachary squinted one eye shut and smacked the left side of his lips. He was a very animated thinker.

"Except if the kids didn't love or even like me very much."

"And you don't consider yourself lovable? But actually you are, Zachary. Trust me. You're just fine. Your kids would adore the hell out of you, and you would adore them. You'd have a mutual adoration society."

He finally laughed and clapped his hands loudly. We usually laugh a good bit when we're together.

"So will you marry me and have my children?" He grinned at me over the top of his steaming cup. "This is a pickup joint, after all. Singles from the Bureau of Labor Statistics and the Government Printing Office come here, hoping to bed staffers from Kennedy's or Glenn's."

"It's the best offer I've had all day. Who called this meeting, anyway? Why are we here at this dive, drinking really bad coffee?"

Taylor slurped his. "Coffee's fairly strong, isn't

it? That's something to be thankful for. What's up, Alex?"

"You interested in another Pulitzer?" I asked him.

He pretended to think it over, but his eyes lit up. "Well, I might be. You see, I need to balance the look of my mantelpiece. One of my dates told me that. Never did see the young woman again. She worked for Gingrich, as a matter of fact."

For the next forty-five minutes or so, I told Zachary exactly what I thought was up. I told him about the 114 unsolved murders in Southeast and parts of Northeast D.C. I detailed the contrasting investigations of the cases of Frank Odenkirk and the German tourist in Georgetown, and those of the black teenagers Tori Glover and Marion Cardinal. I filled him in on the chief of detectives, his proclivities and his biases, or at least my perception of them. I even admitted that I disliked Pittman intensely, and Zachary knows I'm not that way about too many folks who don't murder for a living.

He shook his head back and forth, back and forth, while I talked, and didn't stop when I was finished. "Not that I doubt any of what you're saying, but do you have any documentation?" he asked.

"You're such a stickler for details," I said. "Reporters are such wusses when you come right down to it."

I reached down under my seat and lifted up two thick manila folders. His eyes brightened.

"This should help with the story. Copies of sixty-seven of the unsolved homicide reports. Also a copy of the Glover and Cardinal investigation. Note the number of detectives assigned to each. Check the case hours logged. You'll see a huge discrepancy. That's all I could get my hands on—but the other reports exist."

"Why would this be happening, this malicious neglect?" he asked me.

I nodded at the wisdom of his question. "I'll give you the most cynical reason," I said. "Some Metro cops like to refer to Southeast as 'self-cleaning ovens.' That sound like the beginnings of malicious neglect to you? Some victims in Southeast are called NHIs—that's 'No Humans Involved.' The latter is a phrase used by Chief Pittman."

Zachary quickly leafed through the reports. Then he shook my hand. "I'm going home to my lonely abode, made bearable only by my single Pulitzer. I have all these fascinating police files on NHIs to read, then hopefully a chilling news exposé to write. We'll see. As always, it's been a party, Alex. My best to Damon, Jannie, Nana Mama. I'd like to meet them one day. Put some faces with the names."

"Come to the next Washington Boys Choir performance," I said. "All our faces will be there. Damon is a *chorister.*"

Chapter 38

I WORKED that night until eight-thirty, and then I drove to Kinkead's in Foggy Bottom to meet up with Christine. Kinkead's is one of our favorite restaurants and also an excellent place to listen to jazz and snuggle up to each other.

I sat at the bar and enjoyed the sounds of Hilton Felton and Ephrain Woolfolk until Christine arrived, coming from an event at school. She was right on time, though. She is punctual. Very considerate. Perfect in almost every way, at least in my eyes. *Yes, I will be your wife.*

"You hungry? Want to go to a table?" I asked after we had hugged as if we'd been separated for many years and thousands of miles.

"Let's just sit here at the bar for a few minutes. You mind?" she asked. Her breath smelled slightly of spearmint. Her face was so soft and smooth that I *had* to lightly cup it in both my hands.

"Nothing I'd rather do in the whole wide world," I said.

Christine ordered a Harvey's Bristol Cream and I had a mug of beer, and we talked as the music flowed over, around, and right through our bodies. It had been a long day, and I needed this.

"I've been waiting for this all day long. I couldn't wait. Am I being too corny and romantic again?" I said, and grinned.

"Not for me. Never too corny, never too romantic. That won't happen, Alex." Christine smiled. I loved to see her like this. Her eyes twinkled and danced. I sometimes get lost in her eyes, fall into the deep pools, all that good stuff that people yearn for but few seem to get nowadays, which is sad.

She stared back, and my fingers lightly caressed her cheek. Then I held her under her chin. "Stardust" was playing. It's one of my favorite songs, even under ordinary circumstances. I wondered if Hilton and Ephrain were playing the tune for us, and when I looked at him, Hilton gave me a sly wink.

We moved closer together and danced in place. I could feel her heart beating, feel it right up against my chest. We must have stayed like that for ten or fifteen minutes. No one at the bar seemed to notice; no one bothered us, offered to refill our drinks or escort us to our table. I guess they understood.

"I really like Kinkead's," Christine whispered. "But you know what? I'd rather be home with you tonight. Someplace a little more private. I'll make you eggs, whatever you'd like. Is that all right? Do you mind?"

"No, I don't mind at all. That's a perfect idea. Let's go."

I paid our bar bill and made my regrets about the dinner reservation. Then we went to Christine's.

"We'll start with dessert," she said, and smiled wickedly. I liked that about her, too.

Chapter 39

I HAD been waiting a long time to be in love again, but this was worth it and then some. I grabbed hold of Christine as soon as we were inside her house. My hands began to trace her waist, her hips; they played over her breasts, her shoulders, then touched the delicate bones of her face. We liked to do this slowly, no need to rush. I kissed her lips, then gently scratched her back and shoulders. I pulled her closer, closer.

"You have the gentlest touch," she whispered against my cheek. "I could do this all night. Be just like this. You want some wine? Anything? I'll give you anything I have."

"I love you," I told her, still lovingly scratching her lower back. "We *will* do this forever. I have no doubt of it."

"I love you so much," she said, then I heard her breath softly catch. "So please try to be careful, Alex. At work."

"Okay, I will. But not tonight," I said.

Christine smiled. "Not tonight. Tonight you can live dangerously. We both will. You *are* handsome, and debonair for a policeman."

"Or even for an international jewel thief."

I swept her up and carried her down the hallway to the bedroom. "Mmm. Strong, too," she said. She flicked on a hall lamp as we passed. It was just enough light to see where we were going.

"How about a trip somewhere?" I said. "I need to get away."

"That sounds good. Yes—before school starts. Anywhere. Take me away from all this."

Her room smelled of fresh flowers. There were pink and red roses on the nightstand. She has a passion for flowers and gardening.

"You planned this all along, didn't you?" I said. "You *did*. This is entrapment. You sly girl."

"I was thinking about it all day," she confessed, and sighed contentedly. "I thought about being with you all day, in my office, in the hallways, the schoolyard, and then in my car on the way to the restaurant. I've been having erotic daydreams about you all day."

"I hope I can live up to them."

"You will. No doubt about it."

I took off her black silk blouse in one sweeping motion. I put my mouth to a breast, pulling at it through her demi-bra. She was wearing a brushed leather skirt, and I didn't take it off, just slowly pushed it up. I knelt and kissed her ankles, the tops of her feet, then slowly came up her long legs. She massaged my neck, my back and shoulders.

"You *are* dangerous tonight," she said. "That's a good thing."

"Sexual healing."

"Mmm, please. Heal me all over, Doctor."

She bit down hard into my shoulder, then even harder into the side of my neck. We were both breathing fast. She moved against me, then opened her legs for me. I moved inside her. She felt incredibly warm. The bedsprings began to sing, and the headboard rocked into the wall.

She pushed her hair to one side, behind an ear. I love the way she does that.

"You feel so good. Oh, Alex, don't stop, don't stop, don't stop," she whispered.

I did as I was told and loved every moment, every movement we made together, and I even wondered for a second if we had made a baby.

Chapter 40

MUCH LATER that night, we rustled up some eggs with Vidalia onions and cheddar and mozzarella cheeses, and opened a nice bottle of Pinot Noir. Then I started a fire in August, with the air conditioner turned up high.

We sat in front of the fire, laughed and talked, and planned a quick trip away from Washington. We settled on Bermuda, and Christine asked if we could bring Nana and the kids. I felt as if my life were changing fast, going to a new, good place. If only I could get lucky and catch the Weasel somehow. That could be the perfect ending to my career with the Metro police.

I went home to Fifth Street late, and got in just before three. I didn't want Damon and Jannie to wake in the morning and not find me there. I was up by eight o'clock the next morning, bounding downstairs to the delectable smells of fresh coffee and Nana's world-famous sticky buns.

The terrible twosome were just about ready to dash off to the Sojourner Truth School, where they were taking morning advanced classes. They looked like a pair of shiny angels. I didn't get to feel this good very often, so I was going all the way with it.

"How was your date last night, Daddy?" Jannie said, making her biggest goo-goo eyes at me.

"Who said I had a big date?" I made room for her on my knee. She ate a bite of the humongous sweet bun Nana had set on my plate.

"Let's just say a little birdie told me," she chirped.

"Uh-huh. Little birdie makes good sticky buns," I said. "My date was pretty good. How was yours? You had a date, right? Didn't sit home alone, did you?"

"Your date was *pretty* good? You came home with the milkman." Jannie laughed out loud. Damon was giggling, too. She can get us all going when she wants to; she's been that way since she was a baby.

"Jannie Cross," Nana said, but she let it go. There was no use trying to make Jannie act like a typical seven-year-old at this point. She was too bright, too outspoken, too full of life and fun. Besides, we have a philosophy as a family: He or she who laughs, lasts.

"How come you two don't live together first?" Jannie asked. "That's what they all do in the movies and on TV."

I found myself grinning and starting to frown at the same time. "Don't get me going on the silly stuff they do on TV and in the movies, little girl. They always get it wrong. Christine and I are going to get married soon, and *then* we'll all live together."

"You *asked* her?" they all exclaimed.

"I did."

"And she said yes?"

"Why do you all look so surprised? Of course she said yes. Who could resist being a part of this family?"

"Hooray!" Jannie whooped loudly. I could tell she meant it from the bottom of her little heart.

"Hooray!" echoed Nana. "Thank God. Oh, thank God."

"I agree," Damon piped in. "It's time we had a more normal life around here."

Everybody was congratulating me for several minutes until Jannie finally said, "I have to go to *school* now, *Pa-pa*. I wouldn't want to disappoint Mrs. Johnson by being late now, would I? Here's your morning newspaper."

Jannie handed me the *Washington Post,* and my heart jumped a little in my chest. This was a good day indeed. I saw Zachary Taylor's story at the bottom right of the front page. It wasn't the banner headline it deserved to be, but he'd gotten the story on page one.

POTENTIAL SCANDAL OVER UNSOLVED MURDERS IN
SOUTHEAST D.C. POSSIBLE RACIAL BIAS SEEN IN
POLICE ACTIVITY

"Potential scandal indeed," Nana said, and squeegeed her lower face. "Genocide always is, isn't it?"

Chapter 41

I ENTERED the station house at around eight, and Chief Pittman's assistant-lackey came scurrying up to me. Old Fred Cook had been a bad detective once, and now he was an equally bad and devious administrator, but he was as smooth a butt-kisser as could be found in the department or anywhere else in Washington.

"The chief of detectives wants to see you in his office posthaste. It's important," Fred told me. "Better move it."

I nodded at him and tried to keep my good mood intact. "Of course it is, he's the chief of detectives. You have any helpful hints for me, Fred? You happen to know what this is about, what I should expect?"

"It's a big deal," said Cook, unhelpful and happy about it. "That's about all I can tell you, Alex."

He walked away, leaving me hanging. I could feel bile rising in my throat. My good mood had already deserted me.

I walked down the creaking hardwood floors of the hallway to The Jefe's office. I had no idea what to expect, but I sure wasn't prepared for what I found.

I immediately thought about what Damon had said that morning: *It's time we had a normal life around here.*

Sampson was seated inside the chief's office. Rakeem Powell and Jerome Thurman were both in there, too.

"Come in, Dr. Cross." Chief Pittman beckoned with an outstretched hand. "Please come in. We've been waiting for you to arrive."

"What is this?" I said, pulling up a chair next to Sampson's and whispering in his ear.

"Don't know yet, but it's not too good," he said. "The Jefe hasn't said word one to us. Looks like the canary who ate the cat, though."

Pittman came around in front of his desk and leaned his ample buttocks back against it. He seemed particularly full of himself and bullshit this morning. His mousy gray hair was plastered back and looked like a helmet on his bullet head.

"I can tell you what you want to know, Detective Cross," he said. "In fact, I didn't want to tell these other detectives until you got here. As of this morning, detectives Sampson, Thurman, and Powell have been suspended from active duty. They have been working on cases outside the auspices of this department. Evidence is still being gathered about the full extent of these activities and also if any other detectives were involved."

I started to speak up, but Sampson grabbed my arm—hard. "Be cool, Alex."

Pittman looked at the three of them. "Detectives Sampson, Thurman, Powell, you can go. Your union representative has been informed of the situation. You have questions, or issues with my decision, inform your representative."

Sampson's mouth was set hard. He didn't say a word to The Jefe, though. He got up and left the office. Thurman and Powell trailed close behind him. Neither of them spoke to Pittman, either. The three of them were hardworking, dedicated detectives, and I couldn't stand to watch this happen.

I wondered why The Jefe had spared me so far. I also wondered why Shawn Moore wasn't there. The cynical answer was that Pittman wanted to set us against one another, to make us believe that Shawn had spoken against us.

Pittman reached across his desk and picked up a folded copy of the *Washington Post.* "You happen to see this article today? Bottom right?"

He pushed the newspaper toward me. I had to catch the paper to keep it from falling to the floor.

"'Scandal over unsolved murders in Southeast,'" I said. "Yes, I did. I read it at home."

"I'll bet you did. Mr. Taylor, of the *Post,* quotes unidentified sources in the police department. You have anything to do with the article?" Pittman asked, and stared hard at me.

"Why would I talk to the *Washington Post?*" I asked a question in answer to his. "I told you about the problem in Southeast. I think a repeat killer may be working there. Why go any farther with it than that? Suspending those detectives sure won't help solve the problem. Especially if this sicko is approaching rage, which I believe he is."

"I don't buy this serial-killer story. I don't see any pattern that's consistent. No one else does but you." Pittman shook his head and frowned. He was hot, angry, trying to control himself.

He reached out his hand toward me again. His fingers were like uncooked sausages. He lowered his voice almost to a whisper. "I'd like to fuck you over good, and I will. But for now, it wouldn't be expedient to pull you off the Odenkirk homicide. It wouldn't *look* good, and I suspect it would end up in the *Post,* too. I look forward to your daily reports on the so-called John Doe case. You know, it is time you got some of those unsolved murders off the books. You'll report directly to me on this. I'm going to be all over you, Cross. Any questions?"

I quickly left Chief Pittman's office. Before I hit him.

Chapter 42

SAMPSON, THURMAN, and Rakeem Powell had already left the building by the time I got out of The Jefe's office. I felt as if I could easily go postal. I nearly walked back inside Pittman's office and wiped up the floor with him.

I went to my desk and thought about what to do next, tried to calm myself down before I did anything rash and stupid. I thought about my responsibilities to the people in Southeast, and that helped me. Still, I almost went back after Pittman.

I called Christine and let out some steam. Then, on the spur of the moment, I asked if she could get away for our long weekend, possibly starting on Thursday night. Christine said that she could go. I went and filled out a vacation form and left it on Fred Cook's desk. It was the last thing he and Pittman would expect from me. But I'd already decided the best thing would be to get away from here, cool down, then figure out a plan to move forward.

As I headed out of the building, another detective stopped me. "They're over at Hart's bar," he said. "Sampson said to tell you they reserved a seat for you."

Hart's is a very seedy, very popular gin mill on Second Street. It isn't a cops' bar, which is why some of us like it. It was eleven in the morning, and the barroom was already crowded, lively, even friendly.

"Here he is!" Jerome Thurman saluted me with a half-full beer mug as I walked inside. Half a dozen other detectives and friends were there, too. The word had gotten around fast about the suspensions.

There was a whole lot of laughter and shouting going on. "It's a bachelor's party!" Sampson said, and grinned. "Got you, sugar. With a little help from Nana. You should see the look on your face!"

For the next hour and a half, friends kept arriving at Hart's. By noon the bar was full, and then the regular customers started coming in for their lunch-hour nips. The owner, Mike Hart, was in his glory. I hadn't really thought about having a bachelor's party, but now that I was in the middle of one, I was glad it happened. A lot of men still guard their emotions and feelings, but not so much at a bachelor's party, at least not at a good one thrown by the people closest to you.

This was a good one. The suspensions that had been handed down earlier that morning were mostly forgotten for a few hours. I was congratulated and hugged more times than I could count, and even kissed once or twice. Everybody was calling me "sugar," following Sampson's lead. The "love" word was used, and overused. I was roasted and toasted in sentimental speeches that seemed hilarious at the time. Just about everybody had too much to drink.

By four in the afternoon, Sampson and I were steadying each other, making our way into the blinding daylight on Second Street. Mike Hart himself had called us a cab.

For a brief, clear moment, I was reminded of the purple and blue gypsy cab we were looking for—but then the thought evaporated into the nearly white sunlight.

"Sugar," Sampson whispered against my skull as we were climbing into our cab, "I love you more than life itself. It's true. I love your kids, love your Nana, love your wife-to-be, the lovely Christine. Take us home," he said to the driver. "Alex is getting married."

"And he's the best man," I said to the driver, who smiled.

"Yes I am," said Sampson. "The very best."

Chapter 43

ON THURSDAY night, Shafer played the Four Horsemen again. He was locked inside his study, but through the early part of the night he could hear the sounds of his family throughout the house. He felt intensely isolated; he was nervous, jittery, and angry for no apparent reason.

While he waited to log on with the other players, he found himself thinking back to his wild car ride through Washington. He relived a particular feeling over and over: the imagined moment of sudden impact with an unmovable structure. He saw it as blinding light, and physical objects, and *himself,* all shattering like glass and then becoming part of the universe again. Even the pain he would feel would be part of the reassembling of matter into other fascinating forms and shapes.

I am suicidal, he finally thought. *It's just a matter of time. I really am Death.*

When it was exactly nine o'clock, he began to type in a message on his computer. The other Horsemen were on-line, waiting for his response to the visit and warning by George Bayer. He didn't want to disappoint them. What they had done had made him even more enthusiastic about playing the game. He wrote:

Strangely, Death wasn't surprised when Famine appeared in Washington. Of course he had every right to come. Just as Death could go to London, or Singapore, or Manila, or Kingston, and perhaps Death will pay one of you a visit soon.

That's the beauty of the game we play—anything can happen.

Ultimately, the issue is trust, isn't it? Do I trust that you will allow me to continue to play the fantasy game as I wish? After all, that is what makes the game distinctive and alluring: the freedom we experience.

That *is* the game now, isn't it? We have evolved into something new. We have raised the table stakes. So let's have some real excitement, fellow Horsemen. I have a few ideas to try out on you. Everything is in the spirit of the game. No unnecessary risks will be taken.

Let's play the game as if our lives depended on it.

Perhaps mine already does?

As I told you, we have two new players. They are Washington detectives named Alex Cross and John Sampson. Worthy opponents. I'm watching them, but I can't help wondering whether soon they'll be watching me.

Let me tell you about a fantasy scenario that I've created to welcome them to our game. I'm sending pictures now—Detectives Cross and Sampson.

Chapter 44

IT TOOK us a day to get organized for our trip, but everybody seemed to enjoy the spontaneity, and also the special treat of our all being together on a vacation for the first time. And so Damon, Jannie, Nana, Christine, and I left D.C. in the afternoon and arrived in high spirits at Bermuda International Airport late on Thursday evening, the twenty-fifth of August.

I definitely wanted to be out of Washington for a few days. The Mr. Smith murder case had been followed too quickly by the Jane Doe investigation. I needed a rest. I had a friend who was part owner of a hotel in Bermuda, and it wasn't a particularly long airplane ride. It was perfect for us.

One scene from the airport will always stick in my mind—Christine's singing "Ja-da, ja-da," with Jannie stuck at her side. I couldn't help thinking that they looked like mother and daughter, and that touched me deeply. They were so affectionate and playful, so natural. It was a mind-photo for me to have and to hold, one of those moments that I knew I'd never forget, even as I watched the two of them dancing and singing as if they'd known each other forever.

We were blessed with extraordinarily good weather for our holiday. It was sunny and blue-skied every day, morning until nightfall, when the sky turned a magical combination of reds, oranges, and purples. The days belonged to all of us, but especially to the kids. We went swimming and snorkeling at Elbow Beach and Horseshoe Bay, and then raced mopeds along the picturesque Middle and Harbour roads.

The nights belonged to Christine and me, and we made the most of them. We hit all the best spots: the Terrace Bar at the Palm Reef, the Gazebo Lounge at the Princess, the Clay House Inn, Once Upon a Table in Hamilton, Horizons in Paget. I loved being with her, and that thought kept drifting through my mind. I felt that what we shared had been strengthened because I had backed off and given her time and space. And I felt whole again. I kept remembering the very first time I had seen her in the schoolyard at Sojourner Truth. *She's the one, Alex.* That thought still played in my head, too.

We sat at the Terrace Bar overlooking the city and harbor of Hamilton. The water was dotted with small islands, white sails, ferries going back and forth to Warwick and Paget. We held hands, and I couldn't stop staring into her eyes, didn't want to.

"Big thoughts?" she finally asked.

"I've been thinking a lot about going into private practice again," I told her. "I think it might be the best thing to do."

She stared into my eyes. "I don't want you to do it for me, Alex. Please don't make me the cause of your leaving your job with the police. I know you love it. Most days you do."

"The Job has been tearing at me lately. Pittman isn't just a difficult boss; I think he's a bad guy. What happened to Sampson and the others is just bullshit. They were working unsolved cases on their own time. I'm tempted to give the story to Zach Taylor at the *Post.* People would riot if they knew the truth. Which is why I *won't* give it to the *Post.*"

She listened and tried to help but she didn't push, and I appreciated that. "It does sound like a terrible, complicated, nasty mess, Alex. I'd like to punch out Pittman, too. He's choosing politics over protecting people. I'm sure you'll know what to do when the time is right."

The next morning, I found her walking in the garden, with tropical flowers strewn in her hair. She looked radiant, even more than usual, and I fell in love all over again.

"There's an old saying I've been hearing since I was a little girl," she told me as I joined her. "If you have only two pennies, buy a loaf of bread with one and a lily with the other."

I kissed her hair, in between the flowers. I kissed her sweet lips, her cheeks, the hollow in her throat.

The kids and I went back to Horseshoe Bay

Beach early that afternoon. They couldn't get enough of the deep blue sea, swimming, snorkeling, and building sand castles. And, of course, it was almost time to start school again, so everything about our vacation was extra-special and intense.

Christine took a moped trip into Hamilton to pick up mementos for a few of the teachers at Sojourner Truth. We all waved until she was out of sight on Middle Road. Then back into the water!

Around five o'clock, Damon, Jannie, and I returned to the Belmont Hotel, which sat like a sentinel on lush green hills framed by china-blue skies. All around, everywhere we looked, were pastel-colored cottages with white roofs. Nana was sitting out on the porch, talking to a couple of her new best friends. *Paradise regained,* I thought, and felt something deep and sacred coming back to life inside me.

As I stared out at the cloudless blue sky, I regretted that Christine wasn't there to share it. I actually missed her in just that short a time. I hugged Jannie and Damon, and we were all smiling at the obvious: we loved being here together, and we were so damn fortunate to have one another.

"You miss her," Jannie whispered. It was a statement, not a question. "That's good, Daddy. That's the way it should be, right?"

When Christine still hadn't returned by six o'clock, I struggled between conflicting thoughts of waiting for her at the hotel or driving into

Hamilton myself. Maybe she'd had an accident. *Those damn mopeds,* I thought, having found them fun and perfectly safe just the afternoon before.

I spotted a tall, slender woman entering through the front gates of the Belmont, walking against a background of hibiscus and oleander. I sighed with relief, but as I started down the front stairs, I saw that it wasn't Christine.

Christine still hadn't returned, or called the hotel, by six-thirty. Or by seven o'clock.

I finally called the police.

Chapter 45

INSPECTOR PATRICK Busby from the Hamilton P.D. arrived at the Belmont Hotel around seven-thirty. He was a small balding man who from a distance looked to be in his late fifties or sixties. As he approached the front porch, though, I could tell he was no more than forty, around the same age as me.

He listened to my story, then said that visitors often lost track of time and of themselves in Bermuda. There were also occasional moped accidents on Middle Road. He promised me that Christine would show up soon, with a mild "road rash" or a "slightly turned ankle."

I wouldn't have any of it. She was always punctual, and at the very least, she would have called.

I knew that somehow she'd call if she had a minor accident. So the inspector and I rode together between the hotel and Hamilton, and then we toured the streets of the capital city, particularly Front and Reid streets. I was silent and solemn-faced as I stared out of the car, hoping to get a glimpse of Christine shopping on some side street, forgetful of the hour. But we didn't see her anywhere, and she still hadn't called the hotel.

When she still hadn't turned up by nine, Inspector Busby reluctantly agreed that Christine might be missing. He asked a lot of questions that showed me he was a decent cop. He wanted to know if we'd had any kind of argument or disagreement.

"I'm a homicide detective in Washington, D.C.," I finally told him. I'd been holding it back because I didn't want this to get territorial. "I've been involved with high-profile cases involving mass murders in the past. I've known some very bad men. There might be a connection. I hope not, but that could be."

"I see," Busby said. He was such a precise, neat man with his thin pencil mustache. He looked more like a fussy schoolteacher than a cop, more like a psychologist than I did. "Are there any other surprises I should know about, Detective Cross?" he asked.

"No, that's it. But you see why I'm worried, and why I called you. I'm working on a series of nasty murders in Washington right now."

"Yes, I see a reason for your concern now. I will put out a missing-persons report forthwith."

I sighed heavily, then went upstairs and talked to the kids and Nana. I tried my best not to alarm them, but Damon and Jannie started to cry. And then Nana did, too.

We had learned nothing more about Christine or her whereabouts by midnight. Inspector Busby left the hotel at quarter past twelve. He was kind, actually, and considerate enough to give me his home number; he asked me to call right away if I heard from Christine. Then he said my family and I would be in his prayers.

At three, I was still up and pacing my hotel room on the third floor, and doing some praying myself. I had just gotten off the phone with Quantico. The FBI was cross-checking all of my homicide cases to see if anyone I'd investigated had any connection with Bermuda. The Bureau was now concentrating on the current series of unsolved murders in Southeast. I'd faxed them my profile on the Weasel.

I didn't have any logical reason to suspect that the killer might be here in Bermuda, and yet I feared he might be. It was just the kind of feeling that The Jefe had been rejecting about the murders in Southeast.

I understood that the Bureau probably wouldn't get back to me until later in the morning. I was tempted to call friends at Interpol, but I held off. . . . And then I called Interpol, too.

The hotel room was filled with mahogany Queen Anne furniture and wicker, and had dusty-pink carpets. It seemed empty and lonely. I stood like a ghost before the tall, water-stained dormer windows, stared out at the shifting black shapes against the moonlit sky, and remembered how I held Christine in my arms. I felt incredibly helpless and alone without her. I also couldn't believe this had happened.

I hugged myself tightly and became aware of a terrible pain all around my heart. The tightening pain was like a solid column that went from my chest all the way up into my head. I could see her face, her beautiful smile. I remembered dancing with her one night at the Rainbow Room in New York, and dinners at Kinkead's in Washington, and that one special night at her place when we'd laughed and thought maybe we'd made a baby. Was Christine out there somewhere on the island? She had to be. I prayed again that she was safe. She had to be safe. I refused to have any other thought for more than a couple of seconds.

The telephone in the room rang, a short burst, at a little past four in the morning.

My heart was stuck in my throat. My skin crawled, felt as if it were shrinking and no longer fit my body. I rushed across the room and grabbed the phone before the second ring. My hand was trembling.

The strange, muffled voice scared me: "You have e-mail."

I couldn't think straight. I couldn't think at all.

I'd brought my laptop with me on vacation.

Who knows that I have my computer here? Who could know a small detail like that about me? Who's been watching me? Watching us?

I yanked open the closet door, grabbed the computer, hooked it up, and logged on. I scrolled down the e-mail to the last message.

It was short and very concise.

She's safe for now. We have her.

The curt, cold message was worse than anything I could imagine. Each word was branded into my brain, repeating over and over.

"She's safe for now.

"We have her."

Book Three

ELEGY

SAMPSON ARRIVED at the Belmont Hotel the day after Christine disappeared. I hurried down to the small front lobby to meet him. He threw his large arms around me, clasping me tightly but gently, as if he were holding a child in his arms.

"You okay? You holding up?" he asked.

"Not even close," I told him. "I spent half a day checking the e-mail address I got last night. It came from curtain@mindspring.com. The address was falsified. Nothing is going right."

"We'll get Christine back. We'll find her." He told me what he knew I wanted to hear, but I was sure that he also truly believed it in his heart. Sampson is the most positive human being I've ever met. He won't be denied.

"Thanks for coming. It means a lot to all of us. I can't think straight about anything. I'm really rattled, John. I can't even begin to imagine who could have done this. Maybe the Weasel—I don't know."

"If you *could* think straight now," John said, "I'd

be more worried about you than usual. That's why I'm here."

"I kind of knew you'd come."

"Of course you did. I'm Sampson. Occam's razor and all that other deep philosophical shit at work here."

There were a half-dozen guests in the hotel lobby, and all of them looked our way. The hotel staff knew about Christine's disappearance, and I'm sure that the guests at the Belmont knew as well, as did just about everybody else on the small, chatty island.

"The story's on the front page of the local news-paper," Sampson said. "People were reading copies at the airport."

I told him, "Bermuda is small, mostly peaceful and orderly. The disappearance of a tourist, or any kind of violent crime, is unusual here. I don't know how the paper got the story so quickly. The leak must have come out of the police station."

"Local police won't help us. Probably get in the way," Sampson muttered as we walked over to the hotel registration desk. He signed in, then we trudged upstairs to show Nana and the kids that Uncle John was here.

Chapter 47

THE FOLLOWING morning, the two of us met for hours with the police in Hamilton. They were professionals, but a kidnapping was a rarity for them. They let us set up in their station house on Front Street. I still couldn't concentrate or focus the way I needed to.

Bermuda is a twenty-one-square-mile island. While the British colony is small, we soon discovered that there are more than twelve hundred roads on the island. Sampson and I split up and covered as much ground as we possibly could. For the next two days we went from six in the morning until ten or eleven at night, without a break. I didn't want to stop, not even to sleep.

We didn't do any better than the locals, though. No one had seen anything. We'd reached a dead end. Christine had disappeared without a trace.

We were bone-tired. After we finished at the station house on the third night, Sampson and I went for a late swim at Elbow Beach, just down the road from the hotel.

We had learned to swim at the municipal pool in

D.C. Nana had insisted that we learn. She was fifty-four at the time, and stubborn. She made up her mind to learn and took lessons with us from the Red Cross. The majority of people in Southeast didn't know how to swim back then, and she felt it was symbolic of the limiting inner-city experience.

So one summer, Sampson and I tackled swimming with Nana at the municipal pool. We went for lessons three mornings a week and usually practiced for an extra hour after that. Nana herself was soon able to swim fifty or more laps. She had stamina, same as now. I rarely get into the water without flashing back to those fine summer days of my youth, when I became a reasonably good swimmer.

Now, Sampson and I floated on the calm surface, out about a hundred yards or so from shore. The sky above was the deepest shade of evening blue, sparkling with countless stars. I could see the curving white line of the beach as it stretched several miles in either direction. Palm and casuarina trees shimmied in the sea breeze.

I felt devastated, totally overwhelmed as I floated on the sea. I kept seeing Christine with my eyes open or closed. I couldn't believe she was gone. I teared up as I thought about what had happened, the unfairness of life sometimes.

"You want to talk about the investigation? My thoughts so far? Little things I learned today? Or give it a rest for the night?" Sampson asked me as we floated peacefully on our backs. "Talk? Or quiet time?"

"Talk, I guess. I can't think about anything else except Christine. I can't think straight. Say whatever you're thinking. Something bothering you in particular?"

"Little thing, but maybe it's important."

I didn't say anything. I just let him go on.

"What puzzles me is the first newspaper stories." Sampson paused and then continued, "Busby says he didn't talk to anybody the first night. Not a single person, he claims. You didn't, either. Story was in the morning edition, though."

"It's a small island, John. I told you that, and you've seen it yourself."

But Sampson kept at it, and I began to think that maybe there was something to it.

"Listen, Alex, only you, Patrick Busby, and whoever took Christine knew. *He* called it in to the paper. The kidnapper did it himself. I talked to the girl at the paper who got the call. She wouldn't say anything yesterday, but she finally told me late today. She thought it was just a concerned citizen calling. I think somebody's playing with your head, Alex. Somebody's running a nasty game on you."

"We have her."

A game? What kind of nasty game? Who were the nasty players? Was one of them the Weasel? Was it possible that he was still here in Bermuda?

Chapter 48

I COULDN'T sleep back at the hotel. I still couldn't concentrate or focus, and it was incredibly frustrating. It was as if I were losing my mind.

A *game?* No, this wasn't a game. This was shock and horror. This was a living nightmare beyond anything I had ever experienced. Who could have done this to Christine? Why? Who was the Weasel?

Every time I closed my eyes, tried to sleep, I could see Christine's face, see her waving good-bye that final time on Middle Road, see her walking through the hotel gardens with flowers in her hair.

I could hear Christine's voice all through the night—and then it was morning again. My guilt over what had happened to her had doubled, tripled.

Sampson and I continued to canvass Middle Road, Harbour Road, South Road. Every person we spoke to in the police and the military believed that Christine didn't simply disappear on the island. Sampson and I heard the same song and dance every day for a week. No shopkeepers or taxi or bus drivers had seen her in Hamilton or St.

George, so it was possible that she'd never even arrived in either town that afternoon.

No one, not one witness, remembered seeing her moped on Middle or Harbour roads, so maybe she never even got that far.

Most disturbing of all was that there hadn't been any further communication with me about her since the e-mail on the night she disappeared. An agent at the FBI had investigated the e-mail address and found *it didn't exist.* Whoever had contacted me was a skillful hacker, able to conceal his or her identity. The words I'd read that night were always on my mind.

"She's safe for now."

"We have her."

Who was "we"? And why hadn't there been any further contact? What did they want from me? Did they know they were driving me insane? Was that what they wanted to do? Did the Weasel represent more than one killer? Suddenly that made a lot of sense to me.

Sampson returned to Washington on Sunday, and he took Nana and the kids with him. They didn't want to leave without me, but it was time for them to go. I couldn't make myself leave Bermuda yet. It would have felt as if I were abandoning Christine.

On Sunday night, Patrick Busby showed up at the Belmont Hotel around nine. He asked me to ride with him out past Southampton, about a six-mile drive that he said would take us twenty minutes or more. Bermudians measure distances in straight lines, but all the roads run in wiggles and half-circles, so it always takes longer to travel than you might think.

"What is it, Patrick? What's out in Southampton?" I asked as we rode along Middle Road. My heart was in my throat. He was scaring me with his silence.

"We haven't found Mrs. Johnson. However, a man may have witnessed the abduction. I want you to hear his story. You decide for yourself. You're the big-city detective, not me. You can ask whatever questions you like. Off the record, of course."

The man's name was Perri Graham, and he was staying in a room at the Port Royal Golf Club. We met him at his tiny apartment in the staff quarters. He was tall and painfully thin, with a longish goatee. He clearly wasn't happy to see Inspector Busby or me on his doorstep.

Busby had already told me that Graham was originally from London and now worked as a porter and maintenance man at the semiprivate golf club. He had also lived in New York City and Miami and had a criminal record for selling crack in New York.

"I already told him everything I saw," Perri Graham said defensively as soon as he opened the front door of his room and saw the two of us standing there. "Go away. Let me be. Why would I hold back anything or—"

I cut him off. "My name is Alex Cross. I'm a

homicide detective from Washington. The woman you saw was my fiancée, Mr. Graham. May we come in and talk? This will only take a few minutes."

He shook his head back and forth in frustration.

"I'll tell you what I know. *Again,*" he finally said, relenting. "Yeah, come in. But only because you called me Mr. Graham."

"That's all I want. I'm not here to bother you about anything else."

Busby and I walked inside the room, which was little more than an alcove. The tile floors and all the furniture were strewn with wrinkled clothes, mostly underwear.

"A woman I know lives in Hamilton," Graham said in a weary voice. "I went to visit her this Tuesday past. We drank too much wine. Stayed the evening—you know how it is. I got up somehow. Had to be at the club by noon, but I knew I'd be late and get docked some of my pay. Don't have a car or nothin', so I hitched a ride from Hamilton, out South Shore Road. Walked along near Paget, I suppose. Damn hot afternoon, I remember. I went down to the water, cool off if I could.

"I came back up over a knobbly hill, and I witnessed an accident on the roadway. It was maybe a quarter of a mile down the big hill there. You know it?"

I nodded and held my breath as I listened to him. I remembered the stifling heat of that afternoon, everything about it. I could still see Christine driving off on a shiny blue moped, waving and smiling. The memory of her smile, which had always brought me such joy, now put a tight knot in my stomach.

"I saw a white van hit a woman riding a blue moped. I can't be sure, but it almost looked like the van hit her on purpose. Driver, he jumped out of the van right away and helped her up. She didn't look like she was hurt badly. Then he helped her inside the van. Put the moped inside, too. Then he drove off. I thought he was taking her to the hospital. Thought nothing else of it."

"You sure she wasn't badly hurt?" I asked.

"Not sure. But she got right up. She was able to stand all right."

There was a catch in my voice when I spoke again. "And you didn't tell anybody about the accident, not even when you saw the news stories?"

The man shook his head. "Didn't see no stories. Don't bother with the local news much. Just small-time shit and worthless gossip. But then my girl, she keep talking about it. I didn't want to go to the police, but she made me do it, made me talk to this inspector here."

"You know what kind of van it was?" I asked.

"White van. I think it was maybe a rented one. Clean and new."

"License plate?"

Graham shook his head. "Don't have no idea."

"What did the man in the van look like?" I asked him. "Any little thing you remember is helpful, Mr. Graham. You've already helped a lot."

He shrugged, but I could tell that he was trying to think back to that afternoon. "Nothing special about him. Not as tall as you, but tall. Look like anybody else. Just a black man, like any other."

Chapter 49

IN A small apartment in a suburb of Washington called Mount Rainier, Detective Patsy Hampton lay in bed, restlessly flipping through the pages of the *Post*. She couldn't sleep, but there was nothing unusual about that. She often had trouble sleeping, ever since she was a little girl in Harrisburg, Pennsylvania. Her mother said she must have a guilty conscience about something.

She watched a rerun episode of *ER,* then fetched herself a Stonyfield yogurt with blueberries and logged on to America Online. She had an e-mail from her father, now relocated in Delray Beach, Florida, and one from an old college roommate from the University of Richmond, whom she had never been that close to anyway.

The roommate had just heard from a mutual friend that Patsy was a hotshot police detective in Washington, and what an exciting life she must lead. The roommate wrote that she had four children and lived in a suburb of Charlotte, North Carolina, but added that she was bored with everything in her life. Patsy Hampton would have given anything to have just one child.

She wandered back to the kitchen and got a cold bottle of Evian mineral water. She was aware that her life had become ridiculous. She spent too much time on her job, but also too much time by herself in her apartment, especially on weekends. It wasn't that she couldn't get dates; she was just turned off by men in general lately.

She still fantasized about finding someone compatible, having children. But she was increasingly tired of the depressing and maddening cycle of trying to meet someone interesting. She usually ended up with guys who were either hopelessly boring *or* thirty-something jackasses who still acted like teenagers, though without the charm of youth. *Hopeless, hopeless, hopeless,* she thought as she sent off a cheery lie to her dad in Florida.

The phone rang, and she glanced at her wristwatch—it was twenty past twelve.

She snatched up the receiver. "Hampton speaking."

"It's Chuck, Patsy. Really sorry to call so late. Is it okay? You awake?"

"Sure, no problem, Chucky Cheese. I'm up with the other vampires—yourself included, I guess."

It was kind of late, but she was glad to hear from Chuck Hufstedler, who was a computer geek at the FBI in Washington. The two of them helped each other out sometimes, and she'd recently talked to him about the unsolved D.C. murders, especially the Jane Does. Chuck had told her that he was also in contact with Alex Cross, but Cross had trouble of his own right now. His fiancée had been kidnapped, and Patsy Hampton wondered if it had anything to do with the killings in Southeast.

"I'm wide awake, Chuck. What's up? What's on your big mind?"

He started with a disclaimer that said volumes about his incredibly low self-esteem: "Maybe nothing, but maybe something a little interesting on those killings in Southeast, and particularly the two young girls in Shaw. This really comes out of left field, though."

The FBI computer expert had her attention. "That's where this killer lives, Chuck, in *deep* left field. Tell me what you have. I'm wide awake and listening. Talk to me, Chucky Cheese."

Chuck hemmed and hawed. He was always like that, which was too bad because he was basically a really nice guy. "You know anything about RPGs, Patsy?" he asked.

"I know it stands for role-playing games, and let's see, there's a popular one called Dragons and Dungeons, or Dungeons and Dragons—whatever the order."

"It's Dungeons and Dragons, or Advanced Dungeons and Dragons. Confession time, kiddo: I occasionally play an RPG myself, it's called Millennium's End. I play a couple of hours a day, usually. More on weekends."

"New to me. Go on, Chuck." *God,* she thought, *cyberspace confessions in the middle of the night.*

"Very popular game, even with so-called adults. The characters in Millennium's End work for Black Eagle Security. It's a private organization of troubleshooters who hire out for investigative services around the world. The characters are all good guys, crusaders for good."

"Uh-huh, Chuck. Say six Hail Marys, now make an Act of Contrition, then get to the damn point. It *is* around twelve-thirty, pal."

"Right, I am heartily sorry, and deeply embarrassed, too. Anyway, there's a chatroom on-line that I visited. It's called the Gamester's Chatroom, and it's on AOL. As I speak, there's a fascinating discussion going on about a new kind of game. It's more an *anti*-game, though. All the role-playing games I know are about *good* characters trying to conquer chaos and evil. The game under discussion has a couple of *evil* characters *trying to overcome good.* Specifically, Patsy, one of the characters is attacking and murdering women in the Southeast part of D.C. Lots of lurid detail on the murders. These aren't the actual players, but they know about the game. The game itself is probably protected. Thought you should know. The game is called the Four Horsemen."

Patsy Hampton was definitely wide awake now. "I'm on it. Thanks, Chuck. Let's keep this between the two of us for the moment, okay, Chuck?"

"Yeah. Okay."

It took her a couple of minutes to log on to AOL, then get into the Gamester's Chatroom. She didn't participate, just read what the others had to say. This was interesting. She wondered if she had just stumbled onto her first big break in the Jane Doe case.

The others in the room were named Viper, Landlocked, J-Boy, and Lancelot. They chattered on and on about the hottest fantasy games and cutting-edge magazines, which nearly succeeded in putting her to sleep. The Four Horsemen came up twice, but only in passing, as a point of reference. Lancelot was the one who mentioned it. Chuck was right: these probably weren't the actual players, but they knew about the game somehow.

The fantasy nerds were starting to wear really thin with her by quarter past one. Finally, out of frustration, she typed out a message for the little shitheels. She called herself Sappho.

I came in late, but Horsemen sounds like a neat kind of revolutionary game to me, Lancelot. Pretty audacious stuff, No?
Lancelot shot back:
Not really, *Sappo*. There's a lot of it going around lately. Antiheroes, sickos. Especially in vampire game circles.
Hampton typed:
Haven't I read about murders like these in the newspapers? By the way, it's Sappho, like the poet.

Lancelot replied,

Yeah, but lots of RPGs use current events. No biggie, really, *Sappo*.

Hampton grinned. He was an obnoxious little nerd, but she had him—for the moment, anyway. And she needed him. How much did he know about the Four Horsemen? Could he be a player? She tried to peek at Lancelot's profile, but he had restricted access to it.

You're funny. Are you a player, Laughalot, or just an art critic?

I don't like the basic concept of Horsemen. Anyway, it's a private game. *Strictly* private. Encrypted.

You know any of the players? I might like to try it out myself?

There was no response to the question. Patsy thought maybe she'd pushed too hard, too fast. Damn! She should have known better. Damn, damn! Come back, Lancelot. Earth to Lancelot.

I really would like to play the Four Horsemen. But I'm cool about it. No Biggie. Lancelot?

Patsy Hampton waited, and then Lancelot left the chatroom. Lancelot was gone. And so was her connection to somebody playing a so-called fantasy game about committing gruesome murders in Washington—murders that had really happened.

Chapter 50

I RETURNED to Washington during the first week of September, and I had never felt stranger in my own skin. I'd gone to Bermuda with my family and Christine, and now I was coming home without her. Whoever had taken Christine had contacted me only once. I missed her nearly every moment of every day, and it pained me to think about where she might still be.

It was an unusually cool and windy day when I got back to the city. It almost seemed as if summer had suddenly changed to the middle of fall, as if I had been away much longer than I had. I had been in a fog of unreality in Bermuda, and it was nearly the same once I was back in D.C. It had never been this bad before. I was so lost, so unhinged, so battered.

I wondered if Christine and I were part of a madman's elaborate delusion, what profilers call an escalating fantasy. If so, who was this madman, and where was he now? Was it the Weasel? Did I know him from some time in my past? The heartless, spineless bastard had communicated, *"We have her.*" And that was it. No further word. Now only silence, which was deafening.

I took a cab from the airport and remembered what had happened to Frank Odenkirk, who had innocently taken a cab one night in August and wound up murdered on Alabama Avenue near Dupont Park. I hadn't thought about the Odenkirk case during the past three weeks. I had rarely even had a thought about the Jane Doe murders while in Bermuda, but I was guiltily reminded of them now. Others had suffered painful losses because of the killer.

I wondered if any progress had been made, and who in the department was running the case, at least the Odenkirk part of it. On the other hand, I didn't feel that I could work on any of the other unsolved murders right now. I felt my place was still in Bermuda, and I nearly headed back as soon as I landed.

Then I could see our house up ahead on Fifth Street. Something strange was happening—there was a huge gathering.

Chapter 51

LOTS OF people were standing on the porch
and others were clustered in front of the house
when the cab arrived. Cars were parked and double-
parked all along the street.

I recognized Aunt Tia. My sister-in-law Cilla
and Nana were on the porch with the kids. Sampson
was there with a girlfriend named Millie, a lawyer
from the Justice Department.

Some of them waved as I pulled up, so I knew
everything was all right. This wasn't more trouble.
But what was this all about?

I saw my niece Naomi and her husband, Seth
Taylor, who had come all the way from Durham,
North Carolina. Jerome Thurman, Rakeem Powell,
and Shawn Moore were standing on the front lawn.

"Hey, Alex, good to see you," Jerome's deep
voice boomed out at me as I passed near him on
my way to the porch. I finally set down my travel
bag and started shaking hands, giving out hugs,
receiving back pats and kisses from all sides.

"We're all here for you," Naomi said. She came
over to me and hugged me tightly. "We love you

so much. But we'll go away if you don't want us here now."

"No, no. I'm glad you're here, Scootchie," I said, and kissed my niece on both cheeks. A while back, she'd been abducted in Durham, North Carolina. I had been there for her, and so had Sampson. "It's good that you and Seth are here. It's good to see everybody. You can't imagine how good it is."

I hugged relatives and friends, my grandmother, my two beautiful kids, and I realized again how lucky I was to have so many good people in my life. Two teachers from the Sojourner Truth School had also come to the house. They were friends of Christine's, and they started to cry when they came up to me. They wanted to know if any progress had been made and if there was anything they could do.

I told them that we had a witness to the abduction and that we were more hopeful than ever. The teachers were buoyed by the news, which wasn't nearly as good as I made it sound. Nothing more had come of the one eyewitness account of the abduction. No one else had seen the white van that took away Christine.

Jannie cornered me in the backyard around nine o'clock. I had just spent half an hour with Damon in the basement, talking man to man, shadowboxing a little bit.

Damon had told me that he was having trouble remembering Christine's face, exactly what she looked like. I told him that it happened with people and that it was all right. Then we shared a long hug.

Jannie had patiently waited to talk with me.

"My turn?" she asked.

"Absolutely, sweetheart."

Jannie then took my hand and pulled me forward into the house. She quietly led me upstairs—not to her room, but to mine.

"If you get lonely in here tonight, you can come to my room. I *mean* it," she said as she gently shut the door on the two of us. She is so wise and has such a good perspective on so many things. Both she and Damon are such good kids. Nana says they have "sound character," and it is building nicely. So far, so good.

"Thank you, sweetie. I will come to your room if it gets bad in here. You're very thoughtful and nice."

"I am, Daddy. You helped me be this way, and I'm glad of it. Now I have a real serious question for you, Daddy. It's hard, but I have to ask anyway."

"You go ahead," I told her, feeling uncomfortable under her serious little gaze. I wasn't completely focused, and I didn't know if I could handle one of Jannie's hard questions. "I'm listening, sweetheart," I said. "Fire away."

She had let go of my hand, but then she took it up again, held my big hand tightly in both her small ones.

"Daddy, is Christine dead?" she asked me. "You can tell me if she is. Please tell the true truth, though. I want to know."

I almost lost it, sitting on the edge of the bed with Jannie. I'm sure she had no idea how much her question hurt, or how hard it was to answer.

I was hanging over the edge of a dark abyss, just about gone, but I pulled myself together and took a deep, hard breath. Then I tried to answer my little girl's honest question as best I could.

"I don't know yet," I told her. "That's the truth. We're still hoping to find her, sweetie. We found one witness so far."

"But she might be dead, Daddy?"

"Let me tell you the best thing I know about dying," I said to Jannie. "The very best thing that I know. Just about the only thing, in fact."

"You go away, and then you're with Jesus forever," Jannie said. The way she spoke, though, I wasn't sure if she really believed what she was saying. It sounded like one of Nana's "gospel truths," or maybe she'd heard it in church.

"Yes, that can be a great comfort to know, baby. But I was thinking of something else. Maybe it's the same thing, but a different way to look at it."

Her intense little eyes held mine, wouldn't let go. "You can tell me, Daddy. Please. I want to hear it. I'm very interested in this."

"It's not a bad thing, but it helps me whenever somebody dies. Think about this. We come into life so easily—from somewhere, from the universe, from God. Why should it be any harder when we leave life? We come from a good place.

We leave—and go to a good place. Does that make any sense to you, Jannie?"

She nodded and continued to stare deeply into my eyes. "I understand," she whispered. "It's like it's in balance."

She paused a second, thinking it over, then she spoke. "But Daddy, Christine isn't dead. I just know it. She *isn't* dead. She hasn't gone to that good place yet. So don't you lose hope."

Chapter 52

THE CHARACTER and traits of Death were so much like his own, Shafer was thinking as he sped south along I-95. Death wasn't brilliant, but he was always thorough, and he always won in the end.

As the black Jag raced past the exits for various small towns, Shafer wondered if he wanted to be caught now, if he needed to be unmasked, needed to show his true face to everyone. Boo Cassady believed that he was hiding, even from her, but more important, from himself. Maybe she was right. Maybe he did want Lucy and the kids to see who he really was. And the police. But especially the uptight and sanctimonious staff at the embassy.

I am Death—it's who I am. I am a multiple killer—it's who I am. I am not Geoffrey Shafer anymore; maybe I never was. But if I was, it was a long, long time ago.

Shafer had always had a natural mean streak, a vengeful, nasty way. He remembered it from his early years traveling with his family through Europe, then Asia, and finally back to England. His father had been in the military and was always a real "tough guy" around the house. He struck Shafer and his two brothers often, but not nearly as often as he hit their mother, who died of a fall when Shafer was twelve.

Shafer was large as a boy, and he was one "tough hombre," a real bully. Other boys feared him, even his brothers, Charles and George, who believed that Geoff was "capable of anything." He was.

Nothing in his early days prepared him for being the man who finally emerged once he joined MI6. It was there that he learned he was capable of killing another human being—and he found that he loved it. He had discovered his calling, his true passion in life. He was the ultimate "tough guy"; he was Death.

He continued traveling south on the interstate highway. Because it was late, traffic was light, mostly high-speeding trucks headed toward Florida, he supposed.

He mentally composed a message to the other fantasy game players.

Death goes to Fredericksburg, Maryland, tonight. A good-looking 37-year-old woman lives there with her mirror-image 15-year-old daughter. The woman is divorced, a small-town lawyer, a prosecutor. The daughter is an honor student and a football cheerleader. The two women will be sleeping. Death has come to Maryland because Washington is too dangerous now. (Yes, I took your warning to heart.) The D.C. police are searching for the Jane Doe Murderer. A well-thought-of detective named Patsy Hampton is on the case, and Detective Cross has returned from Bermuda. It will be interesting to see if his character has changed in any way. Character is everything, don't you agree?

I can see the Cahill house up ahead. I can picture both of the lovely Cahill women. They live in a four-bedroom ranch house. The suburban street is virtually silent at 1:00 A.M. No one could possibly connect these two murders to the Jane Does. I wish you could be here with me. I wish you could feel exactly as I do.

Chapter 53

SHAFER PARKED his Jag on the shadowy street and felt strangely alone and afraid. He was actually scaring himself. The things he thought and did. No one had a twisted mind like his—no one thought like this. No one had ever had such outlandish fantasies and ideas, and then acted them out.

The other players also had complicated and very sick fantasy lives, of course, but they paled in comparison to his. Famine claimed authorship of a series of psychosexual murders in Thailand and the Philippines. War liked to think of himself as the uncrowned head of the group—he claimed to "influence" the adventures of the others. Conqueror was confined to a wheelchair and made up stories about using his infirmity to lure his prey close enough for the kill.

Shafer doubted that any of them actually had the guts to play the game out in the real world.

But perhaps they would surprise him. Maybe each of the others was living out a homicidal fantasy. Wouldn't that be something?

The Cahill women thought they were so perfectly safe inside the ranch house, less than fifty
yards away. He could see a green wooden fence surrounding a stone terrace and lap swimming pool in
the back. The house had sliding doors to the pool
area. So many possibilities for him to consider.

He might enter the house and murder both of
them execution-style. Then he would drive directly
back to Washington.

The local police and FBI would be totally baffled. The story might even make network TV. Two
women shot and murdered while they slept, a
mother and daughter whom everybody in their
small town admired. No motive for the horrific
crime, no suspects.

He was hard now, and it was difficult to walk.
That was comical to Shafer, his absurd hard-on
waddle. His mouth formed a smile.

A dog was howling two or three houses down
the street—a small wimpy dog, from the sound of
it. Then a larger dog joined in. They sensed death,
didn't they? They knew he was here.

Shafer knelt beside a maple tree at the edge of
the backyard. He stood in shadows while the moon
cast a soft white light across the yard.

He slid the twenty-sided dice out of his pocket,
then let them fall on the tufts of lawn. *Here we go.
Playing by the rules. Let's see what the night has to offer.*
He counted the numerals on the special dice. They
appeared fuzzy in the dark.

Shafer couldn't believe what he saw. He wanted

to howl like the crazed and bewildered neighbor-hood dogs.

The dice count was *five.*

Death had to leave! This instant! There could be no murders tonight!

No! He wouldn't do it! To hell with the dice. He wouldn't leave. He couldn't. He was losing all impulse control, wasn't he? Well, so be it. Alea jacta est, he remembered from his schoolboy Latin classes—Julius Caesar before he crossed the Rubicon: "The die is cast."

This was a monumental night. For the first time, he was breaking the rules. He was changing the game forever.

He needed to kill someone, and the urge was everything to him.

He hurried to the house before he changed his mind. He was nervous. Adrenaline punched through his system. He used his glass cutter at first, but then just smashed in a small window with a gloved hand.

Once inside, he moved quickly down the dark-ened hallway. He was sweating—so unlike him. He entered Deirdre's bedroom. She was asleep, despite the breaking of the glass. Her bare arms were thrown up over her head, the surrender position.

"Lovely," he whispered.

She was wearing white bikini panties and a matching bra. Her long legs were spread deli-cately, expectantly. In her dreams, she must have known he was coming. Shafer believed that dreams told you the truth, and you had better listen.

He was still hard, and so glad he'd chosen to disobey the rules.

"Who the hell are you?" he heard, suddenly. The voice came from behind.

Shafer whirled around.

It was Lindsay, the daughter. She wore nothing but coral-pink underwear, a brassiere and briefs. He calmly raised his gun until it pointed between her eyes.

"Shhh. You don't want to know, Lindsay," he said in the calmest voice, not bothering to disguise his English accent. "But I'll tell you anyway."

He fired the gun.

Chapter 54

FOR THE second time in my life I understood what it felt like to be a victim of a terrible crime rather than the detective investigating it. I was disconnected and out of it. I needed to be doing something positive on a case, or get back to volunteer work at St. Anthony's—anything to take my mind off what had happened.

I had to be busy, but I knew I'd lost my ability to concentrate, something that had always come so naturally to me. I came across a pair of shocking murders in Maryland that bothered me for some unspecified reason. I didn't follow up on them. I should have.

I wasn't myself; I was lost. I still spent endless hours thinking about Christine, remembering everything about our time together, seeing her face wherever I went.

Sampson tried to push me. He *did* push me. He and I made the rounds of the streets of Southeast. We put the word out that we were looking for a purple and blue cab, possibly a gypsy. We canvassed door to door in the Shaw neighborhood where Tori

Glover and Marion Cardinal had been found. Often we were still going at ten or eleven at night.

I didn't care. I couldn't sleep anyway.

Sampson cared. He was my friend.

"You're supposed to be working the Odenkirk case, right? I'm not supposed to be working at all. The Jefe would be livid. I kind of like that," Sampson said as we trudged along S Street late one evening. Sampson had lived in this neighborhood for years. He knew all the local hangarounds.

"Jamal, you know anything I should know?" he called out to a goateed youth sitting in shadows on a graystone stoop.

"Don't know nothin'. Just relaxin' my mind. Catchin' a cool night breeze. How 'bout yourself?"

Sampson turned back to me. "Damn crack runners working these streets everywhere you look nowadays. Real good place to commit a murder and never get caught. You talk to the police in Bermuda lately?"

I nodded, and my eyes stared at a fixed point up ahead. "Patrick Busby said the story of Christine's disappearance is off the front pages. I don't know if that's good or bad. It's probably bad."

Sampson agreed. "Takes the pressure off them. You going back down there?"

"Not right away. But yeah, I have to go back. I have to find out what happened."

He looked me in the eye. "Are you here with me right now? Are you *here*, sugar?"

"Yeah, I'm here. Most of the time. I'm function-

ing okay." I pointed up at a nearby redbrick building. "That place would have a view of the front
entryway into the girl's building. Any of those
windows. Let's get back to work."

Sampson nodded. "I'm here as long as you want
to be."

There was something about pounding the
streets that appealed to me that night. We talked
to everyone in the building that we could find at
home, about half the apartments. Nobody had
seen a purple and blue cab on the street; nobody
had seen Tori or Marion, either. Or so they said.

"You see any connections anywhere?" I asked as
we came down the steep stairs of a fourth-floor
walk-up. "What do you see? What the hell am I
missing?"

"Not a thing, Alex. Nothing to miss. Weasel
didn't leave a clue. Never does."

We got back down to the entrance and met up
with an elderly man carrying three clear-plastic
bags of groceries from the Stop & Shop.

"We're homicide detectives," I said to him.
"Two young girls were murdered across the street."

The man nodded. "Tori and Marion. I know
'em. You want to know 'bout that fella watchin'
the buildin'? He was sittin' there most the night.
Inside a slick, fancy black car," he said. "Mercedes,
I think. You think maybe he's the killer?"

Chapter **55**

"I BEEN away awhile, y'see. Visitin' wit' my two old-bat sisters in North Carolina for a week of good memories, home-cooked food," the elderly man said as we went up to the fourth floor. "That was why I was missed during the earlier time through here by your detectives."

This was old-school police work, I was thinking as I climbed stairs—the kind of work too many detectives try to avoid. The man's name was DeWitt Luke, and he was retired from Bell Atlantic, the huge phone company that services most of the Northeast. He was the fifty-third interview I'd had so far in Shaw.

"Saw him sittin' there around one in the mornin'. Didn't think much of it at first. Probably waitin' for somebody. Seemed to be mindin' his own business. He was still there at two, though. Sittin' in his car. Seemed kinda strange to me." He paused for a long moment as if trying to remember.

"Then what happened?" I prompted the man.

"Fell asleep. But I got up to pee around three-thirty. He was *still* in that shiny black car. So I watched him closer this time. He was watchin' the other side of the street. Like some kind of damn spy or somethin'. Couldn't tell what he was lookin' at, but he was studyin' somethin' real hard over there. I thought he might be the police. 'Cept his car was too nice."

"You got that right," Sampson said, and barked out a laugh. "No Mercedes in my garage."

"I pulled up a card-table chair behind the darkened window in my apartment. Made sure there were no lights on, so he couldn't see me. By now he'd caught my attention some. Remember the old movie *Rear Window*? I tried to figure out why he might be down there sittin', waitin'. Jealous lover, jealous husband, maybe some kinda night stalker. But he wasn't botherin' anybody far as I could see."

I spoke again. "You never got a better look than that? Man sitting in the car?"

"Around the time I got up to pee, he got out of the car. Opened the door, but the inside light didn't come on. That struck me strange, it bein' such a nice car and all. Fueled my mind even more. I squinted my eyes, get a better look." Another long pause.

"And?"

"He was tall, a blond gentleman. White fella. We don't get too many of them around here at night, or even in the daytime, for that matter."

Chapter 56

DETECTIVE PATSY Hampton's investigation of the Jane Doe murders was starting to show forward movement and positive results. She thought she might have something good in the works. She had confidence in her ability to solve the murders. She knew from experience that she was smarter than everybody else.

It helped to have Chief Pittman and all the department's resources on her side. She had spent the past day and a half with Chuck Hufstedler at the FBI building. She knew she was using Chuck a little, but he didn't seem to mind. He was lonely, and she *did* like his company. She and Chuck were still sitting around at three-thirty in the afternoon when Lancelot entered the Gamester's Chatroom again. *Laughalot,* she remembered.

"He couldn't resist, could he?" Hampton said to Hufstedler. "Gotcha, you fantasy freak."

Hufstedler looked at her, his thick black eyebrows arched. "Three-thirty in the afternoon, Patsy. What does that say? Tell you what it says to me.

Maybe he's playing from work. But I bet our Lancelot is a school kid."

"Or he's somebody who likes to play with school kids." She offered a thought that upset her even as she uttered the words.

This time, she didn't try to make contact with Lancelot. She and Chuck just listened in on a stultifying discussion of several role-playing games. In the meantime, he was trying to trace Lancelot.

"He's pretty good at this, a real hacker. He's built a lot of security into his system. Hopefully, we'll get to him anyway."

"I have confidence in you, Cheeseman."

Lancelot stayed in the chatroom past four-thirty. By then it was all over. Chuck had his name and address: Michael Ormson, Hutchins Place, Foxhall.

At a few minutes before five, two dark-blue vans pulled up in front of the Ormson house on the Georgetown Reservoir. Five agents in blue FBI windbreakers and Detective Patsy Hampton surrounded the large, Tudor-style house with an acre or two of front and back lawn and majestic views.

Senior FBI Agent Brigid Dwyer and Hampton proceeded to the front door and found it unlocked. With weapons drawn, they quietly entered the house and discovered Lancelot in the den.

He looked to be around thirteen years old. A baby geek. He was sitting at a computer in his shorts and black socks.

"Hey, what the heck is going on? Hey! What are

you doing in my house? I didn't do anything wrong. Who are you guys?" Michael Ormson asked in a high-pitched, peeved, but quivering voice.

He was skinny. His face was covered with acne. His back and shoulders had a rash that looked like eczema. Chuck Hufstedler had been right on target. Lancelot was a teenage geek playing with his fancy computer after school. He wasn't the Weasel, though. This boy *couldn't* be the Weasel.

"Are you Michael Ormson?" Patsy Hampton asked the boy. She had lowered her weapon but hadn't holstered it.

The young boy dropped his head and looked ready to weep. "Oh, God, oh, God," he moaned. "Yes, I'm Michael Ormson. Who are you guys? Are you going to tell my parents?"

Chapter 57

MICHAEL'S FATHER and mother were immediately contacted at their jobs at Georgetown University Hospital and the U.S. Naval Observatory, respectively. The Ormsons were currently separated, but they both made it to Foxhall in less than ten minutes, even with rush-hour traffic starting to build. The other two Ormson children, Laura and Anne Marie, had already come home from high school.

Patsy Hampton convinced the parents to let her talk to their son at the house. She told the Ormsons that they could be present, and could interrupt, and even stop the interview anytime they wished. Otherwise, she and Agent Dwyer would have to take Michael to FBI headquarters for the interview.

The Ormsons, Mark and Cindy, agreed to let Michael talk. They were clearly frightened, especially of the FBI personnel, but they seemed to trust Detective Hampton. Most people did, she knew. She was pretty and sincere and had a disarming smile that she used when she needed to.

"I'm interested in the game called the Four Horsemen," Hampton said to the boy. "That's the only reason I'm here, Michael. I need your help."

The teenager dropped his chin to his chest again and then shook his head back and forth. Hampton watched the nervous boy and decided to take a chance with him. She had a hunch that she wanted to play.

"Michael, whatever you think you've done wrong, it's nothing to us. It's *nothing*. We don't care what you've done on your computer. This isn't about you or your family *or* your hacking. There have been some terrible murders in Washington, and there might be a connection to this game called the Four Horsemen. Please help us, Michael. You're the only one who can. You're the only one."

Mark Ormson, who was a radiologist at Georgetown University Hospital, leaned forward on the black leather couch in the den. He looked more frightened now than when he'd gotten home. "I'm beginning to think I better get a lawyer," he said.

Patsy Hampton shook her head and smiled kindly at both parents. "This is *not* about your son, Mr. and Mrs. Ormson. He's not in any trouble with us, I assure you."

She turned back to the teenager. "*Michael,* what do you know about the Four Horsemen? We know you're not one of the players. We know it's a very private game."

The boy looked up. She could tell that he liked

her, and maybe trusted her some. "Hardly anything, ma'am. I don't know too much."

Hampton nodded. "This is very important to us, Michael. Someone is killing people in the Southeast part of Washington—*for real*, Michael. This is not a fantasy game. I think you can help us. You can save others from getting murdered."

Michael dropped his head again. He had hardly looked at his mother and father since they arrived. "I'm good with computers. You probably already figured that out."

Detective Hampton kept nodding, giving the boy positive reinforcement. "We know you are, Michael. We had trouble tracing you here. You're *very* good with computers. My friend Chuck Hufstedler at the FBI was really impressed. When all this is over, you can see where he works. You'll like him, and you'll love his equipment."

Michael smiled, showing off large, protruding teeth with braces. "Back at the beginning of summer, probably late in June, this guy came into the Gamester's Chatroom—where you found me."

Patsy Hampton tried to hold eye contact with the boy. She needed him badly; she had a feeling that this was a big break, her biggest so far.

Michael continued to speak softly. "He sort of, like he took over the conversation. Actually, he was pretty much a control freak about it. He kept putting down Highlander, D & D, Millennium, all the hot games that are out now. Wouldn't let anybody else get a word in. Almost seemed like he was high on something.

"He kept hinting about this completely different game he played called the Four Horsemen. It was like he didn't want to tell us about it, but then he would give out bits and pieces anyway, but not much. He wouldn't shut up.

"He said the characters in Dungeons and Dragons, Dune, and Condottiere were predictable and boring—which, I must admit, they are sometimes. Then he said some of the characters in his game were *chaotic evil* instead of *lawful good*. He said they weren't fake heroes like in most RPGs; his characters were more like people in real life. They were basically selfish, didn't really care about others, didn't follow society's rules. He said Horsemen was the ultimate fantasy game. That was all he would tell us about the Four Horsemen, but it was enough. I mean, you could see it was a game for total psychos."

"What was his call name?" Agent Dwyer asked Michael.

"Call name, or his real name?" Michael asked, and offered up a sly, superior smile.

Agent Dwyer and Hampton looked at each other. *Call name, or his real name?* They turned back to Michael.

"I traced him, just like you traced me. I got through his encryptions. I know his name, and I know where he lives. Even where he works. It's Shafer—Geoffrey Shafer. He works at the British

Embassy, on Massachusetts Avenue. He's some kind of information analyst there, according to the embassy's Web site. He's forty-four years old."

Michael Ormson looked sheepishly around the room. He made eye contact with his parents, who finally looked relieved. Then he looked back at Hampton. "Is any of that stuff helpful to you? Did I help?"

"Yes, you did, Laughalot."

Chapter 58

GEOFFREY SHAFER had vowed he would not get high on pharmaceuticals tonight. He'd also decided he was going to keep his fantasies under control, under wraps. He understood precisely what the psychobabbling profilers on the murder cases would be thinking: his fantasy life was escalating, and he was approaching a rage state. And the profilers would be exactly right—which was why he was playing it cool for a while.

He was a skillful cook—skilled at a lot of things, actually. He sometimes put together elaborate meals for his family, and even large dinner parties with friends. When he cooked, he liked to have the family with him in the kitchen; he loved an audience, even his wife and kids.

"Tonight we'll be eating classic Thai," he announced to Lucy and the children as they watched him work. He was feeling a little hyper, and reminded himself not to let things get out of hand at home. Maybe he ought to take some Valium before he began to cook. All he'd taken so far was a little Xanax.

"What sets Thai food apart from other Southeast Asian cuisines are the explicit rules for proportions of ingredients, especially seasonings," he said as he prepared a centerpiece of carved vegetables.

"Thai is a distinctive cuisine, blending Chinese, Indonesian, Indian, Portuguese, Malaysian. Bet you didn't know that, Tricia and Erica."

The little girls laughed, confused—so much like their mother.

He put jasmine blossoms in Lucy's hair. Then a blossom each for the twins. He tried the same with Robert, but his son pulled away, laughing.

"Nothing too hot tonight, darling?" Lucy said. "The children."

"The children, of course, dear. Speaking of hot, the real heat comes from capsaicin, which is stored in the ribs of these chili peppers. Capsaicin is an irritant and burns whatever it touches, even skin, so it's wise to wear gloves. I'm not wearing gloves, of course, because I'm not wise. Also, I'm a little crazy." He laughed. Everyone did. But Lucy looked worried.

Shafer served the dinner himself, without any help, and he announced the name of each dish both in Thai and in English. "*Plaa meuk yaang,* or roast squid. Delicious." "*Mieng kum,* leaf rolls with 'treasures.' Yummy." "*Plaa yaang kaeng phet,* grilled snapper with red curry sauce. Delectable. A *little* hot, though. Hmmm."

He watched them tentatively sample each course; as they tasted the snapper, tears began to run down their faces. Erica began to choke.

"Daddy, it's too hot!" Robert complained, gulping.

Shafer smiled and nodded blithely. He loved this—the flowing tears, his perfect little family in pain. He savored each exquisite moment of their suffering. He'd managed to turn the dinner into a tantalizing game, after all.

At quarter to nine he kissed Lucy and started off on his "constitutional," as he called his nightly disappearing act. He went out to the Jag and drove a few blocks to Phelps Place, a quiet street without many lights.

He took liberal doses of Thorazine *and* Librium, then injected himself with Toradol. He took another Xanax.

Then he went to his doctor's.

Chapter 59

SHAFER DIDN'T like the arrogant, asshole doormen at Boo Cassady's building, and they didn't like him, he decided.

Who needed their approval, anyway? They were shiftless, lazy incompetents, incapable of doing much more than holding open doors and offering up ingratiating smiles to fat-cat tenants.

"I'm here to see Dr. Cassady," Shafer announced to the familiar black wanker with *Mal* jauntily pinned on his lapel. It was probably there so that he wouldn't forget his own name.

"Right," said Mal.

"Isn't that 'Right, *sir*'?"

"Right, sir. I'll ring up Dr. Cassady. Wait right here, sir."

He could hear Boo through the doorman's staticky phone receiver. She had no doubt left explicit instructions that he be let up immediately. She certainly knew he was coming—they'd talked during the car ride from his house.

"You can go up now, sir," the doorman finally said.

"I'm fucking her brains out, Mal," Shafer said. He waltzed to the elevators with a grin. "You watch that door now. Don't let anyone take it."

Boo was in the hallway to meet him when the elevator cruised to a stop on ten. She was wearing at least five thousand dollars' worth of clothes from Escada. She had a great body, but she looked like a bullfighter or a marching-band leader in the gaudy outfit. No wonder her first two husbands had divorced her. The second husband had been a therapist and treating M.D. Still, she was a good, steady mistress who gave much better than she got. More important, she was able to get him Thorazine, Librium, Ativan, Xanax. Most of the drugs were samples from drug-company representatives; her husband had left them behind when they'd split. The number of "samples" left by the drug reps amazed Shafer, but she assured him it was common practice. She had other "friends" who were doctors, and she hinted to Shafer that they helped her out in return for an occasional fuck. She could get all the drugs he needed.

Shafer wanted to take her right there in the hall, and he knew Boo would like the spontaneity and the passion that were so clearly missing from her life. Not tonight, though. He had more basic needs: the drugs.

"You don't look too happy to see me, Geoff," she complained. She took his face in her manicured hands. Christ, her long, varnished red nails scared him. "What happened, darling? Something's happened. Tell Boo what it is."

Shafer took her in his arms and held her tightly against his chest. She had large soft breasts, great legs, too. He stroked her frosted blond hair and nuzzled her with his chin. He loved the power he had over her—his goddamned shrink.

"I don't want to talk about it just yet. I'm here with you. I feel much better already."

"What happened, darling? What's wrong? You have to share these things with me."

So he made up a story on the spot, acted it out. Nothing to it. "Lucy claims she knows about us. God, she was paranoid *before* I started to see you. Lucy always threatens to destroy my life. She says she'll leave me. Sue for what fucking little I have. Her father will have me fired, then blackball me in the government *and* in the private sector, which he's perfectly capable of doing. The worst thing is, she's poisoning the children, turning them against me. They use the same belittling phrases that she does: 'colossal failure,' 'underachiever,' 'get a real job, Daddy.' Some days I wonder whether it isn't true."

Boo kissed him lightly on the forehead. "No, no, darling. You're well thought of at the embassy. I know you're a loving dad. You just have a bitchy, mean-spirited, spoiled-rotten wife who gets you down on yourself. Don't let her do it."

He knew what she wanted to hear next, so he told her. "Well, I won't have a bitchy wife for much longer. I swear to God I won't, Boo. I love you dearly, and I'm going to leave Lucy soon."

He looked at her heavily made-up face and watched as tears formed and ruined her look. "I love you, Geoff," she whispered, and Shafer smiled as if he were pleased to hear it.

God, he was so good at this.

Lies.

Fantasies.

Role-playing games.

He unbuttoned the front of her mauve silk blouse, fondled her, then carried her inside to the sofa.

"This is my idea of therapy," he whispered hotly in Boo's ear. "This is all the therapy I need."

Chapter 60

I HAD been up since before five that morning. I had to call Inspector Patrick Busby in Bermuda. I wanted to talk to him every day, sometimes more than once, but I stopped myself.

It would only make things worse, strain my relations with the local police, and signal that I didn't trust them to handle the investigation properly.

"Patrick, it's Alex Cross calling from Washington. Did I catch you at a good time? Can you talk for a moment now?" I asked. I always tried to sound as upbeat as possible.

I wasn't, of course. I had been up pacing the house, and already had breakfast with Nana. Then I'd waited impatiently until eight-thirty to call Busby at the station house in Hamilton. He was an efficient man, and I knew he was there every morning by eight.

I could picture the thin, wiry policeman as we talked on the phone. I could see the tidy cubicle office where he worked. And superimposed over everything, I could still see Christine on her moped waving good-bye to me on that perfectly sunny afternoon.

"I have a few things for you from my contact at Interpol," I said. I told him about an abduction of a woman on Jamaica earlier in the summer, and another in Barbados; both were similar, though not identical, to Christine's disappearance. I didn't think they were connected, really, but I wanted to give him something, anything.

Patrick Busby was a thoughtful and patient man; he remained silent until I had finished talking before asking his usual quota of logical questions. I had observed that he was flawed as an interrogator because he was so polite. But at least he hadn't given up.

"I assume that neither abduction was ever solved, Alex. How about the women who were taken? Were they found?"

"No, neither woman was seen again. Not a sign of them. They're still missing."

He sighed into the phone receiver. "I hope your news is helpful in some way, Alex. I'll certainly call the other islands and check into it further. Anything else from Interpol or the FBI?"

I wanted to keep him on the line—the lifeline, as I now thought of it. "A few far-flung possibilities in the Far East, Bangkok, the Philippines, Malaysia. Women abducted and murdered, all Jane Does. To be honest, nothing too promising at this point."

I imagined him pursing his thin lips and nodding thoughtfully. "I understand, Alex. Please keep giving me whatever you get from your sources. It's difficult for us to get help outside this small island.

My calls for assistance frequently aren't returned. I sincerely wish that I had some good news for you on my end, but I'm afraid I don't.

"Other than Perri Graham, no one saw the man with the van. No one seems to have seen Christine Johnson in Hamilton or St. George, either. It's truly a baffling mystery. I don't believe that she ever got to Hamilton. It's frustrating for us, too. My prayers are with you and your wonderful family and, of course, John Sampson."

I thanked Patrick Busby and hung up the phone. I went upstairs and dressed for work.

I still had nothing really substantial on the murder of Frank Odenkirk, and The Jefe was contacting me daily on e-mail. I certainly knew how the Odenkirk family felt. The media heat about the homicide had died down, though, as it often does. Unfortunately, so had the *Post* stories about the unsolved murders in Southeast.

While I was taking a hot shower, I thought about DeWitt Luke and the mysterious "watcher" on S Street. What was the man in the Mercedes doing out there for so long? Did he have some connection with the murders of Tori Glover and Marion Cardinal? None of this was making complete sense to me. That was the truly maddening thing about the Jane Doe murders and the Weasel. He wasn't like other repeat killers. He wasn't a criminal genius like Gary Soneji, but he was effective. *He gets the job done, doesn't he?*

I needed to think more about why someone had

been lurking outside Tori Glover's apartment. Was he a private detective? A stalker? Or was he actually the murderer? One possibility hit me. Maybe the man in the car was an accomplice of the killer. Two of them, working together? I'd seen that before in North Carolina.

I turned up the water, made it hotter. I thought it would help me to concentrate better. Steam out the cobwebs in my brain. Bring me back from the dead.

Nana began banging on the pipes from downstairs in the kitchen. "Get down here and go to work, Alex. You're using up all my hot water," she yelled above the noise of the shower.

"Last time I looked, my name was on the water and gas bills," I shouted back.

"It's still my hot water. Always was, always will be," Nana replied.

EVERY DAY, every night, I was out on the streets of Southeast, working harder than ever, but with nothing much to show for it. I continued to search for the mysterious purple and blue cab, and for the late-model black Mercedes that DeWitt Luke had seen on S Street.

Sometimes I felt as if I were sleepwalking, but I kept at it, sleepwalking as fast as I could. Everything about the investigation seemed a long shot at best. I received tips and leads every day that had to be followed up; none of them went anywhere, though.

I got home at a little past seven that night, and tired as I was, I still let the kids drag me downstairs for their boxing lesson. Damon was showing me a lot of hand speed, and also some pretty good footwork and power for his age. He's always had good spirit, and I was confident that he wouldn't abuse his burgeoning boxing skills at school.

Jannie was more a student of boxing, though she seemed to recognize the value of being able to defend herself. She was quick at mastering techniques, seeing connections, even if her heart wasn't completely in the sport. She preferred to torture her brother and me with her taunts and wit.

"Alex, telephone," Nana called down from the top of the cellar stairs. I looked at my watch, saw it was twenty to eight.

"Practice your footwork," I told the kids. Then I trudged up the steep stone stairs. "Who is it?"

"Wouldn't say who it was," Nana said as I got up to the kitchen. She was making shrimp and corn fritters, and the room was also filled with the glorious smells of honey-baked apples and gingerbread. It was a late dinner for us—Nana had waited until I got home.

I picked up the phone on the kitchen counter. "Alex Cross."

"I know who you are, Detective Cross." I recognized the voice immediately, though I'd heard it only once before—in the Belmont Hotel, in Bermuda. A chill went right through me, and my hands shook.

"There's a pay phone outside the Budget Drugs on Fourth Street. *She's safe for now. We have her.* But hurry. Hurry! Maybe she's on the pay phone right now! I'm serious. *Hurry!*"

Chapter 62

I EXPLODED out the back kitchen door without saying a word to Nana or the kids. I didn't have time to explain where I was going, or why. Besides, I didn't really know exactly what was happening. Had I just spoken to the Weasel?

Hurry! Maybe she's on the pay phone right now! I'm serious.

I sprinted across Fifth Street, then down a side alley and over to Fourth. I dashed another four blocks south toward the Anacostia River. People on the streets watched me running. I was like a tornado suddenly roaring through Southeast.

I could see the metal frame of a pay phone from more than a block away as I approached Budget Drugs. A young girl was leaning against the graffiti-covered wall of the drugstore, talking on the phone.

I pulled out my detective's shield as I raced the final block toward her.

This particular phone gets a lot of use. Some people in the neighborhood don't have phones in their homes.

"Police. I'm a homicide detective. *Get off the*

phone!" I told the girl, who looked nineteen or so. She stared at me as if she couldn't care less that a D.C. policeman was trying to commandeer the phone.

"I'm *using* this phone, mister. Don't care who you are. You can wait your turn like everybody else." She turned away from me. "Probably just calling your honey."

I yanked the receiver away from her, disconnected her call.

"The fuck you think you are!" the girl shouted at me, her face screwed up in anger. "I was talking. The fuck you thinking."

"I'm thinking you better get out of my face. This is a life-and-death situation. Get away from this phone. *Now! Get out of here!*" I could see she had no intention of leaving. "There's been a kidnapping!" I was yelling like a madman.

She finally backed away. She was afraid that I was really crazy, and maybe I was.

I stood there with the phone receiver in my hand, trembling, waiting for the call to come in. I was winded. Sweat covered my body.

I stared up and down Fourth Street.

Nothing obvious or suspicious. I didn't see a purple and blue cab parked anywhere. No one watching me. Somebody definitely knew who I was. He had called me at the Belmont Hotel; he had called me at home.

I could still hear the caller's voice echoing loudly inside my head. I'd been hearing that same deep, wretched voice for weeks.

"She's safe for now.
"We have her."

Those were the words spoken to me six weeks before, in Bermuda. I hadn't heard another word from the caller until now.

My heart was pounding, sounding as if it were amplified in my ears. Adrenaline was rushing like powerful rivers through my bloodstream. I couldn't stand this. The caller had stressed that I *hurry.*

A young man approached the pay phone. He stared at my hand on the receiver. "Wuzup, man? I need to use the phone. The phone? You hear me?"

"Police business." I gave him a hard stare. "Take a walk, please. Go!"

"Don't look like no police business to me," he mumbled.

The man moved away, looking over his shoulder as he retreated down Fourth, frowning, but not stopping to argue with me.

The caller liked to be completely in control, I was thinking as I stood there helpless in front of the busy drugstore. He'd made me wait this long since the Bermuda call, possibly to demonstrate his power. Now he was doing it again. What did he really want, though? Why had he taken Christine? *We* have her, he'd said, and he'd repeated the very same words when he called my house. Was there really a *we*? What kind of group did he represent? What did they want?

I stood at the pay phone for ten minutes, fifteen, twenty. I felt as if I were going mad, but I would stay there all night if I had to. I began to wonder if this was the right phone, but I knew it was. He had been crystal-clear, calm, in control.

For the first time in weeks I allowed myself to truly hope that Christine might be alive. I imagined her face, her deep-brown eyes that showed so much love and warmth. Maybe, just maybe, I would be allowed to talk to her.

I let my anger build toward the unknown caller. But then I cut it off, shut down my emotions, and waited with a cool head.

People came and went, in and out of the drugstore. A few wanted to use the phone. They took one look at me and then moved on in search of another phone.

At five minutes to nine, the phone rang. I lifted the receiver instantly.

"This is Alex Cross," I said.

"Yes, I know who you are. That's already been established. Here's what you should do. *Back all the way off. Just back away. Before you lose everything you care about.* It can happen so easily. In a snap. You're smart enough to understand that, aren't you?"

Then the caller hung up. The line was dead.

I banged the phone with the receiver. I cursed loudly. The manager from the drugstore had come outside and was staring at me.

"I'm going to call the police," he said. "That's a public phone." I didn't bother to tell him I *was* the police.

Chapter 63

WAS IT the weasel who had called? Was I dealing with one killer, or more than one?

If only I had some idea who the caller was and who he meant by *we.* The message scared me just as much as the first one had, maybe even more; but it also gave me hope that Christine might still be alive.

With hope came a jolting surge of pain. If only they would put Christine on the phone. I needed to hear her voice.

What did they want? *"Back all the way off."* Back off from what?

The Odenkirk murder case? The Jane Does? Perhaps even Christine's disappearance? Was Interpol or the FBI getting close to something that had scared them? We weren't close to anything that could solve any of the cases, and I knew timing was critical.

Early Wednesday morning, Sampson and I drove to Eckington. A woman over there knew where a purple and blue cab was garaged. We'd followed up a dozen or so leads like this already,

but it didn't matter. Every lead had to be investigated, every single one.

"Cab owner's name is Arthur Marshall," I told
Sampson as we walked from my car toward a redbrick garden apartment that had seen better days.
"Trouble is, Arthur Marshall seems to be a false
identity. Landlady has him working at a Target
store. According to Target, he doesn't. Never
worked at any Target store. Hasn't been seen
around for a while, according to the landlady."

"Maybe we spooked him," Sampson said.

"I hope not, but you may be right."

I glanced around at the lower-middle-class
neighborhood as we walked. Overhead, the sky
was a bright-blue canvas, nearly empty of clouds.
The street was packed with one- and two-story
homes. Bright-orange fliers were sticking out
from the mailboxes. Every window was a possible
lookout for the Weasel. *Back away,*" he had
warned. I couldn't. Not after what he'd done. I
knew I was taking a risk, though.

He probably spotted us canvassing the streets. If
he was responsible for the Jane Doe murders, he
had been working undetected for a long while. He
was skillful, good at killing, at not getting caught.

The landlady told us what she knew about
Arthur Marshall, which wasn't much more than
the information she needed to rent him a one-bed-
room apartment and the attached garage. She gave
us a set of keys for the place and said we could go
look for ourselves.

The second house was similar to the landlady's, except that it was painted Easter-egg blue. Sampson and I entered the garage first.

The purple and blue cab was there.

Arthur Marshall had told the landlady that he owned the cab and operated it as a part-time job. That was a possibility, but it seemed unlikely. The Weasel was close. I could feel it now. Had he known we would find the cab? Probably. Now what? What came next? What was his plan? His fantasy?

"I'm going to have to figure out how to get some techies in here," I told Sampson. "There has to be something in the cab, or maybe upstairs in the apartment. Hair, fibers, prints."

"Hopefully no damn body parts," Sampson said, and grimaced. It was typical cop humor, and so automatic that I didn't give it a second thought. "Body parts are always popping up in these cases, Alex. I don't want to see it. I like feet attached to ankles, heads attached to necks, even if all the parts happen to be dead."

Sampson searched around the front seat of the cab with latex-gloved hands. "Papers in here. Candy and gum wrappers, too. Why not call in a favor from Kyle Craig? Get the FBI boys over here."

"Actually, I talked to Kyle last night," I said. "The Bureau's been involved for some time. He'll help out if we say the word."

Sampson tossed me a pair of gloves, and I examined the cab's backseat. I saw what could be bloodstains in the fabric of the seat cushion. The stains would be easy enough to check out.

John and I finally climbed upstairs into the apartment above the garage. It was dusty, grimy, without much furniture. Eerie and unpleasant on the eyes. It didn't look as if anyone lived there, but if someone did, he was really weird. The landlady had said as much.

The kitchen was mostly empty. An expensive juicer was the only personal indulgence. Not a low-end model—*expensive.* I took out my handkerchief and opened the refrigerator. There was nothing in it but bottled water and some aging fruit. The fruit was rotting, and I hated to think of what else we might find here in the apartment.

"Health nut," Sampson offered.

"Nut, anyway," I said. "There's a sense of animal fear in here. He gets very tense, excited, when he comes to this place."

"Yeah," Sampson said. "I know the feeling."

We entered the bedroom, which was furnished with only a small cot, a couple of stuffed chairs, nothing else. The sense of fear was here, too.

I opened the closet door, and what I saw stopped me dead. There was a pair of khaki pants, a blue chambray shirt, a blue blazer—and something else.

"John, come here," I called. "John!"

"Oh, shit. Do I have to? Not more bodies."

"Just come here. It's him. This is the Weasel's place. I'm sure of it. It's worse than a body."

I opened the closet door wider and let Sampson see what I'd found there.

"Shit," he groaned. "*Goddamn* it, Alex."

Someone had put up pictures. Half a dozen black-and-white photographs were taped to the wall of the closet. It wasn't a killer's shrine; it was meant to be found.

There were pictures of Nana, Damon, Jannie, me, and Christine. Christine almost seemed to be smiling at the camera, that incredible smile of hers, those big, welcoming eyes.

The pictures had been taken in Bermuda. Whoever had rented this apartment had taken them. Finally, I had something to link Christine's abduction to the murders in Washington. I knew who had taken her.

"Back off.

"Before you lose everything."

I sensed fear again. It was my own.

Chapter 64

PATSY HAMPTON had decided that she wasn't ready to confide in Chief George Pittman just yet. She didn't want The Jefe interfering or crowding her. Also, she flat out didn't trust or like the bastard.

She still hadn't made up her mind what to do about Alex Cross. Cross was a complication. The more she checked him out, the better he looked. He seemed to be a very good, dedicated detective, and she felt bad about keeping Chuck Hufstedler's information away from him. Chuck had been Cross's source first, but she'd used the techie's crush on her to gain an advantage. She didn't like herself for doing that.

She drove her Jeep to the British Embassy late that afternoon. She had Geoffrey Shafer under limited surveillance—hers. She could get more teams, but that would mean going to Pittman now, and she didn't want anyone to know what she had. She didn't want to be crowded.

She had done her preliminary homework on Shafer. He was in the Security Service, which meant he was British intelligence, operating outside England. Most likely he was a spy working out of the embassy on Massachusetts Avenue. His reputation was okay—good, actually. His current assignment supposedly had to do with the British Government's human-rights program, which meant the assignment was bullshit. He lived in Kalorama, a high-rent district, one he couldn't afford on his salary. So who the hell *was* this Shafer chap?

Hampton sat parked in her vehicle outside the embassy on California Street. She smoked a Marlboro Light and started to think things through. She really ought to talk to Cross about where he was with his investigation. Did he know anything that could help? Maybe he was onto Shafer, too? It was almost criminal for her not to contact Cross and share what she'd gotten from Chucky Cheese.

Pittman's dislike for Cross was well known; he considered him competition. She didn't know Cross that well, but he got too many headlines. Still, she wished she knew what Cross had in his files, and especially whether Geoffrey Shafer had appeared on Cross's radar.

There was too much fricking noise on the fricking street near the British Embassy. Workers were doing construction on the Turkish Chancery across California Street. Hampton already had a headache—her life was one big headache—and she wished they would stop pounding and hammering and battering and sawing. For some reason or other, there was a crowd of people swarming all over the National Mosque today.

At a few minutes past five, Shafer got into his Jaguar in a parking lot outside the glass-walled Rotunda.

She'd seen him twice before. He was in very good shape, and attractive, too, though not a physical type she herself responded to. Shafer sure didn't hang around long after the workday ended. Hampton figured he either had someplace to go or really hated his day job. Possibly both.

She stayed a safe distance behind the black Jag, following it along crowded Massachusetts Avenue. Shafer didn't seem to be heading home, and he wasn't going to Southeast, either.

Where are we going tonight? she wondered as she tailed him. *And what does it have to do with the Four Horsemen? What game are you really playing? What are your fantasies?*

Are you a bad man, a murderer, Geoffrey? You don't look like it, blondie. Such a nice, spiffy car for a scumbag killer.

Chapter 65

AFTER WORK, Geoffrey Shafer joined the clogged artery of rush-hour traffic inching along Massachusetts. Turning out of the embassy, he had spotted the black Jeep behind him.

The tail was still there as he drove down Massachusetts Avenue.

Who's in the Jeep? One of the other players? D.C. police? Detective Alex Cross? They've found the garage in Eckington. Now they've found me. It has to be the bloody police.

He watched the black Jeep as it trailed four cars behind him. There was only one person inside, and it looked like a woman. Could it possibly be Lucy? Had she discovered the truth about him? God, had she finally figured out who and what he was?

He picked up his mobile phone and made a call home. Lucy picked up after a couple of rings.

"Darling, I'm coming home, after all. There's a bit of a lull at the office. We can order in or somthing—unless you and the children already have plans."

She blathered on in her usual maddening way.

She and the twins had been going to catch a movie, *Antz,* but they'd rather stay home with him. They could order from Pizza Hut. It would be fun for a change.

"Yes, what fun," Shafer said, and cringed at the thought. Pizza Hut served indigestible cardboard drenched with very bad tomato soup. He hung up, then took a couple of Vicodin and a Xanax. He thought he could feel cracks slowly opening up in his skull.

He made a dangerous U-turn on Massachusetts Avenue and headed toward home. He passed the Jeep going in the opposite direction and was tempted to wave. A woman driver. Now, who was she?

The pizza got to the house at around seven, and Shafer opened an expensive bottle of Cabernet. He washed down another Xanax with the wine in the downstairs bathroom. Felt a little confused, fuzzy around the edges. That was all right, he supposed.

Jesus Christ, he couldn't stand being with his family, though; he felt as if he were going to crawl out of his skin. Ever since he was a boy in England he'd had a repetitive fantasy that he was actually a reptile and could shed his own skin. He'd had the dream long before he read any Kafka; he *still* had the disturbing dream.

He rolled three dice in his hand as he sipped his wine, played the game at the dinner table. If the number seventeen came up, he would murder them all tonight. He swore he would do it. First the twins, then Robert, and then Lucy.

She kept prattling on and on about her day. He smiled blithely as she told him about her shopping trip to Bloomingdale's and Bath & Body Works and Bruno Cipriani at the mall. He considered the supreme irony of his taking truckloads of anti-depressants and only becoming more depressed. Jesus, he was cycling down again. How low could he go?

"Come, seventeen," he finally said aloud.

"What, darling?" Lucy suddenly asked. "Did you just say something?"

"He's already playing tonight's game," said Robert, and snickered. "Right, Daddy? It's your fantasy game. Am I right?"

"Right, son," Shafer replied, thinking, *Christ, I am mad!*

He let the dice gently fall on the dining table, though. He *would* kill them—if their number came up. The dice rolled over and over, then banked off the greasy pizza box.

"Daddy and his games," Lucy said, and laughed. Erica and Tricia laughed. Robert laughed.

Six, five, one, he counted. *Damn, damn.*

"Are the two of us going to play tonight?" Robert asked.

Shafer forced a smile. "Not tonight, Rob Boy. I'd like to, but I can't. I have to go out again."

Chapter 66

THIS WAS getting very interesting. Patsy Hampton watched Shafer leave the large and expensive house in Kalorama at around eight-thirty. He was off on another of his nightly jaunts. The guy was a regular vampire.

She knew that Cross and his friends called the killer the Weasel, and it certainly fit Shafer. There was something uncomfortable about him, something bent.

She followed the black Jag, but he didn't head toward Southeast, which disappointed her. He drove to a trendy supermarket, Sutton on the Run, just off Dupont Circle. Hampton knew the pricey store and called it Why Pay Less.

He parked the sports car illegally, then jogged inside. *Diplomatic immunity.* That pissed her the hell off. What a weasel he was, real Euro-trash.

While he was in the market, Hampton made a command decision. She was pretty sure she was going to talk to Alex Cross. She had thought a lot about it, the pros and cons. Now she figured that she might be endangering lives in Southeast by not sharing at least some of what she knew. If someone died, she wouldn't be able to bear it. Besides, Cross would have gotten the information if she hadn't interceded with Chuck Hufstedler.

Shafer shuffled back out of Sutton on the Run and glanced around crowded Dupont Circle. He had a small bag of overpriced groceries clutched in one arm. Groceries for whom, though? He didn't look in the direction of her Jeep, which was just peeking around the corner.

She followed the black Jag at a safe distance in the light traffic. He got onto Connecticut Avenue. She didn't think he'd spotted her, though he was an MI6 man, so she needed to be careful.

Shafer wasn't far from Embassy Row. He wouldn't be going back to work now, would he? Why the groceries if he was headed to the embassy?

The Jaguar eventually turned into the underground garage of a prewar building in Woodley Park. THE FARRAGUT was engraved on a brass sign in front.

Patsy Hampton waited a few minutes, then pulled into the garage behind the Jag. She needed to look around, check things out if she could.

The garage was public-private, so it wasn't any big deal. She walked over to the attendant in the small kiosk and identified herself.

"The Jag that came in before me, ever see it here before?" she asked.

The man nodded. He was around her age, and

she could tell he wanted to impress her if he could. "Sure. I don't know him to talk to, though. Comes here to visit a lady on ten. Dr. Elizabeth Cassady. She's a shrink. I assume he's a patient. He's got a funny look in his eyes," the attendant said, "but so do most people."

"How about me?" Hampton asked.

"Nah. Well, maybe a little," the attendant said, and grinned.

Shafer stayed upstairs with Dr. Cassady for nearly two hours. Then he came down and went straight back to the house in Kalorama.

Patsy Hampton followed him, then watched the house for another half hour. She thought that Shafer was probably in for the night. She drove to a nearby diner but didn't go inside right away. She picked up her mobile phone before she had too many second thoughts. She knew Cross's street and got the phone number through information. Was it too late to call? Screw it, she was going through with this.

She was surprised when the phone was picked up on the first ring. She heard a pleasant male voice. Nice. Strong.

"Hello. Alex Cross."

She almost hung up on him. Interesting that he'd intimidated her for a moment. "This is Detective Patsy Hampton. I've been doing some work on the Jane Does. I've been following a man who is a suspect. I think we should talk."

"Where are you, Patsy?" Cross said, without hesitation. "I'll come to you. Just tell me where."

"I'm at the City Limits diner on Connecticut Avenue."

"I'm on my way," said Cross.

Chapter 67

I WASN'T totally surprised that Pittman had assigned someone to the Jane Does. Especially after Zach Taylor's article in the *Washington Post.* I was interested in any leads Detective Hampton might have turned up.

I had seen Patsy Hampton around, and she obviously knew who I was. She was supposed to be on a fast track; she was a smart and effective senior homicide detective, though from what I'd heard, she was also a lone wolf. She didn't have any friends in the department, as far as I knew.

She was much prettier than I remembered. She was in very trim, athletic shape, probably early thirties, short blond hair, piercing blue eyes that cut through the diner haze.

She'd put on bright-red lipstick for our meeting, or maybe she wore it all the time. I wondered what was on her mind and what her motives were. I didn't think I could trust her.

"You or me first?" Detective Hampton asked, after we'd ordered coffee. We were seated at a table in the City Limits diner, near a window looking out on Connecticut Avenue.

"I'm afraid I don't know what this is about," I told her.

She sipped her coffee and gave me a look over the cup's rim. She was a strong-willed, confident person. Her eyes told me that much.

"You really didn't know someone else was working the Jane Does?"

I shook my head. "Pittman said that the cases were closed. I took him at his word. He suspended some good detectives for working the cases after hours."

"There's a lot of seriously nasty crap going on in the department. So what's new, though?" she said as she set down her cup. She gave a deep sigh. "I thought I could deal with it by myself. Now I'm not so sure."

"Pittman assigned you to the Jane Does? Personally?"

She nodded, then her blue eyes narrowed. "He assigned me to the Glover and Cardinal murders, and any others I wanted to look into. Gave me free rein."

"And you say you have something?"

"Maybe. I've got a possible suspect. He's involved in a role-playing game that features victims' being murdered, mostly in Southeast. It's all after-the-fact stuff, so he could have read the news stories and then fantasized about them. He works at the British Embassy."

This was a new piece of information, and it surprised me. "How far have you gone with this?"

"Not to Pittman, if that's what you mean. I've done a little discreet checking on the suspect. Trouble is, he seems to be a solid citizen. Very good at his job—supposedly. At least that's the official word from the embassy. Nice family in Kalorama. I've been watching Shafer a little, hoping I'd get lucky. His first name is Geoffrey."

I knew that she was supposed to be a little bit of a loose cannon, and that she didn't suffer fools gladly. "You're out here alone tonight?" I asked her.

Hampton shrugged. "That's how I usually operate. Partners slow me down. Chief Pittman knows how I like to work. He gave me the green light. All green, all day long."

I knew she was waiting for me to give her something—if I had anything. I decided to play along. "We found a cab that the killer apparently used in Southeast. He kept it in a garage in Eckington."

"Anybody see the suspect in the neighborhood?" She asked the right first question.

"The landlady saw him. I'd like to show her pictures of your guy. Or do you want to do it yourself?"

Her face was impassive. "I'll do it. First thing in the morning. Anything revealing in the apartment?"

I wanted to be straight with her. She'd initiated the meeting, after all. "Photographs of me and my family covered a wall in a closet. They were taken of us in Bermuda. While we were on vacation. He was there watching us all the time."

Hampton's face softened. "I heard your fiancée disappeared in Bermuda. Word gets around."

"There were photographs of Christine, too," I said.

Her blue eyes became sad. I got a quick look behind her tough facade. "I'm really sorry about your loss."

"I haven't given up yet," I told her. "Listen, I don't want any credit for solving these cases; just let me help. He called me at home last night. *Somebody* did. Told me to back off. I assume that he meant this investigation, but I'm not supposed to be on it. If Pittman hears about us—"

Detective Hampton interrupted me. "Let me think about everything you've said. You know that Pittman will totally crucify me if he finds out. You have no idea. Trouble is, I don't trust him." Hampton's gaze was intense and direct. "Don't mention any of this to your buddies, or Sampson. You never know. Just let me sleep on it. I'll try to do the right thing. I'm not such a hard-ass, really. Just a little weird, you know."

"Aren't we all?" I said, and smiled. Hampton was a tough detective, but I felt okay about her. I took something out of my pocket. A beeper.

"Keep this. If you get in trouble or get another lead, you can beep me anytime. If you find something out, please let me know. I'll do the same. If

Shafer's the one, I want to talk to him before we bring him in. This *is* personal for me. You can't imagine how personal."

Hampton continued to make eye contact, studying me. She reminded me of someone I'd known a while back, another complicated woman cop, named Jezzie Flanagan. "I'll think about it. I'll let you know."

"All right. Thanks for calling me in on this."

She stood. "You're not in on it yet. Like I said, I'll let you know." Then she touched my hand. "I really am sorry about your friend."

Chapter 68

WE BOTH knew I was in, though. We'd made some kind of deal in the City Limits diner. I just hoped I wasn't being set up by Hampton and Pittman or God knows who else.

Over the next two days, we talked four times. I still wasn't sure that I could trust her, but I didn't have a choice. I had to keep moving forward. She had already visited the landlady who'd rented out the apartment and garage in Eckington. The landlady hadn't recognized the pictures of Shafer. Possibly he'd worn a disguise when he met with her.

If Patsy Hampton was setting me up, she was one of the best liars I'd met, and I've known some good ones. During one of our calls, she confessed that Chuck Hufstedler had been her source, and that she'd gotten him to keep the information from me. I shrugged it off. I didn't have the time or the energy to be angry at either of them.

In the meantime, I spent a lot of time at home. I didn't believe the killer would come after my family, not when he already had Christine, but I couldn't tell that for sure. When I wasn't there, I made sure Sampson or somebody else was checking on the house.

On the third night after I met her, Patsy Hampton and I had a breakthrough of sorts. She actually invited me to join her on her stakeout of Shafer's town house in Kalorama Heights.

He had arrived home from work before six and remained there until just past nine. He had a nice-looking expat family—three children, a wife, a nanny. He lived very well. Nothing about his life or surroundings suggested that he might be a killer.

"He seems to go out every night around this time," Hampton told me as we watched him walk to a shiny black Jag parked in a graveled driveway at the side of the house.

"Creature of habit," I said. A *weasel.*

"Creature, anyway," she said. We both smiled. The ice was breaking up a little between us. She admitted that she had checked me out thoroughly. She'd decided that Chief Pittman was the bad guy in all of this, not me.

The Jaguar pulled out of the drive, and we followed Shafer to a night spot in Georgetown. He didn't seem to be aware of us. The problem was that we had to catch him doing something; we had no concrete evidence that he was our killer.

Shafer sat by himself at the bar, and we watched him from the street. Did he perch by the window on purpose? I wondered. Did he know we were watching? Was he playing with us?

I had a bad feeling that he was. This was all some kind of bizarre game to him. He left the bar around a quarter to twelve and returned home just past midnight.

"Bastard." Patsy grimaced and shook her head. Her blond hair was soft and had a nice bounce to it. She definitely reminded me of Jezzie Flanagan, a Secret Service agent I'd worked with on the kidnapping of two children in Georgetown.

"He's in for the night?" I asked. "What was that all about? He leaves the house to watch the Orioles baseball game at a bar in Georgetown?"

"That's how it's been the last few nights. I think he knows we're out here."

"He's an intelligence officer. He knows surveillance. We also know he likes to play fantasy games. At any rate, he's home for the night, so I'm going home, too, Patsy. I don't like leaving my family alone too long."

"Good night, Alex. Thanks for the help. We'll get him. And maybe we'll find your friend soon."

"I hope so."

On the drive home, I thought a little about Detective Patsy Hampton. She struck me as a lonely person, and I wondered why. She was thoughtful and interesting once you got past her tough facade. I wondered if anyone could ever really get through that facade, though.

There was a light on in our kitchen when I rolled into the driveway. I strolled around to the back door and saw Damon and Nana in their bathrobes at the stove. Everything seemed all right.

"Am I breaking up a pajama party?" I asked as I eased in through the back door.

"Damon has an upset stomach. I heard him in the kitchen, so I came out to get in his way."

"I'm all right. I just couldn't sleep. I saw you were still out," he said. "It's after midnight."

He looked worried, and also a little sad. Damon had really liked Christine, and he'd told me a couple of times that he was looking forward to having a mom again. He'd already begun to think of her that way. He and Jannie missed Christine a whole lot. Twice now they'd had important women taken away from them.

"I was working a little late, that's all. It's a very complicated case, Damon, but I think I'm making progress," I said. I went to the cabinet and took out two tea bags.

"I'll make you tea," Nana offered.

"I can do it," I said, but she reached for the bags, and I let her take them away from me. It doesn't pay to argue with Nana, especially not in her kitchen.

"You want some tea and milk, big guy?" I asked Damon.

"All right," he said. He pronounced it *Ah-yite,* as they do at the playgrounds and probably even at the Sojourner Truth School.

"You sound like that poor excuse for an NBA point guard Allen Iverson," Nana said to him. She didn't much like street slang, never had. She had started off as an English teacher and never lost her love of books and language. She loved Toni Morrison, Alice Walker, Maya Angelou, and also Oprah Winfrey for bringing their books to a wider audience.

"He's the fastest guard in the league, *Grandma Moses*. Shows what you know about basketball," said Damon. "You probably think Magic Johnson is still playing in the league. And *Wilt Chamberlain*."

"I like Marbury with the Timberwolves, and Stoudamire with Portland, formerly with Toronto," Nana said, and gave a triumphant little smile. "*Ah-yite?*"

Damon laughed. Nana probably knew more about NBA point guards than either of us. She could always get you if she wanted to.

We sat at the kitchen table and drank tea with milk and too much sugar, and we were mostly quiet, but it was kind of nice. I love family, always have. Everything that I am flows from that. Damon yawned and got up from the table. He went to the sink and rinsed out his cup.

"I can probably sleep now," he reported to us. "Give it a try, anyway."

He came back to the table and gave Nana and me a kiss before he went back upstairs to bed. "You miss her, don't you?" he whispered against my cheek.

"Of course I miss Christine," I said to Damon. "All the time. Every waking minute." I didn't make mention of the fact that I had been out late because I was observing the son of a bitch who might have abducted her. Nor did I say anything about the other detective on surveillance, Patsy Hampton.

When Damon left, Nana put her hand in mine, and we sat like that for a few minutes before I went up to bed.

"I miss her, too," Nana finally said. "I'm praying for you both, Alex."

Chapter 69

THE NEXT evening at around six, I took off early from work and went to Damon's choir practice at the Sojourner Truth School. I'd put together a good-sized file on Geoffrey Shafer, but I didn't have anything that concretely linked him to any of the murders. Neither did Patsy Hampton. Maybe he was just a fantasy-game player. Or maybe the Weasel was just being more careful since his taxi had been found.

It tore me up to go to the Truth School, but I had to go. I realized how hard it must be for Damon and Jannie to go there every day. The school brought back too many memories of Christine. It was as if I were suffocating, all the breath being squeezed out of my lungs. At the same time, I was in a cold sweat that coated the back of my neck and my forehead.

A little while after the practice began, Jannie quietly reached over and took my hand. I heard her sigh softly. We were all doing a lot more touching and emoting since Bermuda, and I don't think we have ever been closer as a family.

She and I held hands through most of the choir

practice, which included the Welsh folk song "All Through the Night," Bach's "My heart ever faithful, sing praises," and a very special arrangement of the spiritual "O Fix Me."

I kept imagining that Christine would suddenly appear at the school, and once or twice I actually turned back toward the archway that led to her office. Of course, she wasn't there, which filled me with inconsolable sadness and the deepest emptiness. I finally cleared my mind of all thought, just shut down, and let my whole self be the music, the glorious sound of the boys' voices.

After we got home from the choir practice, Patsy Hampton checked in with me from her surveillance post. It was a little past eight. Nana and the kids were putting out cold chicken, slices of pears and apples, cheddar cheese, a salad of endive and Bibb lettuce.

Shafer was still home, and of all things, a children's birthday party was going on there, Patsy reported. "Lots of smiling kids from the neighborhood, plus a rent-a-clown called Silly Billy. Maybe we're on the wrong track here, Alex."

"I don't think so. I think our instincts are right about him."

I told her I would come over at around nine to keep her company; that was the time when Shafer usually left the house.

Just past eight-thirty, the phone in the kitchen rang again as we were digging into the cold, well-spiced, delicious chicken. Nana frowned as I picked up the phone.

I recognized the voice.

"I told you to back off, didn't I? Now you have to pay some consequences for disobeying. It's your fault! There's a pay phone at the old Monkey House at the National Zoo. The zoo closes at eight, but you can get in through the gardening-staff gate. Maybe Christine Johnson is there at the zoo waiting for you. You better get over there quick and find out. Run, Cross, run. Hurry! *We have her.*"

The caller hung up, and I charged upstairs for my Glock. I called Patsy Hampton and told her I'd gotten another call, presumably from the Weasel. I'd be at the National Zoo.

"Shafer's still at his kid's birthday party," she told me. "Of course, he could have called from the house. I can see Silly Billy's truck from where I'm parked."

"Keep in contact with me, Patsy. Phones and beepers. Beeper for *emergencies* only. Be careful with him."

"Okay. I'm fine here, Alex. Silly Billy doesn't pose too much of a threat. Nothing will happen at his house. Go to the zoo, Alex. *You* be careful."

Chapter 70

I WAS at the National Zoo by ten to nine. I was thinking that the zoo was actually pretty close to Dr. Cassady's apartment at the Farragut. Was it just a coincidence that I was so close to Shafer's shrink? I didn't believe in coincidences anymore.

I called Patsy Hampton before I left the car, but she didn't pick up this time. I didn't beep her—this wasn't an emergency—not so far.

I knew the zoo from lots of visits with Damon and Jannie, but even better from when I was a boy and Nana used to bring me, and sometimes Sampson, who was nearly six feet tall by the time he was eleven. The main entrance to the zoo was at the corner of Connecticut and Hawthorne avenues, but the old Monkey House was nearly a mile diagonally across the grounds from there.

No one seemed to be around, but the gardening-staff gate was unlatched, as the caller had said it would be. He knew the zoo, too. More games, I kept thinking. He definitely loved to play.

As I hurried into the park, a steep horizon of trees and hills blocked out the lights of the surrounding city. There was only an occasional foot lamp for light, and it was eerie and frightening to be in there alone. Of course, I was sure I *wasn't* alone.

The Monkey House was farther inside the gates than I remembered. I finally located it in the dark. It looked like an old Victorian railway station. Across a cobblestoned circle there was a more modern structure that I knew was the Reptile House.

A sign over the twin doors of the old Monkey House read: WARNING: QUARANTINE—DO NOT ENTER! More eeriness. I tried the tall twin doors, but they were securely locked.

On the wall beside the doors I saw a faded blue and white sign, the international pictograph indicating there was a phone inside. *Is that the phone he wants me to use?*

I shook the doors, which were old and wooden and rattled loudly. Inside I could hear monkeys starting to scream and act out. First the smaller primates: spider monkeys, chimpanzees, gibbons. Then the deeper grunt of a gorilla.

I caught sight of a dim red glow across the cobblestoned circle. Another pay phone was over there.

I hurried across the square. Checked my watch. It was two minutes past nine.

He kept me waiting last time.

I thought about his game playing. Was this all a role-playing game to him? How did he win? Lose?

I worried that I wasn't at the right phone. I didn't see any others, but there was always the one locked inside the old Monkey House.

Is that the phone he wants me to use? I felt frantic and hyper. So many dangerous emotions were building up inside me.

I heard a long, sustained *aaaaahhhh*, like the sound of a football crowd at the opening kickoff. It startled me until I realized it was the apes in the Monkey House.

Was something wrong in there? *An intruder?* Something or someone near the phone?

I waited another five minutes, and then it dragged on to ten minutes. It was driving me crazy. I almost couldn't bear it any longer, and I thought about beeping Patsy.

Then my beeper went off, and I jumped!

It was Patsy. It had to be an emergency.

I stared at the silent pay phone; I waited a half minute or so. Then I snatched it up.

I called the beeper number and left the number of the pay phone. *I waited some more.*

Patsy didn't call me back.

Neither did the mystery caller.

I was in a sweat.

I had to make a decision now. I was caught in a very bad place. My head was starting to reel.

Suddenly the phone rang. I grabbed at it, almost dropped the receiver. My heart was pounding like a bass drum.

"We have her."

"*Where?*" I yelled into the receiver.

"She's at the Farragut, of course."

The Weasel hung up. He never said she was safe.

Chapter 71

I COULDN'T imagine why Christine would be at the Farragut in Washington, but he'd said she was there. Why would he do that if she wasn't? What was he doing to me? To her?

I ran toward where I thought Cathedral Avenue was located. But it was very dark in the zoo, almost pitch-black. My vision was tunneling, maybe because I was close to being in shock. I couldn't think straight.

My mind in a haze, I tripped over a dark slab of rock, went down on one knee. I cut my hands, tore my pants. Then I was up again, running through thick high bushes that grabbed and ripped at my face and arms.

Animals all around the zoo howled, moaned, bellowed insanely. They sensed that something was wrong. I could make out the sounds of grizzlies and elephant seals. I realized that I had to be approaching Arctic Circle, but I couldn't remember where it was in relation to the rest of the zoo or the city streets.

Up ahead was a high, Gibraltar-like rock. I

clambered up it to try to get my bearings.

Down below I saw a cluster of cages, shuttered gift stores and snack bars, two large veldts. I knew where I was now. I hurriedly climbed back down the rock and started to run again. Christine was at the Farragut. Would I finally find her? Could it actually be happening?

I passed African Alley, then the Cheetah Conservation Station. I came to a vast field with what looked like large haystacks scattered everywhere. I realized that they were bison. I was somewhere near Great Plains Way.

The beeper in my pocket went off again.

Patsy! An emergency! Where is she? Why didn't she call back at the pay-phone number I gave her?

I was soaked in sweat and almost hyperventilating. Thank God I could now see Cathedral Avenue, then Woodley Road up ahead.

I was a long way from where I'd parked my car, but I was close to the Farragut apartment building.

I ran another hundred yards in the dark, then climbed the stone wall separating the zoo from the city streets. There was blood smeared on my hands, and I didn't know where it had come from. The knee I'd scraped? Scratches from swinging branches? I could hear the loud wail of sirens in the near distance. Was it coming from the Farragut?

I headed there in a sprint. It was a little past ten o'clock. Over an hour had already gone by since the call to my house.

The beeper was buzzing inside my shirt pocket.

Chapter 72

SOMETHING BAD had happened at the Farragut. The burping screams of approaching sirens were getting louder as I raced down Woodley. I was reeling, feeling dizzy. I couldn't focus my mind, and I realized that for one of the few times in recent years, I was close to panic.

Neither the police nor the EMS had arrived at the apartment building yet. I was going to be the first on the scene.

Two doormen and several tenants in bathrobes were clustered in front of the underground-garage entrance. It couldn't be Christine. It just couldn't be. I raced across a quadrant of lawn toward them. Was the Weasel here at the Farragut?

They saw me coming and looked as frightened as I felt inside. I must have been quite a sight. I remembered that I'd fallen once or twice inside the zoo. I probably looked like a madman, maybe even like a killer. There was blood on my hands and who knew where else.

I reached for my wallet, shook it open to expose my detective's shield.

"Police. What's happened here?" I shouted. "I'm a police detective. My name is Alex Cross."

"Somebody has been murdered, Detective," one of the doormen finally said. "This way. Please."

I followed the doorman down the steeply sloped concrete driveway leading into the garage.

"It's a woman," he said. "I'm pretty sure she's gone. I called nine-one-one."

"Oh, God," I gasped out loud. My stomach clutched. Patsy Hampton's Jeep was tucked back in a corner space. The door of the Jeep was open, and light spilled outside.

I felt terrible fear, pain, and shock as I hurried around the door. Patsy Hampton was sprawled across the front seat. I could tell she was probably dead.

"We have her." This was what the message meant. Jesus God, no. They murdered Patsy Hampton. They told me to back off. For God's sake, no.

Her bare legs were twisted and pinned under the steering wheel. Her upper body was crumpled over at almost a right angle. Patsy's head was thrown back and lay partly off the seat, on the passenger's side. Her blond hair was matted with blood. Her vacant blue eyes stared up at me.

Patsy was wearing a white knit sport shirt. There were deep lacerations around her throat; bright-red blood was still oozing from the wound. She was naked below the waist. I didn't see any other clothes anywhere. She might have been raped.

I suspected that she'd been strangled with some

kind of wire, and that she'd been dead for only a few minutes. A rope or garotte had been used in some of the Jane Doe murders. The Weasel liked to use his hands, to work close to his victims, possibly to watch and feel their pain—maybe even while he was sexually assaulting them.

I saw what looked like paint chips around the deep, ugly neck wounds. Paint chips?

Something else seemed very strange to me: the Jeep's radio had been partly dislodged, but left behind. I didn't understand why the radio had been tampered with, but it didn't seem important right now.

I leaned back out of the Jeep. "Is anyone else hurt? Have you checked?"

The doorman shook his head. "No. I don't think so. I'll go look."

Sirens finally screeched inside the garage. I saw red and blue lights flashing and whirling against the ceiling and walls. Some of the tenants had made it into the garage as well. Why did they have to come and gape at this terrible crime?

A very bad thought flashed in my head. I climbed out of the Jeep, grabbing Patsy's keys out of the ignition. I hurried around to the back. I pushed the release, and the rear door came open. My heart was thundering again. I didn't want to look inside, but when I did, there was nothing. *Jesus, Jesus, Jesus. "We have her!" Is Christine here, too? Where?*

I looked around the garage. Up near the entrance

I spotted Geoffrey Shafer's sports car, the black Jaguar. He was here at the Farragut. Patsy must have followed him.

I ran across the garage to the Jag. I felt the hood, then the exhaust pipe. Both were still warm. The car hadn't been in the garage very long. The doors were locked. I couldn't break in. I was all too aware of the search-and-seizure constraints.

I stared inside the Jaguar. In the backseat I could see dress shirts on wire hangers. The hangers were white, and I thought of the chips in Detective Hampton's wounds. Had he strangled her with a hanger? Was Shafer the Weasel? Was he still in the building? What about Christine? Was she here, too?

I said a few words to the patrolmen who'd just arrived, the first on the scene after me. Then I took them with me.

The helpful doorman told me which floor Shafer's therapist's apartment was on. The number was 10D, the penthouse. Like all buildings in D.C., the Farragut was restricted to a height no greater than that of the Capitol dome.

I took the elevator with the two uniformed cops, both in their twenties and both scared shitless, I'd bet. I was close to rage. I knew I had to be careful; I had to act professionally, to control my emotions somehow. If there was an arrest, there would be questions to answer, such as what I was doing here in the first place. Pittman would be on my case in a second.

I talked to the policemen on the way up, more to calm myself than anything else.

"You okay, Detective?" one of them asked me.

"I'm fine. I'm all right. The killer might still be in the building. The victim was a detective, one of our own. She was on surveillance here. The suspect has a relationship with a woman upstairs."

The faces of both young cops tightened. It was bad enough to have seen the murdered woman in her car, but to learn that she was a policewoman, a detective on surveillance, made it worse. Now they were about to confront a cop killer.

We hurried out of the elevator to apartment 10D. I led the way and pressed the bell. I saw what appeared to be drops of blood on the hallway carpet near the door. I noticed the blood on my hands, saw the two cops staring at the blood.

No answer from inside the apartment, so I pounded my fist on the door. Was everyone okay in there? "Police, open up! D.C. police!"

I could hear a woman shouting inside. I had my Glock out, the safety off. I was angry enough to kill Shafer. I didn't know if I could hold myself back.

The uniformed patrolmen took their pistols out of their holsters, too. After just a few seconds I was ready to kick down the door, search-and-seizure constraints or no. I kept seeing Patsy Hampton's face, her dead, vacant eyes, the savage wounds in her crushed throat.

Finally, the door to the apartment slowly opened.

A blond woman was standing there — Dr.

Cassady, I assumed. She wore an expensive-looking light-blue suit with lots of gold buttons, but she was barefoot. She looked frightened and angry.

"What do you want?" she demanded. "What the hell is going on here? Do you know what you've done? You've interrupted a therapy session."

Chapter 73

GEOFFREY SHAFER stepped into the doorway and stood a few feet behind his irate therapist. He was tall and imposing and very blond. *He's the Weasel, isn't he?*

"What the hell's the problem here? Who are you, sir, and what do you want?" he asked in a clipped English accent.

"There's been a murder," I said. "I'm Detective Cross." I showed them my badge. I kept looking past Shafer and Dr. Cassady, trying to spot something that would give me probable cause to come inside the apartment. There were lots of plants on the sills and hanging in windows—philodendron, azalea, English ivy. Dhurrie rugs in light pastels, overstuffed furniture.

"No. There's certainly no murderer here," the therapist said. "Leave this instant."

"You should do as the lady says," Shafer said.

Shafer didn't look like a murderer. He was dressed in a navy suit, a white shirt, a moiré tie, a pocket square. Impeccable taste. Completely unruffled and unafraid.

Then I glanced down at his shoes. I almost couldn't believe it. The gods had finally smiled on me.

I pointed my Glock at Shafer. At the Weasel. I went up to him and bent down on one knee. My whole body was trembling. I examined the right leg of his trousers.

"What the *hell* are you doing?" he asked, pulling away from me. "This is completely absurd.

"I'm with the British Embassy," Shafer then stated. "I repeat, I'm with the British Embassy. You have no rights here."

"Officers," I called to the two patrolmen who were still outside the door. I tried to act calm, but I wasn't. "Come here and look. You see this?"

Both patrolmen moved closer to Shafer. They entered the living room.

"Stay out of this apartment!" The therapist raised her voice close to a scream.

"Remove your trousers," I said to Shafer. "You're under arrest."

Shafer lifted his leg and gave a look. He saw a dark stain, Patsy Hampton's blood, smudged on the cuff of his trousers. Fear shot through his eyes, and he lost his cool.

"You put that blood there! You did it," he yelled at me. He pulled out an identification badge. "I am an official at the British Embassy. I don't have to put up with this outrage. I have diplomatic immunity. I will not take off my trousers for you. Call the embassy immediately! *I demand diplomatic immunity.*"

"Get out of here now!" Dr. Cassady yelled loudly. Then she pushed one of the patrolmen.

It was just what Shafer needed. He broke free and ran back through the living room. He rushed into the first room down the hallway, slammed the door, and locked it.

The Weasel was trying to get away. It couldn't happen; I couldn't let it. I got to the door seconds behind him. "Come out of there, Shafer! You're under arrest for the murder of Detective Patsy Hampton."

Dr. Cassady came screaming down the hall after me.

I heard the toilet flush in the bathroom. No, no, no! I reared back powerfully and kicked in the door.

Shafer was pulling off his trousers, standing on one leg. I tackled him hard, knocked him over, then held him facedown against the tile floor. He screamed curses at me, flailed his arms, bucked his lower body. I pushed his face harder into the floor.

The therapist tried to pull me off Shafer. She was scratching my face, pounding my back with her fists. It took both policemen to restrain her.

"You can't do this to me!" Shafer was yelling at the top of his voice, twisting and turning beneath me, a powerful stallion of a man.

"This is illegal. I have diplomatic immunity!"

I turned to one of the officers.

"Cuff him."

Chapter 74

IT WAS a long and very sad night at the Farragut, and I didn't leave until past three. I had never lost a partner before, though I had once come close with Sampson, in North Carolina. I realized that I'd already come to think of Patsy Hampton as a partner, and a friend. At least we had the Weasel in custody.

I slept in the next morning, allowing myself the small luxury of not setting the alarm. Still, I was wide awake by seven. I'd been dreaming about Patsy Hampton, and also about Christine—different, vivid scenes with each of them, the kind of frenetic dreams where you wake up feeling as tired as when you went to bed. I said a prayer for both of them before I finally rolled out of bed. We had the Weasel. Now I had to get the truth out of him.

I slipped on a somewhat worn white satin robe. Muhammad Ali had worn it in his training camp in Manila before the Joe Frazier fight. Sampson had given it to me for my fortieth birthday. He appreciated the fact that while most people would treat the robe as some kind of sacred exhibit in their house, I routinely wear it to breakfast.

I love the old robe, which is unusual for me since I'm not particularly into mementos and souvenirs. Maybe part of it is that I'm supposed to resemble Ali physically, or so people tell me. Maybe I'm a little better looking, but he's definitely the better man.

When I got down to the kitchen, Nana and the kids were sitting at the table watching the small portable TV that she keeps there but doesn't use very often. She prefers to read or chitchat and, of course, cook.

"Ali." Jannie looked up at me and grinned, but then her eyes went back to the TV. "You should watch this, Daddy."

Nana muttered into her cup of tea. "Your British murderer is all over the news this morning. TV and the newspaper, too. 'Diplomatic Immunity May Bar Prosecution of British Embassy Suspect,' 'Spy Linked to Detective Slay.' They already interviewed people in Union Station and on Pennsylvania Avenue. Everybody's mad as a hatter about this diplomatic-immunity disgrace, as they call it. It's just terrible."

"I'm mad. It's not right," Damon said. "Not if he did it. Did he, Dad? Did he do it?"

I nodded. "He did it." I poured milk into my coffee. I wasn't quite ready to deal with Geoffrey Shafer, or the kids, or especially the horrible, senseless murder the night before. "Anything else on the news?"

"The Wizards kicked butt," Damon said with a straight face. "Rod Strickland had a double-double."

"*Shhhh.*" Nana gave us both a mighty look of irritation. "CNN carried stories *from London.* The media there is already comparing this to that unfortunate nanny case in Massachusetts. They say that Geoffrey Shafer is a decorated war hero and that he claims, with good reason, that he was framed by the police. I assume that means you, Alex."

"Yes, it does. Let's watch CNN for a few minutes," I said. Nobody objected, so I switched the channel. A hard knot was forming in my stomach. I didn't like what I was seeing and hearing on TV.

Almost immediately, a reporter came on the screen from London. He introduced himself and then proceeded to give a pompous, thirty-second summary of the previous evening's events.

The reporter looked gravely into the camera. "And now, in a dramatic turnabout, we have learned that the Washington Police Department is investigating a bizarre twist. The senior detective who arrested Geoffrey Shafer might himself be a suspect in the murder case. At least that's what has been reported in the American press."

I shook my head and frowned. "I'm innocent," I said to Nana and the kids. They knew that, of course.

"Until proven guilty," said Jannie, with a little wink.

Chapter 75

THERE WAS a loud hubbub out in front of the house, and Jannie ran to the living-room window to look. She hurried back to the kitchen with wide eyes, loud-whispering, "It's TV cameras and the newspapers outside. CNN, NBC—lots of them, like that other time, with Gary Soneji. Remember?"

"Of course we remember," said Damon. "Nobody's retarded in this house except you."

"Oh, good Lord, Alex," Nana said, "don't they know decent people are eating breakfast?" She shook her head, rolled her eyes. "The vultures are here again. Maybe I should throw some meat scraps out the front door."

"*You* go talk to them, Jannie," I said, and looked back at the TV. I don't know why I was feeling so cynical, but I was. My remark quieted her down for a half second, but then she figured it was a joke. She pointed a finger at herself. "Gotcha!"

I knew they wouldn't go away, so I took my mug of coffee and headed toward the front door. I walked out into a beautiful fall morning, temperature probably in the low sixties.

Leaves rustled merrily in the elm and maple trees, dappled sunshine fell on the heads of the TV crew and print journalists gathered at the edges of our front lawn.

The vultures.

"Don't be absurd and ridiculous around here," I said, and then calmly sipped my coffee as I stared at the noisy press mob. "Of course I didn't kill Detective Patsy Hampton, or frame anyone for her murder."

Then I turned on my heel and walked back inside without answering a single question from any of them.

Nana and the kids were right behind the big wooden door, listening. "That was pretty good," Nana said, and her eyes sparkled and beamed.

I went upstairs and got dressed for work. "Go to school. *Now*!" I called back to Jannie and Damon. "Get straight A's. Play nicely with your friends. Pay no attention to the craziness everywhere around you."

"Yes, Daddy!"

Chapter 76

ON ACCOUNT of his request for diplomatic immunity, we weren't allowed to question Geoffrey Shafer about Detective Hampton's murder or anything else. I was incredibly frustrated. We had the Weasel, and we couldn't get to him.

Investigators were lying in wait for me that morning at the station house, and I knew it was going to be a long and excruciating day. I was interviewed by Internal Affairs, by the city's chief counsel, and also by Mike Kersee from the district attorney's office.

Pay no attention to the craziness everywhere around you, I reminded myself over and over, but my own good advice wasn't working too well.

Around three o'clock, the district attorney himself showed up. Ron Coleman is a tall, slender, athletic-looking man; we had worked together many times when he was coming up in the D.A.'s office. I had always found him to be conscientious, well informed, and committed to rationality and sanity. He'd never seemed very political, so it had come as a shock to almost everyone when Mayor Monroe appointed him the D.A. Monroe loves to shock people, though.

Coleman made an announcement: "Mr. Shafer already has an attorney, and he is one of the bright stars of our galaxy. He has retained none other than Jules Halpern. Halpern's probably the one who planted the story that you're a suspect—which you aren't, as far as I know."

I stared at Coleman. I couldn't believe what I'd just heard. "As far as you know? What does that mean, Ron?"

The D.A. shrugged. "We're probably going to go with Cathy Fitzgibbon on our side. I think she's our best litigator. We'll back her up with Lynda Cole and maybe Stephen Apt, who are also top-notch. That's my take on it as of this morning."

I knew all three prosecutors, and they had good reputations, particularly Fitzgibbon. They were on the young side, but nonetheless tireless, smart, dedicated—a lot like Coleman himself.

"You sound like you're preparing for a war, Ron."

He nodded. "As I said, Jules Halpern is Shafer's defense attorney. He rarely loses. In fact, I don't know if he's ever lost a big case like this one. He turns down all the losers, Alex."

I looked directly into Coleman's dark eyes. "We have Patsy Hampton's blood on the killer's clothes. We have blood in the bathroom drain, and I bet we'll have Shafer's fingerprints somewhere in Hampton's car before the end of the day. We may have the wire hanger he used to strangle her. Ron?"

"Yes, Alex. I know what you're going to say. I know your question. It's the same one I have."

"Shafer *has* diplomatic immunity. So why bring in Jules Halpern?"

"That's a very good goddamn question we both came up with. I suspect Halpern's been hired to get us to drop the charges completely."

"We have substantial evidence. He was *washing Patsy Hampton's blood* off himself in the bathroom. There's residue in the sink."

Coleman nodded and shrank back into his easy chair. "I don't understand why Jules Halpern is involved. I'm sure we'll know before too long, though."

"I'm *afraid* we'll know soon," I said.

I decided to leave the station by the back way that night, just in case there was press lying in wait out front on Alabama Avenue. As I stepped outside, a small balding man in a light-green suit popped out from behind the adjacent stone wall.

"That's a good way to get yourself shot," I told him. I was only half kidding.

"Occupational hazard," he lisped. "Don't shoot the messenger, Detective."

He smiled thinly as he handed me a white letter-sized envelope. "Alex Cross, you've hereby been served with a Summons and Complaint. Have a nice night, Detective," he said in his sibilant whine. Then he walked away as surreptitiously as he'd appeared.

I opened the envelope and quickly scanned the

letter. I groaned. Now I knew why Jules Halpern had been retained, and what we were up against.

I had been named in a civil suit for "false arrest" and "defamation of the character of Colonel Geoffrey Shafer." The suit was for fifty million dollars.

Chapter 77

THE NEXT morning I was summoned to the District of Columbia Law Department offices downtown. This was not good, I decided. The city's chief counsel, James Dowd, and Mike Kersee from the D.A.'s office were already ensconced in red-leather club chairs.

So was Chief of Detectives Pittman, who was putting on quite a show from his front-row seat. "You mean to tell me that because Shafer has diplomatic immunity he can avoid criminal prosecution in criminal court? But he can traipse right into our *civil* court and get protection against false arrest and defamation?"

Kersee nodded and made clucking noises with his tongue and teeth. "Yessirreebob, that's it exactly. Our ambassadors and their staffs enjoy the same kind of immunity in England and everywhere else around the world. No amount of political pressure will get the Brits to waive immunity. Shafer is a war hero from the Falklands. Supposedly he's also pretty well respected inside the Security Service, though lately he seems to have been in some trouble."

"What kind of trouble?" I asked.

"They won't tell us."

Pittman was still badgering the lawyers. "What about that clown from the Baltic Embassy? The one who wiped out the sidewalk café? *He* went to trial."

Mike Kersee shrugged. "He was just a low-level staffer from a low-level country that we could threaten. We can't do that with England."

"Why the hell not?" Pittman frowned and thumped his hand hard against the arm of his chair. "England isn't worth shit anymore."

The phone on Dowd's desk rang, and he raised his hand for quiet. "That's probably Jules Halpern. He said he'd call at ten, and he's an efficient bastard. If it is him, I'll put him on the speaker box. This should be about as interesting as a rectal exam done with a cactus."

Dowd picked up and exchanged pleasantries with the defense attorney for about thirty seconds. Then Halpern cut him off. "I believe we have matters of substance to discuss. My schedule is rather tight today. I'm sure you're hard pressed as well, Mr. Dowd."

"Yes, let's get down to business," Dowd said, raising his thick, curly black eyebrows. "As you know, the police have a qualified privilege to arrest anyone if they have probable cause. You simply don't have a civil case, Counselor—"

Halpern interrupted Dowd before he had finished speaking. "*Not* if that person identifies himself from the outset as having diplomatic immunity, which my client did. Colonel Shafer stood in the doorway of his *therapist's* apartment, waving his British Security Service shield like a stop sign and saying that he had immunity."

Dowd sighed loudly into the phone. "There was blood on his trousers, Counselor. He's a murderer, Counselor, *and* a cop killer. I don't think I need to say any more on the subject. With respect to the alleged defamation, the police also have a qualified privilege to talk to the press when a crime has been committed."

"And I suppose that the chief of detectives' statement in front of reporters—and several hundred million others around the world—isn't slander per se?"

"That's correct, it isn't. There's a qualified privilege with respect to public figures such as your client."

"My client is not a *public* figure, Mr. Dowd. He is a very private individual. He is an intelligence agent. His very livelihood, if not his life, depends on his being able to work undercover."

The chief counsel was already exasperated, possibly because Halpern's responses were so calm, yet always delivered rapid-fire. "All right, Mr. Halpern. So why are you calling us?"

Halpern paused long enough to make Dowd curious. Then he began again. "My client has authorized me to make a very unusual offer. I have strongly advised him against it, but he maintains his right to do so."

Dowd looked startled. I could tell that he hadn't been expecting any kind of deal offer. Neither had I. What was this about?

"Go ahead, Mr. Halpern," said Dowd. His eyes were wide and alert as they roamed around the room looking at us. "I'm listening."

"I'll bet you are, and all your esteemed colleagues as well."

I leaned forward to hear every word.

Jules Halpern continued with the real reason for his call: "My client wants all possibility of a civil case being brought against him waived."

I rolled my eyes. Halpern wanted to make certain that no one could sue his client in civil court after the criminal court case was concluded. He remembered that O. J. Simpson had been set free in the one court only to be bankrupted in the other.

"Impossible!" said Dowd. "There's no way in hell that will ever happen. No way."

"Listen to me. There *is* a way, or I wouldn't have broached the subject. If this is done, and if he and I can be convinced of a speedy route for a criminal trial, my client will *waive diplomatic immunity*. Yes, you heard me correctly. Geoffrey Shafer wants to prove his innocence in a court of law. He insists on it, in fact."

Dowd was shaking his head in disbelief. So was Mike Kersee. His eyes were glazed with astonishment as he glanced across the room at me.

None of us could believe what we had just heard from the defense attorney.

Geoffrey Shafer wanted to go to trial.

Book Four

TRIAL AND ERRORS

CONQUEROR HAD watched her work High Street in Kensington for nearly six weeks. She became his obsession, his fantasy woman, his "game piece." He knew everything there was to know about her. He felt—he knew—that he was starting to act like Shafer. They all were, weren't they?

The girl's name was Noreen Anne, and a long time ago—*three years,* to be exact—she had traveled to London from Cork, Ireland, with lovely dreams of being a fashion model on the world stage.

She was seventeen then, nearly five-ten, slender, blond, and with a face that all the boys and even the older men back home told her was destined for magazine covers, or maybe even the cinema.

So what was she doing here on High Street at half past one in the morning? She wondered about it as she forced a coquettish smile and occasionally waved a hand at the leering men in their slowly passing cars that made the rounds of High Street, DeVere Gardens, Exhibition Road.

They'd thought she was pretty, all right—just not pretty enough for British or American magazine covers, and not good enough, not classy enough, to marry or have as a girlfriend.

Well, at least she had a plan, and she thought it was a good one. Noreen Anne had saved nearly two thousand quid since she began to walk the streets. She thought she needed another three thousand or so, and then she would head back to Ireland. She'd start a small beauty shop, because she did know the secrets of beauty, and also a lot about the dreams.

So, here I am in front of the Kensington Palace Hotel in the meantime, she thought. *Freezing my fine bum off.*

"Excuse me, miss," she heard, and turned with a start. She hadn't heard anyone come up on her.

"I couldn't help noticing you standing here. You're an extraordinary beauty. But of course you know that, don't you?"

Noreen Anne felt relief the moment she saw who it was. This one wouldn't hurt her, couldn't if he tried. She could hurt *him,* if it came to that.

He was old, in his late sixties or seventies; he was obscenely fat; and he was seated in a wheelchair.

And so she went off—with Conqueror.

It was all part of the game.

Chapter 79

THE AMERICANS had promised a speedy route to trial, and the fools had actually delivered.

Five months had passed since the murder of Detective Pasty Hampton. Alex Cross had been shuttling back and forth to Bermuda, but he still had no idea where Christine had disappeared to. Shafer was out of jail but on a very short leash. He hadn't played the game once since Hampton's murder. The game of games had been on hold, and it was driving him mad.

Now Shafer sat in his black Jag in the parking lot directly under the courthouse, feeling hopeful. He was eager to stand trial on the count of Aggravated, Premeditated Murder in the First Degree. The rules of play had been established, and he appreciated that.

The suppression hearing weeks before was still a vivid memory for him. He'd relished every minute of it. The preliminary hearing was held before the jury selection, to determine what evidence would be allowed at the trial; it took place in the spacious chambers of Judge Michael Fescoe. The judge set the rules, so in a way he was the gamemaster. How fabulously droll, how delicious.

Shafer's lawyer, Jules Halpern, argued that Shafer had been in a therapy session at Dr. Cassady's home-office, and therefore had every right to privacy. "That privacy was violated. First, Dr. Cassady refused to let Detective Cross and the other officers come inside. Second, Colonel Shafer showed his identification to the detective. It proved that he was with the British Embassy and had diplomatic immunity. Cross barged into the therapist's office anyway. Consequently, any evidence obtained—if indeed any evidence *was* obtained—is the result of unlawful search."

Judge Fescoe took the rest of the day to consider, then announced his decision the next morning. "As I listened to both sides, it seemed to me that the issues were straightforward and not all that unusual in a murder case. Mr. Shafer does indeed have diplomatic immunity. However, it is my opinion that Detective Cross acted in a reasonable and lawful manner when he went to Dr. Cassady's apartment. He suspected that a grave crime had been committed. Dr. Cassady opened the door, allowing Detective Cross plain view of Mr. Shafer's attire. Colonel Shafer has insisted all along that his diplomatic immunity denied Detective Cross permission to enter the premises.

"I am therefore going to allow the prosecution to use the clothing Colonel Shafer was wearing on the night of the murder, as well as the blood on the carpet outside the apartment door, as evidence.

"The prosecution may also use any evidence found in the parking garage, both in Detective Hampton's car and in Colonel Shafer's," Judge Fescoe continued, and this was the key part of his ruling: "I will *not allow* evidence found once Detective Cross entered the apartment against the stated wishes of both Colonel Shafer and Dr. Cassady. Any and all evidence discovered during the initial or subsequent searches is suppressed and will not be allowed at the trial."

The prosecution was also told not to make any reference, during the trial, to any other uncharged murders that Shafer was suspected of having committed in Washington. The jury was to understand that Shafer was under investigation only for the murder of Senior Detective Patricia Hampton. Both the prosecution and the defense claimed victory at the end of the suppression hearing.

The stone steps outside the courthouse were swarming with a buzzing, unruly crowd on the morning of the first day. Shafer's "supporters" were wearing UK/OK buttons and waving crisp, new Union Jacks. These wondrous fools made him smile as he clasped both hands high over his head in victory. He enjoyed being a hero immensely.

What a glorious time. Even if he *was* a little high and spacey on a few choice pharmaceuticals.

Both sides were still predicting "slam dunk" victories. Lawyers were such fabulous bullshitters.

The press was touting the outrageous charade as

the "criminal trial of the decade." The media hype, expected and ritualistic, thrilled him anyway. He internalized it as tribute and adulation. His due.

He purposely cut quite a dashing figure; he wanted to make an impression—on the world. He wore a soft-shouldered, tailored gray suit, a striped bespoke shirt from Budd, and black oxfords from Lobb's, St. James's. He was photographed a hundred times in the first few moments alone.

He walked into the courthouse as if in a dream. The most delicious thing of all was that he might lose everything.

Courtroom 4 was on the third floor. It was the largest in the building. Closest to the double set of public doors was a gallery that held around a hundred and forty spectators. Then came the "bar area," where the attorneys' tables were situated. Then the "judge's bench," which took up about a quarter of the room.

The trial began at ten in the morning, and it was all a rattle and hum to him. The lead prosecutor was Assistant U.S. Attorney Catherine Marie Fitzgibbon. He already yearned to murder her, and wondered if he possibly could. He wanted Ms. Fitzgibbon's scalp on his belt. She was just thirty-six, Irish Catholic, single, sexy in her tight-assed way, dedicated to high-minded ideals, like so many others from her island of origin. She favored dark-blue or gray Ann Taylor wardrobes and wore a ubiquitous tiny gold cross on a gold chain. She was known in the D.C. legal community as the Drama

Queen. Her melodramatic telling of the gory details was meant to win the sympathy of the jury. A worthy opponent indeed. A worthy prey as well.

Shafer sat at the defendant's table and tried to concentrate. He listened, watched, felt as he hadn't in a long time. He knew they were all watching him. How could they not?

Shafer sat there observing, but his brain was on fire. His esteemed attorney, Jules Halpern, finally began to speak, and he heard his own name. That piqued his interest, all right. He was the star here, wasn't he?

Jules Halpern was little more than five-four, but he cut quite a powerful figure in a court of law. His hair was dyed jet-black and slicked back tightly against his scalp. His suit was from a British tailor, just like Shafer's. Shafer thought, rather uncharitably, he supposed, *Dress British, think Yiddish.* Seated beside Halpern was his daughter, Jane, who was second chair. She was tall and slender, but with her father's black hair and beaked nose.

Jules Halpern certainly had a strong voice for such a slight and small fellow. "My client, Geoffrey Shafer, is a loving husband. He is also a very good father, and happened to be attending a birthday party for two of his children half an hour *before* the murder of Detective Patricia Hampton.

"Colonel Shafer, as you will hear, is a valued and decorated member of the British intelligence community. He is a former soldier with a fine record.

"Colonel Shafer was clearly set up for this murder charge because the Washington police *needed* this terrible crime to be solved. This I will prove to you, and you will have no doubt of it. Mr. Shafer was framed because a particular homicide detective was going through some bad personal times and lost control of the situation.

"Finally—and this is the most essential thing for you to remember—Colonel Shafer *wants* to be here. He isn't here because he has to be; he has diplomatic immunity. Geoffrey Shafer is here to clear his good name."

Shafer nearly stood up in the courtroom and cheered.

Chapter 80

I PURPOSELY, and probably wisely, skipped the first day, then the second and the third day, of the courtroom circus. I didn't want to face the world press, or the public, any more than I had to. I felt like I was on trial, too.

A cold-blooded murderer was on trial, but the investigation continued more feverishly than ever for me. I still had the Jane Does to solve, and the disappearance of Christine, if I could open up any new leads. I wanted to make certain that Shafer would not walk away a free man, and most important, I desperately wanted finally to know the truth about Christine's disappearance. I had to know. My greatest frustration was that because of the diplomatic shenanigans, I had never gotten to question Shafer. I would have given anything for a few hours with him.

I turned the southern end of our attic into a war room. There was an excess of unused space up there, anyway. I moved an old mahogany dining table out from the shadows. I rewired an ancient window fan, which made the attic space almost bearable most days—especially early in the morning and late in the evening, when I did my best work up there—in my hermitage.

I set up my laptop on the table, and I pinned different-colored index cards to the walls, to keep what I considered the most important pieces of the case before me at all times. Inside several bulky and misshapen cardboard boxes, I had all the rest of it: every scrap of evidence on Christine's abduction, and everything I could find on the Jane Does.

The murder cases formed a maddening puzzle created over several years, one that was not given to easy solutions. I was trying to play a complex game against a skillful opponent, but I didn't know the rules of his game, or how it was played. That was Shafer's unfair advantage.

I had found some useful notes in Patsy Hampton's detective logs, and they led me to interview the teenage boy, Michael Ormson, who'd chatted on-line with Shafer about the Four Horsemen. I continued to work closely with Chuck Hufstedler of the FBI. Chuck felt guilty about giving Patsy Hampton the original lead, especially since I'd come to him first. I used his guilt.

Both the Bureau and Interpol were doing an active search of the game on the Internet. I'd visited countless chatrooms myself, but had encountered no one, other than young Ormson, who was aware of the mysterious game. It was only because Shafer had taken a chance and gone into the chatroom that he'd been discovered. I wondered what other chances he'd taken.

Following Shafer's arrest at the Farragut, we did a little search on his Jaguar, and I'd also spent nearly an hour at his home—before his lawyers knew I was there. I spoke to his wife, Lucy, and his son, Robert, who confirmed that he played a game called the Four Horsemen. He had been playing for seven or eight years.

Neither the wife nor the son knew any of the other players, or anything about them. They didn't believe that Geoffrey Shafer had done anything wrong.

The son called his father the "straight arrow of straight arrows." Lucy Shafer called him a good man, and she seemed to believe it.

I found role-playing game magazines as well as dozens of sets of game dice in Shafer's den, but no other physical evidence relating to his game. Shafer was careful; he covered his tracks well. He was in intelligence, after all. I couldn't imagine him throwing dice to select his victims, but maybe that helped to account for the irregular pattern of the Jane Does.

His attorney Jules Halpern complained loudly and vigorously about the invasion of Shafer's home, and had I uncovered any useful evidence, it would certainly have been suppressed. Unfortunately, I didn't have enough time, and Shafer was too clever to keep anything incriminating in his house, anyway. He'd made one big mistake; he wasn't likely to make another. Was he?

Sometimes, very late at night, as I worked in the attic, I would stop for a while and remember something about Christine. The memories were painful and sad, but also soothing to me. I began to look forward to these times when I could think about her without any interruption. Some nights, I would wander down to the piano in the sun porch and play songs that had been important to us—"Unforgettable," "Moonglow," "'S Wonderful." I could still remember how she'd looked, especially when I visited at her place—faded jeans, bare feet, T-shirt or maybe her favorite yellow crewneck sweater, a tortoiseshell comb in her long hair that always smelled of shampoo.

I didn't want to feel sorry for myself, but I just couldn't help feeling miserably bad. I was caught in limbo, not knowing one way or the other what had really happened to Christine. I couldn't let her go.

It was paralyzing me, crippling me, making me feel so damn sad and empty. I knew I needed to move on with my life, but I couldn't do it. I needed answers, at least a few of them. *Is Christine part of the game?* I kept wondering. I was obsessed with the game.

Am I *part of it?*

I believed I was. And in a way, I hoped she was, too. It was my only hope that she might still be alive.

Chapter 81

AND SO I found myself a player in a truly bizarre game that was habit-forming for all the wrong reasons. I began to make up my own rules. I brought in new players. I was in this game to win.

Chuck Hufstedler from the FBI offices in D.C. continued to be helpful. The more I talked to him, the more I realized that he'd had a serious crush on Detective Hampton. His loss, and mine with Christine, united us.

I climbed up to the attic late Friday night after watching *The Mask of Zorro* with Damon, Jannie, Nana, and Rosie the cat. I had a few more facts to check before going to bed.

I booted up the computer, logged on, and heard the familiar message: *You have mail.* Ever since that night in Bermuda, those words had given me a terrible fright, a chill that tightened my body from head to toe.

Sandy Greenberg from Interpol was replying to one of my e-mails. She and I had worked together on the Mr. Smith case and had become friends. I'd asked her to check on several things for me.

Call me anytime tonight, Alex, and I mean anytime. Your irritating doggedness may have paid off. It's vitally important that you call. *Sandy.*

I called Sandy in Europe, and she picked up after the second ring. "Alex? I think we've found one of them. It was your bloody idea that worked. Shafer was playing a game with at least one of his old cronies from MI-Six. You were spot on."

"Are you sure it's one of the game players?" I asked her.

"Pretty sure," she shot back. "I'm sitting here now staring at a copy of Dürer's *Four Horsemen,* on my Mac. As you know, the Horsemen are Conqueror, Famine, War, and Death. What a creepy bunch. Anyway, I did what you asked. I talked to some contacts from MI-Six, who found out that Shafer and this one chap regularly keep in touch on the computer. I have all your notes, too, and they're very good. I can't believe how much you figured out from back there in the colonies. You're a very sick puppy, too."

"Thanks," I said. I let Sandy ramble on for a few minutes. A while back I'd recognized that she was a lonely person, and that even though she sometimes put up a cantankerous front, she craved company.

"The name this chap uses in the game is Conqueror. Conqueror lives in Dorking, Surrey, in England," Sandy told me. "His name is Oliver Highsmith, and he's retired from MI-Six. Alex, he was running several agents in Asia at the same time Shafer was there. Shafer worked under him. It's eight in the morning over here. *Why don't you call the bastard?*" Sandy suggested. "Or send him an e-mail. I have an address for him, Alex."

I started to wonder about the other players in the Four Horsemen game. Were there really four of them, or was that just the name of the game? Who were these players? How was the game actually played? Did all, or indeed any, of them act out their fantasies in real life?

My message to Conqueror was simple and straightforward and not too threatening, I hoped. I didn't see how he could resist answering me.

Dear Mr. Highsmith,
I am a homicide detective in Washington, D.C., Looking for information about Colonel Geoffrey Shafer pertaining to the Four Horsemen. I understand that Shafer worked for you in Asia. Time is of the essence. I need your help. Please contact Detective Alex Cross.

Chapter 82

I WAS surprised when a message came right back. Oliver Highsmith—Conqueror — must have been on-line when my e-mail went through.

Detective Cross. I am well aware of you, since the ongoing murder trial is a rather big story in England, and in the rest of Europe, for that matter. I have known G.S. for a dozen years or more. He did work under me, briefly. He is more an acquaintance than a close friend, so I have no expertise or bias about his guilt or innocence. I hope it's the latter, of course.

Now, as to your question about the Four Horsemen. The game—and it *is* a fantasy game, Detective—is highly unusual in that all of the players assume the role of gamemaster. That is to say, each of us controls his own fate, his own story. G.S.'s story is even more daring and unusual. His character, the Rider on the Pale Horse—death—is deeply flawed. One might even say evil. The Character is somewhat like the person on trial in Washington, or so it seems to me.

However, I must make a few important points. The appearance of any murder fantasies in our game always occurred days *after* reports of murders in the newspapers. Believe me, this was thoroughly checked by us once G.S. was accused. It was even brought to the attention of Inspector Jones at the Security Service in London, so I'm surprised you weren't informed before now. The Service have been to see me about G.S. and were completely satisfied, I assume, since they haven't been back.

Also, the other players—who have themselves been checked out by security—are all represented by positive characters in the game. And as I've said, as powerfully involving as Horsemen is, it is nevertheless only a game. By the way, did you know that by some scholarly accounts there is a Fifth Horseman? *Might that be you, Dr. Cross?*

FYI—the contact at the Service is Mr. Andrew Jones. I trust he will vouch for the veracity of my statements. If you wish to converse further, do so at your own risk. I am 67 years of age, retired from Intelligence (as I like to put it), and a rather famous windbag. I wish you much luck in your search for truth and justice. I miss the chase myself.

CONQUEROR

I read the message, then reread it. *"Much luck in your search?"* Was that as loaded a line as it sounded?

And was I now a player—the fifth Horseman?

Chapter 83

I WENT to court every day the following week, and like so many other people, I got hooked on the trial. Jules Halpern was the most impressive orator I had ever watched in a courtroom, but Catherine Fitzgibbon was effective as well. The verdict would depend on whom the jury believed more. It was all theater, a game. I remembered that as a kid I used to regularly watch a courtroom drama with Nana, called *The Defenders.* Every show began with a deep-voiced narrator's saying something to the effect of, "The American justice system is far from perfect, but it is still the very best justice system in the world."

That may be true, but as I sat in the courtroom in Washington, I couldn't help thinking that the murder trial, the judge, the jury, the lawyers, and all the rules were just another elaborate game, and that Geoffrey Shafer was already planning his next foray, savoring every move that the prosecution made against him.

He was still in control of the game board. He was the gamemaster. He knew it, and so did I.

I watched Jules Halpern conduct smooth examinations that were designed to give the impression that his monstrous, psychopathic client was as innocent as a newborn baby. Actually, it was easy to drift off during the lengthy cross-examinations. I never really missed anything, though, since all the important points were repeated over and over, ad nauseam.

"Alex Cross . . ."

I heard my name mentioned and refocused my attention on Jules Halpern. He produced a blown-up photograph that had appeared in the *Post* on the day after the murder. The photo had been taken by another tenant at the Farragut and sold to the newspaper.

Halpern leaned in close to the witness on the stand, a man named Carmine Lopes, a night doorman at the apartment building where Patsy Hampton had been murdered.

"Mr. Lopes, I show you Defendant's Exhibit J, a photograph of my client and Detective Alex Cross. It was taken in the tenth-floor hallway soon after the discovery of Detective Hampton's body."

The blowup was large enough for me to see most of the detail from where I was sitting in the fourth row. The photo had always been a shocker to me.

In it, Shafer looked as if he had just stepped out of the pages of *GQ*. In comparison, my clothes were tattered and dirty. I had just come off my crazy marathon run from the zoo, and I had been down in the garage with poor Patsy's body. My fists were clenched tightly, and I seemed to be roaring out anger at Shafer. Pictures *do* lie. We know that. The photograph was highly inflammatory, and I felt it could instill prejudice in the minds of the jurors.

"Is this a fair representation of how the two men looked at ten-thirty that evening?" Halpern asked the doorman.

"Yes, sir. It's very fair. That's how I remember it."

Jules Halpern nodded as if he were receiving vital information for the first time. "Would you now describe, *in your own words,* what Detective Cross looked like at that time?" he asked.

The doorman hesitated and seemed slightly confused by the question. I wasn't. I knew where Halpern was going now.

"Was he dirty?" Halpern jumped in and asked the simplest possible question.

"Er, dirty . . . sure. He was a mess."

"And was he sweaty?" the defense lawyer asked.

"Sweaty . . . yeah. We all were. From being down in the garage, I guess. It was a real hot night."

"Nose running?"

"Yes, sir."

"Were Detective Cross's clothes ripped, Mr. Lopes?"

"Yes, they were. Ripped and dirty."

Jules Halpern looked at the jury first, then at his witness. "Were Detective Cross's clothes blood-stained?"

"Yes . . . they sure were. That's what I noticed first, the blood."

"Was the blood anywhere else, Mr. Lopes?"

"On his hands. You couldn't miss it. I sure didn't."

"And Mr. Shafer, how did Mr. Shafer look?"

"He was clean, not mussed at all. He seemed pretty calm and collected."

"Did you see any blood on Mr. Shafer?"

"No, sir. No blood."

Halpern nodded, then faced the jury. "Mr. Lopes, which of the two men looked more like someone who might have just committed a murder?"

"Detective Cross," the doorman said without hesitation.

"Objection!" the district attorney screamed, but not before the damage was done.

Chapter 84

THAT AFTERNOON, the defense was scheduled to call Chief of Detectives George Pittman. The assistant district attorney, Catherine Fitzgibbon, knew that Pittman was on the docket, and she asked me to meet her for lunch. "If you have an appetite before Pittman goes on," she added.

Catherine was smart, and she was thorough. She had put away nearly as many bad guys as Jules Halpern had set free. We got together over sandwiches at a crowded deli near the courthouse. Neither of us was thrilled about Pittman's upcoming appearance. My reputation as a detective was being ruined by the defense, and it was a hard thing to watch and do nothing.

She bit down into a hefty Reuben sandwich that squirted mustard onto her forefinger and thumb. Catherine smiled. "Sloppy, but worth it. You and Pittman are really at odds, right? More like you hate each other's guts?"

"It's serious dislike, and it's mutual," I told her. "He's tried to do me in a couple of times. He thinks I'm a threat to his career."

Catherine was attacking her sandwich. "*Hmmm,*

there's a thought. Would you be a better chief of detectives?"

"Wouldn't run, wouldn't serve if elected. I wouldn't be good cooped up in an office playing political Ping-Pong."

Catherine laughed. She's one of those people who can find humor almost anywhere. "This is just fricking great, Alex. The defense is calling the chief of detectives as one of *its* goddamn witnesses. He's listed as hostile, but I don't think he is."

Catherine and I finished off the rest of her sandwich. "Well, let's find out what Mr. Halpern has up his sleeve today," she said.

At the start of the afternoon session, Jules Halpern did a careful and thorough setup of Pittman's credentials, which sounded reasonably impressive in the abstract. Undergrad at George Washington, then law school at American; twenty-four years on the police force, with medals for bravery and citations from three different mayors.

"Chief Pittman, how would you describe Detective Cross's record in the department?" asked Halpern.

I cringed in my seat. Felt my brow wrinkle, my eyes narrow. *Here we go,* I thought.

"Detective Cross has been involved in some high-profile cases that the department has solved," he said, and left it at that. Not exactly praise, but at least he hadn't gone on the attack.

Halpern nodded sagely. "What, if anything, has changed his performance recently?"

Pittman looked my way, then answered. "A woman he was seeing disappeared while they were on a trip together in Bermuda. Since that time, he's been distracted and distant, quick to anger, not himself."

Suddenly I wanted to speak up in the courtroom. Pittman didn't know the first thing about Christine and me.

"Chief Pittman, was Detective Cross ever a suspect in the disappearance of his girlfriend, Mrs. Christine Johnson?"

Pittman nodded. "That's standard police procedure. I'm sure he was questioned."

"But his behavior on the job has changed since her disappearance?"

"Yes. His concentration isn't the same. He's missed days of work. It's all a matter of record."

"Has Detective Cross been asked to seek professional help?"

"Yes."

"Did you ask him to seek help yourself?"

"I did. He and I have worked together for a number of years. He was under stress."

"He's under a *lot* of stress? Is that fair to say?"

"Yes. He hadn't closed a single case recently."

Halpern nodded. "A couple of weeks before the Hampton homicide, you suspended some detectives he was friendly with."

Pittman's look was somber. "Unfortunately, I did."

"Why did you suspend the detectives?"

"The detectives were investigating cases outside the auspices of the department."

"Is it fair to say they were making up their own rules, acting like vigilantes?"

Catherine Fitzgibbon rose to her feet and objected, but Judge Fescoe allowed the question.

Pittman answered, "I don't know about that. *Vigilantes* is a strong word. But they were working without proper supervision. The case is still under investigation."

"Was Detective Cross part of the group that was making up its own rules to solve homicides?"

"I'm not certain. But he was spoken to about the matter. I didn't believe he could handle a suspension at that time. I warned him and let it slide. I shouldn't have," said Pittman.

"No further questions."

None needed, I thought.

Chapter 85

THAT NIGHT, after he left the courthouse, Shafer was flying high. He thought that he was winning the game. He was manic as hell, and it felt both good and bad. He was parked in the dark garage under Boo Cassady's building. Most manics aren't really aware of it when they're exhibiting signs of a manic episode, but Shafer knew. His "spirals" didn't come out of nowhere; they built and built.

The irony and the danger of being back in her building weren't lost on him. Scene of the crime, and all that rot. He wanted to go to Southeast tonight, but that was too risky. He couldn't hunt—not now. He had something else in mind: the next few moves in his game.

It was unusual, though not unheard-of, for the defendant in a first-degree homicide trial to be out roaming the streets, but that had been one of the prerequisites of his dropping his immunity. What choice did the prosecution have? None at all. If the D.A. hadn't agreed, he had a free pass to keep him out of jail.

Shafer followed a tenant he'd seen several times into the lift from the garage and took it to Boo's apartment. He rang the doorbell. Waited. Heard her padding across the parquet floor. Yes, Act One of tonight's performance was about to begin.

He knew she was watching him through the door's peephole, just as he had watched Alex Cross through it on the night Patsy Hampton got her just desserts. He had seen Boo a few times after his release, but then he'd cut her off.

When he'd stopped seeing her, she lost it. Boo had called him at work, then at home, and constantly on his car phone, until he changed the bloody number. At her worst, she reminded him of the nutcase Glenn Close had played in the movie *Fatal Attraction.*

He wondered if he could still push her buttons. She was a fairly bright woman, and that was a large part of her problem. She thought far too much, double- and triple-think. Most men, especially dull-witted Americans, didn't like that, which made her even crazier.

He put his face against the door, felt its cool wood on his cheek. He started his act.

"I've been petrified to see you, Boo. You don't know what it's been like. One slipup, anything they can use against me, and I'm finished. And what makes it worse is that I'm innocent. You know that. I talked to you the whole time from my house to yours that night. You know I didn't kill that detective. Elizabeth? Boo? Please say something. At least curse at me. Let the anger out . . . Doctor?"

There was no answer. He rather liked that. It made him respect her more than he had. What the hell, she was more screwed up than he was.

"You know exactly what I'm going through. You're the only one who understands my episodes. I need you, Boo. You know I'm manic-depressive, bipolar, whatever the hell you shrinks want to call my condition. Boo?"

Then Shafer actually started to cry, which nearly made him laugh. He uttered loud, wrenching sobs. He crouched on his haunches and held his head. He knew he was a far better actor than so many of the high-priced fakers he saw in the movies.

The door to the apartment slowly opened. "Boo-hoo," she whispered. "Is poor Geoff in pain? What a shame."

What a bitch, he thought, but he had to see her. She was testifying soon. He needed her tonight, and he needed her help in the courtroom.

"Hello, Boo," he whispered back.

Chapter 86

ACT TWO of the evening's performance.

She stared at him with huge dark-brown eyes that looked like amber beads, the kind she bought at her swanky shops. She'd lost weight, but that made her sexier to him, more desperate. She wore navy walking shorts and an elegant pink silk T-shirt—but she also wore her pain.

"You hurt me like no one ever has before," she whispered.

He held himself under control, playacting, a truly award-winning performance. "I'm fighting for my life. I swear, all I think about is killing myself. Haven't you heard anything I've said? Besides, do you want your picture all over the tabloids again? Don't you see? That's why I've been staying away from you."

She laughed bitterly, haughtily. "It's going to happen anyway when I testify. The photographers will be everywhere I go."

Shafer shut his eyes. "Well, that will be your chance to hurt me back, darling."

She shook her head and frowned. "You know I

wouldn't do that. Oh, Geoff, why didn't you at least call? You're such a bastard."

Shafer hung his head, the repentant bad boy. "You know how close I was to the edge before all this happened. Now it's worse. Do you expect me to act like a responsible adult?"

She gave a wry smile. He saw a book on the hallway table behind her: *Man and His Symbols.* Carl Jung. How fitting. "No, I suppose not, Geoff. What do you want? Drugs?"

"I need you. I want to hold you, Boo. That's all."

That night, she gave him what he wanted. They made love like animals on the gray velvet love seat she used for her clients, then on the JFK-style rocking chair where she always sat during sessions. He took her body—and her soul.

Then she gave him drugs—antidepressants, painkillers, most of her samples. Boo was still able to get the samples from her ex, a psychiatrist. Shafer didn't know what *their* relationship was, and frankly, he didn't care. He swallowed some Librium and shot up Vicodin at her place.

Then he took Boo again, both of them naked and sweating and frenzied on the kitchen counter. *The butcher block,* he thought.

He left her place around eleven. He realized he was feeling worse than before he'd gone there. But he knew what he was going to do. He'd known before he went to Boo's. It would explode their little minds. Everyone's. The press. The jury.

Now for Act Three.

Chapter 87

AT A little past midnight, I got an emergency call that blew off the top of my head. Within minutes I had the old Porsche up close to ninety on Rock Creek Parkway, the siren screaming at the night, or maybe at Geoffrey Shafer.

I arrived in Kalorama at 12:25. EMS ambulances, squad cars, TV news trucks were parked all over the street.

Several neighbors of the Shafers' were up and had come outside their large, expensive houses to observe the nightmare scene. They couldn't believe this was happening in their upscale enclave.

The chatter and buzz of several police radios filled the night air. A news helicopter was already hovering overhead. A truck marked CNN arrived and parked right behind me.

I joined a detective named Malcolm Ainsley on the front lawn. We knew each other from other homicide scenes, even a few parties. Suddenly, the front door of the Shafer house opened.

Two EMTs were carrying a stretcher outside. Dozens of cameras were flashing.

"It's Shafer," Ainsley told me. "Son of a bitch tried to kill himself, Alex. Slit his wrist and took a lot of drugs. There were open prescription packets everywhere. Must've had second thoughts, though. Called for help."

I had enough information about Shafer from the discovery interviews preceding the trial, and from my own working profile on him, to begin to make some very educated guesses about what might have happened. My first thought was that he suffered from some kind of bipolar disorder that caused both manic and depressive episodes. A second possibility was cyclohymia, which can manifest itself in numerous hypomanic episodes as well as depressive symptoms. Its associated symptoms could include inflated self-esteem, a decreased need for sleep, excessive involvement in "pleasurable" activities, and an increase in goal-directed activity—in Shafer's case, maybe, an intensified effort to win his game.

I moved forward as if I were floating in a very bad dream, the worst I could imagine. I recognized one of the EMS techies, Nina Disesa. I'd worked with her a few times before in Georgetown.

"We got to the bastard just in time," Nina said, and narrowed her dark eyes. "Too bad, huh?"

"Serious attempt?" I asked her.

Nina shrugged. "Hard to tell for sure. He hacked up his wrist pretty good. Just the left one, though. Then the drugs, *lots* of drugs—doctors' samples."

I shook my head in utter disbelief. "But he definitely called out for help?"

"According to the wife and son, they heard him call out from his den, 'Daddy needs help. Daddy is dying. Daddy is sick.'"

"Well, he got *that* part right. Daddy is incredibly sick. Daddy is a monumental sicko."

I went over to the red and white ambulance. News cameras were still flashing all over the street. My mind was unhinged, reeling. *Everything is a game to him. The victims in Southeast, Patsy Hampton, Christine. Now this. He's even playing with his own life.*

"His pulse is still strong," I heard as I got close to the ambulance. I could see one of the EMT workers checking the EKG inside the van. I could even hear beeps from the machine.

Then I saw Shafer's face. His hair was drenched with perspiration, and his face was as pale as a sheet of white paper. He stared into my eyes, trying to focus. Then he recognized me.

"You did this to me," he said, mustering strength, suddenly trying to sit up on the stretcher. "You ruined my life for your career. You did this! You're responsible! Oh, God, oh, God. My poor family! Why is this happening to us?"

The TV cameras were rolling film, and they got his entire Academy Award–quality performance. Just as Geoffrey Shafer knew they would.

Chapter 88

THE TRIAL had to be recessed due to Shafer's suicide attempt. The courtroom shenanigans probably wouldn't resume until the following week.

Meanwhile, the media had another feeding frenzy, including banner headlines in the *Washington Post,* the *New York Times, USA Today.* At least it gave me time to work on a few more angles. Shafer was good—God, he was good at this.

I had been talking with Sandy Greenberg nearly every night. She was helping me collect information on the other game players. She had even gone and talked with Conqueror. She said she doubted that Oliver Highsmith was a killer. He was late-sixties, seriously overweight, and wheelchair-bound.

Sandy called the house at seven that night. She's a good friend. Obviously, she was burning the midnight oil for me. I took the call in the sanctuary of my attic office.

"Andrew Jones of the Security Service will see you," she announced in her usual perky and aggressive manner. "Isn't that great news? I'll tell you: *it is.* Actually, he's eager to meet with you, Alex. He didn't say it to me directly, but I don't think he's too keen on Colonel Shafer. Wouldn't say why. Even more fortuitous, he's in Washington. He's a top man. He matters in the intelligence arena. He's very good, Alex, a straight shooter."

I thanked Sandy and then immediately called Jones at his hotel. He answered the call in his room. "Yes. Hello. It's Andrew Jones. Who is this, please?"

"It's Detective Alex Cross of the Washington police. I just got off the line with Sandy Greenberg. How are you?"

"Good, very good. Well, hell, not really. I've had better weeks, months. Actually, I stayed here in my room hoping that you'd call. Would you like to meet, Alex? Is there someplace where we wouldn't stand out too much?"

I suggested a bar on M Street in half an hour, and I arrived there a minute or two early. I recognized Jones from his description on the phone: "Broad, beefy, red-faced. Just your average ex-rugby type—though I never bloody played, don't even watch the drivel. Oh, yes, flaming red hair and matching mustache. That should help, no?"

It did. We sat in a dark booth in back and got to know each other. For the next forty-five minutes, Jones filled me in on several important things, not the least of which was politics and decorum within the English intelligence and police communities; Lucy Shafer's father's good name and standing in the army, and the concern for his reputation; and the desire of the government to avoid an even dicier scandal than the current mess.

"Alex, if it were true that one of our agents committed cold-blooded murders while posted abroad, and that British intelligence knew nothing about it, the scandal would be a true horror and a major embarrassment. But if MI-Six *knew anything* about what Colonel Shafer is suspected of doing! Well, it's absolutely unthinkable."

"Did it?" I asked him. "Is this situation unthinkable?"

"I won't answer that, Alex—you know I can't. But I am prepared to help you if I possibly can."

"Why?" I asked, then, "Why now? We needed your help on this before the trial began."

"Fair question, good question. We're prepared to help because you now have information that could cause us a hell of a lot of trouble. You're privy to the *unthinkable.*"

I said nothing. I thought I knew what he was alluding to, though.

"You've discovered a fantasy game called the Four Horsemen. There are four players, including Shafer. We know you've already contacted Oliver Highsmith. What you probably don't know yet, but will find out eventually, is that all the players are former or current agents. That is to say, Geoffrey Shafer might be just the beginning of our problems."

"All four of them are murderers?" I asked.

Andrew Jones didn't answer; he didn't have to.

Chapter 89

"WE THINK that the 'game' originated in Bangkok, where three of the four players were posted in 'ninety-one. The fourth, Highsmith, was a mentor to George Bayer, who is Famine in the Four Horsemen. Highsmith has always worked out of London."

"Tell me about Highsmith," I said.

"As I said, he's always been in the main office, London. He was a high-level analyst, then he actually ran several agents. He's a very bright chap, well thought of."

"He claimed that the Four Horsemen was just a harmless fantasy game."

"It may be for him, Alex. He may be telling the truth. He's been in a wheelchair since 'eighty-five. Automobile accident. His wife had just left him, and he cracked. He's an enormous fellow, about three hundred pounds. I doubt that he's getting about and murdering young women in the scuffier neighborhoods of London. That's what you believe Shafer was doing here in Washington? The Jane Doe murders?"

Jones was right, and I didn't deny it. "We know he was involved in several murders, and I think we were close to catching him. He was picking up his victims in a gypsy taxicab. We found the cab. Yes, we knew about him, Andrew."

Jones tented his thick fingers, pursed his lips. "You think Shafer knew how close you and Detective Hampton were getting?"

"He may have known, but there was also a lot of pressure on him. He made some mistakes that led us to an apartment he rented."

Jones nodded. He seemed to know a great deal about Shafer, which told me he'd been watching him, too. Had he been watching me as well?

"How do you think the other game players might react to Shafer's being so out of control?" I asked.

"I'm fairly sure they felt threatened. Who wouldn't? He was a risk to all of them. He still is." Jones continued, "So, we have Shafer, who's probably been committing murders here in Washington, acting out his fantasies in real life. And Highsmith, who probably couldn't do that, but could be a sort of controller. Then there's a man named James Whitehead, in Jamaica, but there have been no murders of the Jane Doe variety on that island or any other one nearby. We've checked thoroughly. And there's George Bayer in the Far East."

"What about Bayer? I assume you've investigated him, too."

"Of course. There's nothing specific in his

record, but there was an incident, a possible connection, to follow up on. Last year in Bangkok, two girls who worked in a strip bar in Pat Pong disappeared. They just vanished into the noisy, teeming streets. The girls were sixteen and eighteen, respectively, bar dancers and prostitutes. Alex, they were found nailed together in the missionary position, wearing only garters and stockings. Even in jolly old Bangkok, that caused quite a stir. Sound distressingly similar to the two girls who were killed in Eckington?"

I nodded. "So we have at least two unsolved Jane Does in Bangkok. Has anyone actually questioned Bayer?"

"At this point, no, but he's being watched. Remember the politics, the fear of a scandal that I mentioned earlier? There's an ongoing investigation of Bayer and the others, but to some extent our hands are tied."

"*My* hands aren't tied," I said to Jones. "That's what you wanted me to say, isn't it? What you expected? It's why you met with me tonight?"

Jones turned very serious. "It's how the world works, I'm afraid. Let's do this together from here on. If you help us . . . I promise to do what I can to find out what happened to Christine Johnson."

Chapter 90

THE TRIAL resumed sooner than expected—
the following Wednesday, in fact. There was specu-
lation in the press about how serious Shafer's self-
inflicted wounds had been. None of the public's
perverse interest in the case seemed to have been lost.

It seemed impossible to predict the outcome, a
fact of life I tried not to let get me down too much.
Both Shafer and I were present in the packed courtroom that first morning back. Shafer looked pale,
weak—an object of sympathy, perhaps. I certainly
couldn't take my eyes off him.

Things got stranger and stranger. At least they
did for me. Sergeant Walter Jamieson was called
that morning. Jamieson had been at the Police
Academy when I attended it. He had taught me
my craft, and he was still there, teaching others. I
couldn't imagine why he would be called as a witness in Patsy Hampton's murder case.

Jules Halpern approached the witness with a
heavy-looking hardback book open in his hands.

"I read to you from the textbook *Preserving the
Crime Scene: A Detective's Primer,* which you wrote

twenty years ago and which you still use in your classes: 'It is *imperative* that the detective not disturb the crime scene until backup can be brought in to corroborate charges effected by the detective to unearth evidence, lest those charges be misconstrued to be those of the perpetration. Gloves *must* be worn at all times at a crime scene.' Did you write that, Sergeant Jamieson?"

"Yes, I did. Most certainly. Twenty years ago, as you said."

"Still stand by it?" Halpern asked.

"Yes, of course. A lot of things have changed, but not that."

"And you heard earlier testimony that Detective Cross wore gloves both inside Detective Hampton's car and at the Cassady apartment?"

"Yes, I heard the testimony. I also read the grand-jury transcripts."

Halpern turned on the overhead projector in the courtroom. "I direct your attention to prints number one-seventy-six and two-eleven provided by the D.A.'s office. You see the ones denominated?"

"Numbers one-seventy-six and two-eleven. I see them."

"Now, the prints are denominated 'Detective Hampton Belt Buckle: ID: Alex Cross/Right Thumb' and 'Left Side Dashboard: ID: Alex Cross/Left Forefinger.' What does that mean? Can you explain the markings to us?"

"It means that Alex Cross's prints were found on

Detective Hampton's belt as well as on the dashboard of her car."

Jules Halpern paused for a full ten seconds before he went on. "And may we not therefore conclude, Sergeant Jamieson, that Detective Cross himself may be our murderer and rapist?"

"Objection!" Catherine Fitzgibbon stood up and shouted.

"Withdrawn," said the defense attorney. "I'm finished here."

Chapter 91

LAWYERS FOR both the prosecution and the defense continued to appear regularly on Larry King and other TV shows, and to boast that their cases were "slam dunks." If you listened to the lawyers, neither side could lose.

In the courtroom, Jules Halpern had the fierce look and body language of someone brimming with confidence and determination. He was riding the case hard. He looked like a jockey whipping his Thoroughbred to victory.

The bailiff stood and announced, "The defense calls Mr. William Payaz."

I didn't recognize the name. Now what? Now *who?*

There was no immediate response in the courtroom.

No one came forward.

Heads craned around the room. Still, no one responded. Who was the mystery witness?

The bailiff repeated, a little louder, "Mr. Payaz. Mr. William Payaz."

The double doors in the back of the room suddenly opened, and a circus-style clown walked in. The gallery began to whisper loudly, and a few people laughed. What a world we lived in; what a circus, indeed.

The clown took the stand, and both the prosecution and the defense were immediately called forward for a sidebar by Judge Fescoe. A heated discussion ensued that none of the rest of us could hear. The clown issue was apparently resolved in favor of the defense. After being sworn in, the clown was asked his name for the record.

With his white-gloved right hand raised, he said, "Billy."

The bailiff asked, "Last name, please?"

The clown said, "First name, Silly. Last name, Billy. Silly Billy. I had it legally changed," he turned and confided to the judge.

Jules Halpern then took over, and he treated the clown with respect and seriousness. First, he asked him to state his credentials, which the clown did, politely. Then Halpern asked, "And what brings you here today?"

"I did a party for Mr. Shafer out in Kalorama on the fateful and terrible night of the murder. It was his twins' fifth birthday. I did a party when they were four as well. I brought a video along. Want to see?" he said, speaking as if he were addressing a crowd of three-year-olds.

"Of course," said Jules Halpern.

"Objection!" Catherine Fitzgibbon called out loudly.

The video was admitted over the prosecution's objections and after yet another lengthy sidebar. The newspapers had claimed that Judge Fescoe was intimidated by Jules Halpern, which seemed the case.

The tape began with an arresting close-up of a painting of a clown's face. As the camera pulled back, everyone in the courtroom could see it was the sign on Silly Billy's van, which was parked in front of a handsome redbrick town house with a glass conservatory linked to the main building. The Shafer house.

The next scene showed Silly Billy ringing the front bell and apparently surprising the Shafer children at the door.

Once again, the prosecution objected to the videotape. There was another sidebar. The lawyers returned to their seats, and the tape resumed.

The other children at the birthday party then ran to the door. The clown handed out toys from a sack slung over his shoulder—teddy bears, dolls, shiny red fire trucks.

Silly Billy then performed magic tricks and gags on the sun porch, which looked out onto the backyard. The yard was very pretty, with potted orange trees, white climbing roses, a jasmine vine, lush green grass.

"Wait! I hear something outside!" he turned and said into the camera. He ran and disappeared from sight.

The kids all followed. The tension of surprise

and imminent fun showed in the children's eyes.

A cream-colored pony appeared, cantering slowly around the corner of the house. Silly Billy was riding the pony.

But when the clown dismounted, the kids discovered that the clown was actually Geoffrey Shafer! All the kids went wild, but especially the Shafer twins. They ran and hugged their daddy, who seemed the perfect father.

There were heartwarming candid shots of the children eating frosted cake and playing party games. There were more shots of Shafer laughing and playing with several of the children. I suspected that Jules Halpern had supervised the final editing of the tape. It was very convincing.

The adult guests at the party, all dressed up and looking sophisticated, gave glowing testimonials. They said that Geoffrey Shafer and his wife were outstanding parents. No longer in his clown costume but in a smart navy suit, Shafer modestly deflected the tributes. He had changed into the same clothes he wore when he was apprehended at the Farragut.

The tape ended with the smiling and quite beautiful twins telling the camera that they loved their mommy and daddy for making their "dream come true." The lights came up. The judge granted a brief recess.

I felt incredibly angry that the video had been shown. It made Shafer out to be a wonderful father—and such a *victim*.

The jury was all smiles, and so was Jules Halpern. He had argued masterfully that the tape was crucial to establishing Geoffrey Shafer's state of mind shortly before Patsy Hampton's murder. Halpern was so skillful an orator that he'd actually made the outrageous request to show the video sound logical. At any rate, it was moot now.

Shafer himself was smiling broadly, as were his wife and son. It suddenly occurred to me that Shafer had been riding a pale horse at the party for his children. He was Death, from the Four Horsemen.

It was all theater and games to him, his entire life.

Chapter 92

SOMETIMES I wanted to shut my eyes tight and not have to watch another moment of the trial. I wanted things to be the way they'd been before the Weasel.

Catherine Fitzgibbon was doing a very good job with each witness, but the judge seemed to be favoring the defense whenever possible. It had begun at the critical suppression hearing, and it continued now.

Lucy Shafer took the witness stand early that afternoon. The warm, homespun videotaped images of the Shafer family were still fresh in the minds of the jurors.

I had been trying to understand Lucy Shafer's odd and perplexing relationship with her husband since the first time I met her, on the night of Patsy Hampton's murder. What kind of woman could live with an unrepentant monster like Shafer and not know it? Could this woman be that much in denial? Or was there something else that motivated her, somehow held her captive to Shafer? I had seen all kinds of marital relationships in my therapy practice, but nothing like this.

Jane Halpern conducted the questioning, and looked every bit as confident and winning as her father. She was tall and slender, with wiry black hair tied in a bow with a dark-crimson ribbon. She was twenty-eight, just four years out of Yale Law School, but seemed older and wiser.

"Mrs. Shafer, how long have you and your husband known each other?"

Lucy Shafer spoke in a gentle but clear voice. "I've known Geoffrey for most of my adult life, actually. My father was his commanding officer in the army. I believe I was just fourteen when I first met Geoff. He was nine years older. We married when I was nineteen, after my second year at Cambridge. Once, when I was studying for exams, he showed up at university in full military dress— polished saber, medals, shiny black leather riding boots—right in the middle of the library. I was studying in a sweatshirt or some such awful getup, and I don't think I'd washed my hair in days. Geoff told me it didn't matter. He didn't care a bit about appearances. He said he loved me and always would. I must tell you, he's kept that promise."

"Very nice," Jane Halpern said, seemingly utterly charmed, as if she'd never heard the story before. "And has he remained romantic?"

"Oh, yes, even more so. Scarcely a week goes by when Geoff doesn't bring me flowers, or perhaps a beautiful Hermès scarf, which I collect. And then there are our 'ouch' excursions."

Jane Halpern wrinkled her nose, and her dark-brown eyes twinkled. "What are 'ouch' excursions?" she asked with the exuberant curiosity of a morning TV-show host.

"Geoff will take me to New York, or maybe Paris, or back to London, and I get to shop for clothes until he says 'ouch.' He's very generous, that way."

"A good husband, then?"

"The best you could imagine. Very hardworking, but not so much that he forgets about his family. The children adore him."

"Yes, we could tell that from this morning's film, Mrs. Shafer. Was the party an unusual occasion?"

"No. Geoffrey's always throwing parties. He's very joyful, full of life, full of fun and surprises. He's a sensitive, very creative man."

I looked from Lucy Shafer to the jury box. She had the jurors in a spell, and they couldn't take their eyes off her. She was also credible. Even I had the sense that she genuinely loved her husband, and more important, that she believed *he* loved *her.*

Jane Halpern milked the testimony for all it was worth. I couldn't blame her. Lucy Shafer was attractive and seemed nice, kind, and obviously was very much in love with her husband and adored her children, but she didn't appear to be a fool. Just someone who had found exactly the man she wanted and valued him deeply. That man was Geoffrey Shafer.

It was the indelible image the jurors took away with them at the end of the day.

And it was an amazing lie, spun by a master.

Chapter 93

I TALKED things over with Andrew Jones when I got home after court that afternoon. I'd tried to contact Oliver Highsmith again, but so far hadn't gotten any response. Also, there was nothing new to link Shafer to the Jane Doe murders in Washington. Shafer didn't seem to have murdered anyone, at least locally, in the past several months.

After a dinner of chicken pot pie, salad, and rhubarb pie, Nana gave the kids the night off from their chore of doing the dishes. She asked me to stay and help, to be her "partner in grime," as we used to call it.

"Just like the good old days, same as it ever was," I said as I splashed soap and water onto silver and dishes in the porcelain sink that's as old as the house.

Nana dried the kitchenware as quickly as I got it to her. Her fingers were still as nimble as her mind. "I like to think we're older *and* wiser," she chirped.

"I don't know. I'm still the one getting dishwater hands."

"I haven't told you something, and I should have," Nana said, going serious on me.

"Okay," I said, and stopped splashing water and soap bubbles around in the sink. "Shoot."

"What I wanted to say is that I'm proud of the way you've been able to handle the terrible things that have happened. Your strength and your patience have given me inspiration. And I'm not easily inspired, especially by the likes of you. I know it has had the same effect on Damon and Jannie. They don't miss a thing."

I leaned over the sink. I was feeling in a confessional mood. "It's the worst stretch of my life, the hardest thing I've ever had to do. It's even worse than when Maria died, Nana, if that's possible. At least back then I knew for sure she was dead. I could let myself grieve. I could finally let her go and breathe again."

Nana came around the sink and took me in her arms, which always surprised me with their strength.

She looked me squarely in the eyes, just like she always has since I was around nine years old. She said, "Let yourself grieve for her, Alex. Let her go."

Chapter 94

GEOFFREY SHAFER had an attractive, loving wife, and that incongruous and monstrously unfair fact bothered me a lot. I couldn't understand it as a psychologist or as a detective.

The clever testimony of Lucy Shafer continued early the following morning and lasted just over an hour. Jane Halpern wanted the jury to hear more about Lucy's wonderful husband.

Finally, it was Catherine Fitzgibbon's turn. In her own way, she was as tough, and maybe as formidable, as Jules Halpern.

"Mrs. Shafer, we've all been listening to you intently, and it all sounds very charming and idyllic, but I'm troubled and confused by something. Here's what troubles me: your husband tried to commit suicide eight days ago. Your husband tried to kill himself. So maybe he isn't quite what he seems to be. Maybe he isn't so well balanced and sane. Maybe you're mistaken about who he really is."

Lucy Shafer stared directly into the prosecuting attorney's eyes. "In the past few months, my husband has seen his life, his career, and his good name falsely put in jeopardy. My husband couldn't believe that these horrible charges were made against him. This whole Kafkaesque ordeal drove him, quite literally, to despair. You have no idea what it means to lose your good name."

Catherine Fitzgibbon smiled and then quipped, "Sure I do. Of course I do. Haven't you read the *National Enquirer* lately?" That got a laugh from the courtroom audience, even the jury members. I could tell that they liked Catherine. So did I.

She continued, "Isn't it true that your husband has been treated for 'despair' for many years? He's seeing a psychologist, Mrs. Shafer. He suffers from manic depression, or bipolar disorder, correct?"

Lucy shook her head. "He's had a midlife crisis. That's all it is. It's nothing unusual for men his age."

"I see. And were you able to help him with his crisis?"

"Of course I was. Although not with respect to his work. So much of what he does is classified and top-secret. You must understand that."

"I must," the prosecutor said, then quickly went on, "So your husband has a great many secrets he keeps from you?"

Lucy frowned, and her eyes shot darts at the wily prosecutor. "In his *work,* yes."

"You knew that he was seeing Dr. Cassady? Boo Cassady?"

"Yes, of course I did. We often talked about it."

"How often did he see her? Do you know? Did he tell you that? Or was it *top-secret*?"

Jane Halpern shouted, "Objection!"

"Sustained. Ms. Fitzgibbon," warned Judge Fescoe, with an arched brow.

"Sorry, Your Honor. Sorry, Lucy. All right, then. How often did your husband see Boo Cassady?"

"He saw her as much as necessary, I suppose. I believe her name is *Elizabeth*."

"Once a week? Twice? Every day?" Fitzgibbon pressed on, without missing a beat.

"I think once a week. Usually it was once a week."

"But the doormen at the Farragut testified that they saw your husband much more than that. Three or four times a week, on average."

Lucy Shafer shook her head wearily and glared at Fitzgibbon. "I trust Geoffrey completely. I don't keep a leash on him. I certainly wouldn't *count* his therapy sessions."

"Did you mind that Dr. Cassady—*Elizabeth*—was such an attractive woman?"

"No. Don't be absurd."

Fitzgibbon looked genuinely surprised. "Why is that absurd? I don't think it is. I think *I'd* mind if my husband was seeing an attractive woman at her home-office two, three, four times a week."

Fitzgibbon moved swiftly. "Didn't it bother you that Boo Cassady was a surrogate *sex* therapist for your husband?"

Lucy Shafer hesitated, seemed surprised, and glanced quickly at her husband. *She hadn't known.* It was impossible not to feel sorry for her.

Jane Halpern quickly rose from her seat.

"Objection! Your Honor, there is no foundation that my client was seeing a sex surrogate."

Lucy Shafer visibly pulled herself together on the witness stand. She was clearly stronger than she looked. Was she a game player, too? Could she be one of the players? Or did she and her husband play a completely different kind of game?

She spoke. "I'd like to answer the question. Madam Prosecutor, my husband, Geoffrey, has been such a good husband, such a good father, that even if he felt it necessary to see a sex therapist, and did *not* want to tell me about it because of the hurt or shame he felt, I would understand."

"And if he committed *cold-blooded murder*—and did not want to tell you?" the prosecutor asked, then turned to the jury.

Chapter 95

ELIZABETH "BOO" cassady was in her late thirties, slender and very attractive, with lustrous brown hair that she had worn long since she was a young girl. She was a regular shopper at Neiman Marcus, Saks, Nordstrom, Bloomingdale's, and various chic specialty shops around Washington. It showed.

She had gotten the nickname Boo as an infant because she always laughed and laughed whenever she heard the sound of somebody playing peek-a-boo with her. She soon learned to do it herself, muttering *"boo, boo, boo, boo."* In school, right through college, she kept the name, friends said, because she could be a little scary at times.

For her important day in court she'd chosen a single-breasted pantsuit, beautifully cut, very soft and flowy. Her outfit was an eye-pleasing mix of coffee and cashmere cream. She looked like a professional person, and a successful one.

Jules Halpern asked her to state her name and occupation for the record. He was amiable but businesslike, a little cooler than he had been with other witnesses.

"Dr. Elizabeth Cassady. I'm a psychotherapist," she replied evenly.

"Dr. Cassady, how do you know Colonel Shafer?"

"He's a patient of mine, and has been for over a year. He sees me at my office at twelve-oh-eight Woodley Avenue once or twice a week. We increased the frequency of the sessions recently, after Mr. Shafer's attempted suicide."

Halpern nodded. "What time are the sessions?"

"Usually early evening. They can vary according to Mr. Shafer's work schedule."

"Dr. Cassady, I direct your attention to the evening of the murder of Detective Hampton. Did Geoffrey Shafer have a therapy session with you that night?"

"Yes, he did. At nine P.M., from nine until ten. I think he may have arrived a little earlier that night. But the session was scheduled for nine."

"Could he have arrived as early as eight-thirty?"

"No. That isn't possible. We were talking to each other on cell phones from the time he left his house in Kalorama until he arrived at my building. He was feeling a great deal of guilt about his latest dark mood's coming too close to his daughters' birthday party."

"I see. Was there any break in your conversation with Colonel Shafer?"

"Yes. But it was a very short one."

Halpern kept the pace brisk. "How much time passed between the time the two of you stopped talking on the cell phone and his arrival at your office?"

"Two or three minutes—five at the most. While he parked and came upstairs. No more than that."

"When he arrived at your office, did Geoffrey Shafer seem unsettled in any way?"

"No, not at all. He appeared relatively cheerful, actually. He had just hosted a successful birthday party for the twins. He felt it had gone very well, and he dotes on his children."

"Was he out of breath, tense, or perspiring?" Halpern asked.

"No. As I said, he was calm and looked quite fine. I remember it very clearly. And after the intrusion by the police, I made careful *notes* to keep everything accurate and fresh," she said, then glanced at the prosecution table.

"So you made notes for the sake of accuracy?"

"Yes, I did."

"Dr. Cassady, did you notice any blood anywhere on Colonel Shafer's clothing?"

"No, I did not."

"I see. You saw no blood on Shafer. And when Detective Cross arrived, did you see any blood on him?"

"Yes, I saw dark stains or streaks of blood on his shirt and suit coat. Also on his hands."

Jules Halpern paused to let everything sink in

with the jury. Then he asked a final question: "Did Colonel Shafer look as if he had just murdered someone?"

"No, certainly not."

"I have nothing further," said the defense attorney.

Daniel Weston did the cross-exam for the prosecution. He was twenty-nine years old, bright, quick-witted, a rising star—and known to be a ruthless hatchet man in the prosecutor's office.

Dan Weston was also good-looking, blond, and rugged. He got physically close to Boo Cassady. They made a fetching couple, which was precisely the visual idea he wanted to communicate.

"Ms. Cassady, you weren't Mr. Shafer's *psychiatrist,* were you?"

She frowned slightly, but then managed a weak smile. "No, a psychiatrist has to be a medical doctor. You know that, I'm sure."

"And you are not a medical doctor?"

She shook her head. "I am not. I have a doctorate in sociology. You know that, too."

"Are you a *psychologist?*" Weston asked.

"A psychologist usually has a graduate degree in psychology, sometimes a Ph.D."

"Do you have a graduate degree in psychology?"

"No. I'm a psychotherapist."

"I see. Where did you train to be a psychotherapist?"

"American University. I graduated with a Ph.D. in Social Work."

Daniel Weston kept coming at Cassady. There was hardly a beat between answer and question. "This 'psychotherapy office' of yours at the Farragut, what sort of furnishings does it have?"

"A couch, desk, lamp. It's basically very spare. Lots of plants, though. My patients find the atmosphere functional but also relaxing."

"No box of tissues by the couch? I thought that was a must," Weston said with a wry smile.

The witness was clearly annoyed now, and maybe even shaken. "I take my work very seriously, Mr. Weston. So do my patients."

"Was Geoffrey Shafer referred to you by someone?"

"Actually, we met at the National Gallery . . . at the Picasso erotic-drawings exhibit. That's been covered in depth by the press."

Weston nodded, and a thin smile crossed his lips. "Ah, I see. Are your sessions with Geoffrey Shafer erotic? Do you ever discuss sex?"

Jules Halpern rose quickly—a regular Jules-in-the-box. "Objection! Doctor-patient privilege. It's confidential."

The young prosecutor shrugged and flipped back his blond curls with his hand. "I'll withdraw the question. No problem. Are you a sexual surrogate?"

"No, I am not. As I stated earlier, I am a psychotherapist."

"On the evening of the murder of Detective Hampton, did you and Geoffrey Shafer discuss—"

Jules Halpern quickly rose again. "Objection. If the prosecution is inquiring into the patient's privileged disclosures—"

Weston raised both arms in frustration. He smiled at the jurors, hoping they felt the same way. "All right, all right. Let me see. I'll take this out of the so-called doctor-patient realm and ask you, quite simply, if you, Ms. Cassady, a woman, have had sexual relations with Geoffrey Shafer, a man?"

Elizabeth "Boo" Cassady hung her head and stared down at her lap.

Daniel Weston smiled, even as Jules Halpern objected to the question and was upheld by Judge Fescoe. Weston felt that he had made his point.

Chapter 96

"CALL DETECTIVE Alex Cross."

I took a deep breath, composed my mind, body, and soul, then walked up the wide center aisle of the courtroom to testify. Everyone in the room was watching me, but the only person I really saw was Geoffrey Shafer. The Weasel. He was still playing the part of the wronged innocent man, and I wanted to bring him down. I wanted to cross-examine him myself, to ask the real questions that needed to be asked, to tell the jury about all the suppressed evidence, to bring justice down on him with all its crushing force.

It was a hard thing to have worked honestly for so many years and now to be accused of being a rogue cop, someone who had tampered with evidence and perhaps worse. It was ironic, but now maybe I would have the opportunity to set the record straight, to clear my name.

Jules Halpern smiled cordially at me as I sat down in the witness stand. He established eye contact, quickly looked over at the jury, then turned back to me. His dark eyes radiated intelligence, and it seemed an incredible waste that he was working for Shafer.

"I want to start by saying that it is an honor to meet you, Detective Cross. For years I, like most of the jurors, I'm sure, have read in the Washington papers about the murder cases you have helped solve. We admire your past record."

I nodded and even managed a grudging smile of my own. "Thank you. I hope you'll admire my present and future record as well," I said.

"Let's hope so, Detective," Halpern said. He moved on. We parried for half an hour or so before he asked, "You suffered a terrible personal tragedy a short time before the arrest of Colonel Shafer—could you tell us about it?"

I fought the urge to reach out and grab the polite-sounding, insidious little man by the neck. I leaned closer to the mike, struggled for control.

"Someone dear to me was kidnapped while we were in Bermuda on vacation. She's still missing. I haven't given up hope that she'll be found. I pray every day that she's still alive."

Halpern clucked sympathetically. He was good, much like his client. "I really am sorry. Did the department give you adequate time off?"

"They were understanding and helpful," I said, feeling my jaw stiffen with resentment. I hated that Halpern was using what had happened to Christine to unsettle me.

"Detective, were you officially back on active duty at the time of Detective Hampton's murder?"

"Yes, I went back on full-time duty about a week before the murder."

"Was it requested that you stay off active duty for a while longer?"

"It was left up to me. The chief of detectives did question my ability to resume my duties, but he made it my choice."

Halpern nodded thoughtfully. "He felt your head might be elsewhere? Who could blame you if it was?"

"I was upset, I still am, but I've been able to work. It's been good for me. The right thing to do."

There were several more questions about my state of mind, and then Halpern asked, "When you found out that Detective Hampton had been murdered, how upset were you?"

"I did my job. It was a bad homicide scene." *Your client is a butcher. Do you really want to get him off? Do you realize what you're doing?*

"Your fingerprints were on Detective Hampton's belt and on the dashboard of her car. Her blood was on your clothes."

I paused for several seconds before I spoke again. Then I tried to explain. "There was a huge, jagged tear in Detective Hampton's jugular vein. Blood was everywhere in the car, and even on the cement floor of the garage. I tried to help Detective Hampton until I was certain she was dead. That's why my fingerprints were in the car and Detective Hampton's blood was on my clothes."

"You tracked blood upstairs?"

"No, I did not. I checked my shoes carefully before I left the garage. I checked *twice.* I checked because I *didn't* want to track any blood up into the building."

"But you were upset, you admit that much. A police officer had been murdered. You forgot to put on gloves when you first searched the scene. There was blood on your clothes. How can you possibly be so sure?"

I stared directly into his eyes and tried to be as calm as he was. "I know exactly what happened that night. I know who killed Patsy Hampton in cold blood."

He raised his voice suddenly. "No, you do not, sir. That's the point. *You do not.* In frisking Colonel Geoffrey Shafer, isn't it fair to say that you were in physical contact with him?"

"Yes."

"And isn't it possible blood from *your* clothes got onto *his?* Isn't it even likely?"

I wouldn't give him an inch. I couldn't. "No, it isn't possible. That blood was on Geoffrey Shafer's trousers *before* I arrived."

Halpern moved away from me. He wanted me to sweat. He walked over to the jury box, occasionally looking back at me. He asked several more questions about the crime scene, and then said, "But Dr. Cassady didn't see any blood. And the two other officers didn't see any blood, either—*not until after you came into contact with Colonel Shafer.* Colonel Shafer was on the phone for three to five minutes before he met with his therapist. He went straight there from his children's birthday party. *You have no evidence, Detective Cross!* Except what you brought into Dr. Cassady's apartment yourself. You have absolutely no evidence, Detective! You arrested the wrong man! You framed an innocent man!"

Jules Halpern threw up his hands in disgust. "I have absolutely no further questions."

Chapter 97

I TOOK a back way out of the courthouse. I usually did that anyway, but on this day it was essential. I had to avoid the crowds and the press, and I needed to have a private moment to recover from my time on the witness stand.

I'd just had my ass pretty well kicked by an expert asskicker. Tomorrow, Cathy Fitzgibbon would try to undo some of the damage in cross-exam.

I was in no hurry as I walked down a back stairway that was used by maintenance and cleaning people in the building, and also served as a fire escape.

It was becoming clear to me that there was a chance Geoffrey Shafer would be acquitted. His lawyers were the best, and we'd lost important evidence at the suppression hearing.

And I *had* made a bad mistake at the homicide scene, when, in my rush to help Patsy Hampton, I'd neglected to put on gloves.

It was an honest mistake, but it probably created doubt in the minds of the jurors. I'd had more blood on me than Shafer. That was true. Shafer might actually get away with murder, and I couldn't stand the thought. I felt like yelling as I descended the twisting flights of stairs.

And that's exactly what I did. I yelled at the top of my voice, and it felt so damn good to get it out. Relief flowed through my body, however temporary it might be.

At the bottom of the concrete stairs was the basement of the courthouse. I headed down a long, dark hallway toward the rear lot where the Porsche was parked. I was still lost in my thoughts, but calmer after hollering my fool head off in the stairwell.

There was a sharp bend in the hallway near the exit to the parking lot. I came around the turn and saw him. I couldn't believe it. The Weasel was right there.

He was the first to speak. "What a surprise, Dr. Cross. Sneaking away from the madding—or is it 'maddening'?—crowd. Tail between your legs today? Don't fret, you did all right upstairs. Was that you yelling in the halls? Primal screams are the best, aren't they?"

"What the hell do you want, Shafer?" I asked him. "We're not supposed to meet or talk like this."

He shrugged his broad shoulders, wiped his blond hair away from his eyes. "You think I care about rules? I don't give a shit about rules. *What do I want?* My good name restored. I want my family not to have to go through any more of this. I want it all."

"Then you shouldn't have killed all those people. Especially Patsy Hampton."

Shafer smiled. "You're very sure of yourself, aren't you? You don't back down. I admire that, to a degree. I played the game of being a hero once myself. In the army. It's interesting for a while."

"But it's much more interesting to be a raving lunatic murderer," I said.

"See? You just don't back down from your bull-headed opinions. I love it. You're wonderful."

"It's not opinion, Shafer. You know it, and so do I."

"Then prove it, Cross. Win your pitiful, sodding case, will you? Beat me fair and square in a court of law. I even gave you a home-court advantage."

I started to walk toward him; I couldn't help myself. He stood his ground.

"This is all an insane game to you. I've met assholes like you before, Shafer. I've beaten better. I'll beat you."

He laughed in my face. "I sincerely doubt it."

I walked right past him in the narrow tunnel.

He pushed me—*hard,* from behind. He was a big man, and even stronger than he looked.

I stumbled, almost went over onto the stone floor. I wasn't expecting the outburst of anger from him. He held it in so well in court, but it was close to the surface. The madness that *was* Geoffrey Shafer. The violence.

"Then go ahead, beat me. See if you can," he

yelled at the top of his voice. "Beat me right here, right now. I don't think you can, Cross. I know you can't."

Shafer took a quick step toward me. He was agile and athletic, not just strong. We were almost the same size—six-two or -three, two hundred pounds. I remembered that he'd been an army officer, then MI6. He still looked to be in excellent shape.

Shafer pushed me again with both hands. He made a loud grunting noise. "If you've beaten better, then I should be a pushover. Isn't that so? I'm just a *pushover.*"

I almost threw a punch; I wanted to. I ached to take him down, to wipe the smug, superior look off his face.

Instead, I grabbed him hard. I slammed Shafer up against the stone tunnel wall and held him there.

"Not now. Not here," I said in a hoarse, raw whisper. "I'm not going to hit you, Shafer. What? Have you run to the newspapers and TV? But I am going to bring you down. Soon."

He came out with a crazy laugh. "You are fucking hilarious, do you know that? You're a *scream.* I love it."

I walked away from Shafer in the dark tunnel. It was the hardest thing I'd ever had to do. I wanted to beat the answers out of him, get a confession. I wanted to know about Christine. I had so many questions, but I knew he wouldn't answer them. He was here to bait me, to *play.*

"You're losing . . . everything," he said to my back.

I think I could have killed Geoffrey Shafer on the spot.

I almost turned, but I didn't. I opened the creaking door and went outside instead. Sunlight streamed into my eyes, half blinding me for a dizzying moment. Shading my face with an arm, I climbed the stone stairs to the parking area, where I got another unwanted surprise.

A dozen grim-faced members of the press, including some well-known reporters, were gathered in the back parking lot. Someone had alerted them; someone had tipped them off that I was coming out this way.

I looked back at the gray metal door, but Geoffrey Shafer didn't come out behind me. He had retreated and disappeared back into the basement.

"Detective Cross," I heard a reporter call my name. "You're losing this case. You know that, don't you?"

Yes, I knew. I was losing everything. I just didn't know what I could do to stop it.

Chapter 98

THE FOLLOWING day was taken up with my cross-examination by Catherine Fitzgibbon. Catherine did a good job of redressing some of the harm done by Jules Halpern, but not all of it. Halpern consistently broke up her rhythm with his objections. Like so many recent high-profile trials, this one was maddening. It should have been easy to convict and put away Geoffrey Shafer, but that wasn't the case.

Two days later, we got our best chance to win, and Shafer himself gave it to us, almost as if he were daring us. We now realized that he was even crazier than we'd thought. The game was his life; nothing else seemed to matter.

Shafer agreed to take the stand. I think I was the only one in the courtroom who wasn't completely surprised that he was testifying, that he was playing the game right in front of us.

Catherine Fitzgibbon was almost certain that Jules Halpern had advised, begged, and warned him not to do it, but there Shafer was anyway, striding toward the witness stand, looking as if he had been called up there to be ceremoniously knighted by the queen.

He couldn't resist the stage, could he? He looked every bit as confident and in control as he had the night I arrested him for Patsy Hampton's murder. He was dressed in a navy-blue double-breasted suit, white shirt, and gold tie. Not a single blond hair was out of place, nor was there any hint of the anger that was boiling just under the surface of his meticulously groomed exterior.

Jules Halpern addressed him in conversational tones, but I was sure that he felt uneasy about this unnecessary gamble.

"Colonel Shafer, first, I want to thank you for coming to the witness stand. This is completely voluntary on your part. From the very beginning, you've stated that you wanted to come here to clear your name."

Shafer smiled politely and then cut off his lawyer with a raised hand. The lawyers on both sides of the bar exchanged looks. What was happening? What was he going to do?

I leaned way forward in my seat. It struck me that Jules Halpern might actually *know* that his client was guilty. If so, he wouldn't be able to cross-examine him. Legally, he couldn't ask questions that disguised the real facts as he knew them.

This was the only way Shafer could have his moment in the sun: a soliloquy. Once called to the stand, Shafer could give a speech. It was unusual but absolutely legal—and if Halpern knew that his client was guilty, it was the only way Shafer could take the stand and not be incriminated by his own attorney.

Shafer had the floor. "If you will please excuse me, Mr. Halpern, I believe I can talk to these good people myself. I really can manage. You see, I don't need a lot of expert help to tell the simple truth."

Jules Halpern stepped back, nodded sagely, and tried to keep his poise. What else could he do under the circumstances? If he hadn't known before that his client was an egomaniac or insane, he surely knew it now.

Shafer looked toward the jury. "It has been stated here in court that I am with British intelligence, and that I was MI-Six, a spy. I'm afraid that I am actually a rather unglamorous agent— Double-or-Nothing, if you will."

The light, well-aimed jab at himself drew laughter in the courtroom.

"I am a simple bureaucrat, like so many others who toil away their days and nights in Washington. I follow well-established procedures at the embassy. I get approvals for virtually everything I do. My homelife is simple and orderly as well. My wife and I have been married nearly sixteen years. We love each other dearly. We're devoted to our three children.

"So I want to apologize to my wife and children. I am so frightfully sorry for this hellish ordeal they've had to go through. To my son, Rob, and the twins, Tricia and Erica, I'm so sorry. If I'd had any idea what a circus this would become, I would have insisted on maintaining diplomatic immunity rather than trying to clear my name, our name, *their* name.

"While I'm making heartfelt apologies, I'll make one to all of you for being a bit of a bore right now. It's just that when you're accused of murder, something so heinous, so unthinkable, you want desperately to get it off your chest. You want to tell the truth more than anything else in the world. So that's what I'm doing today.

"You've heard the evidence—and there simply isn't any. You've heard character witnesses. And now you've heard from me. I did not kill Detective Patsy Hampton. I think you all know that, but I wanted to say it to you myself. Thank you for listening," he said, and bowed slightly in his seat.

Shafer was brief, but he was poised and articulate and, unfortunately, very believable. He always held eye contact with the jury members. His words weren't nearly as important as the way he delivered them.

Catherine Fitzgibbon came forward to do the cross-examination. She was careful with Shafer at first; she knew he had the jury on his side for the moment. She waited until near the end of her cross-exam to go after Shafer where he might be most vulnerable.

"Your statement was very nice, Mr. Shafer. Now, as you sit before this jury, you claim that your relationship with Dr. Cassady was strictly professional, that you did not have a sexual relationship with her, correct? Remember, you are under oath."

"Yes, absolutely. She was, and hopefully will continue to be, my therapist."

"Notwithstanding the fact that she admits to having a sexual relationship with you?"

Shafer held his hand out toward Jules Halpern, signaling for him not to object. "I believe that the court record will show that she did *not* admit to such."

Fitzgibbon frowned. "I don't follow? Why do *you* think she didn't answer counsel?"

Shafer shot back, "That's so obvious: because she didn't care to *dignify* such a question."

"And when she hung her head, sir, and looked down at her lap? She was nodding assent."

Shafer now looked at the jury and shook his head in amazement. "You misread her completely. You missed the point again, Counselor. Allow me to illustrate, if I may. As King Charles said before being beheaded, 'Give me my cloak lest they think I tremble from fear.' Dr. Elizabeth Cassady was deeply embarrassed by your associate's crude suggestion, and so was my family, and so am I."

Geoffrey Shafer looked at the prosecutor with steely eyes. He then acknowledged the jury again. "And so am I."

Chapter 99

THE TRIAL was almost over, and now came the
really hard part: waiting for the verdict. That
Tuesday, the jurors retired to the jury room to
commence their deliberations in the murder trial
of Geoffrey Shafer. For the first time, I allowed
myself to actually think the unthinkable—that
Shafer might be set free.

Sampson and I sat in the rear row of the courtroom and watched the twelve members depart:
eight men and four women. John had come to
court several times, calling it the "best and sleazi-
est show this side of the Oval Office," but I knew
he was there to give me support.

"The son of a bitch is guilty; he's mad as little
Davey Berkowitz," Sampson said as he watched
Shafer. "But he has a lot of good actors on his side:
doting wife, doting mistress, well-paid lawyers,
Silly Billy. He could get away with it."

"It happens," I agreed. "Juries are hard to read.
And getting harder."

I watched as Shafer courteously shook hands
with the members of his defense team. Jules and

Jane Halpern both had forced smiles on their faces. *They know, don't they? Their client is the Weasel, a mass murderer.*

"Geoffrey Shafer has the ability to make people believe in him when he needs to. He's the best actor I've seen," I said.

Then John left and I snuck out the back way again. This time neither Shafer nor the press was lying in wait downstairs or in the rear parking lot.

In the lot, I heard a woman's voice, and I stopped moving. *I thought it was Christine.* A dozen or so people were walking to their cars, seemingly unaware of me. I felt fevered and hot as I checked them all. None of them was her. Where had the voice come from?

I took a ride in the old Porsche and listened to George Benson on the CD player. I remembered the police report about Shafer's thrill-seeking ride that ended near Dupont Circle. It seemed a strangely appealing prospect. I took my own advice not to try to guess how the jury would decide the case. It could go either way.

I let myself think about Christine, and I choked up. It was too much. Tears began to stream down my cheeks. I had to pull over.

I took a deep breath, then another. The pain in my chest was still as fresh as it had been the day she disappeared in Bermuda. She had tried to stay away from me, but I wouldn't let her. I was responsible for what had happened to her.

I drove around Washington, riding in gently

aimless circles. I finally reached home more than two and a half hours after leaving the courthouse.

Nana came running out of the house. She must have seen me pull into the driveway. She'd obviously been waiting for me.

I leaned out of the driver's-side window. The deejay was still talking congenially on Public Radio.

"What is it, old woman? What's the matter now?" I asked Nana.

"Ms. Fitzgibbon called you, Alex. The jury is coming back. They have a verdict."

Chapter 100

I WAS apprehensive as could be. But I was also curious beyond anything I could remember.

I backed out of the driveway and sped downtown. I got back to the courthouse in less than fifteen minutes. The crowd on E Street was even larger and more unruly than it had been at the height of the trial. At least a half-dozen Union Jacks waved in the wind; contrasting with them were American flags, including some painted across bare chests and faces.

I had to push and literally inch my way through the crush of people up close to the courthouse steps. I ignored every question from the press. I tried to avoid anyone with a camera in hand, or the hungry look of a reporter.

I entered the packed courtroom just before the jury filed back inside. "You almost missed it," I said to myself.

Judge Fescoe spoke to the crowd as soon as everyone was seated. "There will be no demonstrations when this verdict is read. If any demonstrations occur, marshals will clear this room immediately," he instructed in a soft but clear voice.

I stood a few rows behind the prosecution team and tried to find a regular breathing pattern. It was inconceivable that Geoffrey Shafer could be set free; there was no doubt in my mind that he'd murdered several people—not just Patsy Hampton, but at least some of the Jane Does as well. He was a wanton pattern killer, one of the worst, and had been getting away with it for years. I realized now that Shafer might be the most out-rageous and daring of all the killers I'd faced. He played his game with the pedal pressed to the floor. He absolutely refused to lose.

"Mr. Foreman, do you have a verdict for us?" Judge Fescoe asked in somber tones.

Raymond Horton, the foreman, replied, "Your Honor, we have a verdict."

I glanced over at Shafer; he appeared confident. As he had since the trial began, he was dressed today in a tailored suit, white shirt, and tie. He had no conscience whatsoever; he had no fear of anything that might happen to him. Maybe that was a partial explanation for why he'd run free for so long.

Judge Fescoe looked unusually stern. "Very well. Will the defendant please rise?"

Geoffrey Shafer stood at the defense table, and his longish blond hair gleamed under the bright overhead lighting. He towered over Jules Halpern and his daughter, Jane. Shafer held his hands behind him, as if he were cuffed. I wondered if he might have a pair of twenty-sided dice clasped in them, the kind I had seen in his study.

Judge Fescoe addressed the foreman again. "As to count one of the indictment, Aggravated, Premeditated Murder in the First Degree, how do you find?"

The foreman, *"Not guilty,* Your Honor."

I felt as if my head had suddenly spun off. The audience packed into the small room went completely wild. The press rushed to the bar. The judge had promised to clear the room, but he was already retreating to his chambers.

I saw Shafer walk toward the press, but then he quickly passed them by. What was he doing now? He noticed a man in the crowd and nodded stiffly in his direction. Who was that?

Then Shafer continued toward where I was, in the fourth row. I wanted to vault over the chairs after him. I wanted him so bad, and I knew I had just lost my chance to do it the right way.

"Detective Cross," he said in his usual supercilious manner. "Detective Cross, there's something I want to say. I've been holding it in for months."

The press closed in; the scene was becoming smothering and claustrophobic. Cameras flashed on all sides. Now that the trial had ended, there was nothing to prevent picture-taking inside the courtroom. Shafer was aware of the rare photo opportunity; of course he was. He spoke again, so that everyone gathered around us could hear. It was suddenly quiet where we stood, a pocket of silence and foreboding expectation.

"You killed her," he said, and stared deeply into my eyes, almost to the back of my skull. "*You killed her.*"

I went numb. My legs were suddenly weak. I knew he didn't mean Patsy Hampton.

He meant Christine.

She was dead.

Geoffrey Shafer had killed her. He had taken everything from me, just as he'd warned me he would.

He had won.

Chapter 101

SHAFER WAS a free man, and he was enjoying the bloody hell out of it. He'd wagered his life. He had gambled, and he had won big-time. *Big-time!* He had never felt anything quite like this exhilarating moment following the verdict.

Shafer accompanied Lucy and the children to a by-invitation-only press conference held in the pompous, high-ceilinged grand-jury room. He posed for countless photos with his family. All of them hugged him again and again, and Lucy couldn't stop crying like the brain-dead, hopelessly spoiled and crazy child she was. If some people thought *he* was a drug abuser, they'd be shocked by Lucy's intake. Christ, that was how he'd first learned about the amazing world of pharmaceuticals.

He finally punched his arm into the air and held it there as a mocking sign of victory. Cameras flashed everywhere in the room. They couldn't get enough of him. There were nearly a hundred reporters wedged into the room. The women reporters loved him most of all. He was a legitimate media star now, wasn't he? He was a hero again.

A few gate-crashing agents of fame and fortune pressed their cards at him, promising obscene amounts of money for his story. He didn't need any of their tawdry offers. Months before, he had picked out a powerful New York and Hollywood agent.

Christ, he was free as a bird! He was absolutely flying now. After the press conference, claiming concern for their safety, he sent his wife and children ahead without him.

He stayed behind in the court law library and firmed up book-deal details with Jules Halpern and representatives from the Bertelsmann Group, now the most powerful book-publishing conglomerate in the world. He had assured them that they would get his story, but of course they weren't going to get anything close to the truth. Wasn't that the way with the so-called tell-all, bare-all nonfiction published these days? The Bertelsmann people knew this, and still they'd paid him dearly.

After the meeting, he took the slow-riding lift down to the court's indoor car park. He was still feeling incredibly high, which could be dangerous. A set of twenty-sided dice was burning a hole in the pocket of his suit trousers.

He desperately wanted to play the game. Now! The Four Horsemen. Or better yet, Solipsis—*his* version of the game. He wouldn't give in to that urge, though, not yet. It was too dangerous, even for him.

Since the beginning of the trial, he had been parking the Jaguar in the same spot; he *did* have his patterns, after all. He'd never bothered to put coins in the meter, not once. Every day there was a pile of five-dollar tickets under the windshield wiper.

Today was no exception.

He grabbed the absurd parking tickets off the windshield and crumpled them into a ball in his fist. Then he dropped the wad of paper onto the oil-stained concrete floor.

"I have diplomatic immunity," he said aloud, and smiled as he climbed into his Jag.

Book Five
ENDGAME

SHAFER COULDN'T believe it. He had made a very serious and perhaps irreversible mistake. The result wasn't what he had expected, and now his whole world seemed to be falling apart. At times he thought it couldn't have been any worse had he gone to prison for the cold-blooded murder of Patsy Hampton.

Shafer knew that he wasn't just being paranoid or mad. Several of the pathetic wankers inside the embassy watched him every bloody time he stepped out of his office. They seemed to resent and openly despise him, especially the women. Who had turned them against him? Somebody surely was responsible.

He was the white, English O. J. Simpson. A weird, off-color joke to them. Guilty though proven innocent.

So Shafer mostly stayed inside his office with the door closed, sometimes locked. He performed his few remaining duties with a growing sense of irritation and frustration, and a sense of the absurd. It was driving him mad to be trapped like this, to be a pathetic spectacle for the embassy staff.

He idly played with his computer and waited for the game of the Four Horsemen to resume, but the other players had cut him off. They insisted that it was too dangerous to play, even to communicate, and *not one of them* understood why this was the perfect time to play.

Shafer stared out onto Massachusetts Avenue for interminably long stretches during the day. He listened to call-in talk shows on the radio. He was getting angrier and angrier. He needed to play.

Someone was knocking on the door of his office. He turned his head sharply and felt a spike of pain in the back of his neck. The phone had begun to ring. He picked up and heard the temp he'd been assigned. Ms. Wynne Hamerman was on the intercom.

"Mr. Andrew Jones is here to see you," she said.

Andrew Jones? Shafer was shocked. Jones was a hot-shit director from the Security Service in London. Shafer hadn't known he was in Washington. What the hell was this visit about? Andrew Jones was a high-level, very tough prick who wouldn't just drop by for tea and biscuits. *Mustn't keep him waiting too long.*

Jones was standing there, and he looked impatient, almost furious. What was this about? His steely blue eyes were cold and hard; his face was as rigid as that of an English soldier posted in Belfast. In contrast, his brilliant red hair and mustache made him look benign, almost jolly. He was called Andrew the Red back in London.

"Let's go inside your office, shall we? Shut the door behind you," Jones said in a low but commanding voice.

Shafer was just getting past his initial surprise, but he was also starting to lose it. Who did this pompous asshole think he was to come barging into his office like this? By what right was he here? How dare he? The toad! The glorified lackey from London.

"You can sit down, Shafer," Jones said. Another imperious command. "I'll be brief and to the point."

"Of course," Shafer answered. He remained standing. "Please do be brief and get to the point. I'm sure we're both busy."

Jones lit up a cigarette, took a long puff, then let the smoke out slowly.

"That's illegal here in Washington," Shafer goaded him.

"You'll receive orders to return to England in thirty days' time," said Jones as he continued to puff on his cigarette. "You're an embarrassment here in Washington, as you will be in London. Of course, over there the tabloids have re-created you as a martyr of the brutal and inefficient American police and judicial systems. They like to think of this as 'D.C. Confidential,' more evidence of wholesale corruption and naïveté in the States. Which we both know, in this case, is complete crap."

Shafer sneered. "How dare you come in here and talk to me like this, Jones? I was framed for a heinous crime I didn't commit. I was acquitted by an American jury. Have you forgotten that?"

Jones frowned and stared him down. "Only because crucial evidence wasn't allowed in the trial. The blood on your trousers? That poor woman's blood in the bathroom drain at your mistress's?" He blew smoke out the side of his mouth. "We know everything, you pathetic fool. We know you're a stone-cold killing freak. So you'll *go* back to London and stay there—until we catch you at something. Which we will, Shafer. We'll make something up if we have to.

"I feel sick to my stomach just being in the same room with you. Legally, you've escaped punishment this time, but we're watching you so very closely now. We will get you somewhere, and someday soon."

Shafer looked amused. He couldn't hold back a smile. He knew he shouldn't, but he couldn't resist the play. "You can try, you insufferable, sanctimonious shit. You can certainly try. But get in line. And now, if you please, I have work to do."

Andrew Jones shook his head. "Well, actually, you *don't* have any work to do, Shafer. But I am happy to leave. The stench in here is absolutely overpowering. When was the last time you bathed?" He laughed contemptuously. "Christ, you've completely lost it."

Chapter 103

THAT AFTERNOON, I met with Jones and three of his agents at the Willard Hotel, near the White House. I had called the meeting. Sampson was there, too. He'd been reinstated in the department, but that didn't stop him from doing what had originally gotten him into trouble.

"I believe he's crazy," Jones said of Shafer. "He smells like a commode at boot camp. He's definitely going down for the count. What's your take on his mental state?"

I knew Geoffrey Shafer inside and out by now. I'd read about his family: his brothers, his long-suffering mother, his domineering father. Their travels from military base to military base until he was twelve. "Here's what I think. It started with a serious bipolar disorder, what used to be called manic depression. He had it when he was a kid. Now he's strung out on pharmaceutical drugs: Xanax, Benadryl, Haldol, Ativan, Valium, Librium, several others. It's quite a cocktail. Available from local doctors for the right price. I'm surprised he can function at all. But he survives. He doesn't go down. He always wins."

"I told Geoff he has to leave Washington. How do you think he'll take it?" Jones asked me. "I swear his office smelled as if a dead body had been festering there for a couple of days."

"Actually, his disorder can involve an accompanying odor, but it's usually steely, like metal—very pungent, sticks to your nostrils. He probably isn't bathing. But his instincts for playing the game, for winning and surviving, are amazing," I said. "He won't stop."

"What's happening with the other players?" Sampson inquired. "The so-called Horsemen?"

"They claim that the game is over, and that it was only a fantasy game for them," Jones told him. "Oliver Highsmith stays in touch, mostly to keep tabs on us, I'm sure. He's actually a scary bastard in his own right. Says he's saddened by the murder of Detective Hampton. He's still not a hundred percent sure that Shafer is the killer. Urges me to keep my mind open on that one."

"Is your mind open on it?" I asked, looking around the room at the others.

Jones didn't hesitate. "I have no doubt that Geoffrey Shafer is a multiple murderer. We've seen enough and heard enough from you. He is quite possibly a homicidal maniac beyond anything we've ever known. And I also have no doubt that eventually he's going down."

I nodded my head. "I agree," I said, "with everything you just said. But especially the homicidal-maniac part."

Chapter 104

SHAFER WAS talking to himself again that night. He couldn't help it, and the more he tried to stop, the worse it became; the more he fretted, the more he talked to himself.

"They can all bugger off—Jones, Cross, Lucy and the kids, Boo Cassady, the other spineless players. Screw them all. There was a reason behind the Four Horsemen. It wasn't just a game. There was more to it than simple horseplay."

The house at Kalorama was empty, much too quiet at night. It was huge and ridiculous as only an American house can be. The "original" architectural detail, the double living room, the six fireplaces, the long-ago dead flowers from Aster florist, the unread books in gold and brown leather bindings, Lucy's marmite. It was driving him up the twelve-foot-high walls.

He spent the next hour or so trying to convince himself that he wasn't crazy—more specifically, that he wasn't an addict. Recently, he'd added another doctor in Maryland to his sources for the drugs. Unfortunately, the illegal prescriptions cost him a fortune. He couldn't keep it up forever. The Lithium and Haldol were to control his mood swings, which were very real. The Thorazine was for acute anxiety, which was fucking bloody real as well. The Narcan had also been prescribed for his mood swings. The multiple injections of Loradol were for something else, some pain from he couldn't remember when. He knew there were good reasons, too, for the Xanax, the Compazine, the Benadryl.

Lucy had already fled home to London, and she'd taken the traitorous children with her. They'd left exactly one week after the trial ended. Her father was the real cause. He'd come to Washington and spoken to Lucy for less than an hour, and she'd packed up and left like the Goody Two-shoes she'd always been. Before she departed, Lucy had the nerve to tell Shafer she'd stood by him for the sake of the children and her father, but now her "duty" was over. She didn't believe he was a murderer, as her father did, but she knew he was an adulterer, and that, she couldn't take for one moment longer.

God, how he despised his little wifey. Before Lucy left, *he* made it clear to *her* that the real reason she'd performed her "duty" was so he wouldn't reveal her unsavory drug habit to the press, which he *would* have done and still might do, anyway.

At eleven o'clock he had to go out for a drive, his nightly "constitutional." He was feeling unbearably jittery and claustrophobic. He wondered if he could control himself for another night, another minute. His skin was crawling, and he had dozens of irritating little tics. He couldn't stop tapping his goddamn foot!

The dice were burning a bloody hole in his trouser pocket. His mind was racing in a dozen haphazard directions, all of them very bad. He wanted to, needed to, kill somebody. It had been this way with him for a long time, and that had been his dirty little secret. The other Horsemen knew the story; they even knew how it had begun. Shafer had been a decent English soldier, but ultimately too ambitious to remain in the army. He had transferred into MI6 with the help of Lucy's father. He thought there would be more room for advancement in MI6.

His first posting was Bangkok, which was where he met James Whitehead, George Bayer, and eventually Oliver Highsmith. Whitehead and Bayer spent several weeks working on Shafer, recruiting him for a specialized job: he would be an assassin, their own personal hit man for the worst sort of wet work. Over the next two years, he did three sanctions in Asia, and found that he truly loved the feeling of power that killing gave him. Oliver Highsmith, who ran both Bayer and Whitehead from London, once told him to depersonalize the act, to think of it as a game, and that was what he did. He had never stopped being an assassin.

Shafer turned on the CD in the Jag. *Loud,* to

drown out the multiple voices raging in his head. The old-age-home rockers Jimmy Page and Robert Plant began a duet inside the cockpit of his car.

He backed out of the drive and headed down Tracy Place. He gunned the car and had it up close to sixty in the block between his house and Twenty-fourth Street. *Time for another suicidal drive?* he wondered.

Red lights flashed on the side of Twenty-fourth Street. Shafer cursed as a D.C. police patrol car eased down the street toward him. *Goddamn it!*

He pulled the Jag over to the curb and waited. His brain was screaming. "Assholes. Bloody impertinent assholes! And you're an asshole, too!" he told himself in a loud whisper. "Show some self-control, Geoff. Get yourself under control. Shape up. Right now!"

The Metro patrol car pulled up behind him, almost door to door. He could see two cops lurking inside.

One of them got out slowly and walked over to the Jag's driver's-side window. The cop swaggered like a hot-shit all-American cinema hero. Shafer wanted to blow him away. Knew he could do it. He had a hot semiautomatic under the seat. He touched the grip, and God, it felt good.

"License and registration, sir," the cop said, looking unbearably smug. A distorted voice inside Shafer's head screeched, *Shoot him now. It will blow everybody's mind if you kill another policeman.*

He handed over the requested identification,

though, and managed a wanker's sheepish grin. "We're out of Pampers at home. Trip to the Seven-Eleven was in order. I know I was going too fast, and I'm sorry, Officer. Blame it on baby-brain. You have any kids?"

The patrolman didn't say a word; not an ounce of civility in the prick. He wrote out a speeding ticket. Took his sweet time about it.

"There you go, Mr. Shafer." The patrol officer handed him the speeding ticket and said, "Oh, and by the way, we're watching you, shithead. We're all over you, man. You didn't get away with murdering Patsy Hampton. You just *think* you did."

A set of car lights blinked on and off, on and off, on the side street where the patrol car had been sitting a few moments earlier.

Shafer stared, squinted back into the darkness. He recognized the car, a black Porsche.

Cross was there, watching. Alex Cross wouldn't go away.

Chapter 105

ANDREW JONES sat next to me in the quiet, semi-darkened cockpit of the Porsche. We'd been working closely together for almost two weeks. Jones and the Security Service were intent on stopping Shafer before he committed another murder. They were also tracking War, Famine, and Conqueror.

We watched silently as Geoffrey Shafer slowly turned the Jaguar around and drove back toward his house.

"He saw us. He knows my car," I said. "Good."

I couldn't see Shafer's face in the darkness, but I could almost feel the heat rising from the top of his head. I knew he was crazed. The words "homicidal maniac" kept drifting through my mind. Jones and I were looking at one, and he was still running free. He'd already gotten away with one murder—*several* murders.

"Alex, aren't you concerned about possibly putting him into a rage state?" Jones asked as the Jaguar eased to a stop in front of the Georgian-style house. There were no lights on in the driveway area, so we wouldn't be able to see Geoffrey Shafer for the next few seconds. We couldn't tell if he'd gone inside.

"He's already in a rage state. He's lost his job, his wife, the children, the game he lives for. Worst of all, his freedom to come and go has been curtailed. Shafer doesn't like having limitations put on him, hates to be boxed in. He can't stand to lose."

"So you think he'll do something rash."

"Not rash, he's too clever. But he'll make a move. It's how the game is played."

"And then we'll mess with his head yet again?"

"Yes, we will. Absolutely."

Late that night, as I was driving home, I decided to stop at St. Anthony's. The church is unusual in this day and age in that it's open at night. Monsignor John Kelliher believes that's the way it should be, and he's willing to live with the vandalism and the petty theft. Mostly, though, the people in the neighborhood watch over St. Anthony's.

A couple of worshipers were inside the candlelit church when I entered, around midnight. There are usually a few "parishioners" inside. Homeless people aren't allowed to sleep there, but they wander in and out all through the night.

I sat watching the familiar red votive lamps flicker and blink. I sucked in the thick smell of incense from Benediction. I stared up at the large gold-plated crucifix and the beautiful stained-glass windows that I've loved since I was a boy.

I lit a candle for Christine, and I hoped that

somehow, someway, she might still be alive. It didn't seem likely. My memory of her was fading a little bit, and I hated that. A column of pain went from my stomach to my chest, making it hard for me to breathe. It has been this way since the night she'd disappeared, almost a year ago.

And then, for the first time, I admitted to myself that she was gone. I would never see her again. The thought caught like a shard of glass in my throat. Tears welled in my eyes. "I love you," I whispered to no one. "I love you so much, and I miss you terribly."

I said a few more prayers, then I finally rose from the long wooden pew and silently made my way toward the doors of the vestibule. I didn't see the woman crouching in a side row. She startled me with a sudden movement.

I recognized her from the soup kitchen. Her name was Magnolia. That was all I knew about her, just an odd first name, maybe a made-up one. She called out to me in a loud voice, "Hey, Peanut Butter Man, now you know what it's like."

Chapter 106

JONES AND Sandy Greenberg from Interpol had helped get the other three Horsemen under surveillance. The net being cast was large, as the catch could be if we succeeded.

The huge potential scandal in England was being carefully watched and monitored by the Security Service. If four English agents turned out to be murderers involved in a bizarre "game," the fallout would be widespread and devastating for the intelligence community.

Shafer dutifully went to the embassy on Wednesday and Thursday. He arrived just before nine and left promptly at five. Once inside, he stayed out of sight in his small office, not even venturing out for lunch. He spent hours on America Online, which we monitored.

Both days, he wore the same gray slacks and a double-breasted blue blazer. His clothes were uncharacteristically wrinkled and unkempt. His thick blond hair was combed back; it looked dirty and greasy, and resisted the high winds flowing through Washington. He looked pale, seemed nervous and fidgety.

Was he going to crash?

After dinner on Friday night, Nana and I sat out in back of the house on Fifth Street. We were spending more time together than we had in years. I knew she was concerned about me, and I let her help as much as she wanted. For both our sakes.

Jannie and Damon were washing the dishes inside and managing not to squabble too much. Damon washed while Jannie dried. Damon's tape deck played the beautiful score from the movie *Beloved.*

"Most families have a dishwasher and drier these days," Nana said, after she'd taken a sip of her tea. "Slavery has ended in America, Alex. Did you happen to hear about that?"

"We have a dishwasher and drier, too. Sounds like they're in good working order. Low maintenance, low cost. Hard to beat."

Nana clucked. "See how long it lasts."

"If you want a dishwasher, we can buy one—or are you just practicing the fine art of being argumentative before you launch into something more deserving of your talents? As I remember, you are a fan of Demosthenes and Cicero."

She nudged me with her elbow. "Wiseapple," she said. "Think you're so smart."

I shook my head. "Not really, Nana. That's never been one of my big problems."

"No, I suppose not. You're right, you don't have

a big head about yourself." Nana stared into my eyes. I could almost feel her peering into my soul. She has an ability to look very deeply into things that really matter. "You ever going to stop blaming yourself?" she asked me. "You look just terrible."

"Thank you. Are you ever going to stop nagging me?" I asked, smiling at her. Nana could always bring me out of the doldrums, in her own special way.

She nodded her small head. "Of course I will. I'll stop one day. Nobody lives forever, Grannyson."

I laughed. "You probably will, though. Live longer than me or the kids."

Nana showed lots of teeth—her own, too. "I *do* feel pretty good, considering everything," she said. "You're still chasing him, aren't you? That's what you're doing nights. You and John Sampson, that Englishman Andrew Jones."

I sighed. "Yeah, I am. And we're going to get him. There may be four men involved in a series of murders. Here and in Asia, Jamaica, London."

She beckoned to me with a bent, crabbed forefinger. "Come closer now."

I grinned at her. She's such a soft touch, really, such a sweetie, but such a hard-ass, too. "You want me to sit down on your lap, old woman? You sure about that?"

"Good Lord, no. Don't sit on me, Alex. Just lean over and show some respect for my age and wisdom. Give me a big hug while you're at it."

I did as I was told, and I noticed there wasn't any

fuss or clatter coming from the kitchen anymore.

I glanced at the screen door and saw that my two little busybodies were watching, their faces pressed against the mesh wire. I waved them away from the door, and their faces disappeared.

"I want you to be so very, very careful," Nana whispered as I held her gently. "But I want you to get him somehow, someway. That man is the worst of all of them. Geoffrey Shafer is the worst, Alex, the most evil."

Chapter 107

THE GAME had never really ended, but it had changed tremendously since the trial in Washington.

It was five-thirty in the evening in London, and Conqueror was waiting at his computer. He was both anxious and feverishly excited about what was happening: the Four Horsemen was starting up again.

It was 1:30 A.M. in Manila, in the Philippines. Famine was ready for a message, and a new beginning to the game he loved.

And War awaited news of the Four Horsemen at his large house on the island of Jamaica. He, too, was obsessed with how it would end and whether he would be the winner.

It was twelve-thirty in Washington. Geoffrey Shafer was driving fast to the White Flint Mall, from the embassy. He had a lot to accomplish that afternoon. He was revved and manic.

He sped up Massachusetts Avenue, past the British Embassy and the vice president's house. He wondered if he was being followed and supposed it was possible. Alex Cross and the other police were out there, just waiting to get him. He hadn't spotted them yet, which only meant that they were getting serious now.

He made a quick right, hit a traffic circle, and shot onto Nebraska Avenue, heading toward American University. He snaked around back roads near the university, then got on Wisconsin and sped toward the mall.

He entered Bloomingdale's and found the department store sparsely peopled—a little depressing, actually. Good; he despised the American shopping scene anyway. It reminded him of Lucy and her brood. He walked at a leisurely pace through the men's clothing section. He picked up a few overpriced Ralph Lauren Polo sport shirts, then two pairs of dark trousers.

He draped a black Giorgio Armani suit over his arm and took the bundle into the changing rooms. At a security desk inside, he handed the clothes to an attendant on duty, posted there to curtail shoplifters, no doubt.

"Changed my mind," he said.

"That's not a problem, sir."

Shafer then jogged down a narrow corridor that led to a rear exit. He sprinted toward the glass doors and burst through them into a parking lot in back. He saw signs for Bruno Cipriani and Lord & Taylor and knew he was headed in the right direction.

A Ford Taurus was parked there near the F pole. Shafer jumped inside, started it, and drove up the

Rockville Pike to Montrose Crossing, a little over a mile away.

He didn't think anyone was following him now. He passed Montrose and went north to the Federal Plaza shopping center. Once there, he entered the Cyber Exchange, which sold new and used software and lots of computers.

His eyes darted left and right until he saw exactly what he needed.

"I'd like to try out the new iMac," he told the salesperson who approached him.

"Be my guest. You need any assistance, holler," the salesperson said. "It's easy."

"Yes, I think I'm fine. I'll call if I get stuck. I'm pretty sure I'm going to buy the iMac, though."

"Excellent choice."

"Yes. Excellent, excellent."

The lazy clerk left him alone, and Shafer immediately booted up. The display model was connected on-line. He felt a rush of manic excitement, but also a tinge of sadness as he typed in his message to the other players. He'd thought this through and knew what had to be said, what had to be done.

Greetings and Salutations. This glorious and unprecedented adventure of eight years, the Four Horsemen, is nearly at an end now. You have stated your case very logically, and I accept the regrettable conclusion you've reached. The game has become too dangerous. So I propose that we create an unforgettable ending. I believe that a face-to-face meeting is a fitting end. It's the only conclusion that I can accept.

This was inevitable, I suppose, and we have discussed it many times before. You know where the game ends. I propose that we start play on Thursday. Trust me, I will be there for the grand finale. If necessary, I can begin the game without you. Don't make me do that. . . . *Death.*

Chapter 108

AT NINE o'clock on Monday morning, Shafer joined the monotonous, stomach-turning line of workaday morons stuck in traffic going in the direction of Embassy Row. He had the intoxicating thought that he would never again have to work after today. Everything in his life was about to change. He couldn't go back.

His heart was pounding as he stopped and waited at the green light on Massachusetts Avenue near the embassy. Car horns beeped behind him, and he was reminded of his suicide run a year ago. Those were the days, damn it. Then he blasted through on the red. He ran. He had rehearsed his escape. This was for keeps.

He saw two blocks of clear roadway ahead, and he floored the gas pedal. The Jaguar leaped forward with raw, phallic power, as it were. The sports car rocketed toward the puzzle of side streets around American University.

Ten minutes later he was turning in to the White Flint Mall at fifty, gunning the Jag up to fifty-five, sixty, sixty-five as he sped across the mostly empty lot. He was sure no one had followed him.

He drove toward a large Borders Books & Music store, turned right, then zoomed up a narrow side lane between buildings.

There were five exits out of the mall that he knew of. He accelerated again, tires squealing.

The surrounding neighborhood was a warren of narrow streets. Still no one was behind him, not a single car.

He knew of a little-used one-way entrance onto the Rockville Pike. He got on the road, heading out against the barrage of traffic streaming to work in the city. He hadn't spotted any cars speeding behind him inside the mall, or on the side streets, or on the pike.

They probably had only one car, or at most two, on him in the morning. That made the most sense to Shafer. Neither the Washington Metro police nor the Security Service would approve a larger surveillance detail to follow him. He didn't think they would, anyway.

He'd probably lost them. He whooped loudly and started blaring the Jag's horn at all the pathetic suckers and fools stuck in the oncoming lanes, headed for work. He'd been waiting nearly eight years for this.

It was finally here.

Endgame.

Chapter 109

"WE'VE STILL got him?" I asked Jones, nervously looking around at the half-dozen agents working in the crisis room inside the British Embassy. The room was filled with state-of-the-art electrical equipment, including half a dozen video monitors.

"Still got him. He won't get away that easily, Alex. Besides, we think we know where he and the others are going now."

We had a tiny, sophisticated homing device on the Jaguar, but there was a reasonable chance that Shafer would discover it. So far, he hadn't. And now he was running in the Jag, running with the bait—at least that was what we *thought* was happening.

The Horsemen were all on the move. Oliver Highsmith had been followed from his home in Surrey to Gatwick Airport, outside London. Agents at the airport made sure that Conqueror got on the British Air flight to New York, then called Washington to report he was en route.

A couple of hours later, an agent phoned from the Philippines. George Bayer was at Ninoy

Aquino Airport in Manila. Famine had purchased a ticket to Jamaica, with a stopover in New York.

We already knew that James Whitehead had retired to Jamaica, and that he was on the island now. War was waiting for the others to arrive.

"I'm trying to get a fixed pattern for the Four Horsemen game, but there are several points of view at work. That's what they like about the game, what makes it so addictive," I said to Jones as we waited for more information to come in.

"We know that at least three of them have been playing the game since they were stationed in Thailand, in 'ninety-one. Around that time, bar girls and prostitutes began to disappear in Bangkok. The local police didn't spend much time on the investigations. Girls in Pat Pong had disappeared before. The police have somewhat the same attitude here in Washington with respect to the Jane Doe killings. These girls didn't mean much. They were written off. Murders and disappearances in Southeast certainly aren't investigated like ones in Georgetown or on Capitol Hill. It's one of Washington's dirty little secrets."

Jones lit a new cigarette off the butt of his last one. He puffed, then said, "It might be just Shafer who's involved in the actual murders, Alex. Either that or the others are much more careful than he is."

I shrugged my shoulders. I didn't think so, but I didn't have enough concrete evidence to argue my case effectively with Jones, who was himself no slouch as a detective.

"The end of the Four Horsemen is coming, right? Can they really end their little fantasy game?" Sampson asked.

"It sure looks like they're getting together," I said. "Four former British agents, four grown men who love to play diabolical games. In my opinion, four murderers."

"Possibly." Andrew Jones finally admitted that the unthinkable could be true: "Alex, I'm afraid you could be right."

Chapter 110

JAMAICA MUST have been chosen because it was relatively private, and because James White-head owned a large beach house there. But perhaps there were other angles attached to the game of the Four Horsemen. I hoped that we would know soon enough.

Oliver Highsmith and George Bayer arrived on the island within minutes of each other. They met at the baggage claim inside Donald Sangster Airport, then drove for about an hour to the posh Jamaica Inn in Ocho Rios.

We were on the move, too. Sampson and I had gotten there on an early-morning flight from D.C. The weather was glorious. Blue skies, warm breezes. We heard strains of English and Jamaican Creole at the airport, reggae and ska. The rustle of the banana trees as the sea breeze rushed through them was like a soft chorus.

The hotel in Ocho Rios was very private and old-fashioned, just forty-five rooms overlooking the sea. We arrived there simultaneously with four

English teams. There were also two teams of detectives from Kingston.

The English High Commission office in Kingston had been alerted about our presence and our purpose here. Full cooperation had been promised. Everyone was committed to bringing down all four game players, whatever the consequences, and I was very impressed with the English group, and also with the local detectives.

We waited for Geoffrey Shafer. Sampson and I were strategically positioned to watch the narrow, shaded road that led to the hotel. We were on a lush hillside between the hotel and the sparkling blue Caribbean sea. Andrew Jones and another agent were in a second car hidden near the hotel's rear entrance. Six of Jones's agents were posing as porters and maintenance workers at the hotel. The Jamaican detectives were also posted on the grounds.

We'd had no news about Shafer. He had finally lost us. But we believed he would join the others. Jones complained that there weren't enough of us to stop Shafer if he was coming after the others. I agreed; if Shafer was playing kamikaze, there would be no adequate defense.

So we waited and waited. Continual updates came in over the car's short-wave radio. The messages didn't stop all afternoon. They were a kind of electronic heartbeat for our surveillance detail.

"Oliver Highsmith is still in his room. Doesn't want to be disturbed, apparently. . . ."

"Bayer is in his room as well. Subject was spotted on the terrace about ten minutes ago, checking out the beach with binoculars. . . ."

"Bayer has left his room. He's taking a dip in the deep blue sea. Subject is in a red-striped swimming costume. Difficult to miss. Makes the job easier. Not on the eyes, though. . . ."

"Black Mercedes arriving at the front gate. Driver's tall and blond. Could be Geoffrey Shafer. You see him, Alex?"

I reported immediately, "The blond man isn't Shafer. Repeat, it isn't Shafer. Too young, probably American. Young wife and two children tagging along. False alarm. It isn't Shafer."

The radio reports continued.

"Highsmith has just ordered up from room service. Two English breakfasts in the middle of the day. One of our people will take it up to him. . . ."

"Bayer is back from his swim. He's well tanned. Little guy, but muscular. Tried to hit on some ladies. Struck out."

Finally, at around six o'clock, I made another report. "James Whitehead just drove up in a green Range Rover! He's coming inside the hotel. War is here."

Only one more game player to go.

We waited. Death had yet to arrive.

Chapter III

SHAFER WAS in no particular hurry to flash the checkered flag. He took his sweet time thinking through each possible scenario. He had spotted the coast of Jamaica on the horizon several hours before. He had originally flown to Puerto Rico, then sailed from there in a chartered boat. He wanted to be able to leave either by air or by sea.

Now he calmly waited for nightfall, drifting in his boat with the cooling trade winds. It was the famous "blue hour" on the sea, just past sunset, extraordinarily serene and beautiful. Also magical and slightly unreal. He had finished five hundred more push-ups on the deck of the boat, and he wasn't even winded. He could see half a dozen large cruise ships anchored near Ocho Rios. All around him were scores of smaller boats like his own.

He remembered reading somewhere that the island of Jamaica had once been the personal property of Christopher Columbus. It pleased him to think there had been a time when a man could take whatever he wanted, and often did. His body was tight and hard, and he was bronze from the three days of sun during his trip. His hair was bleached even blonder than usual. He'd had the drugs under control for almost a week now. It had been an act of will, and he'd risen to the challenge. He wanted to win.

Shafer felt like a god. No, he *was* a god. He controlled every move in his own life and in the lives of several others. There were surprises left, he thought as he slowly sprayed his body with cooling streams of water. There were surprises for everybody who still chose to be in the game.

His game.

His plan.

His ending.

Because this wasn't just a game; it never had been. The other players had to know that by now. They understood what they had done, and why there had to be payback. It was what the Four Horsemen had been all about from the beginning: *Endgame is payback, and payback is mine . . . or theirs? Who knows for sure?*

His father had taught him and his brothers to sail, probably the only useful thing he'd ever done for Shafer. He actually could find peace on the sea. It was the real reason he'd come to Jamaica by boat.

At eight o'clock he swam to shore, passing several of the smaller sailboats and a few motorboats. He found the physical exertion a neat antidote to his anxiety and nerves. He was a strong swimmer and diver, and good at most other sports as well.

The night air was peaceful and calm and fragrant. The sea was flat. Not a ripple disturbed the surface. Well, there would be plenty of ripples soon.

A car was waiting for him just off the coast road, a black Ford Mustang, glossy and shiny in the moonlight.

He smiled when he saw it. The game was progressing beautifully.

Famine was there to meet him.

No, Famine was there for another reason, wasn't he?

George Bayer was waiting on shore to kill him.

Chapter 112

"GEORGE BAYER isn't in his room. He's not with Oliver Highsmith or James Whitehead, either. Damn it to hell! He's loose."

The alarming message went out over the two-way radio. Sampson and I had been watching the south side of the hotel for close to eight hours, and we were sure George Bayer hadn't come our way.

We heard Andrew Jones's concerned voice on the radio. "Remember that all of the Four Horsemen are agents, like ourselves. They're capable and deadly. Let's find Bayer right away, and be extra alert for Geoffrey Shafer. Shafer is the most dangerous player—at least we *think* he is."

Sampson and I hurried out of our rented sedan. We had our guns out, but they seemed inappropriate at the beautiful and serene resort. I remembered feeling the same way nearly a year before, in Bermuda.

"Bayer didn't come this way," Sampson said. I knew he was concerned that Jones's people had lost Famine. *We* wouldn't have made that mistake, but we were seen as backup, not the primary team.

The two of us quickly walked up a nearby hill that gave us a perspective on the manicured lawns rolling down toward the hotel's private beach. It was getting dark, but the grounds near the hotel were relatively well lit. A couple in bathing suits and robes slowly walked toward us. They were holding hands, oblivious to the danger. No George Bayer, though. And no Shafer.

"How do they end this thing?" Sampson asked. "How do you think the game ends?"

"I don't think any of them knows for sure. They probably have game plans, but anything can happen now. It all depends on Shafer, if he follows the rules. I think he's beyond that, and the other players know it."

We hurried along, running close to the hotel buildings. We were getting nervous and concerned looks from the hotel guests we passed on the narrow, winding sidewalk.

"They're all killers. Even Jones finally admits that. They killed as agents, and then they didn't want to stop. They liked it. Now maybe they plan to kill one another. Winner takes all."

"And Geoffrey Shafer hates to lose," said Sampson.

"Shafer doesn't ever lose. We've seen that already. *That's* his pattern, John. It's what we missed from the start."

"He doesn't get away this time, sugar. No matter what, Shafer doesn't walk."

I didn't answer Sampson.

Chapter 113

SHAFER WASN'T even breathing hard as he made it to the white-sand shoreline. George Bayer stepped out of the black Ford Mustang, and Shafer watched for a weapon to appear. He continued to walk forward, playing the game of games for the highest stakes of all: his life.

"You bloody *swam?*" Bayer asked, his voice jovial yet taunting.

"Well, actually, it's a fantastic night for it," Shafer said, and casually shook water off his body. He waited for Bayer to move on him. He observed the way he tensed and untensed his right hand. Watched the slight forward slant of his shoulders.

Shafer took off a waterproof backpack and pulled out fresh, dry clothes and shoes. Now he had access to his weapons. "Let me guess. Oliver suggested that you all gang up on me," he said. "Three against one."

Bayer smiled slyly. "Of course. That had to be considered as an option. But we rejected it because it wasn't consistent with our characters in the game."

Shafer shook his hair, let the water drip off. As he dressed, he turned halfway away from Bayer. He smiled to himself. God, he loved this—the game of life and death against another Horseman, a master player. He admired Bayer's calmness and his ability to be so smooth.

"His playing is so bloody predictable. He was the same way as an agent and analyst. George, they sent you because they thought I'd never suspect you'd try to take me out by yourself. You're the first play. It's so obvious, though. A terrible waste of a player."

Bayer frowned slightly but still didn't lose his cool, didn't let on what he felt. He thought that was the safest attitude, but it told Shafer his suspicion was true: Famine was here to kill him. He was sure of it. George Bayer's cool demeanor had given him away.

"No, nothing like that," Bayer said. "We're going to play according to the rules tonight. The rules are important to us. It's to be a board game, a contest of strategy and wits. I'm just here to pick you up, according to plan. We'll meet face to face at the hotel."

"And we'll abide by the throw of the dice?" Shafer asked.

"Yes, of course, Geoff." Bayer held out his hand and showed him three twenty-sided dice.

Shafer couldn't hold back a sharp laugh. This was so good, so rich. "So what did the dice say, George? How do I lose? How do I die? A knife? A pistol? A drug overdose makes a great deal of sense to me."

Bayer couldn't help himself. He laughed. Shafer was such a cocky bastard, such a good killer, a wonderful psychopathic personality. "Well, yes, it might have occurred to us, but we played it completely straight. As I said, they're waiting at the hotel for us. Let's go."

Shafer turned his back to Bayer for an instant. Then he pushed hard off his right foot. He sprang at Bayer.

But Bayer was more than ready for him. He threw a short, hard punch that struck Shafer's cheek, rattled and maybe even loosened a few teeth. The right side of Shafer's head went completely numb.

"Good one, George. Good stuff!"

Then Shafer head-butted Bayer with all of his strength. He heard the crunch of bone against bone, saw an explosion of dizzying white before his eyes. That got his adrenaline flowing.

The dice went flying from Bayer's hand as he reached for a gun, or some other weapon. It was tucked in the back of his waistband.

Shafer clutched Bayer's right arm, twisted with all of his strength, and broke it at the elbow. Bayer shrieked in pain.

"You can't beat me! Nobody has, nobody can!" Shafer screamed at the top of his voice.

He grabbed George Bayer's throat and squeezed with superhuman strength. Bayer gagged and turned the brightest red, as if all the blood in his body had rushed to his head. George was stronger than he appeared, but Shafer was speeding on adrenaline and years of pure hatred. He outweighed Bayer by twenty pounds, all of it muscle.

"*Noooo.* Listen to me." George Bayer wheezed and gasped. "Not like this. Not here."

"*Yes,* George. *Yes, yes.* The game is on. The game that you bastards started. Tally-ho, old chap. *You* did this to me. You made me what I am: Death."

He heard a loud, crisp snap, and George Bayer went limp against him. He let his body fall to the sand.

"One down," said Shafer, and finally allowed himself a deep, satisfying breath. He snatched up the fallen dice, shook them once, then hurled them into the sea. "I don't use the dice anymore," he said.

Chapter 114

HE FELT so damn good. So fine. God, how he had missed this! The mainline of adrenaline, the incomparable thrill. He knew it was likely that the Jamaica Inn was being watched by the police, so he parked the Mustang at the nearby Plantation Inn.

He walked at a quickening pace through the crowded Bougainvillea Terrace. Drinks were being served while the wretched song "Yellowbird" played loudly. He had a nasty fantasy about shooting up the terrace, killing several dickhead tourists, so he got away from the crowded area immediately for everybody's sake—but mostly for his own.

He strolled the beach, and it calmed him. It was quiet, restful, the strains of calypso music gently weaving through the night air. The stretch between the two hotels was eye-catching, with plenty of spotlights, sand the color of champagne, thatched umbrellas placed at even intervals. A very nice playing field.

He knew where Oliver Highsmith was staying: in the famous White Suite, where Winston

Churchill and David Niven and Ian Fleming had slept once upon a time. Highsmith loved his creature comforts almost as much as he loved the game.

Shafer despised the other Horsemen, in part because he wasn't of their snobbish social class. Lucy's father had gotten him into MI6; the other players had gone to the right universities. But there was another, more powerful reason for his hatred: they had dared to use him, to feel superior and throw it in his face.

He entered through a white picket-fence gate at the property line of the Jamaica Inn. He broke into a soft jog. He wanted to run, to sweat. He was feeling manic again. Playing the game had made him too excited.

Shafer held his head for a moment. He wanted to laugh and scream at the top of his lungs. He leaned against a wooden post on the path leading up from the beach, and tried to catch his breath. He knew he was crashing, and it couldn't have happened at a worse time.

"Everything all right, sir?" a hotel waiter stopped to ask him.

"Oh, couldn't be better," Shafer said, waving the man away. "I'm in heaven, can't you tell?"

He started walking toward the White Suite again. He realized that he was feeling the same way he had that morning last year when he nearly crashed his car in Washington. He was in serious trouble again. He could lose the game right now, lose everything. That required a change of strategy, didn't it? He had to be more daring, even more aggressive. He had to act, not think too much. The odds against him were still two to one.

At the far end of the courtyard, he spotted a man and a woman in evening clothes. They were loitering near a white stucco portico strewn with flowers. He decided they were Jones's people. They had staked out the hotel, after all. They were here for him, and he was honored.

The man glanced his way, and Shafer abruptly lowered his head. There was nothing they could do to stop or detain him. He'd committed no crime they could prove. He wasn't wanted by the police. No, he was a free man.

So Shafer walked toward them at a leisurely pace, as if he hadn't seen them. He whistled "Yellowbird."

He looked up when he was a few yards away from the pair. "I'm the one you're waiting for. I'm Geoffrey Shafer. Welcome to the game."

He pulled out his Smith & Wesson nine-millimeter semiautomatic and fired twice.

The woman cried out and grabbed the left side of her chest. Bright-red blood was already staining her sea-green dress. Her eyes showed confusion and shock before rolling back into her forehead.

The male agent had a dark hole where his left eye had been. Shafer knew the man was dead even before his head struck the courtyard floor with a loud, satisfying smack.

He hadn't lost anything over the years. Shafer hurried toward the White Suite and Conqueror.

The gunshots certainly would have been heard. They wouldn't expect him to run straight into the trap they'd set. But here he was.

Two maids were pushing a squeaking cleanup cart out of the White Suite. Had they just turned down Conqueror's bed? Left the fat man a box of chocolate mints to nibble?

"Get the hell out of here!" he yelled, and raised his gun. "Go on, now! Run for your lives!" The Jamaican maids took off as if they had just seen the devil himself, and later they would tell their children they had.

Shafer burst in the front door of the suite, and there was Oliver Highsmith freewheeling his chair across the freshly scrubbed floor.

"Oliver, it's you," Shafer said. "I do believe I've caught the dreaded Covent Garden killer. You did those killings, didn't you? Fancy that. Game's over, Oliver."

At the same time, Shafer thought, *Watch him closely. Be careful with Conqueror.*

Oliver Highsmith stopped moving, then slowly but rather nimbly turned his wheelchair to face Shafer. A face-to-face meeting. This was good. The best. Highsmith had controlled Bayer and White-head from London when they were all agents. The original game, the Four Horsemen, had been his idea, a diversion as he eased into retirement. "Our silly little fantasy game," he always called it.

He studied Shafer, cold-eyed and measuring. He was bright—an egghead, but a genius, or so Bayer and Whitehead claimed.

"My dear fellow, we're your friends. The only ones you have now. We understand your problem. Let's talk things through, Geoffrey."

Shafer laughed at the fat man's pathetic lies, his superior and condescending attitude, his nerve. "That's not what Georgie Bayer told me. Why, he said you were going to murder me! Hell of a way to treat a friend."

Highsmith didn't blink, didn't falter. "We're not alone here, Geoff. They're at the hotel. The Security Service team is on the grounds. They must have followed you."

"And *you,* and *Bayer,* and *Whitehead*! I know all that, Oliver. I met a couple of crackerjack agents down the hall. Shot 'em dead. That's why I have to hurry up, can't tarry. The game's on a clock now. Lots of ways to lose."

"We have to talk, Geoff."

"Talk, talk, talk." Shafer shook his head, frowned, then barked out a laugh. "No, there's nothing for us to talk about. Talk is such an over-rated bore. I learned to kill in the field, and I like it much more than talking. No, I actually love it to death."

"You *are* mad," Highsmith exclaimed, his grayish-blue eyes widening with fear. Finally, he understood who Shafer was; he wasn't intellectualizing anymore. He felt it in his gut.

"No, actually, I'm not insane. I know precisely what I'm doing—always have, always will. I know the difference between good and evil. Anyway, look who's talking: the Rider on the White Horse."

Shafer moved swiftly toward Highsmith. "This isn't much of a fight—just the way I was taught to perform in Asia. You're going to die, Oliver. Isn't that a stunning thought? Still think this is a bloody fantasy game?"

Suddenly Highsmith jumped to his feet. Shafer wasn't surprised; he knew he couldn't have committed the murders in London from a wheelchair. Highsmith was close to six feet, and obese, but surprisingly quick for his size. His arms and hands were massive.

Shafer was faster. He struck Highsmith with the butt of his gun, and Conqueror went crashing down on one knee. Shafer bludgeoned him a second time, then a third, and Highsmith dropped flat on the floor. He groaned loudly and slobbered blood and spit. Shafer kicked the small of his back, kicked a knee, kicked his face.

Then he bent and put the gun barrel against Highsmith's broad forehead. He could hear the distant sound of running footsteps' slapping down the hall. Too bad—they were coming for him. *Hurry, hurry.*

"They're too late," he said to Conqueror. "No one can save you. Except me, Conqueror. What's the play? Counsel me. Should I save the whale?"

"Please, Geoff, no. You can't just kill me. We can still help each other."

"I'd love to stretch this out, but I really have to dash. I'm throwing the dice. In *my mind.* Oh, bad news, Oliver. The jig is up. You just lost game."

He inserted the barrel of his gun into Highsmith's pulpy right ear, and fired. The gunshot blew Conqueror's gray matter all over the room. Shafer's only regret was that he hadn't been able to torture Oliver Highsmith for a much, much longer time than he had.

Then Shafer was running away, and suddenly he was struck with a realization that actually surprised him: he had something to live for. This was a wonderful, wonderful game.

I want to live.

Chapter 115

SAMPSON AND I sprinted toward the secluded wing of the hotel where Oliver Highsmith had his suite. There had been gunshots, but we couldn't be everywhere at once. We'd heard the pistol reports all the way on the other side of the Jamaica Inn.

I wasn't prepared for the bloody massacre scene we found. Two English agents were down in the courtyard. I'd worked with them both, just as I'd worked side by side with Patsy Hampton.

Jones and another agent, in addition to a team of local detectives, were already crowded into Highsmith's suite. The room was abuzz. Everything had turned to chaos and carnage in a burst of homicidal madness.

"Shafer went through two of my people to get here," Jones said in an angry voice strained with tension and sadness. He was smoking a cigarette. "He came in shooting, took down Laura and Gwynn. Highsmith is dead, too. We haven't found George Bayer yet."

I knelt and quickly checked the damage to

Oliver Highsmith's skull. It wasn't subtle. He'd been shot at point-blank range, and the wound was massive. I knew from Jones that Shafer had resented the senior man's intelligence, and now he'd blown out his brains. "I told you he liked to kill. He has to do this, Andrew. He can't stop.

"Whitehead!" I said. "The end of the game."

Chapter 116

WE DROVE faster than the narrow, twisting road safely allowed, barreling toward James Whitehead's home. It wasn't far.

We passed a road sign that read Mallard's Beach—San Antonio.

Sampson and I were quiet, lost in our own thoughts. I kept thinking of Christine, couldn't stop the images from coming. *"We have her."* Was that still true?

I didn't know, and only Shafer, or possibly Whitehead, could give me the answer. I wanted to keep both of them alive if I could. Everything about the island, the exotic smells and sights, reminded me of Christine. I tried, but I couldn't imagine a good conclusion to any of this.

We headed toward the beach and soon were skimming past private houses and a few very large estates, some with long, winding driveways that stretched a hundred yards or more from the road to the main house.

In the distance I could see the glow of other house lights, and I figured we had to be close to

James Whitehead's. Was War still alive? Or had Shafer already come and gone?

Jones's voice came in spits over the radio: "This is his place, Alex. Glass and stone house up ahead. I don't see anybody."

We pulled in near the crushed-seashell driveway leading to the house. It was dark, pitch-black and satiny. There were no lights on anywhere on the property.

We jumped out of our cars. There were eight of us in all, including one team of detectives from Kingston, Kenyon and Anthony, both of whom were acting nervous.

I didn't blame them. I felt exactly the same way. The Weasel was on a rampage, and we already knew he was suicidal. Geoffrey Shafer was a homicidal-suicidal maniac.

Sampson and I ran through a small garden that had a pool and cabana area on one side and an expanse of lawn and the sea on the other.

We could see Jones's people beginning to fan out across the grounds. *Shafer came into the hotel with guns blazing,* I thought. *He doesn't seem to care whether or not he survives. But* I *do. I need to question him. I have to know what he knows. I need all the answers.*

"What about this prick Whitehead?" Sampson asked as we hurried toward the house.

It was dark near the water, a good place for Shafer to attack from. Dark shadows stretched out from every tree and bush.

"I don't know, John. He was at the hotel briefly.

He's a player, so he's after Shafer, too. This is it: *Endgame*. One of them wins the game now.

"He's here," I whispered. "I know it."

I could definitely sense Geoffrey Shafer's presence; I was sure of it. And the fact that I *knew* scared me almost as much as he himself did.

Shots sounded from the darkened house.

My heart sank, and I had the most disturbing and contradictory thought: *Please don't let Geoffrey Shafer be dead.*

Chapter 117

ONE MORE target, one last opponent, and then it would be over. Eight glorious years of play, eight years of revenge, eight years of hatred. He couldn't bear to lose the game. He'd shown Bayer and Highsmith a thing or two; now he'd demonstrate to James Whitehead which of them was truly "superior."

Shafer had noisily crashed through thick foliage, then waded waist deep into a foul-smelling swamp. The water was distressingly tepid, and the oily green scum on the surface was an inch or two thick.

He tried not to think about the swamp, or the insects and snakes that might infest it. He'd waded into far worse waters during his days and nights in Asia. He kept his eyes set on James Whitehead's expensive beach house. One more to go, just one more Horseman.

He'd been to the villa before, knew it well. Beyond the swamp was another patch of thick foliage, and then a chain-link fence and White-head's manicured yard. He figured that Whitehead wouldn't expect him to come through the swamp. War was cleverer than the others, though. He'd been committing murders in the Caribbean for years, and not even a blip had shown up to suggest a pattern to the police. War had also helped him in the matter of Christine Johnson, and that had gone perfectly. It was a mystery, inside a mystery, all inside a complex game.

Shafer lost track of everything real for a moment or two—where he was, who he was, what he had to do.

Now, *that* was scary—a little mental breakdown at the worst possible time. Ironically, it was Whitehead who had first gotten him dependent on uppers and downers in Asia.

Shafer began to slosh across the fetid swamp, hoping the water wouldn't be over his head. It wasn't. He came out and climbed over the chain-link fence on the far side. He started across the back lawn.

He had the most powerful obsession about destroying James Whitehead. He wanted to torture him—but where would he find the time? Whitehead had been his first handler in Thailand, and then in the Philippines. More than anyone, Whitehead had made Shafer into a killer. Whitehead was the one he held responsible.

The house was still dark, but Shafer believed War was in there.

Suddenly a gun fired from the house. *War* indeed.

Shafer began to zig and zag like an infantryman thoroughly trained in combat. His heart was thundering. Reality came in odd stop-and-go movements. He wondered if Whitehead had a nightscope on his gun. And how good a shot he was.

Whether he'd ever been in combat.

Was he frightened? Or was he excited by the action?

He figured that the doors to the house were locked and that War was crouched low, hiding inside, waiting to take a shot without too much exposure. He had never done his own dirty work, though; none of them had—not Whitehead, not Bayer, not Highsmith. They had used Death, and now he'd come for them. If they hadn't agreed to meet in Jamaica, he would have come after them one at a time.

Shafer broke into a full sprint toward the house. Gunshots exploded from inside. Bullets whizzed past him. He hadn't been hit. Because he was so good? Or because War wasn't?

Shafer threw both arms up in front of his face. This was it. He dived through the large picture window in the loggia.

Glass exploded everywhere as the window blew into a thousand small pieces. He was inside!

War was here, close by. Where was his enemy? How good was James Whitehead? His mind was filled with important questions. A dog was barking somewhere in the house.

Shafer tumbled across the tile floor and hit the leg of a heavy table, but came up firing anyway. *Nothing.* No one was in the room.

He heard voices outside, in front. The police were here! Always trying to spoil his fun.

Then he saw War trying to run. Tall, gangly, with longish black hair. War had blinked first. He was heading toward the front door, looking for help from the police, of all people.

"You can't make it, Whitehead. Stop! I won't let you get out! Stay in the game."

Whitehead apparently realized he couldn't get out the front door. He turned toward a stairway, and Shafer followed, only a few steps behind. War turned sharply and fired again.

Shafer flicked his hand at a wall switch, and the hall lights flashed on.

"Death has come for you! It's your time. Look at me! Look at Death!" he screamed.

Whitehead kept moving, and Shafer calmly shot him in the buttocks. The wound was large, gaping, and Whitehead screamed like a stuck pig. He whirled and fell halfway down the stairs. His face slammed against the metal railing as he fell.

He finally lay writing at the foot of the stairs, where Shafer shot him again, this time between the legs. War screamed again. Then he began to moan and to sob.

Shafer stood over him, triumphant, his heart bursting. "You think sanctions are a game? Is this still a game to you?" he asked in the softest voice. "*I* believe it's great fun, but do you?"

Whitehead was sobbing as he tried to speak. "No, Geoffrey. It's not a game. Please stop. That's enough."

Shafer began to smile. He showed his enormous teeth. "Oh, you're so wrong. It's lovely! It is the most amazing mind game you could imagine. You should feel what I feel right now, the power over life and death."

He had a thought, and it changed everything, changed the game for him and Whitehead. This switch was so much better than what he'd originally planned.

"I've decided to let you live—not very well, but you *will* live."

He fired the semiautomatic again, this time into the base of Whitehead's spine.

"You will never forget me, and the game will continue for the rest of your life. Play well. I know *I* shall."

Chapter 118

THE MOMENT we heard the gunshots, we ran toward the main house. I raced ahead of the others. I had to get to Shafer before they did. I had to take him myself. I had to talk to him, to know the truth once and for all.

I saw Shafer slip out a side door of the house. Whitehead must be dead. Shafer had won the game.

He was running toward the sea, moving fast and purposefully. He disappeared behind a small sand dune shaped like a turtle. Where was he going? What was next for him?

Then I saw him again. He was kicking off his shoes and getting out of his trousers. What was he doing?

I heard Sampson come running up behind me. "Don't kill him, John! Not unless we have to," I yelled.

"I know! I know!" he called.

I plunged ahead.

Shafer turned and fired off a shot at me. The distance was too great for any real accuracy with a handgun, but still, he was a good shot, and he came pretty close. He knew how to use a gun, and not just from a few feet away.

I glanced over and saw that Sampson was kicking off his sneakers, pulling away his pants. I did the same with my sweats and T-shirt.

I pointed out to sea. "He must have a boat out there. One of those."

We saw Shafer striding into the low waves of the Caribbean, heading into a cone of light made by the moon.

He did a shallow dive and started to swim in a smooth-looking crawl stroke.

Sampson and I were down to our underwear, nothing very pretty. We both made shallow dives into the sea.

Shafer was a very strong swimmer and was already pulling ahead of us. He swam with his face in the water, lifting it out sideways after several strokes to catch a breath.

His blond hair was slicked back and shone in the moonlight. One of the boats bobbing out there had to be his. But which one?

I kept a single thought in my head: stretch and kick, stretch and kick. I felt as if I were gathering strength from somewhere inside. I had to catch Shafer—I had to know the truth about what he'd done to Christine.

Stretch and kick, stretch and kick.

Sampson was laboring behind me, and then he started to fall even farther back.

"Go," I called to him. "Go back for help. I'll be all right. Get somebody out there to check those boats."

"He swims like a fish," Sampson shouted back.

"Go. I'll be fine. Hold my own."

Up ahead I could still see Shafer's head and the tops of his shoulders glistening in the creamy white moonlight. He was stroking evenly, powerfully.

I kept going, never looking back to shore, not wanting to know how far I had come already. I refused to be tired, to give up, to lose.

I swam harder, trying to gain some sea on Shafer. The boats were still a good way away. He was still going strong, though. No sign of tiring.

I played a mind game of my own. I stopped looking to see where he was. I concentrated only on my own stroke. There was nothing but the stroke; the stroke was the whole universe.

My body was feeling more in sync with the water, and I was buoyed as it got deeper. My stroke was getting stronger and smoother.

I finally looked. He was starting to struggle. Or maybe that was just what I *wanted* to see. Anyway, it gave me a second wind, added strength.

What if I actually caught him out here? Then what? We'd fight to the death?

I couldn't let him get to his boat before me. He'd have guns on board. I needed to beat him there. I had to win this time. Which boat was his?

I swam harder. I told myself that I was in good

shape, too. And I was. I'd been to the gym every day for almost a year—ever since Christine disappeared.

I looked up again and was shocked at what I saw.

Shafer was there! Only a few yards away. A few more strokes. Had he lost it? Or was he waiting for me, gathering strength?

The closest boat was no more than a hundred, a hundred and fifty yards away.

"*Cramp!*" he called out. "Bad one!" Then Shafer went under.

Chapter 119

I DIDN'T know what to think or exactly what to do next. The pain on Shafer's face looked real; he looked afraid. But he was also a good actor.

I felt something underneath me! He grabbed hard between my legs. I yelled and managed to twist away, though he'd hurt me.

Then we were grabbing at each other, struggling like underwater wrestlers. Suddenly, he pulled me under with him. He was strong. His long arms were like powerful vises, and he held me tightly.

We went down, and I started to feel the coldest, most serious fear of my life. I didn't want to drown. Shafer was winning. He always found a way.

Shafer stared into my eyes. His eyes were incredibly intense and manic and crazed. His mouth was closed, but it was twisted and evil-looking. He had me; he would win again.

I pushed forward as hard as I could. When I felt him straining against me, I reversed directions. I kicked out with my leg and caught Shafer under the jaw, maybe in the throat. I hit him with all of my strength, and he began to sink.

His long blond hair floated up around his face. His arms and legs went limp.

He began to sink, and I followed him. It was even darker under the surface. I grabbed one of his arms.

I barely caught him. His weight was pulling me with him, toward the bottom. I couldn't let him go. I had to know the truth about Christine. I couldn't go on with my life unless I knew.

I had no idea how deep the water was here. Shafer's eyes had been wide open, and so had his mouth; his lungs must be filling with water by now.

I wondered if I'd broken his neck with my kick. Was he dead, or just unconscious? I took some satisfaction in the idea that I might've broken the Weasel's neck.

Then it really didn't matter. Nothing did. I had no more breath. My chest felt as if it would collapse. There was a fire spreading wildly inside me. Then a severe ringing started in both ears. I was dizzy and starting to lose consciousness.

I let Shafer go, let him sink to the bottom. I didn't have a choice. I couldn't think about him anymore. I had to get to the surface. I couldn't hold my breath any longer.

I swam frantically up, pulled at the water, kicked with all my might. I didn't think I could make it; it was too far to the surface.

I had no more breath.

Then I saw Sampson's face looming above me. Close, very close. It gave me strength.

His head was framed against a few stars and the blue-black of the sky. "Sugar," he called as I finally came up for air.

He held me up, let me get my breath, my precious breath. We both treaded water for a while. My mind was reeling.

I let my eyes explore the surface for some sign of Shafer. My vision was blurred, but I didn't see him. I was certain he'd drowned.

Sampson and I slowly paddled back to shore.

I hadn't gotten what I needed out there. I hadn't been able to learn the truth from Shafer before he drowned.

Once or twice I glanced back to make sure that Shafer wasn't following us, that he was gone. There was no sign of him. There was only the sound of our own tired strokes cutting into the tide.

Chapter 120

IT TOOK two more exhausting days and nights to finish with the local police investigation, but it was good to keep focused and busy. I no longer had any hope of finding Christine, or even discovering what had happened to her.

I knew it was remotely possible that Shafer hadn't taken Christine, that it had been some other madman from my past, but I didn't give that possibility more than a passing thought. I couldn't go there. It was too crazy an idea, even for me.

I'd been unable to grieve from the start, but now the monstrous finality of Christine's fate struck me with all of its brutal force. I felt as if my insides had been hollowed out. The constant, dull ache I had known for so long now became a sharp stab of pain that pierced my heart every waking moment. I couldn't sleep, yet I felt as if I were never fully awake.

Sampson knew what was happening to me. There was nothing he could say, but he made comforting small talk, anyway.

Nana called me at the hotel, and I knew it was

Sampson's doing, though both of them denied it. Jannie and Damon got on the phone, and they were both sweet and kind and full of life and hopefulness. They even put Rosie the cat on for a friendly long-distance meow. They didn't mention Christine, but I knew she was always in their thoughts.

On our final night on the island, Sampson and I had dinner with Jones. We had become friendly with him, and he finally told me some facts he had previously withheld for Security reasons. He wanted me to have some closure; he felt I deserved that much.

Back in 1989, after joining MI6, Shafer had been recruited by James Whitehead. Whitehead in turn reported to Oliver Highsmith, as did George Bayer. Shafer performed at least four "sanctions" in Asia over the next three years. It was suspected, but never proved, that he, Whitehead, and Bayer had also murdered prostitutes in Manila and Bangkok. These murders were obviously the precursors to the Jane Does, and to the game itself. All in all, it had been one of the worst scandals in the history of the Security Service. And it had effectively been covered up. That was how Jones wanted to keep it, and I had no worthwhile objection. There were already more than enough unfortunate stories to keep people cynical about their governments.

Our dinner broke up at around eleven, and Jones and I promised to keep in touch. There was one bit of disturbing news, though no one wanted to overstate the significance of it: Geoffrey Shafer's body still hadn't been found. Somehow that seemed a fitting end.

Sampson and I were due to catch the first flight to Washington on Tuesday morning. It was scheduled to leave at ten past nine.

That morning, the skies were swirling with black clouds. Heavy rain pounded on our car's roof all the way from the hotel to the Donald Sangster Airport. Schoolchildren ran along the side of the road, shielding themselves from the rain with flopping banana-tree leaves.

The downpour caught us good as we tried to dash out from under the cover of the tin overhang outside the rent-a-car depot. The rain was cool, though, and it felt good on my face and head and on the shirt plastered to my back.

"It'll be real good to be home," Sampson said as we finally made it to a shelter under the metal roof painted a bright yellow.

"I'm ready to go," I agreed. "I miss Damon and Jannie and Nana. I miss being home."

"They'll find the body," Sampson said. "Shafer's."

"I knew who you meant."

The rain hammered the airport's roof without mercy, and I was thinking how much I hated to fly on days like this—but it would be good to be home, to be able to end this nightmare. It had invaded my soul, taken over my life. In a way I supposed it was as much a "game" as any that

Shafer had played. The murder case had obsessed me for over a year, and that was enough.

Christine had asked me to give it up. Nana had asked, too, but I hadn't listened. Maybe I hadn't been able to see my life and actions as clearly then as I did now. I was the Dragonslayer, and all that meant, the good and the bad. In the end, I held myself responsible for Christine's kidnapping and murder.

Sampson and I walked past the colorful concession stands without any real interest, barely a passing nod. Street hawkers, called higglers, were selling wooden jewelry and other carvings, but also Jamaican coffee and cocoa.

Each of us carried a black duffel bag. We didn't exactly look like vacationers, I was thinking. We still looked like policemen.

I heard a voice calling loudly from behind, and I turned back to look at the commotion coming up from the rear.

It was one of the Jamaican detectives, John Anthony, shouting out my name in the noisy terminal, running our way. He was several steps ahead of Andrew Jones, who looked powerfully dismayed.

Jones and Anthony at the airport? What in God's name was happening now? What could possibly have gone wrong?

"The *Weasel*?" I said, and it came out like a curse.

Sampson and I stopped to let them catch up

with us. I almost didn't want to hear what they had to tell us.

"You have to come back with us, Alex. Come with me," Jones said, slightly out of breath. "It's about Christine Johnson. Something's turned up. Come."

"What is it? What's happened?" I asked Jones, and then turned to Detective Anthony when the Englishman was slow in answering.

Anthony hesitated, but then he said, "We don't know for sure. It could be nothing at all. Someone claims to have seen her, though. She may be here in Jamaica, after all. Come with us."

I couldn't believe what he had just told me. I felt Sampson's arm wrap tightly around me, but everything else seemed unreal, as in a dream.

It wasn't over yet.

Chapter 121

ON THE road out of the airport, Andrew Jones and Detective Anthony filled us in on what they knew. I could tell they were trying not to build up my hopes too much. I'd been in the same untenable situation many times, but not as a victim of a crime.

"Last night we caught a small-time local thief breaking into a house in Ocho Rios," Anthony said as he drove, the four of us packed tightly in his Toyota. "He said he had information to trade. We told him we would hear what he had to say, and then we would decide. He revealed that an American woman had been kept in the hills east of Ocho Rios, near the town of Euarton. There's an outlaw group lives up there sometimes.

"I learned about it only this morning. I called Andrew, and we hurried to the airport. The man says she was called Beatitude. No other name was used. I contacted your hotel, but you had already left for the airport. So we came out here to get you."

"Thank you," I finally said, realizing I had probably been told as much as they knew.

Sampson spoke up. "So why does this helpful thief appear now, after all this time?"

"He said there was a shooting a few nights ago that changed everything. Once the white men died, the woman wasn't important anymore. Those were his words."

"You know these men?" I asked Detective Anthony.

"Men, women, children. Yes, I've dealt with them before. They smoke a lot of ganja. Practice their hybrid religion, worship the Emperor Haile Selassie, y'know. A few of them are small-time thieves. Mostly, we let them be."

Everyone in the car grew quiet as we hurried along the coast road toward Runaway Bay and Ocho Rios. The storm had passed quickly, and suddenly the island's hellified sun was blazing again. Sugarcane workers with machetes on their hips were tramping back into the fields.

Past the village of Runaway Bay, Detective Anthony turned off the main road and headed up into the hills on Route A1. The trees and bushes here were a thick jungle. The road eventually became a tunnel boring through vines and branches. Anthony had to turn on the headlights.

I felt as if I were drifting through a mist, watching everything as if in a dream. I understood that I was trying to protect myself, but I also knew it wasn't working.

Who was Beatitude? I couldn't make myself

believe that Christine was alive, but at least there was a chance, and I clung to that. I had given up weeks before. Now I allowed myself to remember how much I loved her, how much I missed her. I choked hard and turned my face toward the window. I went deep inside myself.

Suddenly, bright light shone in my eyes. The car had exited the brush after two or three miles that had seemed much longer on the twisting road. We were entering lush hills that looked something like the American South back in the fifties and sixties—maybe Georgia or Alabama. Children in dated clothes played in front of small run-down houses. Their elders sat on uneven, slanted porches and watched the occasional car drive past.

Everything looked and felt so surrealistic. I couldn't focus.

We turned onto a skinny dirt road with a thick, high corridor of grass running between deep tire ruts. This had to be the place. My heart was pumping loudly and sounded like a tin drum being pounded in a tunnel. I felt every bump in the road like a hard punch.

Beatitude? Who is the woman they're holding? Can it possibly be Christine?

Sampson checked the load in his Glock. I heard the mechanism slide and *click* and glanced his way.

"They won't be happy to see us, but you won't need the gun," Anthony turned and said. "They probably know we're coming. They watch the local roads. Christine Johnson might not be here now, if she was ever here at all. But I knew you would want to see for yourself."

I didn't say anything. I couldn't. My mouth felt incredibly dry, and my mind was a blank. We were still involved with the Four Horsemen, weren't we? Was this Shafer's play? Had he known we'd eventually find this place in the hills? Had he set a final trap for us?

We arrived at an old green house with tattered white cloth over the windows and a burlap bag for a front door. Four men immediately came outside, all of them sporting dreadlocks.

They walked toward us, their mouths set hard, their eyes blazing with distrust. Sampson and I were used to the look from the streets of Washington.

Two of the men carried heavy field machetes. The other two wore floppy shirts, and I knew they were armed beneath the loose-fitting clothes.

"Galang. Go back, mon," one of them shouted loudly at us. "Nah woman here."

Chapter 122

"NO!"

Detective Anthony got out of the car with both hands held high. Sampson, Jones, and I followed his lead.

We could hear the beat of traditional drums coming from the woods directly behind the main house. A pair of lounging dogs raised their lazy heads to look at us and barked a few times. My heart was thundering faster now.

I didn't like the way this was going down.

Another one of the men called to us, "I and I would like you to leave."

I recognized the figure of speech: the double pronoun represented the speaker and God, who live together in each person.

"Patrick Moss is in jail. I'm Detective Anthony, from Kingston. This is Detective Sampson, Detective Cross, and Mr. Jones. You have an American woman here. You call her Beatitude."

Beatitude? Could it be Christine?

A man wielding a machete in one hand glared and spoke to Anthony. "Galang bout yuh business.

Lef me nuh. Nah woman here. Nah woman."

"This *is* my business, and we *won't* leave you alone," I said, surprising the man with my understanding of his dialect. But I know Rastaman from D.C.

"Nah woman here. Nah American," the man repeated angrily, looking directly at me.

Andrew Jones spoke up. "We want the American woman, then we'll leave. Your friend Patrick Moss will be home by tonight. You can deal with him in your own way."

"Nah American woman here." The original speaker spat defiantly on the ground. "Turn around, go back."

"You know James Whitehead? You know Shafer?" Jones asked.

They didn't deny it. I doubted we'd get any more from them than that.

"I love her," I told them. "I can't leave. Her name is Christine."

My mouth was still dry, and I couldn't breathe very well. "She was kidnapped a year ago. We know she was brought here."

Sampson took out his Glock and held it loosely at his side. He stared at the four men, who continued to glare back at us. I touched the handle of my gun, still in its holster. I didn't want a gunfight.

"We can cause you a whole lot of trouble," Sampson said in a low, rumbling voice. "You won't believe how much trouble is coming your way."

Finally, I just walked forward on a worn path

back through the tall grass. I passed by the men, lightly brushing against one of them.

No one tried to stop me. I could smell ganja and sweat on their work clothes. Tension was building up inside me.

Sampson followed me, no more than a step or two behind. "I'm watching them," he said. "Nobody's doing anything yet."

"Doesn't matter," I said. "I have to see if she's here."

Chapter 123

AN OLDER woman with long and wildly frazzled gray and white hair stepped out of the front door as I reached the scarred, unpainted steps. Her eyes were ringed with redness.

"Come with me." She sighed. "Come along. You nah need no weapon."

For the first time in many months, I allowed myself to feel the tiniest flash of hope, though I didn't have any reason to, other than the rumor that a woman was being kept here against her will.

Beatitude? Something to do with blessedness and happiness? Could it be Christine?

The old woman walked unsteadily around the house and through light bushes, trees, and ferns out back. About sixty or seventy yards into the thickening woods, she came to half a dozen small shacks, where she stopped. The shacks were made of wood, bamboo, and corrugated metal.

She walked forward again and stopped at the next-to-last shack in the group.

She took out a key attached to a leather strap

around her wrist, inserted it in the door lock, and jiggled it.

She pushed the door forward, and it creaked loudly on a rusty hinge.

I looked inside and saw a plain, neat, and clean room. Someone had written *The Lord Is My Shepherd* in black paint on the wall.

No one was there.

No Beatitude.

No Christine.

I let my eyes fall shut. Desperation enveloped me.

My eyes slowly opened. I didn't understand why I had been led to this empty room, this old shack in the woods. My heart was ripped in two again. Was it some kind of trap?

The Weasel? Shafer? Was he here?

Someone stepped out from behind a small folding screen in one corner of the room. I felt as if I were in free fall, and a small gasp came out of my mouth.

I didn't know what I had been expecting, but it wasn't this. Sampson put out his hand to steady me. I was barely aware of his touch.

Christine slowly stepped into the shafts of sunlight coming from the single window in the shack. I had thought I would never see her again.

She was much thinner, and her hair was braided and longer than I'd ever seen it. But she had the same wise, beautiful brown eyes. Neither of us was able to speak at first. It was the most extraordinary moment of my life.

I had gone cold all over, and everything was moving in slow motion. It seemed supernaturally quiet in the small room.

Christine was holding a light-yellow blanket, and I could see a baby's head just peeking above the crown of the covers. I walked forward even though my legs were trembling and threatening to buckle. I could hear the baby softly cooing in the nest of blankets.

"Oh, Christine, Christine," I finally managed.

Tears welled in her eyes, and then in mine. We both stepped forward, and then I was awkwardly holding her. The little baby gazed up peacefully into both our faces.

"This is our baby, and he probably saved my life. He takes after you," Christine said. Then we kissed gently, and it was so sweet and tender. We held on for dear, dear life. We melted into each other. Neither of us could believe this was actually happening.

"I call him Alex. You were always right here," Christine told me. "You were always with me."

Epilogue

LONDON BRIDGES, FALLING

HIS NAME was Frederick Neuman, and he liked to think of himself as a citizen of the European community rather than of any single country, but if anyone asked, he claimed to be German. His head was shaved close, and it made him look severe, but also more impressive, he thought—an amazing accomplishment in itself.

He would be remembered as "quite tall, thin and bald," or as an "interesting *artiste* type," and several people *did* see him that week in Chelsea in London. *I want to be remembered. That's important.*

He shopped, or at least window-shopped, on the King's Road and in Sloane Street.

He went to the cinema in Kensington High Street.

And the Waterstone's bookshop.

Nights, he would have a pint or two at the King's Head. He mostly kept to himself at the pub.

He had a master plan. Another game was beginning.

He saw Lucy and the twins at Safeway one afternoon. He watched them from across rows of baked beans, then followed them down the aisles filled with shoppers. No harm, no foul—no problem for anybody.

He couldn't resist the challenge, though. The dice started to play in his head. They rattled the number he wanted to hear.

He kept walking closer and closer to the family, careful to keep his face slightly averted, just in case, but still watching Lucy out of the corner of his eye, watching the twins, who were perhaps more dangerous.

Lucy was examining some wild Scottish salmon. She finally noticed him, he was sure, but she did-n't recognize him—obviously. Neither did the twins. Dumb, silly little girls—mirrors of their mother.

The game was on again—so delicious. He'd been away from it for a while. He had the book money, his advance from the trial tell-all, which he kept in Switzerland. He had bummed around the Caribbean after his escape by boat from Jamaica. He'd gone to San Juan and been tempted to act up there. Then on to Europe—first to Rome, Milan, Paris, Frankfurt, and Dublin, and finally home to London. He'd strayed only a couple of times on the whole trip. He was such a careful boy now.

It felt just like old times as he got oh-so-close to Lucy in the shopping aisle. Jesus, his physical tics were back. He was tapping his foot nervously and shaking out his hands.

He'd have thought she'd notice that, but she

was such a vacuous blond cow, such a cipher, such a waste of his time; even now, as he got closer and closer, only a foot or two away, she still didn't recognize him

"Oh Loo-cy . . . it's Ricky," he said, and grinned and grinned. "It's me, *darling.*"

Swish. Swish. He swiped at her twice, back and forth, as they passed like strangers in the aisle at Safeway. The blows barely crisscrossed Lucy's throat, but they cut it inches deep.

She dropped to her bony knees, both hands clutching her neck as if she were strangling herself. And then she saw who it was, and her blue eyes bulged with shock and pain and finally with what seemed to be a terrible sadness.

"Geoffrey," she managed in a gurgling voice, as blood bubbled from her open mouth.

Her last word on Earth. His name.

Beautiful for Shafer to hear—the recognition he craved—revenge for all of them. He turned away, forced himself to, before he did the twins as well.

He was never seen again in the Chelsea neighborhood, but everyone would remember him for as long as they lived.

God, would they remember.

That tall bald monster.

The one in all-black clothes, the inhuman freak.

The heartless killer who had committed so many horrible murders that even *he* had lost count.

Geoffrey Shafer.

Death.

CONDOR DREAMS

Western Literature Series

OTHER BOOKS BY GERALD W. HASLAM

Fiction

Okies: Selected Stories

Masks: A Novel

The Wages of Sin: Collected Stories

Hawk Flights: Visions of the West

Snapshots: Glimpses of the Other California

The Man Who Cultivated Fire and Other Stories

That Constant Coyote: California Stories

Many Californias: Literature from the Golden State (*editor*)

Nonfiction

Forgotten Pages of American Literature (*editor*)

The Language of the Oil Fields

Western Writing (*editor*)

California Heartland: Writing from the Great Central Valley (*coeditor*)

A Literary History of the American West (*coeditor*)

Voices of a Place: Social and Literary Essays from the Other California

The Other California: The Great Central Valley in Life and Letters

Coming of Age in California: Personal Essays

The Great Central Valley: California's Heartland

Gerald W. Haslam

Afterword by Gary Soto

UNIVERSITY OF NEVADA PRESS   Reno   Las Vegas   London

Condor Dreams

& Other Fictions

Western Literature Series Editor:
John H. Irsfeld

A list of books in the series appears at
the end of the book.

The paper used in this book meets the
requirements of American National
Standard for Information Sciences –
Permanence of Paper for Printed
Library Materials, ANSI Z39.48-1984.
Binding materials were selected for
strength and durability.

Library of Congress
Cataloging-in-Publication Data

Haslam, Gerald W.
Condor dreams and other fictions /
Gerald W. Haslam ; afterword by
Gary Soto.
p.   cm. — (Western literature series)
ISBN 0-87417-227-6 (alk. paper)
ISBN 0-87417-232-2 (pbk. : alk. paper)
1. Working class – California – Central
Valley (Valley) – Fiction.   2. Men –
California – Central Valley (Valley) –
Fiction.   3. Central Valley (Calif. :
Valley) – Fiction.   I. Title.
II. Series.
PS3558.A724C66   1994
813'.54 – dc20   93-33531
                                                CIP

University of Nevada Press
Reno, Nevada 89557 USA
Copyright © 1994 University of
Nevada Press
All rights reserved
Design by Richard Hendel
Printed in the United States
of America
9 8 7 6 5 4 3 2 1

To the memory of my grandparents . . .

Ramona Silva and Jack Johnson,

Marie Martin and Fred Haslam

CONTENTS

CONDOR DREAMS

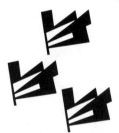

Standing with his nearly empty coffee cup in one hand, Dan gazed into tule fog dense as oatmeal. It obscured the boundary between sky and earth, between breath and wind, and he was momentarily uncertain where or what he was. He could see nothing. He could not be seen. This must be what nothingness is, he thought, what extinction is . . . like what's happened to the condors. Then he chuckled at himself: Don't lose it, pal. Don't lose it. Stress will do that to you.

He rubbed his chest where it was again tightening. This field is real and those critters are gone, as defunct as family farmers soon will be. As I'll be, Dan thought. His chuckle turned grim.

Nearly fifty years before, on a morning as sunny and clear as this one was foggy and obscure, he had stood next to his father in this same field and seen for the first time a wonder soaring high above – a vast black shape like death itself. Frightened, he moved closer to his father. Then he noticed the bird's bare head and its vast wings. Those dark sails were cored with white, their farthest feathers spread like fingers grasping sky. It appeared to belong to another, sterner time.

"Look, Daniel," his father said, "that's a California condor. See, its wings, they never move. It rides the wind."

"It rides the wind? How, Papa?"

"Ahhh . . . it is just a wind rider, I guess."

"Can I be one?"

"Only in your dreams, Daniel."

"Where did he come from, Papa?" Dan asked.

His father pointed southeast, where the Tehachapi Mountains loomed, where mysterious canyons slashed into them. "There," he explained. "They live where men can't. Years ago, when I come here from the old country, those condors they'd fly out here over the valley every spring to eat winter kills. Sometimes fifty or sixty of 'em. Sometimes maybe a hundred. You could hear their beaks clicking. Now, only four or five ever come."

"Why, Papa?"

"Why?" His father had migrated here from the Azores and worked for other people until he could buy a patch of worn-out range, which he'd then turned into this farm. "I don't know," he finally replied. "Things they changed, eh? Maybe some ranchers they shoot 'em 'cause they think those condors take calves . . . or for the fun of it. Maybe there's not so much for 'em to eat no more. All I ever seen 'em eat is winter kills. I don't know . . ." His voice trailed off, and he seemed genuinely puzzled. A few years later, the boy's father had been a winter kill, drowned by a freak flood pouring from one of those mountain canyons.

Just a few days before his father's death, the two of them had stood on the edge of this very field and spied a dot high against the mountains. They leaned on their shovels and watched it grow larger, closer, since by then appearances of condors over the valley had become rare indeed. A young heifer had died and, as was his habit, his father had left the carcass next to the reservoir, and a cluster of buzzards busied themselves cleaning it up.

Neither man said anything and they stood waiting: Perhaps the great condor might strip this heifer's bones. As though tantalizing them, it approached slowly, so slowly, its white-splotched wings tipping, never pumping, as it sailed far above, then began to swing lower, its great shadow sliding over these acres. Finally, the antique flier swooped down from the wind, and the smaller, squabbling birds quickly bounced away and scrambled into the sky. As the condor began to feed, father and son turned and smiled at one another; they were gazing at a California older than memory.

Dan stood now on the land his family had reclaimed, and he could not see the sky because of the fog that had risen, as it so often did following rains, obscuring nearly everything. If the condors were out there anymore, they were as hidden as other people's dreams. If they were there. Crazy thoughts.

He walked up one long row, grapevines staked on both sides of him, their bare branches trained on wires. Normally the campesinos would be pruning them now, but not this year. Not any year, perhaps. Dan had grown up working these fields that his father and uncle had originally cleared and plowed, that his brothers and sisters and he had irrigated and cultivated and reaped. Now a bank would take it all, the land and the memories. It was grinding to accept. One part of him wanted to weep, another wanted vengeance. He wandered the field now because he could not bring himself to tell Mary everything he had heard the day before at the bank. It was the first significant thing he had ever withheld from her, and that too compounded his tension. Thank God the kids were grown.

He stopped, far from house or road, surrounded by the gray-velvet haze, and listened closely. He had heard a voice. Then he realized it was his own, arguing with himself. That's what this was doing to him, driving him nuts. It would take nearly $300,000 to convert his fields to profitable crops now that table grapes with seeds no longer sold well, but five consecutive losing years had so eroded his credit that he could not raise that kind of backing. His note was due and the once friendly banker demanded payment.

Dan tilted his face skyward and stared into the colorless miasma surrounding him, wanting to scream like a dying animal. Were there condors left up there? Would they come clean his bones? He trudged back toward the house to give his wife the bad news.

The next morning, they sat at the dinette table sipping coffee and gazing out the window at fog as soft as kittens' fur. "Another cold one," he sighed, meaningless talk to fill the silence.

"Why don't you start the pruning?" his wife asked. "It's not like you to give up."

"What's the point?" His voice edged toward anger, for he'd sensed reproach even before she spoke. She didn't understand. This land was his body, and now it would be torn from him. Her way was to stay busy; when her mother'd died, Mary had cooked for three days. But you can't stay busy when your land, your flesh, is being devoured like so much carrion. She didn't understand that.

No, Dan simply wanted revenge. But on whom? The banker who had urged him to expand and had staked him for so many years? The public that ate only Thompson seedless grapes and Perlettes? The county agriculture agent who hadn't warned him about changing tastes? Who?

There was the sharp sound of a car door slamming, then a light knock at the kitchen door. It was 6:45 A.M., and the two glanced at each other across the table before Dan stood and strode to the door.

"Buenos días, Señor Silva," said the old man who stood there, battered five-gallon hat in hand. "Estoy aquí para trabajar." His chin was not quite half shaven, and his faded jeans were only partly buttoned.

"Come on in, Don Felipe," Dan smiled. "You want coffee?"

"Sí, por favor."

"Como? Americano o Mexicano?" It was an old joke between them.

"Solo Mexicano, por favor." The grin was nearly toothless.

Despite the gentle humor, here was one more problem. Felipe Ramirez had been working on this land as long as Dan could remember. His father had originally employed the old man years before. Despite his name and fluent Spanish, he was more than half Yokuts – local Indian. In his prime he had been a vaquero in those far away condor mountains. Dan had always liked him, with his strange but amusing yarns, his unabashed belief in the supernatural – which he said *was* natural.

The old man now lived with a niece in Bakersfield, and Dan annually hired him to help prune grapevines, then kept him on over the summer as a general helper. He was a link to the past, to Dan's own father. Don Felipe remained a strong worker, but his peculiar tales – amusing during good times – would be a burden now.

At the table, Don Felipe bowed to Mary, who smiled and greeted him. He seated himself and accepted a steaming mug of coffee into which he spooned a great mound of sugar. Their conversation was, as always, conducted in two languages, a comfortable weaving of Spanish and English. "Where are the others?" asked the old man.

Dan was suddenly embarrassed. "We haven't begun pruning yet."

"It is too wet?"

"No."

There was a long silence, for the old man would not ask why. It was not his way to probe. "It will be a fine growing year," he finally observed, "all this rain. In my dream, the great green gods were touching you."

"It could be a good year," Dan responded.

"Tell him," said Mary. Her husband briefly glared at her. This was difficult enough without being rushed. She had never understood how men speak to one another . . . or don't speak to one another about some things.

Again there was silence. The old man did not appear anxious. "Would you like some tobacco?" he asked, extending his pouch of Bull Durham.

"No thanks."

Don Felipe knew Mary did not smoke, so no tobacco was offered her. Instead, he rolled a drooping cigarette, carefully twisting both ends. "Do you no longer wish to employ me, Daniel?" He pronounced the name "Don-yale."

"We are losing our ranch, Don Felipe. A bank will take it. But I want you to work with me because there are still some things to be done."

"I am your servant."

"Just take it easy today. Tomorrow I'll have a list of jobs."

"As you wish, Daniel."

Two hours later, a brisk wind broke from the mountains and cleared the fog. Dan emerged from the barn when he heard its swift whine, and walked into cold sunlight, then noted on what they called the old section a lone figure among the vines. What the hell? He strode to the place where Don Felipe pruned grapes.

"Why are you doing this?" he asked, almost demanded, for this land would soon no longer be his, and to work it was suddenly a personal offense. He had not even told Mary that it was rumored the bank would subdivide ranchettes here, a prospect too painful for words.

"It must be done."

"Don't you understand, I won't own this land much longer. I won't harvest grapes this year."

"Daniel," the old man said in a tone Dan had heard before, "no one owns the land. The earth must be nurtured, never owned. Your father knew that and you, deep within, you know that too. It is like a woman, to be loved but never owned. It is not an empty thing but full of life. And these vines are our children."

"Tell the bank that," Dan spat.

"They will build no houses here."

"Houses? Who won't?"

"The bank will build no houses here."

"Of course not. Who said they would?" How had the old man guessed that?

A smile lit the leathery face and the eyes rolled skyward. "Your father started here with only eighty acres, true?"

"Yes."

"How many do you plant now?"

"About thirteen hundred. Why?"

"I am pruning the old eighty acres. You must save them. No houses here, Daniel."

This conversation was crazy. He didn't need it; he had problems enough. "I'm saving all of it or none of it," he snapped. His chest began tightening as he fought rage. Why didn't the old man sense the trouble he was causing? Dan was tempted to call Don Felipe's niece and have her come back for him.

Wind was picking up, blowing north from the distant mountains, and dust was beginning to pepper them. The old man removed a thong from one pocket, wrapped it over his sombrero, and tied it under his chin. "It is the dust of the condors," he said, squinting toward the peaks and canyons to the south. "They will protect this land."

"The condors are dead."

The old man's eyes seemed to crackle for a second, then he smiled. "No, not all of them."

"I'll need some condors, or buzzards maybe, when the bank is through with me."

"The condors, my son, are not mere carrion birds. They bring life from death. They renew, that is why their dust is a good sign. It will be a good year."

"For the bank," Dan said, and he turned toward the house.

That night he could not relax. In the cusp between sleep and wakefulness near dawn, he saw the earth rupture and a gray flatus ooze out, then a great inky bird seemed to swim from it while he struggled to find light . . . find light. He awoke, his breast tight, and immediately stared out the window: Heavy fog pressed against the glass, the world rendered low-contrast and colorless. He couldn't even see the land he was about to lose, and the compression in his chest and jaw were edging toward pain.

He rose quietly, but Mary stirred. "Getting up?" she asked drowsily.

"Yeah." He headed for the bathroom, where he gulped two antacid tablets, then pulled on his jeans and boots, shrugged on a shirt, and finally washed up. In the kitchen, he started coffee, one hand holding his aching breast, then put on his hat and walked out the back door to smell the morning fog.

As he stood in that near-darkness, he heard – or thought he heard – an irregular clicking. Condors? Condors' beaks? For a moment he was puzzled, rubbing his chest, then realized what it had to be: Someone was pruning grapes.

On the old field, he confronted Don Felipe. "Why are you doing this? I'm going to lose the ranch, don't you understand?"

The leathery face smiled, and the old man, still bent with pruning shears in one hand, replied, "When I was a young man, I worked with an old Indian named Castro on the Tejon Ranch in those mountains. He was what you call it? a . . . a wizard, maybe, or a . . . a medicine man. He could do many strange things. He could turn a snake by looking at it. One time I saw him touch a wolf that had killed some sheep and the wolf understood; it never came back. No horse ever bucked him.

"That guy, one time he told me that this life we think is real isn't real at all. He said we live only in the dreams of condors. He said that us Indians

were condors' good dreams, and you pale people were their nightmares."
The old man smiled, then he continued, "He said we can live only if
those birds dream of us."

Dan didn't need this nonsense. "Condors are extinct," he pointed out.
He was sure he'd read that in the newspaper.

The old man only grinned. "Then how are we talking? We are still
here, Daniel, so the condors cannot be gone. You are still here." The old
man paused, then added, "I think that guy he *was* a condor."

Too much, this was just too damned much. He would have to call
Don Felipe's niece as soon as he returned to the house. He just didn't
need this mumbo jumbo on top of the distress he was already suffering.
"Why do you think that?" the younger man snapped.

"Because one day he flew away up a canyon into the heart of the
mountains, and we never saw him again. He said that if the condors
disappeared, so would their dreams. That's what that old Indian told me."

"*Right*," said the despondent farmer, turning away. Why couldn't this
old man understand? Why couldn't he deal with reality? Dan was becoming agitated enough to fire Don Felipe on the spot.

Before he could speak, though, the pain surged from his chest into his
arm and jaw. "Listen . . . ," he began, but did not finish, for breath left
him. "Listen . . . ," he croaked just before he swayed to the damp soil.

"Daniel!" Don Felipe cried. He knelt, and his hard old hands, like
talons, touched the fallen man's face. Dan was straining to speak when
he sensed the fog beginning to swirl and vaguely saw the old man's body
begin to deepen and darken and oscillate. A shadowy shape suddenly
surged and a liquid wing swelled beneath Dan, lofting him from his pain.

A startled moment later, he hovered above a great gray organism that
sent misty tendrils into nearby canyons and arroyos, that moved within
itself and stretched as far north into the great valley as his vision could
reach. It was . . . all . . . so . . . beautiful, and his anxiety drained as he
skimmed wind far above the fog, far beyond it, as he rode his own returning breath, and below the mist began clearing. His fields focused as the
earth-cloud thinned. The land too was breathing, he suddenly realized,
its colors as iridescent as sunlight on the wings of condors. It was all so
alluring that he stretched a hand to touch . . . touch . . . it.

"Dan," Mary's voice startled him, "are you all right?" She cradled his head in her hands and her own face was tight with fear.

It was like waking from his deepest dream but, after a second of confusion, he managed a smile. "I'm okay." An edge of breathlessness remained, that and pain's shadow, so he hesitated before, with her help, climbing to his feet. Past his wife's shoulder he saw the old man, whose dark eyes merged momentarily with his. "I just let tension get to me," he explained. Rising, he brushed wet earth from his jeans. "I'll drive into town and see the doc just in case."

The easy tone of his voice seemed to reassure his wife. "Let's go have our coffee," she urged.

"Sure," he replied, putting an arm around her waist, his relief at being able to touch her as tangible as breath itself, then turning toward the old man. "Don Felipe, are you coming in?"

"I must finish the field."

"Okay," Dan replied, "I'll bring something out, and I'll give you a hand when I get back from the doctor's." This place, even eighty acres of it, was worth saving. There had to be a way.

"I will be grateful," the old man nodded.

After Dan and Mary turned, they could hear Don Felipe's shears clicking like a condor's beak. Arm in arm, they walked toward home. The fog had dissipated enough so that their house shone sharp and white across the field of dormant vines. Behind it, bordering the hazy valley, those mountains, the Tehachapis, bulked like the land's surging muscles: creased and burnished and darkened with bursts of oaks and pines, flexing into silent summits and deep canyons where valley winds were born, into the hidden heart of the range where Dan now knew a secret condor still dreamed.

COWBOYS

This old boy named Shorty Moore used to haul mud out to the rig, see. Shorty he could whup a man and he never ducked a fight, so not many guys in the oil fields ever give him much trouble.

One time old Shorty he was sittin' around the doghouse at quittin' time discussin' this new pistol he'd just bought while us guys changed to go home, and a engineer looked at Shorty's duds, then asked real smart alecky if he was a cowboy. All of us on the crew just set back to watch Shorty stomp the bastard, see, but old Shorty he fooled us. He looked around, kind of grinned, and said real quiet: Naw, I ain't no cowboy. Never have been. But I wear these boots and this belt and shirt because they're western, see, workin' men's clothes. And I feel western. I ain't no college sissy with a necktie and pink hands. I'm a man and that's what my clothes say. Any old boy that doubts it ain't got but to jump and I'll kick his ass for him.

That was that. The engineer never said nothin' more, so old Shorty just let things slide and I guess everyone was happy to get out of the doghouse that afternoon.

But, you know, every time a guy turns around in Bakersfield nowadays, seems like, some pasty-faced bastard's eyein' your belt buckle or boots, and you just know he's a-thinkin' *cowboy* and laughin' at you to hisself. They all think they're high powers. I ain't like old Shorty; things like that just eat on me. I work as hard as any man does for my wages, a-buckin' pig iron on a drillin' rig, and I can't take some pencil-necked fairy that works in a office looking down his nose at me. I'll break his nose for him, by God.

Last summer, whenever the college kids come out to replace guys goin' on vacation, wouldn't you know we'd get us a hippie. And it was comical as hell whenever this kid first drove up to the rig. We'd just spudded in, see, a-hopin' to hit gas on Suisun Bay up near Fairfield. It was tower change and my crew was workin' daylights. About the time we walked out of the doghouse, and old Turk Brown's crew was comin' off, see, up sputters a little red sports car with this great big long-haired kid a-drivin' it. Well, he gets out of the car, all the guys kinda standing back watchin' him, and he commences talkin' to the pusher. That kid was so huge, and his car was so small, he looked like a big old snake coming out of a little basket: more and more of him kept coming after you just knew the car couldn't hold all of him.

Old Arkie Williams he made a kissin' sound with his mouth and the kid looked at him. I seen cold eyes before, but that kid looked like he could put a fire out starin' at it. And I could see that even though Arkie kept on bullshittin', he knew he'd made a mistake. Is it a boy or a girl? Arkie said. He never did have enough sense to admit he was wrong after he started spoutin' off. The pusher told us to get up on the rig and pull them slips, and the kid he was still just a-lookin' at Arkie, not sayin' nothin'; I figured Arkie was into it. Too bad for him too. He never could fight a lick.

The kid he went to work that mornin' and spent the whole tower helping Buford Kileen clean out the pumps. Come quittin' time, we all headed for the doghouse hot to get changed and go drink us some beer. Just about the time Arkie walked up to the doorway from between pipe racks, the new kid he stepped in front of him and bam! one-punch-coldcocked him. Jesus, could that big old kid hit! And that ain't all; Arkie hadn't but hit the ground and the hippie had him kicked three or four times. We grabbed the kid and had one hell of a time holdin' him while two boys from the crew that was just comin' to work helped Arkie. The pusher he took the kid into his office and told him, I guess, any more fightin' and he'd be canned. And the pusher took Arkie aside and told him he'd got just what he deserved.

What really disturbed me though was that the new kid never said nothing. After it was over he just climbed out of his work clothes and into them suede drawers with fringes on 'em, and high cowboy boots, and a western belt with a big turquoise buckle. He put on some little colored beads and a leather sombrero and out he walked, no shirt a-tall. He climbed into his little red car, see, and drove off without saying good-bye or kiss my ass or nothin'.

After he was gone some of the guys commenced kidding about the highfalutin cowboy clothes the kid wore. I'll bet he never rode nothing but that little red car, old Buford said, 'cept maybe a few of them college coeds. Everyone laughed. Yeah, Easy Ed Davis said, he's a real cowpoke, that one, must think he's Buffalo Bill with that long hair. Reckon we ought to buy him some ribbons to go with them beads? I asked. Arkie never laughed, then pretty soon he ups and says that if the kid ever messed with him again, by God, there'd be one more cowboy on Boot Hill. Shorty Moore showed up a little later at this beer joint where we usually went, and he said he didn't have no use for hippies period. No use a-tall.

The kid turned out to be one hell of a worker; he give a honest jump for his wages, I'll say that much. He never let none of the boys on the job get real friendly with him, but he seemed to like it when they commenced callin' him Cowboy. He didn't know that most of the guys wanted to call him Dude, but they thought better of it. He was a big old boy.

I could tell he really didn't give a damn for none of us. Whenever he did talk to us it was to show off all of his book learnin' and to hint at how ignorant he figured we was. You know, one of us might say he thought the Dodgers would go all the way this year, and young Cowboy he'd kind of sneer: It all depends on whether they can exploit more blacks than the other teams, he'd say – shit like that. Hell, he couldn't stand to see us enjoy nothin'; he liked to wreck things for everyone, it seemed like.

Cowboy he was studying to be a college pro-fessor and he had about that much sense.

A couple of months after he first come to work, we finally lifted the kid. He was tougher than most summer hires to trick because he didn't talk much, and he didn't seem to give a damn about what we thought of him. But old Easy Ed, our derrick man, he finally bullshitted the kid into it. Easy Ed could talk a coon white if you give him half a chance. He just kept a-gabbin' at Cowboy all the time, see, telling him he didn't know what a strong man was. Hell, old Ed would say, a young buck like you ain't seen a stout man till you seen a old-timer like me hot after it. There ain't many old boys in this oil patch can lift as much weight as me, by God. I can pick up three guys at one time. Easy Ed's just a little bitty fart, and the kid would kind of look at him funny but not say nothin'. It was comical, really. Cowboy would bring all these books with him to read when he ate, but he'd no more than get his dinner bucket open than Easy Ed would be a-chewing on his ear. I believe that kid finally give in just to shut Ed up.

We was circulatin' mud and waitin' for the engineers to give us the go-ahead on making more hole that day; everyone was pretty bored. We'd just finished unloading sacks of chemicals off Shorty's truck, and we was kind of layin' around on the mud rack chewin' tobacco and tellin' lies. Pretty soon up comes Easy Ed and he right away starts in on Cowboy. Before long the kid said okay, let's see you lift three guys.

So everybody trooped around behind the rig, and old Ed he laid down a length of rope on the ground. Then he said: three of you boys lay down on her. Heavy, he said to me, you take one side. Shorty, you take the other. Cowboy, you crawl in the middle. I want you to know there ain't no trick to it. We three got down on our backs while the other guys stood around us. Ed just kept a-jabbering, see. I swear, that guy should of been a preacher; he damn sure coulda talked some sisters into the bushes.

Well, anyways, old Ed he tells us three to wrap our arms and legs around each other (me and Shorty knowin' this stuff from way back but not lettin' on, so the kid won't suspect nothin'). Now make her real tight, Ed tells us, I don't want nobody slippin' whenever I pick y'all up. Me and Shorty really cinched up on the kid's arms and legs, see. We had him pinned to the ground, and I could tell he was catchin' on.

Ed, a-yackin' all the time, commenced unbuttonin' Cowboy's fly and Buford handed Ed the dope brush. The kid tensed up, then kind of chuckled and relaxed. Ah, shit, he said, laughin' a little. I figured then it was gonna be a easy liftin', and that the kid wasn't half bad after all. But just about the time Easy Ed started painting the kid's balls with dope, old Arkie couldn't keep his mouth shut. He kind of spit at the kid: In the position you let us get you in, weevil, just thinka all the things we *could* do to you. Then he made that kissin' sound.

Oh Jesus! The kid just exploded! I'm a pretty stout old boy myownself, see, but Cowboy just sort of shook me loose, then kicked Ed in the slats with his free foot. I've helped lift maybe a hundred weevils in my day, and nobody never just shook me off before. Old Shorty hung on and in a minute the two of them was rollin' around in the dust and puncture vines. Shorty don't know how to give up in a fight, and he held on to that big old boy like a dog on a bull.

We knew the pusher would can the kid if he seen him fightin', so we all jumped in and broke her up. When we managed to get 'em apart, the kid's eyes locked on Shorty, and Shorty he stuck his finger in the kid's face and said: Name the place, Cowboy. We'll finish her where there ain't nobody gonna get in the way. The kid just kept starin' and said anyplace was fine with him.

There was this little beer joint at a eucalyptus grove between where we was drillin' and Rio Vista. That's where Shorty and the kid decided to meet after work. The whole crew drove right over there and drank beer while they waited for Shorty to get back from Lodi where he left his truck in the chemical company's yard every evenin'. The kid he stayed outside a-leanin' on his little red car, see, his sombrero tilted back, his long hair a-blowin' in the wind. Them frozen blue eyes of his just glowed. Damned if he don't look like some old-time gunfighter, Buford said, lookin' out the window. I told him that was one cowboy I didn't want to tangle with. You notice he never messes with me no more, Arkie bragged, and all the guys laughed, but old Arkie was serious and he didn't see nothin' funny. Naturally, Easy Ed took to laying bets: I taken old Shorty, he said, and I'll put five bucks on him. Buford covered him right away. Arkie bet on Shorty too, and Buford covered him. Ain't you a-bettin',

Heavy? Ed asked me, but I said no. I never felt too good about the whole thing.

Shorty he drove up directly and crawled out of his Chevy. It was near sundown and the light it'd turned all funny like in a movie. For a minute him and Cowboy just stood there starin' at each other, then Cowboy he bent over and reached into his car and pulled out a gunbelt, the old kind with ammunition loops and long thongs danglin' from the holster. He slipped her on and tied the thongs around his right thigh. Hey! I heard Buford say and when I looked away from the kid, I seen old Shorty he was doin' the same thing.

All of us guys froze. Cowboy and Shorty they pulled their six-guns from the holsters, spun the cylinders and kinda blew on the sights. Then they slid the revolvers back into leather and commenced walkin' toward each other. What the hell is this? Easy Ed whispered, but I couldn't answer, my heart was a-stompin' inside my chest and I couldn't even swallow. I wanted to holler, but I just stood there.

When they was about twenty-five or thirty foot apart – real close – Cowboy and Shorty stopped, then spread their legs like they was gonna pick up somethin' heavy. It's yer play, dude, Shorty said, his eyes pointed straight at Cowboy's. Cowboy he kinda rocked back on his heels: You've been alive too long, he croaked. You've outlived yourself.

Then a roar! For what seemed like forever, they dipped their right shoulders and threw their right hands straight down. There wasn't no fancy grabbin' and wingin', movie-style, just two short, efficient moves, like when a good worker shovels. ·

And Shorty busted backwards, almost up in the air, then fell, a puppet without no strings, empty, his gun in the dirt. A cloud of blue smoke hung where he'd stood.

Oh sweet lovin' Jesus! I cried out, and I run over to Shorty, but he'd had it. He was all sprawled out, his eyes lookin' like egg-whites. Little frothy bubbles was comin' from his brisket, but not much blood. He coughed, choked maybe, and a gusher shot up from his mouth and from the hole in his middle, then the bubbles quit.

Get your ass away from him, I heard Cowboy say. I looked at the kid. He still held his six-gun, and some of the blue smoke still hung there in front of him; there wasn't no wind. I looked back down at Shorty and seen a great big puddle of blood was growing underneath him, peekin' out, not red but maroon, almost black. Get! Cowboy hollered again, so I walked back to where the other boys stood. I couldn't do old Shorty no good.

Cowboy he holstered his pistol, untied the thong, then slipped the gunbelt off and dropped it into his car. You guys gonna buy me a beer? he asked. None of us said nothin'. I didn't figure so, he said. He climbed into his car, backed up – me afraid he was a-gonna run over Shorty but he was real careful not to – then started out onto the road. Then he done something real funny; he slowed down, almost stopped, and flashed us one of them V-peace signs hippies are always makin'. He drove away toward Fairfield, up over a low hill into the fadin' sun.

Jesus, Buford said, what're we gonna do?

Easy Ed he just kept lookin' from where Shorty lay with a big old blow-fly already doin' business on his bloody lower lip, then back toward the hill where Cowboy'd disappeared. We might could form a posse, he said.

IT'S OVER . . .

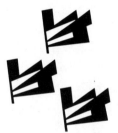

Over Wynonna's shoulder, I see Elaine chatting with friends, then I grin at the attractive woman standing directly in front of me and reply, "Sure, why not?"

"For old times' sake," she adds. "Right, old-timer?"

"Right, old-timer," I chuckle, and we join other couples on the floor.

The first time I ever danced with Wynonna was in this same high school multipurpose room nearly thirty years ago. We were fourteen-year-old freshmen at an afternoon sock hop. There was a girls'-choice dance, and her cronies dared her to ask a boy. Saucy, she bounced to the stag line and without hesitation pulled me onto the floor.

We went steady for the next four years until she departed for college and a much larger world than Bakersfield promised, leaving me devastated by the certain knowledge that my plans – my assumptions – had been wrong and would never be realized. Shortly thereafter, I was drafted into the army and began the odyssey that would lead me from a dead-end job at a gas station to college, then graduate school. Nearly thirty years ago it had started in this very room . . .

It's over.

All over,

And soon somebody else

will make a fuss over you

but how about me?

As a singer purrs, my high school love and I move together, facing one another, bodies still familiar. Despite my casual smile, I am breathless. "Your wife is lovely, Nicky," Wynonna smiles. "She really is. I'd heard that, but she's even nicer and prettier than I expected."

"Elaine's a great gal."

"You've been lucky."

"Yeah, I have . . . we have. And you?" It is an unintentionally thoughtless question. She's been married three times, I know.

Without hesitation, she grins. "Mixed bag. All big shots, dot the o's, if you get my meaning." Her legal practice in Santa Barbara is elite, mutual friends have told me. Little wonder she encounters big shots, dotted o's or not.

"I'm sorry."

"*You're* sorry"; she raises her eyebrows. Her voice is thick with wine, and mine is too, I guess. We're well into the evening.

From the moment Wynonna entered the reunion – our class's twenty-fifth – I had fought not to stare at her: It had been so long and she looked so trim, so youthful, so . . . yes . . . so expensive. While she hugged old chums and laughed with them, I managed to exchange a quick handshake with her, a moment of eye contact, while I sensed the gaze of others on us, then drifted away to those old friends with whom Elaine and I remained close.

So many years ago, Wynonna and I had explored life's currents and channels, learned together some mysterious lessons that have not left me. We had, of course, invented sex – secret and overwhelming – and it became deliciously central to our relationship. But there had been another, less understandable, less escapable bonding: not sister and brother, something deeper and more enduring. It can still swoop my stomach at odd times.

"Do you remember our first dance, Nicky?" she asks. My wife – everyone else, in fact – calls me Nick.

"Yeah." She should ask if I remember breathing.

"You asked me right in this room when we were freshmen."

"No, it was girls' choice. You asked me."

"No, I didn't. *You* asked me," she giggles.

There had been hints late in our senior year – she had less time for dates, we had no more noon rendezvous, my phone calls increasingly went unanswered – signs that her interests were turning from me, and the plans we'd made, toward the universities that beckoned a top student. Although my job at the service station paid little, I had simply and naively assumed that we'd graduate, marry, and live happily ever after, as the popular songs promised.

One terrible Saturday afternoon Wynonna had emerged with an icy face from her house to greet me. She looked delicious in pink shorts and a white blouse while I stood on her porch, fresh from work, wearing an oil-stained shirt with "Nick" sewn on one pocket. I don't think I'd ever wanted to hold her more, but she curtly informed me that she would leave the following August to attend the University of California in Los Angeles. Our marriage would have to wait until after she graduated. Her tone told me far more, and that evening I'd picked a fistfight with a guy I didn't know.

"You have four kids now?" she asks.

"Two boys, Dan and Nick; two girls, Kelly and Kit."

"Do you worry about your girls? You sure made my folks worry about me – for good reason, as it turned out." Her laugh is deep and intimate.

"No, I really don't, not about *that* anyway. Or about my boys either. What we did all seems pretty innocent today . . . so – what's the word? – so *sincere*, so *earnest*."

"Yes," she replies, and her eyes leave mine. Her voice has suddenly lost its happy edge.

"And your family?" I ask, changing the subject.

"I have the one boy, Bradley, from my first marriage. He's at Dartmouth."

"Danny and Kelly are both attending Cal Poly."

"Oh," she says with – or do I merely imagine – the tiniest hint of condescension.

If we had actually married immediately after high school, I wouldn't have been drafted, wouldn't have qualified for the GI Bill and wouldn't have been able to attend college; I certainly wouldn't have become principal of the local junior high school. What either of us would be doing now is anyone's guess. Whether I'd have been the first of a string of husbands, whether she'd be another frustrated housewife or ex-wife struggling through college in her forties, whether we'd be mired in debt and hopelessness and mutual disdain or be one of those rare and enchanting couples who somehow have managed to keep it all together – it's anybody's guess.

While the music sweeps, she says, "My folks were relieved to be rid of you." Her eyes still look away, her voice remains deep.

"Your folks? I thought they liked me."

"They said you were going nowhere, that you were irresponsible and didn't have any ambition. They even said you'd probably get tired of me and leave me."

"Your folks? They said that? I *really* thought they liked me." I have never heard this before and am both shocked and pained by it.

"Oh, they did. But they *loved* me, and they were ambitious for me. They wanted me to have chances they didn't have. You were an obstacle."

Still uncomfortable about what she has revealed, I reply, "Not much of one, as it turned out."

"They said you weren't dumb but that you weren't motivated."

"I was young and in love," I point out, having to clear my thickening throat.

"Yes," she says, her own voice softer. We fall silent once more, and her head is suddenly on my shoulder, her cheek next to mine. "Do you remember when we broke up, Nicky?" she breathes into my ear.

"I remember that we unraveled like a bad braid."

"No. I mean what happened at Don and Donna's party?"

We had been at Don Smith and Donna Pasquinni's wedding reception, just before Wynonna left for UCLA. We had danced – the last time until tonight – then sipped champagne at a corner table while she delicately explained that, after talking with her mother, she had decided that each of us should date others while she was away at school. "Is that all?" I asked. "Do we do anything besides 'date'?"

"I wouldn't do *that* with anyone else." Her eyes glistened, and one hand reached across the table and took mine, but I was receiving another, darker message, the final shredding of my dream.

"Do you really want someone else's babies?" I demanded in a cracking voice. Irrational as it seems now, it was my soundless heart's most honest cry. I'd sensed even before this conversation that other forces now determined her life and that I was powerless, but at least I could speak what I felt.

Her eyes flashed. "I didn't say *breed*, I said *date*," she snapped, her rationality and resolve negating my plea.

A moment later, I stood and said, "I've gotta go."

"I want to stay till Donna throws her bouquet." Wynonna remained seated. My eyes were imploring, hers implacable.

"Fine," I said. "I'll see you." I turned and walked away, my heart crumpling, my pride intact. Yearning immediately dislodged my innards as I drove away, a desolation I would not fully escape for years, and I kept glancing at the rearview mirror hoping that she'd emerge from the increasingly distant doorway to join me, but she didn't. For the first time since childhood, I wept.

Wynonna's voice grows even softer, her breath warmer on my ear where her lips brush. "I wanted your baby, Nicky, I really did, but my folks put so much pressure on me . . ." I feel that odd-but-not-unfamiliar sensation of her warm tears wetting my cheek. There is a sigh so deep that I seem to feel her lighten, then she adds, "I still want it."

Our bodies are moving together, her breath lurching into my ear and that distant, familiar passion again dislodges my heart. I cannot breathe. I cannot move my head to reply. And I cannot allow the music to stop.

But it does.

SCARS

. . . on left calf. Unobtrusive. No surgery recommended.

No. 16 *(age 11)*: Chicken pox. Pitting on forehead and both cheeks. Cosmetic surgery recommended but declined.

No. 17 *(age 12)*: Bicycle accident. Severe contusion and laceration of lower jaw. Large cicatrixive seam on chin. Cosmetic surgery successful.

No. 18 *(age 12)*: The smell of alcohol and perfume awakened him, those and her touch. "What?" he asked groggily. No reply, but he felt her hands moving, caressing him there. "Momma?" he said. "What're you doing?" The hands moving, then the mouth on him. "Momma? What're . . . *ohhhh!*" Psychotherapy continues.

No. 19 (age 14): Football. Fractured nose. Slightly askew after healing. Adds character. No surgery recommended.

No. 20 (age 16): "Hey, pretty boy! You look like a queen to me. Come 'ere. I wanna feed you through this tube. Come 'ere sweetness, I got a tube steak for you." Psychotherapy continues.

No. 21 (age 17): Fistfight. Lacerated right upper lip. Cracked right incisor. Tooth later capped. Cicatrix on lip. Adds character. No surgery recommended.

No. 22 (age 17): He flipped on the light and a nude stranger jerked upright from the couch, blinking. Then he heard his mother's mushy voice – "Who'sh there?" – and she sat up. Also naked. Psychotherapy continues.

No. 23 (age 17): Basketball. Severe laceration of left ocular region. Disfiguring keloid extending from mid-eyebrow, around outer portion of ocular depression onto upper cheek. Cosmetic surgery only partially successful.

No. 24 (age 17): "Hey, Paul, look at this guy's picture in the paper that got sentenced to prison in L.A. He looks just like you, and he's even got the same name. He's not your *dad*, is he? Ha-ha!" Psychotherapy continues.

No. 25 (age 17): "I mean it, man. She wants to have you. Nobody at school knows she screws but me. I been tappin' her since sophomore year. Now she wants to try you. Hey, I can share. Pussies don't wear out. Come on, man. Come on." Psychotherapy continues.

No. 26 (age 18): Football. Major disruption of collateral ligaments of right knee. Surgically repaired. Further participation in contact sports barred. Keloid on knee obtrusive. Psychotherapy continues.

No. 27 (age 20): "Do you really, Paul? Do you really love me? Do you. . . . Uhhh! Uhhh! Uhhh! Ohhh! Dooo! Youuu?" Psychotherapy continues.

No. 28 (age 21): Second-degree burn on palm of right hand. Keloid in unobtrusive location. Surgery postponed pending further evaluation.

No. 29 (age 22): "Listen, you're a good-lookin' kid. I can use you for the part. Now sit down, relax, have a drink with me. Unbutton your shirt, why don't you? No one's gonna interrupt us here in my office." Psychotherapy continues.

No. 30 (age 23): Laceration of left elbow. Patient shows increasing tendency to produce keloids. Further evaluation pending.

No. 31 . . .

MAL DE OJO

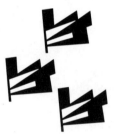

My grandmother really didn't want me hanging around Mr. Samuelian's yard, but I did anyways. He was the old poet who lived next door to Abuelita and me, and for some reason she didn't like him; she said he was crazy, but us guys all loved him. He was the only grownup in the neighborhood who treated us like friends, not kids. That week me and Flaco Perez and Mando Padilla we were working with him on a big birdhouse – "a hotel for our little friends," he called it.

"Friends!" huffed Grandma when I told her. "Those birds eat my garden. They leave the nasty white spots! First that mad Armenian *feeds* them, and now he *houses* them. He is *loco!*" She sounded genuinely agitated.

"They're just birds, Abuelita," I pointed out.

"You have no idea the damage they do. Like that crazy Armenian, they are a menace."

What could I say? "Okay."

"I warn you, *mijito*. Avoid that Armenian. He is *peligroso*."

"Dangerous?"

"He reads all those books."

"Oh," I said.

Abuelita prided herself in being plainspoken. My father had once said to me, "Your grandmother not only calls a spade a spade, she calls a lot of other things spades too."

She had not liked the poet much since that first day when he'd moved into the neighborhood and she'd asked if he wasn't an Armenian. He said no, his parents had been Armenians but he was an American, born and raised in Fresno. That answer displeased Abuelita, who always identified people by nationalities . . . or her version of nationalities, anyways.

Mr. Samuelian, in response, asked what nationality she was and, like always, my grandma said, "Spanish."

"Spanish," he grinned, "what part of Spain are you from?"

Abuelita really didn't like that – the words or the grin – since she, like me, had been born in Bakersfield. "My *people* were from Spain," she spat. What's funny is that my Mom told me our family came from Mexico, not Spain.

"*Voy a pagarlo en la misma moneda*," Abuelita had mumbled after that encounter, but I didn't understand what she meant, something about paying him the same money. My father was a gringo and he hadn't let my momma use much Spanish around me – before they got divorced, I mean – and I had come to live with my grandma so Momma could go to L.A. and find a good job.

Anyways, me and Flaco and Mando were working on the hotel that next afternoon while Mr. Samuelian was at the library. We were finishing it up, really, when a big shiny car swooped into the dirt driveway of the yard. Since our neighbor owned only a bicycle, I had rarely seen an automobile here.

A husky man who favored Mr. Samuelian, but real suntanned like he worked outside all the time, he swung from the door. He had the same burst of white hair, the same hook of a nose; his eyebrows were black and he had a ferocious black mustache. One of his eyes was covered by a dark patch. "Hello, my lads!" he called. "Where is Sarkis Samuelian?"

"He went to the library," I answered.

"Always reading. He will destroy his vision yet. And who are you young men?"

"I'm Gilbert. I live next door. This is Flaco and Mando."

"Well, young gentlemen, I am Haig Samuelian, brother of Sarkis Samuelian. And what do you work on?"

"It's just this birdhouse," Mando answered.

"Be careful with those tools, my lads. See this?" he tugged at the patch that covered his eye. "A stray screwdriver can put your eye out!"

"Oh!" I said involuntarily. I'd heard all my life about the variety of implements that might put an eye out, but this was my first contact with someone to whom it had actually happened.

Before I could inquire further, the poet returned toting a load of books. "Ahhh!" he called. "My little brother visits! Why aren't you in Fresno counting your raisins?"

"Only a fool counts his raisins and ignores his grapes!" responded the one-eyed man, and he hugged Mr. Samuelian. "I've just been commiserating with your associates here."

"Oh," grinned our neighbor, "these young scamps. They're doing a fine job on the new birdhouse, though. Come in, Haig, we must have coffee. How's Aram? Where is Malik's son now? And Dorothy, still a dancer?" They disappeared into the house.

As soon as they were gone, Flaco said, "That guy I think he got his you-know-what poked out."

We enlivened the remainder of the afternoon discussing his poked eye. "I wonder what's left. I wonder is it just a hole there," said Mando.

"Maybe it's all dried up like Mrs. Lopez's dried-up old hand," Flaco suggested.

"Grossisimo!" It was a word we'd invented, so we giggled together.

"Maybe it's like that place where there use to be a boil on your brother Bruno's neck," I told Mando.

"Grossisimo!" he said.

Before we went home that night, Haig Samuelian handed each of us a small bag of pomegranates. "Those are from Fresno, my lads. They are the finest in the world."

"Gee, thanks."

I took mine to Grandma, but she would not touch them. "You got these from that Armenian *pirata?* Him with his *mal de ojo?*"

"Bad of eye?" A lot of the stuff she said in Spanish wasn't clear to me.

"The *evil* eye, *mijito,* the *evil* eye."

"Evil eye? Abuelita, that's just Mr. Samuelian's brother . . ."

"Another of those Armenians!" she hissed.

". . . and he got that eye poked out by a screwdriver."

"You are young," she told me. "You haven't seen behind that mask. You do not understand the realm of evil."

"The realm of evil?"

She stopped then and gazed directly at me. "If you ever look deeply into *un mal de ojo* you will see Hell itself."

"Hell itself?" I didn't have a clue what she was talking about.

"Pray your rosary," she cautioned.

"Okay."

"And don't be working outside in the sun with those two *malcriados,*" she added.

"Why?"

"It will make you dark like a *cholo.* You must wear a hat, *mijito.*"

Like a *cholo?* That's the name the guys at school called all the kids — mostly Indians — who'd just come from Mexico. Hey, I *wanted* to be dark like them so I wouldn't look different from the other kids in my class. At Our Lady of Guadalupe School, I was the only Ryan amidst Martinezes and Gonzalezes and Jiminezes. I'll tell you a secret: One day, when Abuelita wasn't home, I even put black shoe polish on my hair, but it looked real dopey. I had a heck of a time washing it out before she got back.

Anyway, the morning after our *cholo* talk I couldn't wait to dash outside into the sunlight and slip over to our neighbor's yard, maybe steal a glance behind that patch. The large car was still there, but its owner wasn't in sight, so I helped Mr. Samuelian water his weeds. Then he busied himself reciting his latest verse — "Great unconquered wilderness is calling, calling me! Its crystal peaks and wooded glens all yearn to set me free!" — while staking up peas. Before long, the man with a hole in his face emerged from the small house and began picking and sampling ripe plums from a tree in the overgrown yard. "These are wonderful," he said, "almost as good as the ones in Fresno."

After a moment, his tone deepened: "You see those sharp stakes Sarkis carves. Beware of them! My eye . . ." he said heavily, pulling at his patch.

I gulped.

Later that day, me and Mando and Flaco we were erecting the bird hotel when this big mean kid named David Avila, who had chased us home from school more than once, he swaggered up and stood on the dirt border between the yard and the pitted street. A week before he'd caught me and given me a Dutch rub and a pink belly too; he especially liked to pound my pale skin because it turned red so easily. Avila he looked like a large brown toad and he was almost that smart, but he had real biceps and the beginnings of a mustache. Only a year ahead of us at Our Lady of Guadalupe School, he was already a teenager.

Anyways, the big toad he kind of studied us, sneered, then hollered, "Hey, leettle *pendejos*, I can't wait for them birds. I got me a BB gun and I'll keell 'em all. Maybe I'll shoot you three leettle *pendejos* too. You just wait!"

"No, *you* just wait, young criminal!" I heard a shout, and Mr. Samuelian's brother dashed from the plum tree's foliage – I don't think Avila had noticed him there. In a moment, he had the bully by the neck and was shaking him with one hand while he thrust an open wallet into his face with the other. "Do you see this badge?" he demanded. "I'll have you in jail for *years* if you bring a BB gun around here! Do you understand? Do you see this patch? A BB gun!" He shook Avila again.

The bully had wilted quickly under Haig Samuelian's storm, and once released, he scurried away.

"Scalawag!" the one-eyed man shouted after him. "Scoundrel," he continued fuming as he returned, his fierce mustache twitching. "I can have him jailed!" He thrust his wallet toward us and displayed a small badge that said, "Friend of the Fresno County Sheriff's Department."

"Ah, Haig! Haig!" called Mr. Samuelian, emerging from his pea patch to pound his brother's back. "Ever the crusader!"

"BB guns!" said Haig Samuelian, and he spat vehemently on the ground and jerked his patch momentarily.

"Come," urged Mr. Samuelian, "let me give you a glass of tea, Haig," and they entered the small house.

"I bet it's a glass eye under that patch is what," said Mando. "I tried to look under when he was pickin' plums, but I couldn't see nothin'."

"I think it's a big ol' bloody hole," suggested Flaco.

"With worms, maybe," I added. "I'll bet there's big worms in it."

"Grossisimo!" chorused my pals.

I joined my grandma talking to our other neighbor, Mrs. Alcala, when I arrived home for dinner. "Esperanza, you didn't actually *eat* the pomegranates that *brujo* gave you?" Abuelita demanded.

"Of course," smiled old Mrs. Alcala, who was Flaco's grandmother. "They were delicious. And he's not a *brujo*, Lupe, he's just another Samuelian, a gentleman but . . . ah . . . *very* enthusiastic."

"Enthusiastic?"

"And very friendly," added Mrs. Alcala.

"*Two* of those Armenians now," my grandma said. "Both of them *loco*."

Mrs. Alcala was smirking when she added, "The Samuelians aren't the only *locos* in this neighborhood."

"And what is *that* supposed to mean, Esperanza?"

"Oh nothing," replied the old woman, grinning as she hobbled away on two canes. "Hasta la vista, Lupe."

That long, warm evening the Samuelian brothers sat in wooden lawn chairs talking, and after Grandma freed me from chores I wandered over to listen. "That was the day I fought Dikran Nizibian, the terror. Remember, Sarkis? I fought him for an hour and fifteen minutes nonstop, the longest and fiercest battle in the history of Fresno. We fought all the way up Van Ness Avenue to Blackstone, and then we fought for a mile down Blackstone. Our sweat flowed through the gutters. The police stood back in awe to watch such a battle. Businesses closed. Priests held crosses to their hearts. Doctors averted their eyes. Strong women prayed. Strong men fainted."

"Who won? Who won?" I asked, breathless.

"Who won?" he paused. Mr. Samuelian's brother twitched his mustache and tugged his patch. "I'll tell you who won. Do you see this eye?" he pointed at the cloth covering his empty socket. "The evil Dikran Nizibian tried to *gouge* it out in the middle of Blackstone Avenue in

Fresno forty years ago, but . . ." another pause, another twitch, another tug . . . "he regrets it to this day because I knew a secret: Never use more when less will do! Never use two when one will do! I had saved my final strength. With it, I threw the ruthless Nizibian from me and broke everything on him that could be broken. I broke several things that *couldn't* be broken. He never fought again, did he, Sarkis?"

"Not that I remember," replied Mr. Samuelian.

"He never bullied anyone again."

"Not that I remember."

"Nizibian the terror was finished," Haig Samuelian nodded with finality, pulling absently at his patch.

"*Gouged* his eye out," I mumbled as I wandered home.

I told my pals the story of the great Fresno fight the next day at school. We were all eager to hurry back that afternoon and hear more from Mr. Samuelian's brother. On our way, however, while discussing the vast pit that had been gouged in Haig Samuelian's face by the evil Nizibian, and hoping at last to catch a glimpse of its depths, we spied David Avila striding toward us. Oh, no! We immediately began sprinting, each in a different direction, in the hope the bully might be confused.

Unfortunately for me, he wasn't. I was the only blond at Guadalupe School, so when Avila selected a target, I was usually his first choice. I didn't feel honored by that. I didn't have time to feel anything but scared because I was too busy sprinting. The bully was after me at a dead run. Although I was carrying my slingshot, it never occurred to me to use it because I was too busy trying to escape.

I was pretty fast for a little kid, and I got even faster with David Avila on my tail, so at first I kept him way behind me. I was sprinting and glancing back, sprinting and glancing back, juggling my book bag. Before long, though, I realized that Avila the terror was closing the gap between us, his toad eyes slits of rage. I worked even harder to escape, but my breath was growing hot and shallow and my thighs were beginning to tighten and burn.

I shot another look behind me, and he was so close that I saw the shadow of a mustache on his upper lip and the pink pimples decorating his bronze chin. My breath was searing me and my knees couldn't seem to lift anymore; my book bag swung wildly from side to side.

Just as I turned the corner of my block, I lost control of my book bag and it dropped, spilling its contents. I was nearly safe, but if I didn't pick up my things I'd never see them again – and I knew the evil Avila had to be reaching for me.

Hesitating over my books and papers, I glanced back despondently, ready for the twisted arm, the Dutch rub, or the pink belly that was certain, and to my astonishment I realized that Avila had halted. He thrust his hands into his pockets and turned away. When I spun around, I saw the one-eyed Samuelian standing in front of his brother's yard, hands on hips, glaring at David Avila. When I peered once more at the bully, he was retreating rapidly.

I was so relieved that I almost forgot to pick up my books and papers. When I finally did, though, I hurried to our neighbor's house. The large car was being loaded with a suitcase, and Haig Samuelian said to me, "Remember, never use more when less will do, and that young hoodlum will soon learn to leave you alone."

Then the two older men returned to what seemed to be a conversation in progress. "No matter, Sarkis," the younger brother said. "I'll pass the message on to Aram. He will understand." The men hugged, then Haig Samuelian noticed what I carried and said, "Don't let this young man play with that slingshot. You remember my eye, don't you?" He pointed toward his empty socket as he swung into the driver's seat.

His brother smiled, "I remember."

"Well, I must be on my way. I have grapes to tend in Fresno." The two brothers shook hands. The larger man tugged his patch and smiled out the window as he started the engine. "Farewell, young man," he said to me.

I didn't reply because I'd noticed something a moment before when Haig Samuelian had tugged at his small mask while sitting there, his face level with mine. I noticed that there was no fair, untanned skin beneath the patch or the string that tied it.

No fair skin.

Beneath the wristwatch Abuelita had given me last Christmas my own surface was pale as a baby's. Then I realized what that had to mean: "You been changin' eyes!" I thought aloud.

"What is that?" the driver inquired.

"Your patch, it's on the other eye. You been changin' eyes," I spoke as I began to realize what had to have been happening: "You been changin' every day."

Haig Samuelian lifted his patch and winked with a twinkling eye I thought I'd never seen before, and said to his brother, "Beware of *this* one, Sarkis. He will go places."

Then he drove north toward Fresno.

MEDICINE

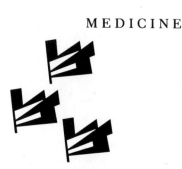

First time I ever seen Lonnie he was drunker 'n hell, and a mite ornery. It was a Saturday night right after I'd took that job at Bob Manhart's ranch, and I was at the Buckhorn just outside Springville, me and other boys that worked ranches 'round there, givin' them town gals a twirl and drinkin' a little tonsil varnish just to stay loose.

Anyways, a bunch of us boys had went outside to watch two fellers have a pissin' contest, when up roars this old Ford with one door open; it throwed gravel all over us whenever it stopped. Well, I started to go whip the driver after I seen he wasn't nothin but a wrinkled old Indi'n, but Johnny Johns, this wrangler, he grabbed me. "Wes," he hissed in my ear, "don't tangle with old Lonnie less'n your insurance is up to date."

That old Indi'n climbed out of his Ford, then swayed there, his eyes little and red like a boar's, mean-lookin', him watching them two boys try to pee farther than one another. Finally he whipped out his own pecker and shot a stream clean over the hood of his car, scatterin' spectators right smart. I never seen nothin' like it before. Then he grunted: "I win. Who buys beer?"

Well, Johnny Johns he was laughin' to beat hell, and he sang out that he was buyin'. When Lonnie walked up to him, Johnny asked: "Where's Dorothy?"

Lonnie rocked on his heels for a minute, looked around, then staggered back to his car. He walked slowly around it, stoppin' next to the open door on the passenger side. "God damn," he said, "Dorothy he fall out." I laughed. Dorothy was a old gal, but Lonnie never got the "he" versus "she" stuff in English too good. Then Lonnie walked into the Buckhorn for his beer.

We was all standin' at the bar next to the door, listenin' to Johnny tell stories about Lonnie, the dancers still cuttin' a purty mean rug on the floor, when the front door busted open and in wandered the damndest specimen of a Indi'n woman, all beat up, scraped and scratched, dirty like she rolled in a ditch. She walked right up to Lonnie, and he said: "God damn, Dorothy. Where you been?"

"Fall out," Dorothy answered.

Lonnie pushed a cowpoke aside at the bar to make room for Dorothy. "God damn," he said.

It got to where I seen Lonnie regular after that, him ridin' with us at spring roundup, workin at Manhart's sugar beet spread down in the valley when he wasn't up at the ranch. He was one hell of a worker, I'll tell you; I never seen nothin' like it before. He'd work any three hands into the ground. And tough too. Whenever the Mexicans come north to thin the sugar beets, Lonnie took to whippin' them one by one till he worked his way through the whole crew. And, hell, he must've been sixty years old then.

Him and Dorothy they had 'em three boys: Elmer, he was about my age; Charley, he was around twenty; and Millard, he was just a kid, maybe fourteen. They was top hands, hard workers, and the young one was doing real good at the county high school.

Well, Elmer he taken sick. Lonnie and Dorothy they tried doctorin'

him, but he just got weaker and weaker. I recollect how Elmer kept sayin'
his head hurt, then he finally just passed out. Finally, old Bob Manhart
got wind of what was happenin', and he had Doc come out from Springville to check Elmer, but Doc said he couldn't tell right off what was
wrong with him. They carried Elmer clean up to San Francisco to the
big hospital so's they could run some tests, but before they could get him
started, he died. I never did hear what killed him.

One day not long after they buried Elmer, I was drinkin' Ripple after
work with Lonnie and Dorothy in their Ford; we was parked in front of
the Springville store just in case we needed to buy us some more. Anyways, this queer-lookin' Indi'n come walkin' up the street. He seen the
Ford settin' there, so's he made for it. Lonnie seen him comin', and he
said somethin' real fast in Yokuts to Dorothy. I couldn't savvy it, but he
sounded hot.

This Indi'n walked right up to Lonnie, and I seen he had what the boys
call flat eyes – the kind that don't show no white, all darkness – so his face
looked like a mask with an animal lurkin' behind it. He barked somethin'
in the window at Lonnie, him talkin' Yokuts, of course. Dorothy tensed
right up, and I seen Lonnie's face turn all chalky. Lonnie looked away
from the queer-lookin' Indi'n, shakin' his head no, then that other Indi'n
he turned around and walked away.

Soon as he's gone, I asked Lonnie who that was. He never answered
for a long time, pullin' long and hard on the Ripple. Finally, he told me:
"Name Coyote. Medicine man."

I waited, but that's all he said. "What did he want?" I asked.

"Money."

"Money?"

"Money."

"For what?"

"You nosey bastard," Lonnie said, so I took the hint and climbed out
of his car. I walked into the store and bought my own damn Ripple, then
walked back to where my pickup was parked. Lonnie stood there waitin'
for me, and I was afraid I'd have to fight him.

Soon as I got close, though, Lonnie said: "When Elmer sick, Dorothy
he call medicine man. Medicine man he say give five hundred dollars
and Elmer get well. I told him go hell."

"Is he still tryin' to get the five hundred for Elmer?"

Lonnie shook his head. "Naw. He say give five hundred dollars or Charley get sick."

"And you told him no?"

Lonnie nodded.

"Well, old Charley's healthy as a fresh-serviced mare," I said, but Lonnie's eyes was uncertain.

And sure enough, not more than a week later Charley took sick. It was the same thing that got Elmer, headaches and feelin' weak, so Bob Manhart he had Doc rush right out and they got Charley to the hospital before he lost consciousness. But it didn't do no good. He died anyways.

Lonnie slowed down some after that. He never hit the Buckhorn no more, and didn't talk hardly at all. He still worked like a whole crew, but he was gettin' darker, lookin' more and more like he didn't give a damn for nothin'. I never seen nothin' like it before. It was just my luck that I was to their cabin when things come to a head.

Dorothy she used to make buckskin gloves and shirts that all the boys at the ranch bought; they was twice as good as you could buy in a store and cheaper. So one afternoon I drove out to their cabin to buy me some new gloves and maybe swap tales. When I got there, I walked right in the kitchen door like always. Lonnie he set at the little table drinkin' whiskey. "What hell you want?" he asked, and I could tell he was gettin' mean drunk. I told him what I wanted, and he just grunted, his eyes little and red.

"What's wrong, Lonnie?"

He glared at me. "Go hell," he said.

"I ain't takin' no shit off you, Lonnie," I told him, knowin' good and well he could whip me.

He stood up, reached for the bottle like he was gonna belt me with it, then handed it to me. "Drink," he ordered. I drank and it was awful stuff, Thrifty Drugstore special. He finally said: "Millard he sick like Elmer, Charley." Then I savvied why Lonnie was sore.

"Oh, Jesus," I said. "I'll go get Doc."

But Lonnie shook his head. "Doc he no good," he told me. "Medicine man come."

Dorothy come shufflin' into the kitchen, lookin' all shriveled and sad.

She touched my shoulder. "Come," she said. Dorothy led me into the little room where the boys all had slept, and there was Millard on his bunk, pale, his breath shallow and ragged. I figured him for a goner. I never seen nothin' like it before, all three of them boys took sick the same way. "He's gotta see Doc," I told Dorothy.

She just shook her head. "My boys good boys," she said as much to the room as me.

"I 'preciate that, Dorothy," I answered, "but Millard's lookin' bad. He better see Doc."

She sighed and, without lookin' toward me, said: "No. Lonnie call Coyote. Lonnie make medicine with Coyote."

"You mean Lonnie's got five hundred dollars?" I asked, remembering what Lonnie'd said about the medicine man before, and knowing his fortune hadn't changed much between then and now. I couldn't figure how Lonnie could pay. Me, I had three hundred, maybe three-fifty, stashed away; I was saving for a Mexican saddle. But lookin' at that kid laying there on his bunk more dead than alive, it seemed like I didn't need a new saddle too bad. It wouldn't be much to pay for a kid's life. "Let me drive back to the ranch," I told Dorothy. "I'll scare up a little cash."

I run out the front door to my pickup, and I'd just opened the truck's door when I heard a scream, pullin' and suckin' at my brain like a wild animal's cry, but it was a guy's voice all right, and he sounded desperate. I stood froze for a minute tryin' to figure where the sound come from; when the scream cut loose one more time, I knew. I busted to the kitchen door and flew in.

Lonnie knelt on that medicine man's chest, hands white around his throat; Coyote's flat eyes wide and dark, he gurgled a little, that's all; his legs jerked and his arms flailed in slow motion. Then they stopped flailin' at all. Lonnie held on for another long minute, my heart poundin' like crazy; key-rist, I just seen him kill a man.

When he let go, Lonnie done somethin' I'll never forget: he reached down and, one at a time, pulled both the medicine man's eyes out, them murky in Lonnie's hands, and he called Dorothy in Yokuts. She come scuttlin' in, steppin' over Coyote's body like it was a sleepin' dog, and took the lid off a pot that held boiling water. Lonnie dropped the eyes in.

Then he turned to me, and I noticed he was breathin' heavy, but his own eyes was clear and untroubled. He sounded relaxed when he told me to grab Coyote's feet. For some silly reason I done just that, and we toted him out and tossed him in the bed of *my* pickup. "Drive up canyon," Lonnie said, and I did, my belly tight, my eyes wanderin' to the rearview mirror.

Lonnie set like a statue next to me as we wound up the dirt track alongside the creek, his eyes readin' the land. Right after we forded the second time, he pointed up the stream; "Stop!" he grunted. I eased up the pickup to a wide spot off the dirt road, not wanting it clobbered by some drunk hunter buzzin' back toward town. Don't ask me why, but I slipped the .30-.30 from the rack behind the seat, and slung it over my shoulder before me and Lonnie commenced to totin' Coyote. Lonnie led the way. We huffed up a side canyon, then a draw – a place I'd never even saw before – then all of a sudden the draw just opened up into the damndest meadow. Lonnie stopped and dropped Coyote, the medicine man stiffenin' up a little so it was like droppin' lumber. "You stop," Lonnie ordered. Since he'd already dropped his end, I could either stop or plow a row with Coyote's nose. I stopped.

"Now go," he ordered.

"Why?"

"You go!"

"Why?" I asked again, comfortable with that loaded .30-.30 on my shoulder.

Lonnie's eyes narrowed. "I shove rifle up ass," he said.

Well, I'd just saw old Lonnie kill a man with his bare hands, and that .30-.30 didn't look like it'd fit real comfortable, so I walked back down the draw and waited at the pickup.

After a spell – it was dark by then – down come Lonnie, his face hid but his eyes just glowin'. He climbed into the cab and said: "Go." We went.

When we got back to the cabin, I naturally let Lonnie lead the way, and lead he did. We hurried right through the kitchen door, steamed right through the kitchen to Millard's room. Dorothy was next to the bunk, spoonin' broth into Millard's mouth, and Millard he was awake, his cheeks already colorin' up. By damn! He'd been most dead when we left.

"Millard drink eyes?" Lonnie asked, and I liked to shit.

Dorothy nodded.

"Drink eyes?" I asked. I didn't mind killin' some bastard, and totin' his body off, but drinkin' his eyes? Jesus, it was uncivilized. I stood stunned for a minute. Then my own fears busted out; I couldn't stop 'em. "Jesus, Lonnie," I said, "what if the sheriff finds the body?"

"Coyote in tribal earth," he said.

"I'm hungry," said Millard.

Dorothy laughed.

Me, I just went for the kitchen door, but when I got there Lonnie was with me. He grabbed my sleeve. "Stop," he ordered. He picked up a spoon from the boilin' pot, raised it up in front of his face with both hands like I seen a preacher do in meetin' one time; he blowed on the steamin' broth, and sipped. Then he nodded.

Just as I was fixin' to turn and leave, he stuck that spoon in my face, and ordered: "Drink."

"Drink?"

"Drink," he repeated, lookin' straight at me.

Well what the hell, I'd did damn near ever' other crazy thing a man could that night, so I took me a sip. Lonnie he grinned and I had to grin back. It tasted a damn sight better'n that Thrifty Drugstore whiskey.

THAT BLACKBERRY WILDERNESS

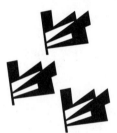

Their hands brushed not quite accidentally, then snapped back. For both it was an electric instant. A moment later, embarrassed not by the touch but by their mutual quick withdrawal, they smiled at one another. "Like a couple a kids," he remarked, and her deep chuckle moved him nearly as much as the fleeting touch had. Seeing those bright eyes smiling at him through the campfire's orange glow, he reached for her hand and grasped it firmly, intertwining his fingers with hers. "Ma'am," he said, "I hope you don't mind."

"Honored," she responded, and her hand squeezed his. She noticed that several other campers had been watching them, so she basked them with a smile, then leaned into his shoulder. As their hands warmed together, an oddly soothing excitement invaded their bodies and they were immediately alone in spite of the other fourteen people who surrounded the fire, howling camp songs with aggressive atonality.

Later the group tripped through darkened woods to a granite slab along the creek where they might lie and gaze into a sky so salted with stars that it appeared hoary, the man and woman side by side, eyes turned upward, vision turned inward, toward one another. Their hands clasped lightly, comfortably. They spoke little – no one in the group said much – the stream's gentle chuckle filling their ears. Alone there amidst the party, they allowed something as old as the stars to innocently work between them.

When the two finally wandered back toward camp, leaving the group stargazing, they still held hands and their continued silence posed questions that neither would ask. With each step, both the man and the woman felt the urgency of their attraction rising in the dark woods like the wind that now urged primordial music from swaying treetops.

At her tent, he squeezed her hand and tapped her cheek with a kiss. "Thanks, Ardith, for a wonderful evening," he said, his voice tight with desire.

"Cal?" she said, those bright eyes wide and visible even in the antique darkness.

His arms were around her before thought could interfere: She was another man's wife, he was another woman's husband, but at that moment, as their lips touched, their mouths opened, and their bodies folded together, memory and convention failed them. Later, a moment or an hour later, in their final breathless words before passion overwhelmed them, they said almost simultaneously, "I wish these damned mummy bags would zip together." The bags didn't.

Ardith awoke startled in the pale glow of pre-dawn, a lone mosquito practicing viola in her ear. For a moment she was disoriented, then her eyes focused and she searched for Cal. He was gone. The bastard. How could he just kiss and run like some high school kid? What was wrong with her, anyway, allowing circumstances and ingenuous passion to sweep her?

Then she noticed him fifty yards away, kneeling near the campfire circle, his tan, bald head wrapped in that crazy red bandana. He was mixing some concoction or other, probably pancake batter. Of course, he was on kitchen duty that morning. No wonder he was gone. At that moment he looked up, noticed her, and waved, a crooked grin on his face. Darn, she was just beginning to enjoy regret, and was contemplating hating him . . . as well as herself. Instead, she sat up and waved, having to scramble to avoid baring a breast in the process. She wished immediately that he was in the bag with her.

So much for remorse.

She finally arose a catnap later, dressed, and began rolling her sleeping pad and stuffing her down bag. Just as she was attaching them to her backpack, one of the younger girls, Lisa, slipped next to her and whispered, "I think it was so *cute*, you two holding hands last night."

Ardith smiled. "You think it's cute?"

"I think it's *darling*."

"Darling?"

"I mean," the girl explained, "you two're like *grand*parents."

"Yes, we are," the older woman smiled, but her voice was unkind. "Hasn't it occurred to you that without a little handholding between people like Cal and me there wouldn't be any grandchildren?"

Lisa giggled.

Six days before, when the group had gathered, such candid conversation had been rare. It was an assemblage of strangers drawn together as volunteers to clean a section of wilderness for the National Park Service, and everyone seemed uncertain how to act. Most were college-age singles like Lisa, although there were supposed to be older volunteers as well, people like Cal and herself, both married to nonbackpackers and grateful for the trip. All had initially been on their best behavior.

In fact, Ardith had been downright uncomfortable that first day because — as was usual for her — she was the first arrival at the assembly point, and as the group gathered, it increasingly appeared that Jed, the group's youthful leader, had failed in his stated attempt to muster a gang reflecting a range of ages. She had felt as though she was the token representative of "over forty" until, quite late that evening, a battered Chevrolet pickup swerved into the parking area. Jed had seemed relieved: "It's gotta be Cal."

A moment later a lean, bald man approached Jed and extended his right hand. "Hi," he smiled, "I'm Cal Chandler. Sorry I'm late, but I had a premature baby to deliver."

So he was the trip doctor, she mused during those first few moments while he was introduced to his fellow campers. Even then she had been riveted by his slate eyes. He sounded pleasant and smiled easily, but there was a tempered core in him. Still, she would not have picked him out of a crowd as anyone special, she knew; he looked like an aging rancher. Well, at least he was a peer. Two weeks of listening to college students' prattle did not appeal to her.

He, on the other hand, would have noticed her in any throng. While he experienced immediate relief that he wasn't the only mature participant, he observed even more intensely the woman's youthful figure and glowing smile. She was one of those rare beauties who had aged well, obviously content to be an attractive middle-aged woman rather than becoming a cosmeticized caricature of a twenty-year-old.

A few minutes of conversation had revealed differences to her. Oh, he was a physician, a Berkeley graduate no less; still, their backgrounds could scarcely have been less similar. She had been born into, raised with, and remained a part of San Francisco society; her family had been among the founders of the Sierra Club. His parents, on the other hand, had been migrant farm laborers from Oklahoma, and he had attended college thanks to the GI Bill. While she and her attorney husband championed liberal causes in the Bay Area, he ran a rural health clinic outside Fresno. When she wondered innocently why he hadn't selected a more lucrative practice, his response had stung her: "I had a responsibility to people like my folks, and I see my responsibilities through. Somebody's gotta work the front lines." Those slate eyes had hardened and she'd known better than to pursue the subject.

Aside from age and being married to nonbackpackers, they did find other areas of common interest. Both were addicted to fly-fishing and were avid readers of fiction. Both had recently become grandparents for the first time. It wasn't much, each had noted, but enough perhaps to allow them to spend two pleasant – or less unpleasant – weeks in one another's company. They certainly hoped so, since no alternatives presented themselves. They agreed on that too, each laughing at their mutual candor.

As the trip progressed, however, she found that she sought Cal's companionship not because he was the least-onerous choice but because he was a man whose vitality and humor resonated with something deep within her. And she had noticed at a stream fording when he had stripped to his shorts in order to swim a safety line across that his body retained lean, hard contours unmatched by most of the younger men. That had interested her too. What she didn't know, couldn't know from his friendly but decidedly unseductive behavior, was that he had coveted her from the moment they had first shaken hands, and that his own desire frightened him.

As the initial week wore on, they increasingly walked, worked, and ate together. One morning while they rested during a trail restoration project, he remarked, "These youngsters jumpin' from sleeping bag to sleepin' bag seem to confuse proximity with intimacy. We're only up here fourteen days. Nothin's gonna atrophy in that time."

Although she laughed, she also wondered if he wasn't covertly explaining his reserve to her. "Let them have fun," she responded. "That excitement wears off soon enough."

He flashed that crooked grin at her. "That's a fact," he said. "I'm probably just jealous."

Luckily there were no medical emergencies among the campers, but Ardith nonetheless saw enough of her new friend in action to admire the way he did business. One morning the group had set out cross country to clear away old fire rings from the shore of a small lake located off the trail. Somehow Jed became disoriented and led them too far west. As soon as it became clear to him that there was a problem, yet without giving anyone else any indication of what was wrong, Cal directed Jed back toward their proper course, then unobtrusively melted back into the group. She liked that performance. Her husband, a successful corporate attorney, would have appointed a committee.

By week's end they had discussed not only most abstract issues of mutual interest but also personal histories, leading Ardith to remark as they sat by the campfire that night, "You probably know more about my family than any living human being."

"I'll be billin' you at fifty bucks an hour," he answered, "my usual fee for psychiatric consultation."

"Where do I send *my* bill? I seem to be hearing a lot about Nell and your daughters and that little grandson of yours."

"Oops," he winced in exaggerated guilt.

"It's funny, isn't it," she continued, "fourteen days isn't such a short period when you're together constantly. A lot of us will see more of one another, under a wider range of circumstances, than we have people we call best friends at home. It'll be hard to keep our masks on for two complete weeks."

He nodded. "Yeah, that girl who fell at the ford yesterday was an inch away from having to be sedated. She was just plain terrified. And so was I before we fished her out, and I told her so. And when the momma bear chased Jed and me the other afternoon, all our college degrees and male boldness just flat disappeared. This old experienced mountaineer nearly wet his britches."

"You move pretty well for an old codger."

"I was just warmin' up. If she'd a got a step closer, I'd've hit the afterburner! I'm sure glad you and Lisa distracted that sow or I might still be runnin'," he laughed.

"You see what I mean? How many people have seen a tough hombre like you scared?"

"Not many. Course, I don't run across momma bears all that often."

"Is that the only thing that scares you?"

"No," he responded, his voice softening, "you do."

She knew immediately what he meant because he frightened her too. A moment later their hands touched.

When he finished his kitchen duty that next morning, washing the last of the pots and pans, she asked what he planned to do that day. The group was splitting, one segment building a bridge over a nearby creek deemed too dangerous to ford, while the other would troop to a distant lake and clean up a mess left by packers. "Well," he hesitated, "I thought I might go to the lake. I've worked on bridges before, but I've never seen that lake."

She guessed from his tone that he didn't want her along, so she smiled and said, "I'm working on the bridge."

Throughout that long day her emotions swerved between sorrow and outrage. After that wonderful night, why had he abandoned her? Perhaps she had been right, he *was* a bastard. But, of course, that couldn't be true, not of the man she had come to know. What was wrong? She had dreamed of a day of hidden smiles and secret touches. Instead she felt as alone as she could ever remember.

When the lake group finally returned just before supper, she did not walk out to greet them with the others, his voluntary absence having finally festered into a pocket of pain. She would not force herself on him or anyone else. Instead, she knelt, busying herself with her pack. Soon she heard the crunch of boots approaching behind her, then his voice: "Howdy, Blackberry. I missed you today."

Blackberry. She wore a purple T-shirt with "Blackberry" printed across the back. In spite of herself, her eyes glistened when she stood and turned to face him and he, without hesitation, leaned forward and kissed her, then hugged her in his wiry arms.

"I had to think some things out," he explained softly, "but mostly I just thought about you and wished you were with me."

"I know," she said. But she hadn't known; she'd only hoped.

That night their bodies blended with less awkwardness. His hands were knowledgeable yet pleasantly tentative on her firm flesh. He was so used to Nell's ample, comforting terrain that he felt a little like an excited explorer. To her, his body seemed almost boyish, so tight was it in contrast to the harbor seal alongside whom she regularly slept. Together they ventured into an urgent wilderness, a region beyond reticence and self.

He awakened before dawn, the sky lightening, the sun a pink promise behind an eastern ridge. Turning his head, he saw only her tousled gray hair protruding from the sleeping bag next to him, so he reached over and delicately pulled the material down until her face was exposed. For long moments he gazed at her – small nose, cleft chin, large eyes now closed, large lower lip. Her right eyelid twitched, so he inclined toward her and kissed it softly. The green eyes fluttered open, and Ardith yawned, then smiled.

"Mornin', Blackberry," he smiled back.

She grinned. Blackberry, she really liked that name.

"Shall I move my bag before everyone notices we slept together?" he asked.

For a moment she thought he was teasing, but his slate eyes revealed that he wasn't. "No," she assured him. "I don't think this sack-hopping group will be very judgmental." His eyes remained uncertain, so she patted his hand, then kissed its open palm. "What'll we do today?" she asked.

It was a rest day, with everyone free to make their own plans. When asked by Jed during breakfast what he'd devised, Cal smiled. "Well, Ardith and I are gonna find us a nice pond, take a dip, eat our lunch, read our books, maybe pick berries, and take a nap," which was exactly what they did. It was a day as free and happy as either could ever remember. Both felt as though they had always held hands and shared secrets, that they always would. "My God," Ardith mused aloud, "I finally know what it's all about, and I'm living it. Don't pinch me."

Two nights later, while they sat talking at the campfire, time began to tumble. He observed, innocently but insensitively, "It's almost over." He was correct, of course. In just three days they would emerge at the trailhead and head back toward those distant lives they had so comfortably forgotten.

"We've still got two nights," she pointed out.

"We've got that," he agreed, patting her hand, but his touch betrayed something deeper than doubt. What it betrayed, if only to him, was the sweep of his passion, his wonder at the need for her that had ripened so swiftly. He was in love, and the most shocking aspect of that realization was that it was a new sensation. He had never loved, at least not this way, before – never so suddenly, so deeply, so completely.

That night, multitudes of stars clouding the blackness above, they once more journeyed toward their mutual wilderness. Afterwards, as they cuddled side by side, her forefinger traced a path around his eyes, his nose, then stroked his lips until he smiled. "You feel guilty, don't you?" she asked.

The smile left him. "Don't *you?*"

"No," she answered honestly. "I feel grateful. This . . . this love" – it was the first time either of them had used that word – "has brought me so much. I feel more alive than I ever have."

In the darkness, she felt his eyes leave hers, gaze beyond her for a moment, then return. "No, I don't feel guilty about what we've done either. It's been spontaneous and innocent and, well, wonderful. I feel like a kid who's finally old enough for somethin' – a watch or long britches, maybe. I'm finally old enough for what we feel." He kissed the hand she had extended to rub his rough cheek. "But I do feel guilty because I love you in a way I've never been able to love Nell, and because of what I'm gonna want to do when this trip's over: the schemin' to see you, the lies I'll be willin' to tell, all the dishonesty that'll destroy the innocence and turn us into cheaters cuckoldin' two good people."

"Oh, Cal," she murmured, caressing him, "the burden you carry."

The next night – their last – they once more traveled that wild and secret region they had discovered, desperate energy driving them. "God, Blackberry," he sighed as they lay spent in one another's arms, "how can I live without you?"

"You don't have to," she whispered. "Whatever else happens, we've got to stay in touch, we've got to stay friends. We can't let all this go." She felt his body tighten as he only grunted. Frightened, she asked, "We can, can't we?"

"I can't," he replied in a choked voice sounding like a man about to weep. "I just can't, Blackberry."

"But *why?*"

"Because it's all gone too far. I want to walk with you, talk to you, touch you, breathe you. If we never make love again, I'll still be crazy to be with you. The only choices I've got are to leave Nell and the family and the clinic and follow you to San Francisco, or just accept the pain of stoppin' now."

As pleased as she was by his declaration of love, she was even more confused. "But I love you, Cal. We love one another. We've got to at least stay in touch." The alternatives he'd mentioned were not the only ones, she knew, but the power of his statement made arguing difficult.

His answer stunned her: "I've been readin' in books all my life that word 'bittersweet.' I think I finally know what it means."

"So because we really care, we can't stay in touch?" She fought the desperate tone that had crept into her voice.

"We just can't."

She rolled away from him, burying her face in her sleeping bag, then pulling the drawstring until she was alone in a soft cave to weep quietly over what she already knew would be the sweetest and saddest of memories. She felt Cal's arm circle her bag, but her own silent sobs masked his grief from her.

They hiked the final miles to the trailhead together the next day, not discussing the previous night's dispute but instead carrying on a civil, uncomfortable conversation ranging over impersonal topics. Good-bye, however, was not so easily contrived.

After making the rounds of other trip members, they wandered to her car and faced one another. He said exactly the wrong thing, or the right one: "Good-bye, Blackberry. This has been the greatest two weeks of my life. I finally know what it means to be alive, thanks to you. I'll miss you so much . . ." His voice trailed into that tone of controlled tears she had heard once before, his hard slate eyes glistened. He cleared his throat, then added, "We've gotta say good-bye and it won't get any easier, so let's not drag it out. You know how I feel, how I'll always feel, about you."

"I know, Cal," she whispered, as his arms circled her, yearning to reason with him – why couldn't they at least write to one another? – but sensing not only the futility of asking, sensing also the damage it might do to so beautiful a memory, she merely held him.

When he stepped back and she started the car's engine, he raised his right hand. "Good-bye, Blackberry," he sighed, then he blew her a kiss. His lips said silently, "I'll always love you." She felt as though a vital organ had been wrenched from her, and that sensation intensified as she motored across the state toward San Francisco, the four-hour trip accomplished in a kind of trance so that she almost missed the contrast between the country she was leaving and the urban web she entered. Only the great wound of loneliness seemed real by the time she traveled the Bay Bridge; Cal had grown as remote and uncapturable as the mountains themselves. In fact, when she wheeled into her driveway, turned off the car, and sat behind the wheel, she could no longer tell who or what was real, other than that terrible wound.

She was better in the morning, although her thoughts were occupied by events of the backpack trip, unsystematically reliving every word, every touch as she walked from room to room, then out into the garden. As days passed into weeks, she began healing that wound within herself with carefully arranged and coveted memories, each seeming more precious than the last.

Ardith realized that she and Cal had been together a very long time, but not long enough, and that he had brought something absolutely new to her, something that only maturity made possible. Cal's integrity, his honor, the very characteristic that now caused her such pain, was the deepest reason for loving him.

Bittersweet, indeed. As much as she hated their separation, she loved that wilderness within themselves they had discovered – or, perhaps, re-discovered – that blackberry wilderness of touched hands and touched hearts and touched lives, and she would never lose it.

Never.

CHINA GRADE

What a wife that ol' boy had! One time me and him we come screechin' down China Grade from this bar up on the bluffs, not more'n two tires on the pavement till we hit bottom and the road it straightened out, us whizzin' past steam plumes and oil creeks, past pumps and derricks, the whole place smellin' a sulfur and crude. Course we never paid it no mind. I mean, we had higher octane in us than the car did, and we's havin' a hell of a time.

Me and Cleophus we done that a lot, flew down China Grade full a giggle juice, I mean. Me, I wasn't married in them days and Cle' wished to hell he wasn't, so we hit this bar up on the bluffs real reg'lar. It's a nice place with country music and the cutest little barmaids. You could look down from this big huge picture window at oil fields spread as far as you could see. Directly under us was the refinery where me and Cle' worked and there was usually steam and this thick black smoke churnin' up from burnin' oil sumps, smoke so heavy it looked about like that greenish sky was a tore octopus a-leakin' ink. Me, I's always glad to be on top a China Grade. Somehow even the beer tasted better when us guys was up there lookin' down. The joint it had a happy hour and me and Cle' we got happy pretty steady.

Anyways, whenever we pulled up to his place in Oildale that evenin' and climbed outta my car, we's plannin' on stayin' happy, but no sir. Here come that witch steamin' out from the house. "You drunks!" she screeched.

I figured I'd kid her a little, so I said real fancy, "We just quaffed a few medicinal spirits so's we could clear obstructions from our throats." Me, I graduated high school and I can come up with them big words.

She never laughed. She grabbed big Cle' and snapped as nasty as could be, "Cleophus Titsworth, you get in that house this minute!" He give me a sick grin and done what she said. Soon as he's gone, she turned to me. "If I's your wife, I'd slit your throat," she spit.

"Hey, if you's my wife, lady, I'd slice my damn wrists!" I spit right back at her. Hell, a little tonsil varnish never hurt nobody.

Well, maybe it hurt Cleophus some, special after he took to seein' things, but that was two, three years later, just before he died. If you never knowed Cle', you missed a good ol' boy. He's might popular with all us guys 'cause we could always count on him to be there if we needed him.

Not only that, he's about as stout as they come. I seen him whup a few fellers that claimed couldn't nobody give 'em a battle, and I seen him win one hell of a lotta contests to see who's strongest. Seems like there's always somebody wanted to test a big man in a oil-field town. One of the funniest, though, happened the time that chubby slicker moseyed into the Tejon Club trailin' this big long-haired kid that was wearin' a vest without no shirt underneath; the kid had giant tattooed arms that looked like long road maps.

Ol' chubby he announced he's the kid's manager. He talked real quick and high like someone was a-playin' his record too fast. After we got to where we could understand him, we figured out that he claimed he's a big wrist-wrestlin' promoter from upstate in Petaluma and his boy, ol' what's-his-name, he could pin anybody in Kern County without even breakin' a sweat.

"You reckon?" asked Cleophus real pleasant.

"Damn right," snapped the slicker.

"Well, we might could have a little contest if you'll show me how."

"Oh, I'll show you," rattled Chubby. "But first let's see if any of your friends are willing to wager."

I couldn't resist. "I'd bet on Cleophus even if it's pecker wrestlin'," I said. "Let's see your green."

Well, once all the bets was laid, Cleophus broke that big kid's arm and shut Chubby's big mouth at the same time. Popped like a shotgun – the arm, I mean. I never noticed if the kid sweated, but ol' chubby sure as hell did whenever he had to pay off.

Don't get me wrong, Cle' wasn't never no troublemaker. In all the years I knowed him – I mean, ever since we's kids – I never seen him go out a his way to start trouble. I also never seen him swerve too hard to avoid it, but he saved a lotta ol' boys' skins by not bein' too damn rough, like the time that Marine sergeant got tight in Trout's Bar and commenced sayin' what a bunch a saps us civilians was. Cleophus picked him up and carried him out to his car, endin' the ruckus.

Miz Titsworth, though, she had his number. He couldn't handle her a-tall. It's like she had some kind a hex on him, and she's a rough customer. We's all at this dance out to the fairgrounds a few years back, and she seen Cle' sneak a little sip from this bottle a Four Roses I'd brung with me. She socked him hard, twice, right on the face, then she tried to give her purse to another woman, sayin' for all the world to hear, "Hold this so's I can clobber the bastard!" She cussed like a trooper whenever she forgot herself. Cleophus coulda eat her without burpin', but he just stood there and took it, lookin' like a man facin' the gallows. It was somethin' strange about her.

I mean, if a gal treated me or you thataway, we'd get shed of her, right? But Cleophus never. He just went about his life with that thorn in the big middle of it. He never even talked about it much, but one day I recollect his ol' lady she'd called Trout's and demanded he come home directly. He just shrugged and mumbled somethin' about birth control, so ol' Arkie Harris that was workin' behind the bar he asked Cle' if it's family night. The big man rolled his eyes and asked, "Are you shittin'? Hell no!" He went on, "I's just wishin' her folks'd used some."

Worst of it is that she's always claimin' he's up to somethin'. If it'd been me, I'd a damn sure been out tomcattin' but Cle' wasn't me. I mean, he never messed with no gals. Then word got around to the Tejon Club that Miz Titsworth had went and called the sheriff's office and claimed her husband had tried to choke her in her sleep, but the cops ignored her, sayin' there wasn't no marks on her neck. Cleophus was real hurt. He said the first thing he knowed about it was when a deputy woke him outta a sound sleep. "Shit," he spit, "if I'uz a killer she'd a been dead a long time ago."

He hit the bottle real hard after that, and it showed. He could whup any man thereabouts, but he had a hell of a time fightin' that whiskey. Wasn't too long before word got out that his wife had went and called the cops again, same ol' story, sayin' he choked her. And he was sound asleep. But it got to him. Not only was folks lookin' at him strange, but he begun to wonder about hisself: Was he crazy? Was he doin' that stuff and not rememberin'?

"Hell, Cle'," I told him, "if you's chokin' her there'd damn sure be finger marks on her neck, and the sheriffs never found none. She's just screwy."

He only grunted.

His wife, though, did one hell of a lot more than grunt. She talked to ever'one, spreadin' lies about Cle', and him takin' it just like he done that time she socked him, not fightin' back, gettin' sadder 'n' sadder.

Then one night, after he'd been a-workin' purty hard on the booze, he busted into my place, just a-blabberin' and a-carryin' on. I figgered he's naturally drunk. "Calm down," I urged. "Calm right down!" I started to offer him a drink, but I thought better. "What's wrong?"

"Oh, Jesus, Buck," he said, "I *am* goin' crazy!"

"No, you're not. What's wrong?" I patted his big ol' back.

"Jesus," he gasped, "I cain't stop shakin'."

"It's okay. What happened?"

"Leona, she sleeps like a damn rock," he told me, all the time lookin' around like he's real scared, "so I been stayin' up the last couple nights watchin' her. I wanted to see if it's somethin' really chokin' her. There I sets in the doorway of the bedroom so's I could watch this movie on the TV in the other room, whenever I hear her start to gag. I turn to look and – Jesus! – she's turnin' to a monster with two heads, her face is crawlin'!"

"What?"

"Just crawlin'. God! Two awful ugly heads!" He raised up his hands and squeezed his temples, tears in his eyes. "I just cain't . . ." he mumbled. "I just cain't . . ." He jumped up and, before I could stop him, he run out the door and jumped into his pickup and off he roared. By the time I got dressed and run outside, he's nowheres to be seen, so I made me a pot of coffee – it's 3 A.M. – and just set at the table a-waitin', this terrible feelin' in the pit a my stomach.

Sure enough, not a quarter hour later, there come a knock at my door, and whenever I answered there stood a deputy. "You know a Cleophus Titsworth?" he asked.

"I surely do," I answered.

"Well, we're looking for him. We want to talk to him about a possible assault on his wife tonight."

I couldn't see no reason to lie. "He'uz here a while back, but he took off. He never said where he's goin'."

The cop was a nice young kid, and he believed me. He thanked me and advised me to tell Cleophus to get in touch with the sheriff if I seen him. He said there wasn't no charges, just a investigation. He said so long and I closed the door, but before I could decide whether to go to bed or not, I heard the door bein' knocked again.

I opened it and there stood that same cop. "I'm afraid I've got some bad news," he said real quiet. "I just heard over the radio that they found your friend's truck down at the bottom of China Grade. He didn't make the turn. He's dead."

All through the funeral and after, when folks was eatin' at the widder's house, I had this funny feelin' about what Cleophus'd told me that night. I mean, I never said nothin' to nobody, but I felt about like sockin' that widder woman, her makin' it clear to ever'one that she wasn't too sad about gettin' shed a Cle'. I knowed then what I had to do and I determined to do 'er. It'uz a gamble but I owed ol' Cle' that much.

First I killed me a bird and stuck Miz Titsworth's name in its beak, then I snuck it under her porch with the head pointin' north. That part'uz easy. Seven days later, it got tough. Like my ol' granny'd told me way back when, I boiled a cabbage in salt water, hopin' I remembered all the stuff I'uz supposed to do, then wrapped it in towels so it'd stay warm, and I drove fast over to Miz Titsworth's house.

It was after midnight, and Cle' had told me his wife slept real sound, but I's still worried whenever I jimmied the back door – a little trick I'd learned back in school. No problem, though. I sneaked into the room where she's snorin', her mouth wide open. I stood for a minute thinkin' of poor Cleophus married to that wolverine, then got on with it. I took this special vinegar I'd bought and real light made a teeny cross on each one of her shoulders, then on her forehead – her stirrin' just a little. I rubbed my hands in nutmeg powder before I finally unwrapped the cabbage and held it like a warm green crystal ball in front of me, the smell of it real strong.

Slowly, I lowered it toward her face and that gapin' mouth: slowly, slowly, not quite lettin' it touch her, liftin' it a little, then lowerin' it again, chantin' real quiet:

> Evil can't resist good,
> termite can't resist wood,
> night can't resist dawn,
> gone, devil, get gone!

I chanted that three times. Just when I was gonna start again, I heard this low moan, a choke, then Miz Titsworth commenced gaggin' to beat hell.

I was scared, but I stood my ground and for a minute I never seen nothing, just her buckin' there on the bed, mouth open, grabbin' at her throat, then I seen it, a long, yeller, puke-headed thing with big white eyes squirmin' outta her mouth, ugly as sin itself. The devil! I sprung back and dropped the cabbage. Shit! I never wanted no devil jumpin' into me.

After a minute, it dawned on me. That wasn't no devil. Couldn't be. It was a worm, I mean a giant worm. Lord, but it's a ugly booger. There I stood, not knowin' what to do. I's in too deep to get away.

That thing was half outta her mouth, squirmin' there like a sinner's soul, and Miz Titsworth seemed only semi-awake, gaggin' and scratchin' all the same. Much as I hated to, I grabbed that nasty thing – the worm, I mean – and give it a jerk. A bunch of it come out in my hands.

Miz Titsworth woke up then, seen me, then let out a war whoop. "You're the one!" she hollered. "You're the one that's been tryin' to kill me! Help! Po-lice!"

I never knew what else to do, so I held that half a worm out to her, it dangling with just the littlest jerks and jumps. Her hands rushed to her chest and she stared at it. After a minute, she gasped, "What *is* that thing?"

"It come outta you," I said. "It's what was chokin' ya." She stared at that worm and I stared at her. Wasn't nothin' else I *could* do, me expectin' the cops at any minute. After a minute, neither of us sayin' nothin', I just dropped that nasty thing right on the edge of her bed and walked out. To hell with it, let the cops come and get me. Anything'd be better'n her and her worm.

But to tell the truth, I never stopped worryin'. Even a week later, if I seen a police car, I ducked. Ever' time the phone rang, I flinched. I mean, the cops wouldn't have no reason *not* to think I's the guy they'd been lookin' for whenever Miz Titsworth had called before. But nothin' happened. No cops, no nothin'.

After a couple weeks, I relaxed some, still wary, still tryin' to figure out what I'd tell the sheriff whenever he come for me, but not duckin' no more ever' time a car passed my place. Course, I never seen Miz Titsworth either, not that I expected to, unless some deputy brung her. I mean, we never traveled in the same circles.

I's up at the Safeway on the top of China Grade doin' my grocery shoppin' that Saturday. I'd moved up there to a different apartment after Miz Titsworth caught me in her house. I just never felt real safe down below no more. Anyways, I's pushin' a grocery cart down one a them aisles, grabbin' this and that, not payin' too much mind to other folks – the store it was real full – when my cart run smack into another'n that was just bein' pushed around a corner. I looked up and there stood Miz Titsworth, us only separated by them two shoppin' carts.

I figured she'd start right in on me or commence whoopin' for a cop, one, so I hunkered down into my collar the way a guy does whenever he feels a punch whistlin' at him. Wasn't no place to hide. Our eyes they locked for a second and I seen – at least I thought I seen – somethin' flicker in hers. Not sayin' nothin', she pulled that cart back and skedaddled.

Me, I just stood there tremblin' like a mouse that had just escaped a gopher snake.

I never felt like shoppin' no more after that, so I hustled to the check-stand, paid my money, then hurried out onto the parkin' lot a-carryin' my bag a groceries. Just when I reached my car, I noticed this dark sedan settin' off by itself with these two eyes, scared-lookin' they was, just peerin' over the dashboard at me like some mad animal lurkin' in the dark: Miz Titsworth.

I'd had enough. I dropped my damn groceries right there in the parkin' lot and made for her. I don't know if I'd a socked her or told her off, but I never found out because that car it fired up so fast that all I could see was big white eyes as it blowed past me, them and a yeller, puke-headed blur. Jesus! I staggered back a step on the blacktop and stared after that thing in the dark car just fishtailin' away, off the bluffs down China Grade into the whistlin' white steam and boilin' black smoke.

THE KILLING PEN

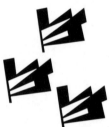

Must of been late that summer when Sam Dawkins died, cause I still remember how brown the foothills and flats had become, and dull too, not like the gold of May or June. Even the warty old oaks on the knolls and in the arroyos and the clusters of willows around streams didn't add much color. The air was hot and heavy.

Grandaddy and me we'd found old Sam collapsed late that spring in the big stock barn, his eyes glazed, one of his legs jerking like a spine-shot buck's. Directly, Grandaddy and some hands put Sam in a wagon and carried him to town. It seemed like a long time before they came back without him. But he wasn't dead, Grandaddy told me, just real sick. They left him in the county hospital.

None of us knew exactly how old Sam was, but he was older than Grandaddy. He'd been a slave on my great-grandfather's spread back in East Texas before the war, and he was already a top hand back when

Grandaddy was just a boy. In the days right after the war, a lot of ex-slaves stayed on as hands, so Great-grandaddy had made Sam a foreman. "They don't make 'em no tougher," Grandaddy told me. "Ol' Sam could live on rawhide and sweat when he had to, by God. If you had some range cows lost out in the thicket, you'd just send ol' Sam and he'd drag 'em back."

Sam taught Grandaddy most of what he knew about horses and cows and men. He taught my daddy too, and he was teaching me and the other ranch kids. He was always telling stories and showing us kids how to do things.

One time Joaquin Dominguez he skipped school then faked a note so he fooled the schoolmistress. But he no sooner got away with it than he started bragging on himself. Then the teacher she got wind of it and whipped him good. Well, old Sam sniffed things out, so he herded a bunch of us kids out to the stock barn where it was cool and he told us a story his momma told him.

Back during the old days, he said, there was this here slave named John who got so he could sneak away from chores without getting caught. "One day John he hidin' out in the thicket, and he come across this ol' white skull a-layin' under a tree. Wellsir, that skull give ol' John a start, don't ya know." We all giggled. "Of a sudden, that skull speak right up to John and like to scare water out of him. 'Tongue brought me here,' it say. John he lit out fast." We all laughed and Sam he winked at us.

"John he tol' ol' Massa everything what happen, but Massa think John just tellin' a lie so's he won't get beat for runnin' off. John say he show Massa, and Massa he strap on his pistol and say 'Let's go.' By 'n by they come to the skull and John say, "Tell Massa what you tole me." Skull it don't say nothin'. Massa he gettin' hot." Us kids giggled, a little tense now since we all liked John better than ol' Massa whenever Sam told us stories about them.

"John beg that skull. He cuss it. He threaten. He do everything he can think of, but ol' skull just won't talk. Directly Massa pull out his gun and shoot John dead. Then he ride away."

We gasped, but before we could say anything Sam he went on. "No sooner'n ol' Massa gone, skull say to John: 'Tongue brought me here and now it's brought you.'"

All of us looked at one another, and Sam gave us the fish-eye. Then Joaquin he said, *"Yo entiendo."*

Sam waited for several moments, then he said: "Don' tell nobody nothin' you don' have to." He repeated it in Spanish just to make sure we all understood. We did.

As far back as I can remember Sam was always kind of bent and skinny with just a little gray fuzz on his head, not that we often saw it, for he wore his battered old hat nearly all the time. His hands were large and strong. He knew more knots than anyone I ever knew, and he could rope most anything. ("Sam can lasso horseflies," Grandaddy said once.) He didn't ride much anymore because of a stiff hip. Mostly he just took care of tack and helped Grandaddy break in new hands.

Afternoons you'd find Sam and Grandaddy playing checkers in the tack room, sometimes with Linc, the blacksmith, and a vaquero or two there just to give them unwelcome advice and listen to their stories. Often as possible us kids joined them. The stories were really something. "You call these things cows?" Sam demanded one time of a young cowpoke who'd broken his arm in a loading chute. "Back in the old days they was real cattle. Them devils stamp into a thicket and come out with a *tigre* hangin' off'n one horn and bear hangin' off'n t'other. I 'mind the first time ol' Jeff there" – he nodded at Grandaddy – "tried to tangle with one. You never seen such a bloody mess in your life." Grandaddy grinned under his curving mustache, but he said nothing.

The younger hands would brag about fights they'd had, but Sam he'd scoff. "Don't bother with no box-fightin'," he'd tell them. "If some ol' boy want a fight make him sorry. Find you a stick or a rock and bash 'im. Keep bashin' 'im 'til he ain't gon' bother you no mo'." The young guys looked like they wanted to laugh, but they could see Sam wasn't joking. And Sam could fight, or at least that's what Grandaddy told me. "He licked a hell of a lot of cowboys in his time. He was foreman and by God all the hands knew it." Grandaddy told me about a group of ex-Reb soldiers who "figgered they'd whup themselves a nigger and they picked Sam. Well they whupped 'im, but they picked the wrong nigger."

"They really whupped him?" I asked, not wanting to believe it.

"They whupped 'im bloody and near dead, but two of them *was* dead, and the other near it. Ol' Sam didn't play around none. He'd hit you with a horse, if that's all there was for him to use. And he could shoot a handgun mighty good."

Grandaddy turned real serious then: "You're a-gonna run this spread one day," he said, chilling my belly with the avoided realization that he too must eventually die, "and I'll tell you this: If you're a-gonna run a ranch you need the best vaqueros, not the whitest or the purtiest. The best. A lot of ranchers hereabouts wouldn't hire nothing but white cowpokes after the war. Fine with me. I hired the best and that's one reason we're still in business and most of them others're long gone."

Holidays, like Christmas or Juneteenth, Grandaddy threw a big dinner for hands and there was music and dancing and whiskey. Lots of things happened on those days, dancing and contests and no school, lots of things, but I remember most of all the stories Sam would tell when he was drinking liquor because they were so sad, and they were most always about slave days: those strange old days so long before I was born, those days that never seemed to die. He told different stories, but he always repeated one about the slave woman who kept having babies and the master just kept selling them away from her as soon as they were weaned. "Lawd," he'd say, "that po' woman just pine and pine." Sam's voice always turned to a mixture of pain and rage. "She have a new baby and she just determine ol' Massa ain't gonna take this lil chile from her." He kind of gulped and brushed at his eyes. "So she done the onliest thing she could figger: she give the baby pizen and took some her own self. Then she lay down and hol' her little baby to her breas' and they die."

That story haunted me. I dreamed of it, and worried over it. I couldn't imagine a woman who would *kill* her own baby. Not in my wildest thoughts did it seem possible. Whenever I asked Grandaddy about it, he answered only "Slavery," with a sort of faraway grunt. Then he added, "That's all past nowadays. Don't bother yourself none with them old days." But they did bother me.

A couple of weeks after Sam took sick, Grandaddy and Linc they brought him home from the county seat. One arm swung loose at his side, and he dragged one foot and leaned on a shiny new cane. Us kids rushed to greet him, but his face was a scary mask to us, with one eye and half his mouth drooping, so we pulled up short. Sam caught it. He saw the sudden fright in our eyes and it hurt him.

Grandaddy moved Sam into the main house with the rest of the family, into my daddy's old room. Sam took his meals with us, of course, but food dribbled out of his mouth and embarrassed him so bad, he found excuses to eat alone in the kitchen as often as he could. But gradually we all got use to each other again. Us kids we learned to understand Sam's newly slurred speech, and Grandaddy didn't let the old man just hide in his room. "You better get on out to that tack room before them young bucks wreck ever'thing. Half of 'em wake up in a new world ever' morning. Besides," he added, "there ain't nobody out there for me to whup at checkers." Sam fussed a little, but pretty soon he was back in the tack room.

My Uncle Jingles – Jacob, really, who was a doctor of veterinary medicine way up in Montana – was scheduled for his annual visit home. He was Grandaddy's only surviving son, so everyone was excited. Besides, he always brought presents. I had to clean my room specially good, and do my chores because Grandaddy was on the prod, checking everything. He had a prime bull calf moved into the killing pen next to the slaughter shed. It just happened that we had a lot of cows, some with suckling calves, on the large pasture bordering the killing pen, and that bull calf's momma stayed right next to the pen nuzzling her big old baby through the whitewashed fence.

We were walking out to the tack room after breakfast – Sam and Grandaddy and me – whenever Sam noticed the cow and calf close together, and he stopped. "Jeff," he called after us, for we'd kept on walking. We returned to where he stood. "It ain't right," he added thickly.

"What ain't?" Grandaddy asked.

"Looky there," Sam pointed his cane toward the cow and calf. "That's just what they done to my Momma and me. You know it ain't right." His face wore that expression of sad rage I'd seen before.

Grandaddy stopped dead. "Go on in the house, boy," he ordered me, and I snapped to it because his voice had turned low and ominous. I watched them out the window. They were talking, arguing almost, both men spitting violently on the ground.

I was baffled. Later, we ate a tense, silent lunch together, and after lunch old Sam he skipped his nap. Instead, he hobbled out to the killing pen and leaned on the rails. I followed him. "You musta seen a thousand calves in that pen before, Mr. Sam," I said. "Why does this one bother you?" His red-rimmed eyes turned toward me. "Some things don't strike a man till he ready to see 'em," he responded.

"Yeah . . ." I started to continue, but he cut me off.

"Ask yo' Granpappy," he ordered. He spent most of that long, hot afternoon, I guess, just leaning on the rails of the pen watching that cow and her bull calf.

Me, I wandered away, confused and a little sore, and found Joaquin. We mumbly-pegged and tried to make a straitjacket out of old harness straps and sacks. Finally we wandered over toward the tack room, stopping at the blacksmith's shed to talk to Linc, but he was quiet and tense. All the black vaqueros, in fact, seemed uneasy, like they felt involved in Sam's private anger. Eventually we reached the tack room and found it empty. I looked out back toward the killing pen and didn't see Sam there either, so Joaquin and me we started for the kitchen in hope of a snack when we saw what looked like a lone leg sticking out near the side of the barn.

It was Sam, crumpled and spraddle-legged: it looked like he'd tripped. His greasy old hat was off and I could see his fuzzy head bleeding bright where it'd struck the ground. He wasn't moving. "Go get Grandaddy," I told Joaquin. Something white-hot had commenced burning in the middle of my belly.

Grandaddy came right away and Linc followed him directly. They knelt next to Sam and Grandaddy felt for a pulse, then looked at Linc, Grandaddy's whole body, even his mustache, drooping; Linc nodded. "Dead," Grandaddy said finally, his pale eyes squinting hard, his voice sighing. Then he stood, looking very straight and tall, his tobacco-stained mustache twitching, and he walked, slowly at first, then fast, to the killing pen. He opened the gate and angrily shooed the bull calf with his hat until it returned to the pasture where the cow stood waiting. "Get in there, you little son of a bitch," Grandaddy said.

Grandaddy walked back to Sam, and knelt again next to the sprawled body. He took off his own hat and, real sudden it seemed, his head was resting in one hand and he was shaking right in front of all of us, a thin stream of tears streaming down one cheek. He reached for Sam and touched the chalky-dark face. "Damn it anyway," Grandaddy said. Linc was looking away. I stood next to Joaquin, too frightened to cry.

Grandaddy finally stood, holding Sam's battered hat in his hand. He cleared his throat, turned toward Joaquin and me, then handed me Sam's greasy old hat. "Grow into this, boy," he ordered.

ELEPHANT TIPS

I got me a job, man, a fuckin' gig. On my way to easy street – *E-Z Street* – because this dude I know, Tommy Giacomini, his uncle runs a classy restaurant out at the country club, and he's gonna make me a waiter. So I struts into Manuel's Chili Palace to tell my partners that will naturally be overjoyed, right?

"You what?" asks Big Cleve, who ain't worked since Nam, unless you consider breakin' and enterin' work.

"Got me a fuckin' gig, man."

"Sheee'."

Artie he just chuckles. He ticks me off sometimes, man. "Yeah," he finally says real loud, lookin' all around, "my man is moooving on up. He's going to circumcise elephants at the zoo. The pay isn't much, but he gets to keep the tips."

Everybody in Manuel's, even the ugly waitress, laughs to beat hell.

"You're a funny fucker, Artie," I tell him.

"What *is* your job, then?" He asks.

I tell him and he don't look so smart when he hears. He'd figured I'll be scrapin' up dog turds for the Parks Department or somethin', man, not a real gig, not a class one.

Cleve he says, "They need anybody else, bro'?" He's serious, man.

Before I can answer, Artie grins again and suggests, "Maybe Merlene here can give you some pointers." He winks at his honey, the waitress that has more tattoos than the three of us combined, and wrestles two weight classes above Big Cleve. She specializes in licking chili off her thumb after ploppin' a plate in front of a customer.

"Thanks," I say. "That'd be real nice." After she lurches away, I add, "Maybe she can teach me to walk like an orangutan too."

Cleve cracks up. "Chi-chi-chi!"

Even Artie smiles. "Hey, she keeps the kid in smokes," he says.

Just then T.J., lookin' like the ass end of bad luck, sways into the cafe. "What the fuck did we drink last night?" he asks as he climbs onto a stool. "I feel like shit."

His problem, man, ain't *what* he drank, it's how much. You drink that much *water* and you'll get sick. He was in the slammer for nine months, man, nine long months employed as a license-plate specialist, and he's been out for eight days tryin' to drink all the booze he missed while he was inside.

"You better slow down, my man," advises Artie. "You never see the kid putting away hooch like you. You never see *anybody* put away hooch like you. Your liver must look like a saddle."

"Fuck you, doctor," growls T.J. "Where's the fuckin' coffee? What's that fuckin' waitress doin'?"

"She's in back havin' her flea bath," I suggest.

"You guys are talking about the woman I love," grins Artie.

Big Cleve cracks up: "Chi-chi-chi! Man, the bitches you make it with."

Artie has an answer. "At least the kid makes it." We heard it a million times.

After T.J. puts the fire out with the brown water Manuel sells for coffee, we repair to the local Goodwill store so I can buy some waiter clothes, a couple used suits, a couple shirts, and these three ties. I let Cleve talk me into one tie with big Hawaiian flowers on it, and he promptly takes it out of my sack and puts it on when we hit the street. It looks great with his sleeveless blue workshirt, but his eighteen-inch biceps convince me not to say nothin'. "How's it look, bro'?" he asks.

"Fine as wine," I answer, havin' sampled his right cross on a couple occasions.

"Thunderbird wine," grunts T.J.

Cleve scowls, "Say, man . . ."

I'm not sure whether it's a comment on the tie or a request for a drink, but before things can get heavy, I say, "Look, once I make a little jingle, we can all buy some shit to wear."

"The kid needs some new threads," acknowledges Artie the great lady killer. Hell, he's the only one of us that's got any decent clothes, and that's because the badgers he loves up keep him clean. He's one slick chili choker, man.

T.J. and Cleve drop me off that afternoon – Artie havin' scheduled a rendezvous with the missing link – and we drive through these big gates and up a long, circular road with bushes that've been trimmed into shapes, like triangles and balls, alongside it. We can see golfers out on the hills all around, drivin' those funny little carts like they're all ice cream men, and wearin' fag clothes – bright little knee pants and pink sweaters and little caps, crazy shit, man; their old ladies must dress 'em. All the hogs in the parkin' lot are Cads and Jaguars and MB's, so T.J.'s Ford, which looks like Patton's command tank, it stands out.

I see these two security types eyein' the Ford when I get out, so I tell the guys to split and pick me up at seven because Mr. Giacomini is only usin' me for the early shift until I get broke in real good. I guess he don't want me spillin' gravy on somebody's pink sweater.

Inside, it's not like the mess hall in Nam, and it's damn sure not like Manuel's Chili Palace either. It looks like a fuckin' hospital, man. Tommy's there and he introduces me to his uncle that's wearin' a silk suit with a flower in his lapel, that introduces me to this guy named Earl, that reintroduces me to himself as "Mr. Romain" as soon as the other two are gone. He's gonna teach me how to wait tables. Earl turns out to be a snotty bastard, actin' like he can just barely tolerate me, and he damn sure doesn't wanna slip up and touch me or somethin', but I stay cool. I need the fuckin' gig, man. Besides, I think he's a fairy.

So after about an hour of instructions, ol' Earl he kinda sighs like he's done all he can, then sends me out to this table where three guys have just sat down. "They'll only want coffee or drinks," he adds, meanin' that I'm not up to carryin' a burger and fries. "Thanks, Earl," I say, thinkin' that the day will come when I'll serve him a fuckin' knuckle sandwich. He don't answer because he don't like me callin' him Earl.

I take three menus to the table and I say, "May I help you gentlemen?"

"A blonde for me and redheads for each of my friends," says this gray-haired dude in knee pants. Just my luck to get Bob Hope.

I smile, but don't say nothing.

One of the other guys says, "Coffee, please. What're you having, Ray?" Ray was having a draft beer.

"Do you have Pimm's Cup?" asks Bob Hope, his eyes all twinkly.

How the fuck do I know? Pimm's Cup? I don't know a Pimm's Cup from a jock cup. "I'll see, sir." I hoofs to the bar and asks. We do. So back I trot to the table. "Yes sir, we do," I say real polite.

"Well, that's a wonderful thing to carry. I'll have coffee." He grins like a shit-eatin' dog.

I try not to look at him while I jot the order down, then collect the three menus. I don't like people fuckin' with me, man. I don't fuck with other dudes and I don't want them fuckin' with me. But, I tells myself, he just saw I was new and wanted to have a little fun. Okay, I'll give him that one.

"What took so long?" Earl demands soon as I get back.

"That old dude sent me to look for Pimm's Cup."

"Dr. Gaspari is a card, but you've got to snap to it."

I'm about to snap him, put a fuckin' knot on his bald gourd, when he send me to another table, this one next to the big window where you can see most of the golf course plus the Sierra in the background. From inside this fancy place the mountains look real good. When you're out sleepin' under the fuckin' freeway like me and the guys've been, they look like freezin' to death.

This old dude is sittin' with a cherry chick, young with a body that won't stop. She's wearin' this low-cut dress and I'm standing over her, lookin' into her Pimm's Cups. The guy, that don't exactly act like her father, he orders cocktails while I eye his honey, thinkin', baby, I could make you forget that old fart so fast.

Back at the waiters' station, Earl is pissed: "You were *looking* at Mrs. Ruggles!"

"I sure as hell was. Is that his *wife?*"

"It most assuredly is! Don't you *ever* let me catch you looking at a woman like that again," he warns.

Now, I'd just about heard enough from ol' Earl. I can take some correctin', but this *warnin'* shit, well, it don't sit too good. "Lookin's not against the law," I point out, tryin' to stay cool. This gig ain't all I thought it'd be.

"It is definitely against the rules here for the help to *ogle* customers."

We're alone, so I ask real quiet, "What the fuck's the difference between a ogle and a look, *Earl?*" I spit his name so hard that he blinks like I lit a firecracker.

After a minute – it finally dawns on him that he's fuckin' with his pulse – he scurries away, sayin', "Mr. Giacomini will hear about this." Fuckin' fairy.

I deliver the cocktails and the guy nods. The chick, man, swear to God, she gives *me* the eye, that look that tells you if the time and place were right we'd be breathin' heavy. I get blue balls walkin' back to my station. And I also get blue, thinkin' about what money can buy. Well, fuck it.

Pretty soon, ol' Earl is back with this smirk on his face. "You are to obey me *or else*," he says. He looks like he expects me to faint.

"Look, asshole," I whisper, "I'll do what you say, but if you keep actin' like your shit don't stink, *somebody's* gonna knock a fuckin' hole in your lung and nobody, not even Mr. Giacomini, will be able to save your ass. Think about it, *Earl.*"

While he's blinking again, I head to another table where these four guys just sat down, and I'm wonderin' if I still got a job, but at least I'm happy that Earl finally understands what's goin' down. I can't figure people out, man. You try to do your work and they mess with you. The four guys all want draft beers, and one wants a club sandwich. When I get back to the station, I expect Earl will be gone, runnin' to report me to Mr. Giacomini, but he's not. "That was better," he says.

"Thanks," I say.

The way they do it, waiters don't go back to the tables to pick up tips – that's not classy, man; the busboys pick up what customers leave and put it in this box. That's why, when the next group comes in – two middle-aged guys in tennis clothes – I'm shocked when one of them says to me after I deliver their little bottles of water, "Would you like your tip now?"

"Well . . . sure," I stammer.

"Buy low and sell high," he says, and both of 'em crack up.

I just turn around and walk away, afraid I'll lose it, when I hear one of 'em say, "He doesn't seem amused." Then the other one says real loud, "He doesn't understand. They don't exactly hire geniuses here."

These are the jokers I fought to protect in Nam, that my buddies got killed to protect. I stalk back to their table. "You want that racquet stuffed up your ass, man?" I ask him, my eyes burnin' into his. I ain't kiddin' and he knows it.

He tries to grin his way out of it and, out the corner of my eye, I see his friend kinda scoot away from the table. "Now just a minute . . ."

"If you can't talk right, man, don't say shit to me."

He looks away, so I turn and walk back to my station. By the time I get there, those two guys're gone. Good fuckin' riddance. A couple minutes later, though, I'm on my way out, too.

This time it's Mr. Giacomini himself that comes stormin' up to me and calls me into his office.

"What did you say to Dr. Collier?"

"Who?" I know damn good and well who he's talkin' about.

"Dr. Collier, the gentleman in tennis togs."

"In what? *Togs?*"

Mr. Giacomini is this little short bastard with a big neck that smokes cigars; he looks like he's smolderin'. "Are you trying to provoke me?" he demands.

The truth is that I am. I mean, what the fuck, I can see that he's on their side, so why not? "Me? No," I says.

"You cursed at one of our best customers, and a close personal friend of mine. Don't you understand that these are people of the finest class: doctors, lawyers, businessmen? You can't come in here and act like a common hoodlum."

"Wait a minute, Mr. Giacomini," I tells him. "I was just doin' my job the best I could. If these people're so classy, why do they treat somebody workin' to make a livin' like he's a turd? If they're so classy, why don't they respect other people's feelin's? You got class mixed up with money, which they got. I know guys on the street that'll never do nothin' to fuck up another guy's gig, but these assholes . . ."

"That's the final straw," he says. "You can't even keep a civil tongue in your head. You're dismissed. I want you off these premises *immediately!*"

"Okay," I says, and I'm fingerin' the Goodwill trousers I just spent my last jingle on, and lookin' at this toad in front of me. "I'd rather not be a whore like you anyways, sellin' my respect so's I can get some doctors and lawyers to act like they like me."

His face turns purple and he jumps to his feet. "Nobody talks to Aldo Giacomini that way! You get your friggin' ass the frig outta here! I'm *connected* and I'll have you dumped in a friggin' lake."

The little wop has lost it. So I gives him one more shot: "Give me any more lip and you'll be *dis*connected, you sawed-off sack a shit." Then I glare at him a second and leave. After all I seen in Nam, guys gutted and kids burned and old people starved to death, this little fuckin' number in his silk suit isn't jack. I slam the door and walk away.

So ain't life grand. I start the day with my first job since Nam and I end it with the fuckin' Mafia on my ass. The more I think about it, I shoulda kicked Giacomini's butt, I mean if they're gonna put me in cement shoes anyway. But hell, he's Tommy's uncle and Tommy's a good dude. He lost his damn hand in Nam.

I get on the horn and call Manuel's Chili Palace and, sure enough, the guys're there. I tell 'em to come pick me up and to bring some fuckin' beer, since T.J. that I'm talkin' to, he sounds like he's already in the bag.

He is. I see his hog weavin' up the fuckin' road to the country club and this kid that parks cars, he says, "Jeez, it looks like that guy's shit-faced." So is Big Cleve that's sitting in the front seat with his eighteen-inch brown biceps hangin' out the window. He's laughin' at the fuckin' golfers in their turquoise pants and lavender sweaters. Soon as they pull up, I jumps in the back seat. "Gimme a fuckin' brew, man," I say.

Cleve passes one to me and says, "You see all these cats, dressed like a bunch a mo'fuckin' punks, man." Then he grins and asks, "Wha's happenin', baby?" Drunk outta his fuckin' gourd.

"The motherfuckers fired me."

"The mo'fuckahs do what?"

"Canned my ass."

"Why, man?"

"Because I told some snotty bastard I'd shove a tennis racquet up his ass."

Big Cleve grins. He likes that kinda action. "Where the mo'fuckah be? I kick his mo'fuckin' ass."

"Hold it," says Artie, who sits next to me in the back seat and who, as usual, is the great voice of reason. Also the great voice of chickenshit. Sometimes I'm glad I didn't serve in his outfit overseas, man. "Do not cause trouble here," he advises. "The kid does not need ninety days in orange coveralls at the county road camp. This is *the* club, where the D.A. and the Mayor and Police Chief, and all the money too, hang out. The kid says cool it."

"Fuck the kid," I say. "We gotta do *somethin'*. I ain't gonna back away from this place." I finish inhalin' beer number one and start on number two. "These assholes treated me like dirt, man."

"Why don't you guys moon the bastards on our way back to the fuckin' gate, man?" suggests T.J.

Cleve is one big grin. "Moon the mo'fuckahs. Right on!" He's already workin' on his belt. He digs it. His cinnamon rolls have been viewed by more people than any other buns in Sacramento, man. Fastest fuckin' moon in the West.

Sounds good to me, too, but Artie almost shouts: "Stop the car! Indecent exposure equals six months. The kid will walk back to town and be by the phone at Manuel's when you *locos* call for bail."

We're used to it, man. We don't even argue. He always pussys out. T.J. slows to about ten miles per hour, then says, "Hit the road."

"Hey, you're still movin'."

"It's a tough fuckin' life," grins T.J., real sympathetic.

"Hey, the kid could break his leg."

All of sudden Big Cleve speaks up. "Get the fuck out, mo'fuckah." Artie is interfering with the moonin', which Cleve is ready to launch.

Artie ain't too bad a fighter when you get him goin', but he don't want no parts of Cleve. He stumbles out and staggers, almost straightens to a jog, then jags until he tumbles on his face as we move away real slow. We all laugh to beat hell.

"Moon time!" calls T.J. as we approach this bunch a golfers right next to the road, and me and Cleve hang buns. They all look shocked. The next group does too, and we're havin' a ball, so T.J. hangs a left away from the gate. "Let's tour this fucker before we take off," he says. Me and Cleve open fresh beers, our asses nice and cool in the afternoon breeze. We're comin' up on this golf cart with these two dudes in it and for a minute I think one's that jerk doctor that got me fired, so I jam my butt so far out the window that I almost hit the driver with it. It's not him though.

Just then T.J. says, "The fuckin' pigs!"

Me and Cleve look around and, sure enough, a red light is flashin' behind us. "Let's get outta here," I says, trying to pull my ass in from the window, but I jammed it so far out that I'm stuck. Cleve is sittin' in the front seat drinkin' more beer, with his drawers down around his ankles. He wants to get as much brew into him as he can before the pigs nab us, man . . . if they do. Meanwhile, T.J. is makin' for the gate, not speedin', but gettin' there as quick as he can just the same.

Just when I'm about to get myself free from that damned window, I hear T.J. kinda sigh, "Ho-ly shit!"

I look up and see the whole fuckin' Sacramento police force waitin' for us at that gate. Red lights, blue lights, guys in bulletproof vests, shotguns, the whole fuckin' banana, man. I quit trying to wiggle my butt loose. Fuck it, man, there's no way to fight rich bastards. They always win. I shoulda just duked that faggot doctor when I had the chance.

"What'll I do?" asks T.J.

"Stop and show 'em you mo'fuckin' license," Big Cleve advises, gigglin'. He don't give a shit, man.

"I ain't got one," T.J. says, soundin' real tense.

"You in big trouble then, bro'," Cleve says, still gigglin'.

I can tell by the wind on my pearly white ass that we're slowin' down as we reach the road block, but I don't care either. "You'll probably get a fuckin' ticket," I add and Big Cleve spits a mouthful a beer laughin', man. He don't even bother to pull his fuckin' pants up.

"Let's all sing 'God Bless America,' " I suggest.

Cleve cracks up again: "Chi-chi-chi! Don' know the mo'fuckin' words, man."

Just as the car stops and the pigs come swarmin' up like they caught Public Enemy Number One, I sees Artie standin' by the gate, his clothes dirty from where he rolled, his hands stuck in his pockets, lookin' real sad. Fuck it, man.

GOOD-BYE, UNCLE SEAMUS

It's funny the things you remember about people. Sylvester Duggan was the first guy I ever saw sock a woman. We were at a dive on the east side celebrating a high school play-off victory, drinking beer and dancing with fancy women, a gang of us – Denny McCann, Sean Daly, Billy Dunn, Mike Shaw, Vester, and me.

Ves, an all-league tackle and huge by the standards of that time, was a gentle giant if ever there was one. Oh, he was a devastating boxer in P.E. classes – he'd battered tough-talking Denny, the only lad his size – but never had to fight otherwise, so never did.

Anyway, he was dancing with a cute little whore when a thick woman with tattooed arms and a face like putty swaggered onto the floor and punched the gal Ves was twirling. The aggressor screeched, "You slut! I'll teach you to steal tricks from me!" She grabbed the smaller girl's hair with one hand and began pummeling her with the other one.

For a second, big Ves just stood there looking like a confused angel, those red curls framing his freckled face. His erstwhile partner was crying, "Help me! Somebody please help me!" as the larger woman beat her. We all thought we were tough football players, but this scene was beyond us: the shrieks, the curses, the dark floor shattering with spears of light from the globe twirling on the ceiling. I, for one, was suddenly frightened, and I froze. But Vester moved.

He reached into the melee, grabbed the older woman's thick neck in one mitt, and popped her with the other, a short crisp left hand that anesthetized her mid-curse: "Son of a . . ." *thunk!* She fell without a quiver to the waxed floor, and nobody, not even the bouncer, laid hands on Sylvester.

Denny, known as "the flower" to his classmates in deference to a noxious habit of his, whispered to me, "It's a brute that'd hit a woman." He was still sore, I'm sure, because Sylvester had humiliated him in that P.E. bout.

"I think that woman's the brute."

He only snorted, "Hunh!" Then he loosed a fart.

That next year, over the protests of his family, Vester went away to college on a football scholarship instead of attending the seminary. You could hear the howls all over the neighborhood because his mother and aunts had assumed that he would become a priest. They never really forgave him. You see, when his father, Tommy Duggan, died – "It was the drink got him," my mother reported at the time – Ves was just a kid; his mother'd moved in with her two unmarried sisters, Rose and Mary Martha Wicklow, and the three of them conspired to raise the boy, to plan his life.

Sylvester was an exceptionally bright kid, it was agreed, and he was targeted for great things by everyone at St. Vincent de Paul School, but by the time he reached high school his brains had become a burden; he *had* to earn A's or he was considered a failure. And all those A's were pointed in one direction: I remember clearly his Aunt Mary Martha telling my mother, "It's a gift of God that will be given Holy Mother Church, isn't it?" I recall that especially, since it was said before noon mass the day after Vester had coldcocked the whore. "Our boy will be takin' the Holy Orders, won't he?" Mary Martha went on.

"A wonderful thing, isn't it?" my mother had replied, then she'd riveted me with her eyes. "There's some could learn from a fine lad like your Sylvester."

The irony, of course, is that now I *am* a priest – Viet Nam, what I saw there, sent me to the seminary – and Ves is a gynecologist out in sunny California. Even the black crows – that's what we called the nuns – would never have guessed that outcome, I'll bet.

For instance, I stood up with Ves when he married Maureen O'Connor. It was just before I went overseas and just after he finished his degree at Penn State and left for medical school at UCLA. In many ways, the ceremony seemed like a funeral. Although he was marrying a neighborhood girl, his mother and aunts were stone-faced because his marriage made it certain that he would not become a priest. They hinted darkly that Maureen had employed the darkest of passions, what they called "sec," to lure their boy.

"There's some don't need *that*, isn't there?" his mother said to mine the week before the wedding. I was driving the two ladies to an altar society meeting at the church, and before I could ask what "that" meant, Mrs. Duggan continued: "The flesh, it's the flesh and the divil that's taken our boy," she clucked and dabbed at her eyes. "It was them atheists at that college turned his head. Now, once he's lost his purity . . . like his father . . ." she muffled sobs with her handkerchief.

You have to understand that Vester's mother and aunts went to mass and received communion daily. They even dressed like nuns: dark clothing that covered their bodies, heads swathed in dark kerchiefs, worn rosaries in their hands, scapulars around their necks. They always planted themselves in the first row and were aggressively the first to stand, the first to kneel, the first to sit during services, their moves so certain that it was clear to all they were choreographed by some Higher Power. If an altar boy or – heaven forbid – a priest made a mistake the Wicklow women could be heard clucking. Until he went away to college, Ves had to go with them and if he didn't receive holy communion, they grilled him, so he always received.

In any case, I'll never forget Vester's bright-red face at his wedding as he knelt next to Maureen before the altar, listening to the soft, funereal sobs from his aunts and mother during the ceremony. His bride appeared stunned and Father Tim was angry. It was not an auspicious beginning, and the young couple made only a token appearance at their own reception in the Duggan flat, then quickly departed for faraway California.

During that period while Ves was in medical school on the West Coast, Maureen took a terrible working-over from her new in-laws: "She lured our boy with the flesh, didn't she." It was not a question. "*Sec.* No better'n a common whore. Not a bit. It was her fancy tastes took him out to *that* place, wasn't it?" Finally, old Father Tim spoke to them about the sin of scandal, and for a while they ceased attending St. Vincent, instead traveling across town to St. Mary Magdalene parish.

Sadly, Maureen was back three years later, with two babies and a broken heart. I don't know the particulars, but since her own parents were dead, she moved in with Vester's mother and aunts – they who had been vilifying her the whole time. After the divorce, they began referring to her as "his one true wife" instead of "that woman." Moreover, Mrs. Duggan and her sisters ceased speaking about their boy then and began to pray the death prayers for him. Because he and I corresponded, I knew Ves had eventually received an annulment – a tangle of church politics that I'd rather not get into – and remarried, that he was in fact living a remarkably conventional life out in exotic California: PTA, Sunday Mass, Little League, and a dog.

Just back from Nam myself, I spoke to Maureen immediately after she returned and she told me then only that she dreaded the winters here and the narrowness. When I asked why she hadn't remained on the coast, she looked away for a moment, then said only, "The children need family." Maureen had been taking classes at a junior college herself before the split, and she knew it would be tough to continue her education here, because there were far fewer such opportunities. I urged her to try night school, which was better than nothing.

When I returned to the parish a few years later as a priest, sad to report she had assimilated – dark clothes, dark demeanor – and her two children were being raised as Ves had been. She approached me shortly after I arrived, a pinched, smileless caricature of the Maureen I had known. She wanted me to intercede with the court that had granted Vester visiting privileges and that allowed him to take the children – a boy and a girl, named after their parents – during the summer. "He's no right to expose my children to *that* place." In fact, I told her, he had every right according to both church and civil law.

"He's fallen away and living in sin and I won't have my children exposed to him," she spat with the tone Catholics use when they're certain that clerics have gone soft. "I'll go to His Eminence," she warned. "It's that *California!*" She spun away and I've seen little of her since because, like her in-laws, she attends a Latin mass held weekly in the Knights of Columbus hall.

The parish itself changed dramatically during the years I was gone. It was now at least half black. When we were kids, it had been populated almost exclusively by shanty Irish, the second and third generation that had not managed to fully emerge from immigrant poverty, but by the time I returned, many of those families had moved to lace-curtain suburbs.

The parish was in disarray, and I found myself toiling in a different neighborhood, one that was haunted by racism both covert and overt, by a sense of hopelessness that led to drugs and casual sex, so I stressed revitalizing the schools to make them the focus of parish life. I wanted to thrust our youngsters, black and white, Catholic and non-Catholic, out of the terrible cycle of poverty that trapped them. Along with parents, I determined to make St. Vincent's elementary and secondary schools the finest in the city, and they're well on their way right now. We've won the Academic Olympics three of the last four years, and our basketball team is a thing to behold.

In any case, it's fortunate that the bishop backed my plan, because many older parishioners did not, deeply resenting my close ties with leaders in the black community, especially with clergy from other denominations. Many had also resented my even opening the school to non-Catholics, which is to say "them black Protestants," as Mrs. Duggan delicately put it. As a matter of fact, "Vinnie's," as we alums call it, had become underpopulated and was on the brink of closure when His Eminence approved my plan.

I'd hired a gifted Negro woman as principal after old Sister Mary Dominic retired, and the Irish really howled. Mrs. Duggan, her two sisters, and her daughter-in-law had written a joint letter to the bishop – he sent a copy to me – complaining that "Holy Mother Church" should concern herself with souls, not "race mixing." They predicted a spate of "mixed marriages," and they meant it both ways, I suppose.

Except to pick up and return his kids, Vester never visited the old neighborhood. In fact, he rarely came east at all; I knew from the occasional notes he sent me. Seamus Tynne's death finally brought him home for something like a real visit after all those years. Uncle Seamus, as we all called him, had been our high school football coach and P.E. teacher. He had been especially close to Vester, a second father to a boy dominated by women. After retiring, Seamus had remained in the parish, where he was a major figure in the Knights of Columbus and an invaluable aid to me. For a number of years after retiring, he had donated his time to organize and run a P.E. program at the grade school, helping those young black athletes as he had helped a couple generations of young white ones. I wrote to Ves, informing him of Uncle Seamus's death, and he called to say that he'd be flying in for the rosary, wake, and mass. Could I pick him up at the airport? I could and would.

Himself strode into the terminal, tan and bearded, leaner and more muscular than I'd expected, garbed in a stylish suit and tie. California seemed to agree with him. He looked, in fact, younger than he had ten years before. "Hey, Hollywood!" I called.

Vester stopped, grinned, then said, "Ah, the good father, you son of a gun!" and we shook hands, hugged, then shook hands again.

"How're my kids doing at Vinnie's?" he asked.

"They're fine as near as I can tell, top students and popular. Your aunts and mother don't trust them," I answered.

"That's a good sign. The kids sure seem great to me. I love to see them and they seem to have a good perspective. You know they've both decided to come out to California to college when they finish Vinnie's?"

"No," I replied. "How's that going over?"

"Like a turd in the punch bowl. But the law's on their side – our side – so they'll eventually join me, thank God."

"Poor Maureen," I said, and he understood.

"I'm sorry about Maureen. She's a fine woman, and now she's caught in everything I had to escape, and one day her own children will escape too." He shook his head. "I don't think she's ever understood how much it hurt when she left me without telling me why, but . . . I wish we could at least be friends."

I said nothing. That was private between them. If he wanted to discuss it, I would, but I wasn't going to push the issue. "It's not always fun being a grown-up," I said.

Driving back toward Uncle Seamus's wake, I told him that old Father Tim, now retired, was gravely ill.

"I'm sorry to hear that," he sighed. "Things change."

"Some things," I said.

"You still go down to the east side on weekends?" he asked innocently, his eyes creasing. "To minister to the whores" – he still pronounced it "hooers" in the old neighborhood fashion – "I mean. Like Pat when he sees a rabbi sneak into a whorehouse and says: 'Would you look at it, then, Mike. He ministers to his flock all week, then frolics with the fancy women.' A minute later they see a priest sneak in the same door and Pat says to Mike, 'Sure there must be sickness in the house.'"

"Oh, yeah," said I with equal innocence, "I spend a good deal of time on the east side. I've got to minister to *your* illegitimate children."

He smiled: "*My* illegitimate children!" Then he launched into another story: "Well, the priest says to the rabbi, 'Tell me, Goldstein, have you ever eaten pork?' Goldstein looks both ways, then nods: 'Yes, once, when I was young,' he says. 'And you, O'Reilly, tell me,' says the rabbi, 'have you ever made love to a woman?' The priest looks both ways, then whispers, 'Yes, once, when I was young.' The rabbi winks at him and says, 'A lot better than pork, isn't it?'"

I chuckled and shook my head, then dropped into the Mick dialect we neighborhood lads had always employed when together: "Arghh, boyo, sure and it's a *praist* yer talkin' to. And it's a mind like a racehorse ya have: It runs best on a dirt track."

"And do ya remember who told me that very tale these fifteen years past, then? A certain feller that's wearin' the collar now," he countered, "and foine broth of a lad wi' the lasses in his day."

"Sure 'tis the divil himself talkin'.'"

"That's what me mither says."

"Your mither," I replied, "says I'm the divil because I don't speak the Latin and I do speak to them *Knee-grows*."

"Are they black Protestants, then?"

"The blackest," I grinned.

"Arghh. At least they ain't orange." We both laughed at that one. He changed the subject: "Is this to be a drinkin' wake, then?"

" 'Tis that, knowin' Seamus Tynne. He'd spin in his grave if forced to depart dry."

"Indaid he would. A foine man. One of the foinest," Ves nodded, and I heard sadness in his voice from years of exile when he had not visited the old man who had been his real father, that man now dead. "I'll have no trouble prayin' for him, will I?" he added. We said no more for a while.

"You going to visit the kids while you're home?"

He nodded. "I'll call tomorrow after the burial. No need alerting the enemy that I'm here."

The rosary was uneventful. As was customary, the body was laid out in an open coffin in the parlor of the deceased's house, which was crowded to bursting with faces black and white. Vester's various womenfolk wouldn't be attending services for the man who had coached their boy to the football scholarship that had "stole him from Holy Mother Church," although Denny McCann, alias "the Flower," who had been trying to keep company with an indifferent Maureen, would likely show up.

Even without the Wicklow women, the soul of Uncle Seamus was given a solid boost toward the heavenly reward we all expected it would receive. After praying the rosary, folks had dutifully filed through the kitchen to collect food and drink. It was a while before the affair thinned, but when it did, I was left with most of the Knights of Columbus – in their formal regalia, complete with brass buttons, plumed hats, and swords – old teammates, plus a few neighborhood layabouts eager for free drink. It seemed a propitious time to begin the toasts, so I ushered most of them into the parlor where Uncle Seamus lay with an angelic look on his tough old mug.

"Boyos," I said, raising a glass of Bushnell's finest, "here's to the coach who made us champions. May his flowers always bloom; may his feet never stink; may his eyes never cross; may he always have drink." Laughter and applause, plus a loud, collective slurp, followed my toast.

Vester was next: "Here's to a lad who was foine wi' the ladies, the Mollies, the Sallies, the Maggies, the Sadies. Here's to a lad wi' a brogue and a wink, who taught us to win and taught us to drink. Here's to a lad who never gave up, I honor him now wi' the tilt o' me cup." More laughter, more applause, and many cups tilted.

By then tongues were loose indeed, and one toast followed another, some smooth, others crude, but all at least mildly funny and all sincere in their appreciation of Uncle Seamus. The several new black members of the Knights seemed to especially enjoy the toasts, and Robert Reed, whose two boys had been coached by Uncle Seamus, offered one of his own: "Here's to a man that had him some soul, who called all the plays and paid all the toll. When he meet his Maker, may his Maker say, come on in and join us, champ, time for to play." I waited until all the oral poets seemed to have exhausted their creativity before making the announcement I'd been saving for just the right moment.

Standing over the coffin, I raised my hands: "Boyos!" I called, "I've something special to tell you." They quieted and gathered around. "It was Uncle Seamus's last request that I present his sword" – I picked up the ceremonial weapon in its sheath from atop the closed half of the casket and held it in both hands – "to the lad he believed was the finest he ever coached." I paused for effect, and names were whispered all around me. Finally, I announced: "Sylvester Duggan!"

Applause and shouts of congratulations mingled with friendly barbs – Billy Dunn: "He couldn't carry my jock!" Sean Daly: "He *needs* a damn sword! Mike Shaw: "That bench warmer?" – as Vester, grinning from ear to ear, but with glistening eyes, accepted the ornate instrument.

Then a boozy growl cut through the others: "He don't deserve it! He's fallen away!" It was Denny McCann, drunk and sounding angry. His presence, save for an occasional noxious aroma that filled the room, had been happily ignored. Now he bulled his way through the crowd, his plumed hat askew, his face like a tight red balloon. He was a big man,

Denny, a big man gone to fat, and he wedged a large space in front of the coffin, across it from Ves and me, then growled, "You're not in the Knights, ya bastard. You're livin' in sin out in that damn California! Look at ya, wearin' them fairy clothes. Gimme that!" He reached across the coffin and tried to grab Seamus's sabre, but I quickly moved in front of him.

"Cool off, Denny," I advised.

"And you, a man of the cloth, defendin' that bastard that's no better'n a Protestant." Denny pushed me aside and drew his sword, it dull as his wits, but a dangerous bludgeon.

"Put that down," warned Vester, shrugging those muscular shoulders. He did not back up.

"I'll settle your hash, ya queer, ya!" cried the Flower, and he waved his weapon while everyone on his side of the coffin scrambled to avoid the wild swings.

"Damn!" I heard Robert Reed grunt when he dodged.

Vester ducked and blocked a blow with his own sheathed weapon and I hit the floor. I heard two more sharp *clanks!* while Denny huffed and swung his blade, then a loud *smack!* followed by a dead *plop!* when the Flower hit the floor across from me, his plumed hat landing three feet away.

I climbed to my feet, and Vester was shaking his head, puffing more from excitement than effort, a look of disgust on that freckled face framed with fading red curls, and I heard Sean Daly from the back of the room whistle between his teeth and call, "Did ya see that left, then? It sure wilted the Flower. Uncle Seamus would've loved it." He was correct, of course, and laughter sprinkled the room, then grew to a roar. "And the good father, scramblin' for his ecclesiastical life!" added Sean. More laughter.

I grinned. "I was just down there givin' the last rites to poor Denny." Another roar. When it subsided, I continued: "Wee Sean, on the other hand, instead of defendin' his fellow Knight, Denny, was on his way to Atlantic City as fast as his size sixes would carry him when the good doctor here applied his anesthesia." More laughter.

"Was the good doctor just drummin' up business, then?" called Billy Dunn, as Vester examined the prostrate Flower.

"He's okay," called the medic. "Just resting."

"And does Dr. Duggan specialize in kayoin' his patients, then?" asked Billy, a copper who's seen a few scraps in his day.

Mike Shaw almost sang an answer: "Oh no! I believe the lad's got another professional interest." Giggles and guffaws from the crowd.

"And what *is* the good doctor's specialty, then?" winked Billy.

"The same thing it always was," wee Sean replied. "He's a lad whose dreams've come true." Another roar.

Standing beside me, Vester smiled and raised his hands over his head like the champ. At the same time he whispered out the corner of his mouth to me, "I *wish*," and his eyes rested momentarily on Uncle Seamus lying placidly amidst the clamor.

MADSTONE

Well, hell, I never believe them vaqueros. I mean they're good workers and all, but *superstitious*. Me, I don't never fall for none of that stuff. Like the night we're workin' on coffee and swappin' stories round the fire back when old Eight Ball Kelley was bear sign artist. Now Eight Ball he's a broke-down cowpoke from East Texas, ghost country, so you know he ain't no great shakes with haints and such. No man on earth can scare him, no critter either, but a haint turns him pale blond. He's plum levelheaded next to them vaqueros, though.

So this night me and Eight Ball and about four vaqueros is all squatted, chawin' tobacco, and damn near havin' to chaw the coffee too, it bein' the bottom of the pot, when these here big white owls kinda fluff over us quiet as beer farts, more like reverse shadows than birds, if you get my meanin'. Just as old Eight Ball is about to finish the story he's been drag-gin' out, I noticed them Mex'cans has quit breathin', then so does Eight

Ball, cause them vaqueros they of a sudden show more eyes than face.

"Los Chisos!" barks Jesse Avilos, then every one of them boys taken off like wolf-spooked jackrabbits.

There we sets, me and Eight Ball. "Mex'cans," he chuckles, then he hauls for his bedroll, so there sets me all alone. Just when I'm fixin' to turn in, here comes Ramon Dominguez, the foreman.

"Where's all the boys?" asks he.

"They got spooked by some birds," says I.

"Birds?" He pours hisself some coffee.

"Yeah," I tells him. "Big white owls they looked like."

He squats there next to the fire for a spell, rollin' that coffee around in his cup, his eyes narrowin', his head tiltin' just a little. "Los Chisos?" he asks me.

"That's what old Jesse said."

He groans, "Madre de Dios." Then off he runs, not even botherin' to eat his coffee first. Well, hell. I turns in. I have to ride drag next day, so to hell with it.

Mornin', old Eight Ball can't raise them four vaqueros nowheres. Pretty soon, up rides Ramon with the night guards. Eight Ball tells him about the missin' men, but Ramon says he already knows. He says they're sick, took with *la luna*.

Eight Ball he's kind of the crew doctor too, so him and me we rides over to the gully where Ramon tells us them vaqueros has hid their bedrolls, and sure enough they're all cooned up with chills and fever. "This don't look like no moon sickness to me," declares Eight Ball. "Naw, looks like grippe. Nothin' I can do. Let 'em rest some. Leave somebody back to watch 'em. They can catch up."

Just when we're fixing to haul, up canters Ramon with this here stray man that's been ridin' the grub line of late. He's a Mex'can too, named Cruz. They dismounts, so old Eight Ball and me we dismounts too. Ramon leads this stray man over to the boys and they talks some, Ramon askin' Cruz if it was too late (Eight Ball he winks at me), and this Cruz answerin' real solemn that no, he figures *maybe* he might pull 'em through. He never says *what* he's pullin' 'em through, but I sees Eight Ball roll his eyes, and I figures maybe we oughta stick around.

Well, hell, while old Ramon tethers their horses, and I sees to ours, this stray man he fishes in the roll he takes off his mount (it, the mount I mean, lookin' more wild than tame, and him, Cruz I mean, lookin' to me like he belongs in a gun outfit). Eight Ball keeps a close eye on that stray man, and he tells me that all this Cruz takes from his roll is a rosary that he kisses and puts around his neck, and a white silk kerchief.

Directly, old Cruz drops to his knees and starts prayin' next to them four sick vaqueros, and fiddlin' with that silk kerchief. I can't rightly savvy him, then I catches on that he's sayin' his prayers backwards. Ramon, by then, is on his knees too. My knees is a little weak because everything of a sudden feels funny, though I figures it's just the sight of two growed men actin' so silly.

Eight Ball catches on to that funny feelin' too, and he jabs me and says, "Looky there." The stray man he's tyin' little knots in his kerchief while he chants them prayers. Every time he finishes one of them knots, Cruz lets out a war whoop that likes to scare water out of me. "That's another'n," Eight Ball he says, and I can tell it's gettin' to him cause his lower lip looks bigger and bigger.

When Cruz finishes the thirteenth knot, he howls even louder, then collapses limp as a old man's pecker. Me and Eight Ball runs to help Ramon tote him, then I notices that more than three of us is workin' on Cruz: It's them four vaqueros, all fit and ready to cut a rusty caper.

Eight Ball he takes off. I mean he's *gone*. I stands there a minute real casual, then tells Ramon I have to get gone too, not that he pays any mind to me, he's too busy slappin' them four boys on the back and proppin' up that stray man. I catches up to Eight Ball about a mile from where we'd been, and that old mossy mare he rides is puffin' to beat hell. "Slow up!" I calls to him, but he keeps his head down and his butt up. "Whoa, dammit!" I hollers, and he finally seems to notice me, then he looks back over his shoulder, his eyes all over his face. Finally, he slows down some. But just some.

. "What the hell's wrong?" I asks him.

"What's wrong?" He looks at me like he figures me for crazy. "Them boys took with grippe, and that witch change 'em, that's what's wrong. I don't study no devil!"

I can't help but laugh. Well, hell, I'd just saw what Eight Ball'd saw, and I admit it's a mite weird, but it's just a damn Mex'can trick and I told him so. Hell, he'd rode with Mex'cans as long as me, but he won't hear nothin' I say. "Them boys have grippe," he keeps repeatin', "and now they cured." I can't reason with him, so I gives up.

Three days later I'm ridin' point through scrubby brush when I hears a big commotion in a thicket up ahead. I rides up to it real quiet, then dismounts and creeps through brush until I sees a prairie wolf kinda staggering against a piñon tree, its head lollin' funny, a greenish-white froth on its mouth. I ain't but ten foot from that wolf, but it never even notices me, it worryin' that tree right smart. It's took with hydrophobia I sees right off, madder'n a gut-shot grizzly. Well, hell, I ain't no great pal to prairie wolves, but I don't like to see no critter suffer like that, so I steps out from the brush and levels my pistol at that poor devil, me fixin' to put him out of his misery.

But my handgun misfires and that wolf he sees me. I cocks my pistol again – the wolf staggerin' in my direction – and my damn gun misfires again. I cocks it once more and it fires this time, killin' the poor critter just after it bites my left leg.

I sets down then, knowin' that goddamned wolf has killed me just when I'm fixin' to help him, knowin' I'm gonna go crazy in a couple weeks and chaw dirt and bite folks then die in the awfulest way, and knowin' there ain't nothin' can be done. I looks at that bite on my leg and at that wolf's carcass and at my damned handgun that's let me down. Well, hell, I figures, might as well make it clean. I puts the muzzle against my head and squeezes the trigger. The sonofabitch misfires.

I puts it against my head once more, then bang! I'm on my butt. Miguel Ybañez, that's been ridin' swing behind me, has kicked the pistol out of my hand and caught my head too. "¿Qué pasó?" he asks. I nods at that wolf, then points at my leg. "Aye, Madre!" he says. Then we hauls toward Ramon and Eight Ball and the chuck wagon.

It's funny, really, that even when you know good and well that somethin' won't kill you for a spell, you still get all faintified. By the time we gets back to camp, I can't even stand up. I just slumps against one of the chuck wagon's wheels. Eight Ball makes a poultice as quick as he can, but he never looks too happy. Ramon takes off in a hurry.

I'm still there propped against that wheel with Eight Ball's poultice on the wound, him trying to get me to drink some coffee, when up rides

Ramon with Cruz, that he's hired on by then. They come right over to where I'm sprawled and that stray man takes the poultice off my leg. (Eight Ball disappears when he sees Cruz.) Well, hell, that stray man he looks into my eyes, then back at that bite, then jumps up and trots to his saddle roll.

He comes back with a funny lookin' rock or some such. Ramon says it's a madstone, took from the belly of a deer and that it can suck the poison out of a wound. What the hell do I have to lose? Cruz kneels next to me and commences jabberin' some kind of prayer, swirlin' that madstone round and round his head with both hands while he carries on, then he puts it right smack where that wolf bit me.

The stone sticks like a leech, hanging there by itself, and I feels this powerful pull. I kinda jumps, but that stray man tells me to set. All the time that stone is suckin' and pullin', I can feel it. It even looks a little like it's gettin' bigger, like dry bread soppin' in soup. But I never says nothin' cause I'm flat scared by then.

I don't know how long that stone is on my leg, but directly it falls off onto the white silk kerchief that Cruz has put under it. "Leche!" He hollers, and here comes Miguel Ybañez with a pail of hot milk he's just took from the fire. The stray man drops his madstone into the pail, careful not to touch it, and the milk directly turns green. "Veneño," says the stray man, grinnin' for the first time. Ramon and Miguel they both laugh.

"You feel better?" asks Ramon and, you know, I do. "Finish your coffee, wrap that wound up, and get back to work," he orders. "We got cattle to drive to Bakersfield." Then them three Mex'cans rides off, the pail of green milk going with 'em.

Soon as they're gone, here comes ol' Eight Ball. "Now what you think?" he asks.

Well, hell, I know he's fixin' to give me a bad time, so I just shrugs and says real casual, "You know how them Mex'cans is."

He pours me a fresh cup of coffee, lookin' at me all the time. "I knows how *you* is," he grunts. Then he fills his own cup, shakes his head, and says, "Loco."

RETURN, PRODIGAL

They'd all but given up on him, the critics had I mean; they'd written him off. After all, when a potentially outstanding artist is roasted by reviewers, then takes a job at a hick college, well you naturally figure he's thrown in the towel.

But Gio Leoni was no ordinary artist. Those of us who knew him weren't surprised when his name appeared in the *Times* a couple of years after he'd quit San Francisco. It was a small story written by Ron Kinney, the art editor, saying that Gio claimed to have developed a new genre, something he called "holoform." Kinney referred to Gio as an "erstwhile boy wonder who claims to have developed an ultimate form of organic art." The story featured a small photo of Gio wearing a cowboy hat.

The new art form would be first presented at a show here in the city, at Beddecker's, the very gallery where Gio's last exhibit had been held, the one so badly slammed by Ron Kinney and company.

Well, great, I figured. Anything that brings Gio back to town is okay with me. You've got to understand that Gio and I became close friends as undergrads at State College. Both of us had been married – both since divorced – and both took advantage of the GI Bill. We swilled gallons of wine together, and wenched together, and solved the world's problems several times over. And we've picked one another's livers more than once too. We had one running argument that lasted about three years. He could never understand how I survived a chemistry major. "Too stifling," he'd say. "It would kill my creativity."

"Oh, balls!" I would delicately answer. "What you need is some scientific discipline to free your cluttered mind."

"Free!" he'd shout. "Free! You don't know the meaning of the word!" And then we'd be into it till the wine ran out or dawn forced us to call it a draw.

I remember one evening when I argued for science as a creative endeavor, telling Gio that Art (with a capital A) had vitiated due to its own incest. Did he ever blow up over that. "Artist die for art," he shouted. "Art lovers die for it. But people only die *because* of science, not for it." That got to me, so we again debated all night, but the point is we never really got angry.

Another thing we disagreed on was his second show. He had received favorable reviews with his first set of displayed paintings, but scheduling his next showing so soon after the first, and at a big gallery like Beddecker's – well, I sensed disaster. And I was right. Gio was experimenting with a fly-sprayer for all his paintings at that time, spreading an incredibly fine filigree of feeling on massive canvases. The trouble was that critics seemed unable to see merit in anything but little, gutsy pseudo–Van Goghs and something they called "organic art," what the hell ever that was. Gio's work was doomed, but he said no, they'll recognize originality when they see it.

Well, the critics didn't recognize any originality in Gio's second showing – they characterized his work as "contrived and weak" – so he and I had to go into hock to pay his outstanding debts and let him get away for a while. He took an artist-in-residence position at Desert State College over near Bishop and, save for an occasional note, disappeared. One letter, I remember, tersely stated: "I'm into something good now, an original synthesis," but he never explained the synthesis and I knew better than to push him.

Came the *Times* article, though, and I knew I'd see him soon – probably a phone call in the middle of the night would rouse me and I'd hear his Groucho Marx voice: "Hello, you fat kike," he'd say with great reverence. "If you can stop playing with yourself long enough, come get me. I'm at the airport." I would reply with an accurate description of his mother's vocation (and avocation) and would then drive out to South City and pick him up. We'd probably be debating before my car had traveled a block.

· Sure enough, one night just as I crawled in bed to enjoy an Agatha Christie, the phone rang. "Hello, you Zionist bastard," Groucho's voice said. I cut him short: "You have the wrong number," I replied in a thick pasta accent, "this is the Italian-American Civil Rights League. Who you want us to kill?" Gio broke up. "Aw," he chanted, "your momma's a tool grinder. I'm at the airport. Come get me." I fetched him home.

Gio was pooped, but we stayed up and drank rot-gut wine and talked. I finally found out what his latest creation was and, I have to tell you, I was astounded. He claimed he got the idea from me, with a little help from Bernard Berensen's writings and Kenneth Clark's. He said that the last two had shown him that new insights in one art form are quickly adapted to other forms. "You know," he said, "you develop something like baroque or rococo in one genre, and pretty soon you've got correlates popping up all over, right?" I nodded. "Well, you add a little McLuhan to the other two, and your own brilliant insights, of course" – I blushed appropriately – "and it just seemed to me that the world was waiting for someone to put it all together at once.

"Well, we've got the technology now to do just that, so I have. Remember all that crap you used to throw my way about the creative potential of the sciences. Okay, I've taken you up." He suddenly metamorphosed into Bela Lugosi: "Meester RRRenfield, I haf created a moonstair," he leered, rubbing his green hands all the while. Then he flew into the kitchen and poured himself another glass of Red Mountain blood. "How the hell can bats drink wine hanging upside down?" he asked.

"They have hollow legs," I responded with scientific gravity.

"Oh," he said, climbing down from my chandelier.

I kept pushing Gio to tell me more about this thing he called "holo-form." He said it would replace Lydia Pinkhams in the hearts of the people. "It's better than hash, grass, and lucky number score cards," he claimed, rolling Jerry Colonna eyes.

"I believe, Great Mufti," I salaamed, "but what the hell *is* it?"

Finally he said that he had created a total artistic experience. "Holo-form is a piece of living sculpture. I mean you can see it and touch it, right? But you can enter it too. And once you get inside," W. C. Fields said, "you will experience thrills and delights, de-lights." He placed his top hat on the end of his cane and staggered through the room juggling two small boys and a dog. "And as for you, my little Jewish poltroon," he said, "I hope a sexually crazed Arab voodoo queen sticks pins in the crotch of your likeness." W.C. teetered into the kitchen, goosing himself with the doorknob, then returned holding a full glass. "Ahhh," said he, "spiritus fermenti."

"But what the hell's inside?" I asked.

"Nuns!" Gio answered surreptitiously. "Wildly passionate nuns driven into a sensual frenzy by a nude photo of the Marquis de Sade!" He sobbed, his face in his hands. "Oh, my secret is out. Pray, kind sir, I was not always as you see me now." He wiped his hands on a cat.

"Peter Sellers," I said.

"You saw that one too. Good. One of the all-time greats. Well, anyway, about holoform, you get caressed by warm, slick membranes when you're inside." Within, he told me, holoform was precisely the temperature the computer at his college had advised. Moreover, a gentle electronic music played just what the computer ordered. And there was more: The dark-ness within holoform was livened by a light diffuser prepared by a physics prof at Desert State that shattered and blended colors. And a couple of organic chemists at the school had developed a pleasant musk aroma that was, as Groucho put it, "verrry stimulating" (he raised and lowered his eyebrows several times). "To women, it smells like primed man; to men, it smells like primed woman."

His last revelation was that a mild hallucinogen was sprayed into the air within holoform. "But cool it," he requested, "it's slightly illegal." In fact, before the night was over, he made me promise not to tell anyone anything about holoform. Both Peter Lorre and Sydney Greenstreet aided him in convincing me I'd best not squeal.

While he brought several of his other things – some conventional sculpture and chronology of his paintings – along to help fill the gallery, there was no question that holoform was the whole show. I asked him if he wasn't counting too much on one piece, and for a moment he flared at me: "Haven't you understood anything I've been telling you? There has never been anything like this. *Never.*" He quickly cooled off and said no, he'd thought about it a long while before making a public announcement, but it was also a question of time, for he knew of several other artists working on similar projects and he keenly understood the value of being first.

Gio spent most of the next couple of days at Beddecker's preparing holoform and the other pieces for the show. Evenings we partied with old pals, including some women I'd somehow foolishly forgotten. Every morning, my mouth tasting as though a marmot drive had passed through it during the night, I'd creak out of bed and find Gio brewing coffee with chocolate in it. He showed no signs of wear. "Work! Work!" he'd say, stalking the kitchen, raising his eyebrows and puffing an imaginary cigar.

On the evening before the show was to open to the general public, there was the usual reception for the select few, mainly critics, plus a sprinkling of fellow artists and, of course, a gang of edible models. Liquor flowed freely, and funny little cigarettes were puffed openly, while the crowd milled around the massive holoform, which stood draped in the middle of Beddecker's main gallery room. You could tell everyone wanted to get started, but Gio guarded his creation like a new father. About the time various critics began glancing at their watches, Herman Beddecker and Gio called everyone to the sculpture and without fanfare, Gio pulled the cord and holoform was exposed.

Wow! The entire audience gasped. It was an earth brown monolith, shaped with the muscular smoothness of an animal form, yet unlike any animal I'd ever seen. I found myself immediately attracted to it. I was standing right next to the holoform and to me it seemed to be pulsing, so lifelike was its exterior, and I thought I heard a vague purring sound, probably feedback from the microphone Gio had used in assembling everyone.

"Well," announced Gio in his usual off-the-wall manner, "let's allow the gentlemen of the press to explore the de-lights within holoform first. Mr. Kinney?"

Dapper Ron Kinney separated his plump form from a tall black girl and, with bemused grin, gave us a thumbs-up and slipped into holoform's glistening crease; I caught a flash of pink as he entered; the purring and pulsing increased slightly. Gio let Kinney have holoform to himself for several minutes, then let other critics enter. I could see Gio's satisfaction as the gentlemen of the press disappeared.

"Give them time to really dig," Gio ordered. "The rest of you can join them in a few minutes. More drinks?" So we all drank until Gio finally gave us the go sign.

I entered first, sliding tentatively into the dark crease, blinded until my whole being suddenly lifted: tingling, tasting, smelling, existing pleasure. Soft, warm sides pressed gently on me as an odor awakened my body. Passionate breath engulfed me; my being orgasmed.

Outside again, I needed a nap. Everyone glowed. "That thing's gotta be illegal," whispered a blonde model I'd been trying to score with all evening. "It's too *good*." And I knew what *good* meant. Did I ever.

One artist friend of Gio's and mine kind of leaned on me and said, "My God, he's actually done it. It *is* a total experience. It's like your first hit of smack, only better. A total experience. A new space. I can't get over it." In fact, everyone who was willing, or able, to talk praised Gio and his holoform. Herman Beddecker looked like one big grinning dollar sign. What a night for Gio! What a comeback!

When we finally returned home, Gio and I enjoyed a nightcap – morning-cap, really – and gabbed for a few more minutes. We rehashed the whole show, step by step, word for word. "You really showed those smug bastards," I told him. "You made them back off."

"One of 'em, anyway," he answered.

"One! All of them. Every damned one! Man oh man, were their mouths open," I told him. "What ever happened to Ron Kinney? Did he rush out to retract a postdated review? He's famous for writing reviews before he even attends shows, you know."

"I know. But that dude has filed his last public crucifixion." Gio looked drunkenly conspiratorial. "Arrrrrgh," breathed Long John Silver, "can ye keep a secret?"

"What do you mean? Do you think you can get his job?"

"Arrrrrgh, who needs his job? I've got the lubber a'ready. Er at least me holoform has. Arrrrrgh."

"Got him?"

"It ate him."

"Ate him?" He was putting me on, per usual.

"Aye, boots, buckles, and all. Arrrrrgh. The boots be tastin' better than his wormy carcass did."

He sounded too serious beneath Long John's speech, and I felt a bubble of doubt growing in my throat. "What do you really mean, ate him?"

Gio poured himself another stiff brandy. "Man," he said, "you are one dense dude. Ate him. Devoured him. Gobbled him all gone. Dig?" He shook his head at my imperception.

"But . . ."

"Look," he said with painful patience, "holoform is alive. How else do you think it can do all those things at once? The critics wanted organic art, didn't they? Well now they've got it. Let's see what the sons of bitches do with it."

I could see he was serious. "What the hell are you saying? You mean you killed Kinney?"

"I didn't lay a glove on him."

"But you say he's dead."

"Maaan," answered Step'nfetchit, "he ain' jus' daid, he *et!*"

"Then how did the rest of us get out?"

He poured more brandy. "You really don't know much about nature for a guy with a Ph.D. It's like a big snake, it only eats about once a week, usually a dog I get at the pound. Old chubby Kinney will last two weeks, I bet." He chuckled. "It's no sweat. I just let it get good and hungry and I can feed it anything I want."

I stood and stalked the room, growing more aghast as the impact of what he revealed struck me. I turned to face him several times but could say nothing. "The police are sure to find out," I finally sputtered.

"Why?"

"Why? Because they'll find the remains, that's why."

Again he laughed at me. "There aren't any," he said, "at least not any that the police will recognize; just a fine gray powder that looks like ashes."

I stood again and walked to the window, then returned to my chair. "But you can't just let it devour critics. It . . . well . . . it just isn't *right*."

Gio looked at me rather sadly, shaking his head a bit, then he finished his brandy and stood. "Why not?" he finally said. "Critics have been devouring artists since day one."

THE LAST ROUNDUP

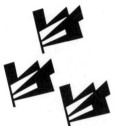

"Come on, all you cowboys and cowgirls," urged that announcer's voice from the radio, "join us at the Last Roundup Saloon in Modesto for the wet T-shirt contest next Saturday night. You cowgirls can win a hundred dollars cash if the judges select you, and all entries will receive free Last Roundup T-shirts."

Some real fast country music without no sangin' come on, then that announcer's voice it talked again: "Don't forget, the wet T-shirt contest at the Last Roundup Saloon in Modesto next Saturday, cowboys and cowgirls, with live music for your dancing pleasure."

"That there's where I wanta go," I said to Uncle Fud Murray that was sippin' coffee at the counter. He's a ol' fart, Uncle Fud, a ex–ranch hand with nothin' to do in Oakdale but drink coffee at the Big Or'nge where I work and bullshit. Usual, he tells some purty good stories too, but sometimes he acts downright devilish.

"You ain't no cowboy, Delbert," he snorted, "and Judas Priest you don't look worth a shit in no T-shirt anyways." Before I could answer him back, ol' Fud went and switched to what he'd been a-talkin' about: "Yessir, just like I's sayin', it's kids nowadays look too damn much alike. A bunch of damn Barbie dolls. Hell, whenever I's a boy back in Bowlegs, folks had character. Like my Aunt Mabel Proudy that had a goiter on her neck the size of a mushmelon. Wadn't nobody else in Bowlegs like her. Anybody seen that goiter, even if they never met 'er before, they knowed it was Aunt Mabel.

"And Dad Murphy that had buck teeth he could play a pianer with, and him a pinhead to boot, but that never slowed the ol' boy down. Run him a good feed bidnis and had fourteen younguns. Went around in the tiniest Stetson you ever seen, like a doll's."

"I look a hell of a lot better'n you do in a T-shirt," I finally got a chance to say. I wasn't lettin' any Fud Murray get the better of me. "Besides, that man he was talkin' about gals in wet T-shirts."

"Ya don't say?" Fud grinned, winkin' at Jake Garcia, this cattle rancher that was settin' next to 'im, and I think he was a-kiddin' me. Just when I's fixin' to answer him real snappy, he started again.

"There was Mutt Powers that had a face like a Mexican Hairless and could yodel better'n any white man in Oklahoma, and Wilma Watson with a harelip that could dance real good, and Tody Parker that had pockmarks on his face so it looked like somebody'd shotgunned him. He owned about half the county. Them folks looked like folks, not plastic dolls." He paused and slurped some coffee and nodded at Jake like he just proved somethin' real important.

"Nowadays," Fud went on, "all these damn kids got braces and that plastic surgery stuff and all. Judas Priest, it seems like there's a doctor behind ever' bush, and the kids they come out lookin' like Dee-troit cars, all the damn same, a-thankin' they're purty, but how can they be purty if they're all the damn same is what I wanta know?"

"That man said they got a band and all them cowboys and cowgirls are a-gonna be there," I said.

Uncle Fud grinned again at Jake.

"Besides," I added, "they even got a mechanical bull at the Last Roundup."

"Bet them cows truly 'preciate that," Fud said real smart-alecky. "Is it like one of them vibrators or what?"

"Huh?" I said. Jake was laughin'.

"Besides," added Uncle Fud, "there's a whiteface bull down the road worth ten thousand dollars. Out to stud."

"That's where I'm a-goin', anyways," I told him, not givin' in.

"Out to stud?"

"Huh?" I said.

Jake was laughin' louder: "Hah! He-he-he!"

"Yessir, out to stud, this boy, and hung like a boar mouse," added Uncle Fud.

"I never said that!" I snapped quick as I could.

"Hah!" Jake busted out even louder. "He-he-he!"

Uncle Fud wouldn't let go, talkin' faster 'n faster. "Gonna service all them little heifers at the wet T-shirt contest."

"I never even said that!"

"Hah! He-he-he!"

"Gonna make that mechanical bull look like a hobby horse!"

"Hah! He-he-he!"

"I never said that!" It's hard keepin' up with him oncet he gets goin'. Just when I's about to sock Fud, in walked that family, and him and Jake clammed right up, but they kept lookin' at me through their eyebrows and I seen their eyes a-laughin'.

Anyways, a man and a woman – they both ordered big or'nges – plus two little knob-knockered girls and even littler boy that looked like he set fire to haystacks for fun – them three had Cokes – set in a booth by the front door. Bigger'n hell, them kids had more chrome in their mouths than a Cadillac does on its grill, and you shoulda seen the I-told-you-so look ol' Fud give me.

By the time them folks left, I wasn't so sore at Uncle Fud no more, and him and Jake was carryin' on about them kids and their braces. "Like a bunch a damn robots," Fud concluded, "all of 'em look exactly alike."

For a minute or two nobody said nothin', me happy for the silence, then Jake said, "Wet T-shirt contest, huh? I've never seen one a those." He sounded interested.

"They got a live band and ever'thang," I added.

"Didn't thank they'd have a dead one, did ya?" Fud asked.

"Huh?"

"Ladies in wet T-shirts, eh?" Jake kinda sighed, tappin' his cup for a refill. While I scrambled over to the pot, then filled his cup, he kept talkin' real quiet: "Wet T-shirts. Uh-huh. Well, boys, let's go take a look at those women in wet T-shirts. Uncle Fud, can your old heart take it?"

"You bet!"

"How 'bout you, Delbert?" he asked me.

"You mean it, Jake? You really gonna take us to the Last Roundup clean over at Modesto?"

"Yeah, I am. I'll have my stock moved by then. Why not?"

"Oh, boy!" I felt about like sangin'. "Boy, oh boy!" I really wanted to see one a them real cowboy places and this was my chance.

I never thought Saturday'd ever come. That ol' week it just dragged and dragged, with me ever bit as excited as the time I went to Disneyland. After work I'd go to my trailer and try on that dandy straw hat with big feathers in front that I'd bought last winter in Fresno. I'd look in the mirror and see that I looked just like the guys in the movie had, like one a them guys that drives a four-wheel-drive pickup, the kind that sets so high off the ground you need a stepladder to climb into it, the kind with white writin' on the tars and all. I'm a-gonna get me one a them someday, too.

Anyways, come the big night – it still light, of course, 'cause it was summer – up drove Jake from his ranch in his pickup, in two-wheel drive with mud and cowshit on the tars, and so low I could step right into the cab. Well, he'd probably have to park down the road from the Last Roundup, so none a them cowboys or cowgirls would see what we was drivin'.

Soon as I popped into the cab, I noticed what Jake was wearin': a suit and tie topped by a green baseball cap with "Skoal" wrote on the front of it. Oh, hell. "Jake," I told him, "you gotta go home and change clothes. You gotta dress like a cowboy to go to the Last Roundup."

"I got my good boots on, Delbert," he answered, sounding a tad pissed. "Besides, if I turn this truck around, it ain't goin' nowhere but home."

I felt about like spittin'. "Couldn't you at least go home and get your hat?"

"I ain't got but two hats. My good one's out being blocked and my work one looks like, well, a work one. I'm driving to Modesto. You can stay or go. Make up your mind."

Hell, he was ruinin' ever'thang. Here we was going to a high-class cowboy and cowgirl joint, and he was dressed like a damn clodhopper. Just when I's about to really tell him off, Jake said, "Where in God's name did you get that war bonnet, anyway?"

That done it. "I . . . I . . ." I couldn't thank a nothin' to say right then, so I made my mind up to travel with him, but not to talk. I'd show Jake Garcia, by God. "This here's a real cowboy hat," I finally told him. Then I give him the silent treatment.

It never lasted too long, though, because that damn ol' Fud came out from his trailer dressed more like a rodeo clown than a cowboy. He had on these baggy slacks, a white Western shirt with red and green cactuses on it that musta been all the rage back about 1940 whenever ol' Gene Artury wore the same thang, yellow shoes like nobody else ever wore, and one a them Smokey-the-Bear hats rangers wear, the kind with dents on the side. "He ain't goin!" I told Jake, and I meant it too.

"Hell, he's all dressed up," Jake answered, never crackin' a smile.

Fud swang into the cab, smelling like a barbershop. "All right, boys," he announced, "let's have at them wet T-shirts."

"You ain't going!" I told him plain and simple.

"Somebody ain't going if you don't shut your face," Jake growled at me. "I'm getting tired of your bellyaching."

"What's a matter with Delbert?" Fud asked, grinnin'.

Well, I wasn't settin' with them two at no Last Roundup. I just made my mind up I'd travel with 'em, but that was all. I was through with 'em. Then I noticed ol' Fud eye'n my clothes real close. "Judas Priest!" he spouted. "Where'd you rustle that getup, Delbert?"

My getup! I's fixin' to tell him off. Before I could, though, he got that motor mouth of his to workin'.

"Hell's bells, you're just a-provin' what I said the other day about young folks all lookin' alike cause if they cain't change their faces, then they try to dress alike: flashy pearl-button shirt, big ol' belt buckle, hat that dips down in front and back and – boy howdy! – how many chickens had to die so's you could wear them feathers? You look like you's stamped outta the same machine as all them citified peckerheads.

"Why, ol' Tody Parker that owned half a Bowlegs, he's a real cowboy from the git go, and he wore a derby hat from England. Nobody else had one. Whenever they seen a derby hat around Bowlegs, wadn't but one guy they knew could be a-wearin' it: Tody Parker."

Even Jake got into it, adding: "Look at ol' Fud's hat. I'll bet you don't see another one like it in Modesto."

I's just fixin' to say somethin' real clever to shut 'em up when Jake he changed the subject and commenced talkin' about how he's gonna buy a Brangus bull to toughen his herd and that led Fud back to Bowlegs and a guy that used a Brahma to service his whitefaces and stuff like that. I let 'em go on, but I never forgot. I's fixin' to tell 'em off but I's afraid I'd lose my ride. They was damn lucky, I'll tell you that much.

The band it was real loud in the Last Roundup, and the joint was real crowded, and I was right about how cowboys dressed, by God, I seen that directly. Jake he fetched us three beers from the bar and found us a table next to the dance floor. He's a big ol' boy, Jake, neck like a bullfrog and arms bigger'n most guys' legs, so he's good to follow in a crowd. To my surprise, nobody give him and Fud the horse laugh for bein' dressed so funny, at least not that I noticed anyways, and one little ol' cowgirl winked at Fud and said sweet as can be, "Love your hat. It's outrageous." She never said nothin' about my sombrero.

We set there for a while, music loud enough to knock the fillin's outta your teeth boomin' from these great big speakers on the sides of the band-stands. All the musicians was hippies with long hair and beards. But cowboy hippies, by God, with feathers on their hats and ever'thang. Jake he tore off pieces of a napkin and stuffed 'em in his ears. "Where the hell's the women?" he asked me. "I don't see anything but a bunch of pencil-necks in cowboy costumes."

For a fact there wasn't a lot a cowgirls showin', and the few I did see had droves of cowboys around 'em, but at least they knew how to dress, not like some folks I could mention.

We's on our second beers whenever they started that mechanical bull-ridin' contest, and had just ordered our thirds whenever the damned thang went and broke down, spittin' sparks and smokin' so bad this one cowboy got his butt burned, fancy chaps or not. Fud went crazy, cacklin' like a damn hen. "Ya reckon it's got the bloat?" he asked Jake, who laughed too. "It sure blowed a parful fart!" said Fud. Then he turned to me: "Where's all them gals at, Delbert?"

"They're a-comin'," I snapped, but to tell the truth I's a little worried myself. Thangs they wasn't exactly like I'd thought they'd be and I's afraid of the raggin' them two would give me whenever we got back home.

Just then the announcer, this fat guy in a sequined suit, he called for the wet T-shirt contestants to report to the bandstand, and everbody give a big war whoop. I could tell it's mainly what they'd been a-waitin' on. Like a mir'cle, a line of gals appeared up there, signed on, and he give each one a T-shirt, then they disappeared into the john to change while the band commenced playin' softer than before and even Jake took out his earplugs. Meanwhile that announcer he said funny thangs like "These ladies wanta get something off their chests" and "Hope you boys don't miss any points of interest," real clever stuff like that. I's laughin' to beat hell whenever the gals come out from the can in their T-shirts, but Fud looked half-solemn and Jake just looked.

The announcer and a helper had spread big ol' mats on the dance floor and they had these pitchers a water on a foldin' table they'd set up. "All got the same T-shirts on," said Fud, soundin' kinda breathless, "just like I said, all trying to look alike," but it never sounded like he meant it, his eyes massagin' them gals.

The man commenced pourin' water over the front of the first little ol' gal, a real cute redhead, and her cupcakes they stood straight out under that clingin' shirt. I heard Uncle Fud gasp, "Judas Priest!" whenever she danced a few steps to the music.

The next cowgirl's bigger'n the first, with black hair and real crisp eyes like flint. Once they got her good and damp, her cantaloupes just glistenin', she danced a bit and I heard ol' Fud gasp, "Jud-das Priest!" Jake hissed, "Now that's my kinda woman," his own eyes locked on her.

Number three was another blackheaded gal, the kind with banana boobs that pointed left and right once her shirt was wet, and bounced in opposite directions whenever she danced. I liked to slipped off the table where I'd climbed to see better, and ol' Fud did fall, moanin' "Juuu-das Priest" just before he landed with a thud! It never killed him though, and he bounced back onto that table like a tennis ball. He sure as hell wasn't fixin' to miss nothin'.

The only blonde in the contest was number four, and her little lemons pointed damn near straight up at the ceilin' fan when her shirt was wet. Once she was dancin', them little boogers jumped like ground squirrels in a bag, and old Fud timbered again, calling "Juuu-dass Priest!" as he fell.

That's when this cowboy standin' next to me, he turned and growled, "Get that old fart outta here before somebody kicks his ass."

Jake, who'd been too busy devourin' them gals with his eyes to pay much mind to Fud, heard that guy, and said, "What?"

"You heard what I said, man, get the old fart outta here right now or I will." That young buck he had a lotta beer talkin' for him. "He's buggin' the hell outta me!"

Well, Jake's blood was already warmed a bit anyways, so he just looked that cowboy in the eye and said, "Mind your own business." From the way he said it I knew he wasn't gonna say no more, so I slipped off my good cowboy hat and surveyed the crowd: Young buck had four pardners all ballin' their fists, all of 'em beered up and brave.

Directly there was only three total because Jake he blasted young buck to the floor so quick I never seen the punch, then he put a choke hold on another'n and crumpled him too. Two others they jumped on his back, and I peeled one off with my beer bottle, and damned if ol' Uncle Fud didn't kick the other'n in the nuts and fold him up. There wasn't but one left and when he seen Jake comin' for him he took off like a spooked quail right through the wet T-shirt contest, knockin' the announcer and his helper ass over teakettle in the process.

Even the bouncer, whenever he come for us, he give Jake a wide berth. "Sorry, boys," he said, a real big guy that looked like a horse trailer, "house rules. All fightin' and fighters outside."

"You kickin' out those punks that started it?" Jake demanded.

"They're gone," answered horse trailer.

"Then we'll just join 'em in the parking lot."

Horse trailer nodded. "Good. We don't want any trouble with you boys."

Before I realized what happened, we's out in the parkin' lot, but them other guys was nowheres to be seen, though two of them big four-wheel-drive pickups with fog lights on top and chrome exhausts they roared out just as we hit the pavement. "I reckon them tough cowboys swallowed the olive," Uncle Fud observed.

"Let's go back inside and see who wins the wet tit . . . I mean T-shirt . . . contest," I suggested.

"They won't be letting us back in there tonight, Delbert," Jake told me. "We're kicked out."

"Kicked out! I left my hat in there."

"Judas Priest," spit Fud, "just when it's a-gettin' good."

We climbed into the cab of Jake's pickup, me feelin' so bad about my lost hat I couldn't even talk. Finally, I asked, "Are you sure they won't let me go back in for my hat?"

Fud shook his head. "Not after the way you operated on that one feller's carbunkle. Sweet as a surgeon and with a beer bottle too."

"That great big bouncer'd put a dent in your head if he saw you," added Jake. "You're better off with a head than a hat, feathers or not. Besides, they'll probably save it and we can pick it up next week."

"Next week?" I asked.

"Next week!" gasped Fud.

"Hell, yeah," Jake chuckled. "I wouldn't want to miss out on all those cowboys and cowgirls. Speaking of that, Fud, I've got one question for you."

"What's that?"

"Do you still think all young folks look alike?"

Fud broke out laughin'. "Judas Priest, I's talkin' 'bout faces, not knockers. I bet if there's a way to put braces on 'em they'd do 'er, but for now there's still somethin' to be said for the way they are. There's still a little variety left, by damn."

"Yeah," I stuck in real quick.

"You got me there, Delbert," he admitted. "You sure as hell got me there," pattin' me on the back.

I felt better all the way home.

STOLEN GLANCES

"Hey, you!" He heard the voice and turned. Across the street he saw the blue blur of a man, who began striding toward him, so he stopped and lowered his plastic bag of aluminum cans to the sidewalk and waited, his eyes lowered.

"Let's see your ID," the policeman demanded.

Up close, Winfield could see well enough to tell this man was young, despite his rough voice. "I got this," he said, and he handed the policeman his discharge paper.

"*You*, a veteran," sniffed the cop, his tone saying it all. Then he handed the frayed paper back. "Where're you livin' at?"

"I'm on the road right now," said Winfield.

"You got a job?"

"I collect these cans."

"Yeah, and steal anything that ain't nailed down. You just keep movin' on, buster, if you don't want hard time. We don't tolerate vagrants around here."

"Yessir." This kid was young enough to be his son. He surely hadn't even been born when Winfield was dodging bullets across France and Germany.

"Now move it."

"Yessir." He hefted the plastic sack and shuffled toward the bridge under which he'd stashed his pack and bedroll, mumbling to himself: "Before you was even born. . . . You need to treat me like a man, not a damn bum," he demanded, one arm flailing, his voice rising as he continued walking. All around him, colored blurs moved to sound, but he concentrated only on each step. His belly boiled, though, for he resented the implication that because he was on the street he was automatically a thief. If he was, he wouldn't be scrounging for these damned aluminum cans. He was a working man out of work.

"Buster!" he spat. "I'm not no buster. I got a name."

What really burned him was the kernel of truth in what that cop had said: he had, just lately, twice stolen pairs of glasses, so guilt compounded his outrage. He knew a real thief wouldn't feel guilt, but that was no solace. "Damn son of a bitch!" he heard, then realized it was his own voice. He was shouting as he walked, and other pedestrians were swerving far around him. Well, to hell with 'em. "Christ on a crutch!" What did they know, anyways?

He wasn't any damn thief, but his eyes were going and he had to see. He had first realized something was wrong when, watching television at the farm near Red Bluff where he'd picked two summers before, the screen had never seemed to be properly focused. At a flophouse in San Francisco he'd had a fistfight with a wino who insisted the TV was okay. After that, when all the other stiffs had agreed with the wino, he realized something wasn't right with his eyes.

Only when everything lost focus did he lift that first pair of glasses from the assistant preacher at the Fresno Rescue Mission. They'd made things look different, longer mostly, and they'd swerved his brain like cheap wine. He returned to the softened edges and blended colors that had gradually become his world, though he kept those glasses just in case.

He stole a second set from a flophouse manager near the railroad yard in Dunsmuir. He liked them better because they flattened and curved what he saw like a funhouse mirror. He often wore them when he walked through city crowds, laughing at the bulging clowns all around him.

Glancing up before crossing the main street, he noted patches of color, thousands of patches, seeming to glow in the afternoon sun. For a moment he smiled. Then one suddenly flashed green and he crossed the street, looking at his own shoes – he could still see them, even the laces – and he pulled at his beard. "He he he!" he chuckled as other walkers delicately skirted him.

Under the bridge, he fumbled a can of chili from his pack and opened it with his pocketknife. Then he carefully scooped the cold beans into his mouth with the blade – they would be his only meal that day and he didn't want to drop even one. From the shade in which he sat, he could see an orange tone settle over the late-afternoon landscape on both sides of him. He liked it, a cantaloupe color that livened the gentle tans and browns of the vacant lots, the vague outlines of buildings beyond. Even in the bridge's shade, the growing glow warmed him.

How many bridges? How many years? There had been jobs after the war, some good ones, but always someone seemed to invent a machine to do what he did, and Winfield had to move to something else, to start again, until one summer he'd found himself, a veteran of W. W. II, picking grapes next to guys who couldn't even speak English. And he had been married for a while, until the day his stepdaughter'd told her mother and him about her dream, and Winfield had reflexively interrupted the girl: "I never touched her!" They both – the daughter, the mother – had gazed at him with surprise, then sorrow, knowing immediately that he had. He'd departed that night and never seen either again. Departed for bridges. Departed for years.

"Son of a bitch!" he shouted. "Bastard!" and his voice echoed from the bridge's cement piers across the lapping water. Then he noted what could have been a large shadow slinking across the far lot toward this very bridge. It was the movement that first alerted Winfield. He could not clearly discern a shape, but the way the thing was approaching – like a damn coyote – warned him. Keeping his eyes on the approaching dark form, he placed his knife on the earth next to him, bolted the rest of his chili, running one finger carefully around the inside of the can, then licking it so that no morsel would be lost. All the while he followed the prowling motion, the blemish moving over the golden lot, until it paused in the sunlight just outside the bridge's shadow and assumed the large, loose figure of a man.

Entering the shade, the coyote was again difficult to see, although he was close enough for his breath to burst white-port sweet on Winfield. "Hey, brother," the bearded and bespectacled face called, and the older man felt the coyote's eyes scanning him, searching his kit. "What you got in that plastic bag, brother?"

"Just got me some cans," Winfield grunted.

"Hey, brother, you're gonna share 'em, aren't ya?" The false friendliness of the coyote's voice hung more ominously than a threat. He was big and assured, this coyote, and Winfield felt peril as tangible as the heavy odor of the man's body, but he also felt something else, and he welcomed it: a scavenger's scorn for carrion.

Winfield had not survived on the streets for all these years without learning how to deal with danger, so he immediately rattled the bag of cans with his right hand to distract the younger man while slowly moving his left down his side where his knife lay shielded from view.

"What else you got, brother? What's in that pack? That's a good bedroll," crooned the cocky voice.

While the coyote jostled Winfield's sleeping bag, the older man carefully lifted the knife.

The coyote's wide face was much closer now, and Winfield felt his pack being tugged. "What's this here?" The younger man was in no hurry. He was confident that he could do anything he wanted. "Hey, brother, you got some beans it looks like." He had pulled open the pack's top and was rummaging through it.

Silently, Winfield opened the blade.

"How 'bout money, brother? You been workin'?" It was a demand, not a question.

The knife was poised.

"No talk, huh? You one of those crazy bastards? Only talk to yourself? Well," the coyote's voice deepened to a growl, "just gimme that bedroll and pack before I fuck you up, brother. And gimme your fuckin' money too."

"I ain't your brother," Winfield hissed. "I'm a veteran. I got a name."

The coyote chuckled as he leaned forward and grabbed Winfield's sleeping bag; his pale face was inches from the old man's but he did not seem to know the knife was coming until he lurched back and screamed as his face peeled open. "You fucker! You cut me, you fucker!"

"I got a name," the older man repeated in a tight whisper as though talking to himself, his blade balanced at his side.

Half the pale face poured crimson as the coyote – still backing away – touched it, looked at his stained hand, and screamed once more as though he couldn't believe it – "You cut me, you fucker!" Then he scrambled from the bridge into the fading orange light of the lot, seeming to dodge aimlessly in the decaying light like a gut-shot dog.

"Son of a bitch!" Winfield shouted. "Bastard!"

After a second – still twisted by tension – he hurriedly secured his pack, tightened his sleeping bag, then hoisted them. He needed to travel before the cops got curious about that yelping coyote. He had just moved when he felt something under his right knee and reached down: Glasses, the ones the coyote had worn, and they weren't broken.

Hesitating a moment, he held the spectacles in one hand, then he put them on and stared out into the light, but immediately covered his eyes with his hands – the images were like razors. He blinked and thrust his fingers under the lenses to rub his eyes. Once more – slowly, gradually – he opened them and gazed tentatively toward the light, his eyes little more than slits.

Through lashes, images again sliced at him as though someone had etched each shape, sharpened every edge. They hurt. Far across the lot loomed the distinct edges of distant buildings, and in the nearby lot were the filthy clumps of gutted cars, clumps of garbage – here an old mattress, there a deteriorating shopping cart – and the crazed figure of a large man, his face masked with blood, running and screaming.

Averting his eyes, he noted that the nearby walls of the bridge's cement abutment were covered with imprecise drawings of women's bodies and of vast, erupting male sex organs, with boasting messages and telephone numbers. Feces had been smeared on the cement surface to shape a swastika. In front of him the river water was gray with what appeared to be turds floating in it, along with a dead fish.

"This world is ugly. Ugly!" he declared.

Winfield removed the glasses and flung them into the water, rubbing his eyes again, then he turned toward the soft, the comforting blur of the lot and began walking toward that great orange glow beyond, hefting his plastic bag of cans and treading across the bare lot toward the vague distance.

"I'm not no Buster. I'm a veteran!" he proclaimed, one arm punching the sky.

THE SOUVENIR

"Do you think I could talk Myrtle into flyin'?" the white-haired man chuckled, and his wife – her own hair a shade of blue invented in a laboratory – smiled primly, still not confident of her new teeth. "That's a fact," she lisped, adding, "Baldwin ain't gettin' me to climb into nothin' I cain't climb out of." She smiled once more, her dentures even and white.

They sat in a clattering railroad lounge car, sipping coffee and talking to another couple – the man bald, the woman also sporting blue hair – while the train swept them up the heart of California's San Joaquin Valley, acres after endless acres of reclaimed desert now green as a tropical rain forest on both sides of them, the engine's silver snout plunging everyone north toward San Francisco.

"So you folks're from Bakersfield," observed the bald-headed man.

"Oildale," Baldwin corrected.

"It's the same as bein' from Bakersfield," recorrected his wife, shooting him an annoyed glance. "He always says Oildale, but it's just part of Bakersfield. Anyways, we're not original from there. We come out from Checotah in '37, me and Baldwin, just married and too young to have good sense."

"We're natives," interjected the other woman.

"Ain't that nice," observed Myrtle tonelessly. "Anyways, Baldwin found work in the oil fields and he's been at it ever since, forty-two years up till he retired last March, workin' for Shell Oil. Not like some of these youngsters jumpin' from job to job. *If they work a-tall.*"

"Isn't it the truth," agreed the native woman, whose teeth seemed to fit securely. "Dan just retired too. He was a salesman for Ward's."

"Uhm. I bet that's inter'stin' work," lisped the new teeth.

The bald man nodded, his eyes twinkling.

"The stories he could tell!" remarked his wife.

While the women continued talking, their conversation drifting toward grandchildren, then recipes, finally to the fact that ladies in San Francisco always wore hats and gloves. The two men sparred for topics, touching on the general rudeness of the younger generation, the fact that *some people* should be forced to speak English if they want to collect welfare or vote, and the assurance that Muhammad Ali couldn't lace up Jack Dempsey's gloves. There was a pause, then the bald-headed man asked, "You folks get up to Frisco often?"

"Naw, not for years," Baldwin replied. "Me and Myrtle just thought, why not? It's time to travel some." He smiled and his own large yellow teeth gave him the appearance of a happy mule. He shifted his heavy shoulders. "Yessir, why not? But do you think I could talk her into flyin'?"

The salesman's smile faded into a knowing scowl. "Well," he intoned, "you won't know Frisco. It's been taken over by beatniks and hippies. Our daughter lives up in El Cerrito and she took us over there last summer. You'll really be surprised at what's on the street."

Again the yellow teeth grinned. "Well, I don't mind if I do see me a hippie. Like I told Myrtle, I'm gonna get my pitcher took with one a them boogers for a souvenir."

His wife, although in the midst of a list of grandchildren's accomplishments, remarked, "You *are* not." She smiled at the other woman, raised her eyebrows, and sighed, *"That* man." The lady with the fitted teeth chuckled knowingly.

Baldwin ignored them. "Yessir," he continued, "seen some a them suckers on TV, but I never seen a real one. I'll find me one, though, and get my pitcher took."

His wife paused, glancing first at him then back toward the native woman. "I *swear,*" she said. Once more the other lady nodded and chuckled.

They detrained at Oakland, bidding good-bye to their new friends, whose daughter met them with a car. Then they walked to a waiting bus that would take them to the terminal in San Francisco, Myrtle scurrying ahead, pillbox hat firmly planted atop her blue hair, white gloves covering her hands. Once Baldwin had plopped into the seat beside her, he asked, "What 'uz the big rush? You damn near run to the bus."

"*You* may not mind bein' stared at by coloreds," she responded tartly, "but *I* do."

"Oh, hell, them boys wasn't starin' at you."

"Hah!" she snorted, and he patted her hand. A few moments later, as the bus wound its way toward a freeway, she observed, "You'd think we was in *Aferca* is where. The co-*loreds!* I never seen so many. Just look at 'em." Baldwin also stared out the window at the dark faces and strange costumes, examining houses and stores and cars, all of it as alien as another nation. "Ain't this somethin'," he said to himself. "Would you look at that!"

Soon the bus swerved up onto the freeway, then across the Bay Bridge, muddy water swirling far below them, and Baldwin felt his stomach lighten. His wife stared stonily ahead. "Looky at that water," he remarked, but she ignored him. He knew she hated bridges.

At the terminal in San Francisco, they gathered their suitcases – him commenting again that she'd brought enough clothes for a month – and asked the Amtrak man how to get to the Busby Hotel, where they had reservations. He instructed them to walk to the front of the building and hail a cab. "How much'll that run us?" asked Myrtle, but before the man could answer, Baldwin had departed for the front of the building; abandoned, she rushed after him, holding her hat on with one gloved hand while she caught up. "Would *you* wait!" she demanded.

They had only walked a short distance in the large building when they saw the first one, a young man dressed in Army fatigues, a pirate's red bandana around his head, and no shoes. "L-O-V-E" was printed neatly just above his eyebrows in green. "Looky there, Myrtle," Baldwin said, his yellow teeth exposed in a great grin, "a hippie. I believe I'll go get my pitcher took with that sucker."

His wife, who cringed from the oblivious young man, hissed, "You *will* not," and increased her pace slightly, but Baldwin stopped and followed the buccaneer with his eyes. "*Baldwin!*" Myrtle cried, torn between the desire to escape this building and the need not to be alone.

While the older man eyed him, the pirate twice accosted people, demanded money, and received it, the donors scurrying away as though embarrassed while the young man with L-O-V-E on his forehead counted the bounty in his hand before thrusting it into a pocket, then scouted for other potential patrons. "Would you *look* at that," observed Baldwin. "Them folks're givin' him money," he grinned to Myrtle, who tugged desperately at his arm. "Come *on*," she urged.

Baldwin had to hurry to keep up with her, his eyes nonetheless scanning everything, everyone. He nearly ran into a post when a long-haired colored girl in a 1940s dress passed them. "Would you *look* at that," he remarked, but Myrtle didn't answer. Just before they reached the heavy glass doors at the front of the building, Myrtle swerved to avoid another barefooted youngster, a girl dressed in jeans and an old blue work shirt. The youngster wore flowers in her hair and no gloves. "Peace," she murmured as Baldwin passed, and he showed her his yellow teeth.

Just as Myrtle and Baldwin emerged from the building, the lone taxi they had sighted through the large glass doors, and toward which they had been hastening, pulled away. "Now what?" asked Myrtle, sounding heartbroken.

Her tone caused Baldwin to wink at her. "Oh," he observed, "I reckon there's more'n one taxi in Frisco. Another'n'll be along d'rectly." He put down the two suitcases and opened the smaller one.

"Now what're you doin'?" asked his wife, her voice still ragged.

"I'm gettin' out the Brownie so's you can take a pitcher of me with a hippie."

"You *are* not."

"I sure as hell am. I never come clean up here not to get my pitcher took with no hippie." His tone was firm.

"*Baldwin*," her voice raised an octave, "you *are* not."

He had just removed the camera and rezipped the bag when he felt his wife's gloved hand grip his arm. "What?" he asked, not looking up. When Myrtle didn't reply, but only squeezed his arm tighter, he glanced up, annoyed. She nodded to their left, where a pale girl stood with one bare hand extended. Someone had drawn a red-and-blue star on one of her cheeks. "Got any spare change?" she asked dreamily.

Baldwin felt his wife shudder. He examined the girl, young and thin with dark eyes and hair, no makeup except that star. She wore a kind of smock over faded jeans that had brightly colored patches on both knees. Around her neck hung a string of eucalyptus buds. "Want your pitcher took, little lady?" he asked.

For a moment the girl didn't reply, then she asked, her voice slightly less dreamy, "Do you got a quarter?"

Myrtle's grip tightened and the lines at the corners of her mouth slashed downward as though extending beyond her chin into the pavement itself. "*Baldwin*," she begged.

"Right over there by the flower stand'd be good," Baldwin told the girl. "My wife here can take the pitcher."

The girl blinked. "What's wrong with you, man? Don't you even got a dime?" Her voice had hardened considerably, and she edged a step away from the muleface.

"Come right on over here, little lady," Baldwin insisted, grabbing the girl's thin arm and leading her to the flower stand, dragging along his wife, whose glove seemed welded to him. "You get right there, and Myrtle here'll snap our pitcher."

"I *will* not."

"Hey, man!" the girl protested, her dark eyes wide, her voice grown rough.

He thrust the camera toward his wife, who suddenly dropped his arm and hurried back to their suitcases. "Myrtle!" he called, but she refused to even turn around and acknowledge him, standing like a gloved, hatted statue facing the street. "Damn it, anyways," he said.

"Tommy! Tommy!" he heard the girl call, and he followed the line of her vision until he saw slouching toward them the same red-bandanaed pirate in Army fatigues he'd noticed earlier. The buccaneer seemed in no hurry, but when he arrived, he extended his hand. "Got any spare change, man?" he asked in a tone that sounded more like "Stick 'em up."

Baldwin handed him the camera. "Back up there by the curb so's you can get them flowers in," he said.

"Huh?" responded the pirate.

"Hey, man!" the girl seemed to moan.

"And make sure you get us in that little square," Baldwin ordered. The buccaneer blinked his eyes, then backed up to the curb.

Baldwin turned to the girl. "Smile, little lady," he directed. She smiled the way a fighter does when he's caught a good right hand.

"It won't work," the pirate said.

"You never wound it," explained Baldwin patiently. "Wind that little doodad on top. Yeah, that's it."

Again the two smiled, and this time there was a soft snap. Over the photographer's shoulder, Baldwin could see his wife's blue hair and white hat like a blossom decorating the background. He retrieved his camera, still grinning, and said, "Much obliged." He returned to his wife.

The pirate followed him, but the girl kept her distance. "How 'bout that spare change?"

"What spare change? I ain't got no spare change. I worked for what little I got and I need it."

The buccaneer stared at the large, white-haired man in front of him. "Okay," he said, "then how 'bout our modeling fee?"

"Your what?" Baldwin stared at the L-O-V-E on the younger man's forehead.

"Modeling fee." The pirate's eyes narrowed; his jaw thrust forward.

For a moment, the old man seemed stumped. His wife hissed out of the corner of her mouth, "Bald-win, *give* 'em somethin'."

"Modelin' fee, eh?" Baldwin chewed on it like a fresh tobacco plug, and the pirate boldly stepped closer until his hand almost touched the older man. Then the mischievous mule grin reappeared: "Well, since you took the pitcher and I's in it, you owe *me* a modelin' fee."

"Bald-*win!*" insisted his wife.

"Hey, man! I want my money!"

"Your money! You got some money?" grinned the hulking old man.

"Tom-*my!*" the pale girl called to the pirate, keeping her distance.

"Yessir," said Baldwin, "I never knew they paid no modelin' fees in Frisco or I'd a come up sooner."

The buccaneer's mouth hardened to a gash. "Okay, man, I'm calling a cop."

Still smiling, the old man pointed across the street. "Want a cop? There's one right over there. Hey, officer!" he shouted.

The pirate and his lady immediately fled into the terminal, eyes wide as they glanced back over their shoulders, even though the policeman didn't acknowledge Baldwin's call. "Would you *look* at that," the old man observed. "I guess they never wanted no cop after all."

For a long moment his wife did not speak, then she said slowly, "I just *hate* it whenever you act like that."

"Like what? We come up here to have fun, didn't we?"

She clattered her new teeth at him, too exasperated to speak. It seemed that a cab would never arrive. Baldwin was unconcerned. Grinning, he scanned the area, the assorted cars and people, then his eyes locked onto a bewhiskered specimen wending his way toward them from the far corner. The man wore an ankle-length overcoat that sagged like an elephant's skin, and he sipped furtively from a brown paper bag. He appeared to be carrying on an active conversation with himself, complete with shouts and angry gestures. "Would you *look* at that," Baldwin said, then he handed the camera to his wife, who absently accepted it, her eyes straining for a glimpse of a taxi. She no longer cared how much it might cost. When she finally darted a glance toward him, her husband was moving toward the man in the overcoat.

"Baldwin?" she called.

"I'm just gonna go have me a word with that booger," he explained over his shoulder.

"Bald-*win!*"

SOJOURNER

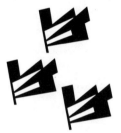

We are only sojourners on this Earth,
waiting to be called Home.
    Rev. Gary Chu, Pastor, Stockton,
    California, 1981

Afternoons he liked to face the gradually lowering sun, to feel it smooth his ridged and canyoned face, soothe his sightless eyes. Lulled by its warmth, he registered shrill voices of children from the playground and allowed them to evoke the one shrill voice he'd not heard for more than half a century, that he could never again hear but would never cease listening for. Beyond, just over the levee, sucked the great river, the Sacramento. During such somnolent moments he imagined it was the mighty Shuang sweeping past.

So, so far away, all of it: his land, his life, his people. Yet never deserted. He carried all within, where he could often return, especially on long, warm afternoons.

He had traveled to this heathen land originally in search of the golden dream. Since his older brother had occupied their ancestral home when their parents died, Wing Nu set out in search of his own best opportunities, first as a laboring peasant in the fields of others until great floods destroyed crops and forced him to eke out a subsistence cutting wood in Fukien's nearly denuded hills.

Tied to no man, he was young, sinewy, and clever, clever enough to realize that his abilities would be wasted in Fukien unless nature itself changed dramatically, something he neither expected nor bothered to hope for. He could do any job and do it well, and he could both read and write a bit, but what was the point if work promised no improvement in his conditions?

He had heard, of course, of the mountains of gold across the sea. Rumors of great fortunes spread where poor men gathered, gossip of kinsmen who had migrated and, within a week, gathered enough gold to return home rich beyond the dreams of the emperor. For a woodcutter, however, the very trip to the mountains of gold was hopelessly expensive.

Gnawing himself within, he stalked the lanes of his village seeking a loan, but could arrange none. Then he saw the posted sign:

Laborers wanted for California in the United States of America. There is much work. Food and housing supplied. Wages are generous. There is no slavery. You will be treated considerately. All is nice.

The ship is going soon and will take all who can pay for their passage. Persons having property can have it sold for them by my agents or borrow money for passage against it from me. I cannot take security on your wife or children but if you are a good worker, I will loan you passage money which you repay from your wages in California.

The ship is substantial and convenient.

The poster was signed "Ah Chang," and an address in Fuchou was listed below the name. Wing Nu read the poster to himself, then read it aloud to other men gathered around. He reread the part that began, "I will loan you passage money," and the men gathered round him chattered excitedly. He had no money, but he was a good worker and an educated man. He would climb those mountains of gold.

Voices, voices, voices:

"What else could I do? Crops had failed and floods had ruined our field. There was no wood left to cut in the hills. What else could I do?"
Lu Ng, laborer, Sacramento, California, 1854

"I remember the mornings on the river at home, the sounds of women calling to one another, the laughter of children. I miss them most."
Ying Nu, laborer, Auburn, California, 1856

"My father sold me when I was nine. He had no choice."
Jade Ping, prostitute, San Francisco, California, 1858

From downstream the old man heard the hoarse hoot of a steamer's whistle, and he strained his ears for the slap-slap of its wheel churning through the water. Before his eyes had dimmed he had much enjoyed pausing in his work to watch the large white ships that plied the Sacramento, and had been amused at the sometimes rude gestures and shouts that passengers made at the lone man waving to them from a field. These Americans, he had thought, so immature, so uncertain, so frightened.

Like the red-faced man who had confronted him at Silva's Bar on the Consumnes River. "I don't give a good goddamn what the law says," the Yankee had growled to the constable, "I say when American miners quit, these goddamn chinks gotta quit too. They got no goddamn business workin' longer'n white men. It ain't natural!"

"Well," chuckled the constable, whose main occupation appeared to be avoiding mayhem to himself while breaking up fights, "seems like to me, Jake, it was you told me a Chinaman couldn't work as long or as hard as an American whenever these boys come to the diggin's. Said they was too little and weak and dumb. I recollect you sayin' how these little fellers'd burn out in no time."

Wing Nu stood impassively before the two men, lightly holding a spade. He understood enough of their difficult tongue to know he was in danger, and he was prepared to defend himself.

"I don't know why a bunch of goddamn Chinee pirates can come from nowheres and dig American gold and take it back to their king or who-the-hell-ever."

"These here little fellers all pay the foreign miners' tax, Jake. And look what they're scrubbin' dust from. Why, you boys finished with this bar months ago, claimed it was played out." The constable's arm gestured at the pile of tailings on which the Chinese worked. "Hell, they're workin' second-hand gold."

"First-hand or second, the boys deputized me to come stop these damn chinks from workin' overtime and to make 'em observe the Sabbath like Christians. Hell's fire, ain't no human bein' can work like these heathens. There's somethin' wrong with 'em. They don't have feelin's like normal folks. They ain't human, and we can't have 'em workin' when we ain't."

The constable rocked on his heels. "Wellsir, I disremember you boys holdin' any church service on the Sabbath."

The big man's neck swelled like a horned toad. "This ain't no damned joke! The new miners' law at Silva's Bar is that no goddamn chink works longer'n us Americans work or they'll all lose a hell of a lot more than their pigtails."

Still grinning, the constable had turned toward Wing Nu, who acted as captain of the Fukinese miners. "You heard 'im, Chinaman. No more work until I say so." Wing had merely nodded, his gaze straight and unblinking. He had to acquiesce, but he did not want these Americans to think they intimidated him. In fact, they reminded him of a Northern Chinese he had met on the boat to California. That man, expensively dressed and traveling on the upper deck, had spat that Wing and the other Fukinese were barbarians and had laughed at their plight. When the Northerner's remark was translated for him, Wing had struck the man. These Yankees, however, were too numerous and too well armed, so Wing Nu kept his counsel.

Three weeks later, carrying only what they could secrete on their persons, all seventy-one Fukinese miners were driven from Silva's Bar by a mob of drunken heathens. The volunteer fire department marching band and drum corps had accompanied the grim procession, and their presence probably saved many Chinese lives, for the music lightened the mood of the drunken Yankees, who contented themselves with cutting queues and a few slaps and punches to keep Wing Nu and his friends moving.

Voices, voices, voices:

"We had saved enough so that all four of us could return to Canton rich men, but a Yankee bandit stole it from us in broad daylight. When we complained to the sheriff, he laughed."

Yu Wang, laborer, Reno, Nevada, 1866

"They are in many respects a disgusting element of the population but not wholly unprofitable."

Editorial, *Record-Avalanche*, Silver City, Idaho, June 23, 1867

"No one bothered me, except when they were drunk. Most people left me alone, and I avoided them. I became a Christian."

Au Li, herbalist, Mariposa, California, 1871

From the labor contractor's office across the street, the old man heard voices of laborers returning from the fields, piling out of wagons in mid-afternoon, then drifting in small groups toward saloons or camps or the park where Wing Nu rested. Many of them spoke tongues he did not understand – Spanish, Portuguese, Italian – and they smelled unlike the people he knew well. But he did understand their toil and their fatigued relief at the workday's end.

Despite the congratulations and cries of envy from other Fukinese laborers, there had been little triumph in Wing Nu's step that first morning following his return to Mr. Schmidt's farm outside Stockton. True, he had visited his small village in Fukien, a rare enough occurrence in itself. Moreover, he had married and sired a son there, the cause of great celebration among his fellows.

But a more harsh and immediate reality made it impossible for him to rejoice: He was back in California while his wife and son remained in China. One part of him acknowledged his good fortune, while another ached for his wife and the little brown bundle he feared he would never again see.

At least he knew they would be well cared for. Each month he turned most of his wages over to the *hui kuan*, his clan, which in turn forwarded it to his village. The question of whether he would ever see his family again was entirely up to him. He would work. He would save. Someday he would return to his village a wealthy and respected man.

It would take a great fortune, though, to accomplish that, as he had learned on his first visit home. With nearly 1,500 American dollars he had saved or won gambling, Wing Nu had assumed he could return and remain. But his money had disappeared more quickly than he had imagined possible.

Conditions had changed, and the entire country seemed to be run by soldiers and petty officials. He had been forced to pay off a minor magistrate and the man's lackeys in order to leave the port. Then his aging uncle had to be rescued from bankruptcy. He loaned his older brother a substantial sum. When all was done, he had barely enough money left to marry, buy a small house, and provide for his family when he finally returned, far too soon, to the gambling halls and whorehouses and opium dens of America.

Back in California, he knew his next fortune would come more slowly than his first. There was no more gold to be dug. He would now dig another man's vegetables or irrigate another man's fields. On the boat taking him away from those he loved, he had fantasized that one day his son would join him and help accumulate wealth for the family.

That had only been a dream and, standing in the searing sunlight of a San Joaquin Valley morning, his comrades still teasing and praising him, everything and everywhere else seemed unreal. The ache in his loins was real, the ache in his heart was too. In front of him, heat waves shimmered from Mr. Schmidt's fields, and Wing Nu strode forward, certain in his secret self that he would never see his wife and son again, not in this world anyway. That realization was his first death.

Voices, voices, voices:

"I liked working on the farm. It was good work, outdoors, with animals. If only my family could have been with me, then I could have been truly happy."
Lin Ho, laborer, Fresno City, California, 1879

"We cut through mountains for the railroad, chipping stone, blasting it, hauling it away. We spanned rivers. It was hard, but I was young and strong. Afterwards I was able to return home."
Pyau Ng, merchant, Kwantung, China, 1881

"They killed my brother and they tried to kill me. I was beaten. My queue was cut. I was stripped and my clothes were thrown into the stream. They left me to die, but I did not die."

Woo Soo, laborer, Rock Springs, Wyoming, 1885

Caught in a dragon's bowels, Wing struggled with the bulky sacks of laundry, sweating, almost unable to breathe. No longer young, he was wearied by the tough toil. His eyes had so dimmed that he could not do the farm work he preferred and, forced into this humid basement to earn a living, he could no longer hear birds sing or feel breeze on his skin. Another part of him died then.

Nonetheless, he toiled, struggling through hissing, grinding mechanical monsters. Through the bragging of fellow workers, through the steam that seemed to enter and sap him, he labored. He was trapped in these bowels, but it had been the only job the *hui kuan* could arrange for him, and he had to work. That much was certain.

Each evening he bumped through crowded streets to the small alleyway cafe where Fukinese workers gathered to eat and talk about home, then he would slump on to his tiny room, too exhausted to even try to read the newspaper the restaurateur saved for him each week. Less frequently, he would visit a fantan parlor, more for companionship than gambling. For the same reason he would occasionally patronize one of the bordellos so available in Chinatown. Somehow, even they brought little joy.

Although he had plenty of people to talk to in the city, plenty of people who could understand his feelings and hopes, he felt trapped here. All his life he had loved the outdoors. Now only once a week or so could he wander to the new park being built near the levee on the town's west edge and gaze across the river at the open land beyond. Those were the best times of all.

Voices, voices, voices:

"It is quite simple. We provide entertainment for lonely men. In exchange, we earn a profit. Occasionally we must protect our interests, but we are not violent men."

Lin Jay, Tong leader, San Francisco, California, 1893

"Cities are filthy, but what choice have I? I cannot operate my business without customers. Besides, I can speak a civilized tongue again here, and perhaps begin a family."

Yang Lee, laundryman, Los Angeles, California, 1899

"I am strongly of the opinion that, but for the presence of the Chinese, California would not now have more than one-half or two-thirds of her present population; Chinese labor has opened up many avenues and new industries for white labor, made many kinds of business possible."

Alva Griffin, State Senator, Sacramento, California, 1903

Meeting Mr. Reilly had been one joy of his late years. Retired like himself, Reilly also had no family and few friends, and he was also blind. Every sunny day, the old Irishman's servant deposited him on a bench in the town's square – it was there the old men met – and he would sun, chatting with Wing Nu as the outer heat fought their dimming inner fires, two travelers near journey's end.

Each had trouble understanding the other at first, although both spoke English, "or so we t'ought," chuckled Mr. Reilly. Both were immigrants – each regaling the other with tales of his youth, of strange green lands and long-dead friends – but Reilly's fortune had been considerably better than Wing's: He owned a restaurant and a home and several rentals. Still, aging and alone save for his servant, ignored if not disdained except by those coveting his property, his emptiness was no less. For him, too, the golden dream had come to dust.

While Wing yearned for the wife and child he'd not touched for over fifty years, Reilly – who'd never married – pined for a girl he'd left in Ireland half a century before, "gone dead in the convent these twenty-seven years," and for the children they'd never had. Rich or poor, loneliness was the same.

But the two men did not mire themselves in maudlin memories. Having acknowledged the pain of estrangement, they found many lively topics to discuss, conversing through most afternoons, laughing frequently about episodes from their lives or those of others, debating points of religion or philosophy or politics, resolving nothing. It was the fray they enjoyed, the respect each paid the other's ideas. Those conversations were the liveliest moments either man experienced anymore.

Passersby often noted with amusement the two old men who had never seen one another animatedly debating in near-incomprehensible accents the doctrine of Original Sin or farm labor practices. From a distance, in fact, it was difficult to notice their physical differences, and their tones revealed little.

Voices, voices, voices:

"No greater scourge in the history of mankind has been recorded. The heathen mongol must be stopped. He breeds like an animal and soon Christianity and Democracy will be dead. If the Chinaman is allowed to resume his invasion, the White Race faces mongrelization."
Benjamin Franklin Burns, Congressman, Washington, D.C.
October 9, 1906

"All we do is sit. No family here. Just us old men. Just us. I only hope to return home someday."
Ko Yip, retired, Seattle, Washington, 1914

"Edward, my son, returned home from school crying yesterday. He said a gang of bullies had chased him and called him 'Ching-chong Chinaman.' We must move to a better neighborhood."
Mrs. Lin Chen, housewife, San Francisco, California, 1918

The aging man trudged the stairs to his room, resting every few steps, his breath seeming to grow shorter each day. Fumbling his key into the lock, Wing Nu snapped the door open, entered, then closed it. Evening had come. He felt the slight chill and heard the sounds of night begin to replace those of day, traps and carriages rattling by on the street below, and even a few automobiles.

He slumped to his bed and sat for several moments before stretching out. It had been a full day for an old man far away from home. Yet – and only fatigue prompted such a question – where was home? He had lived three-quarters of his life in California. He knew its rivers and fields better than he had ever known Fukien's. With his wife dead and his son disappeared, his only true friend remained here in Sacramento.

It was no question, really. America had tolerated and used Wing Nu; it had never accepted him. Only dreams of Fukien motivated him. He was Fukien: It dwelled within him, as tangible as the bed on which he rested, and soon his third death would free him from this tiny room, this alien town. Then the *hui kuan* would transport his body back home, to the soil that had given him life. Then, at last, he could rest.

Still, lying in darkness, nearly asleep, hearing familiar sounds from the street, smelling familiar odors, feeling a familiar breeze, it was difficult to separate places, as though there were only one place with many names, one life with many journeys, and he – this weary sojourner – was about to begin another.

WIDDER MAKER

Things they's a-jumpin back in them days. Ever'one fig-
gered there was oil under their land, and wildcatters was a-raisin' rigs so
fast the whole of Kern County looked about like a forest. Me, it was just
my luck I hired on to a dirt-poor wildcatter out of McKittrick who run
this here old cable tool rig, and I mean old. He couldn't pay nothin',
but he kept us in grub, and us roughnecks was a-gonna get 5 percent of
whatever we struck. It beat sittin' on our butts.

Brownie, the wildcatter, he had this arrangement with a farmer whose
place was right next to where the Shell done real good, so we commenced
putting up that big damn rig, workin' our tails off while that farmer he just
stood around spittin' tobacco juice on the ground and figgerin' how to
spend the oil money he'd make. He never offered us no water or nothin'.

Whenever we was hoistin' the walkin' beam into place, Brownie's
A-frame just a huffin' and puffin', damned if the cable didn't bust and

bite ol' Clarence, this colored boy from Langston that was on our crew. Well, the farmer's wife she carried ol' Clarence in the car to the county hospital. That left us one man short just whenever we needed everyone most, so Brownie he asked that farmer to come give us a hand, but not him. Naw, he just sucked on his tobacco quid for a spell, then turned and grinned. "Well?" ol' Brownie'd asked. That farmer he kindly puffed up at Brownie and barked: "I'm payin' you boys to do the oil work. If you can't handle her, I believe I can find me another outfit to drill here."

Well, he was right about findin' another outfit. It was a good spot and we all knowed it. So Brownie he just turned around and stuffed a little more snuff under his lip and we all went back to work. And I seen that farmer just a-grinnin' while we liked to killed ourselves getting that damn rig together.

If Brownie hadn't been down on his luck, that farmer'd of been one big bruise, but when you're eating the labels off last week's bean cans, well, you just take them thangs, but you don't forget 'em. Ain't none of us forgot 'em. We was sure as hell happy that next week whenever ol' Clarence got back.

Before long we was makin' hole, that big ol' mother hubbard just a bitin' through clay formation. Brownie he spent about his last buck to have a mud smeller come check what we was a-bringin' up. Well, that geologist he said it looked good, real good. He figgered we was only a few hundred foot from makin' a strike. But it was a long ways when we was out of casin', then we lost our damn bit in the hole and had to fish for it. I commenced wonderin' if maybe we wasn't lookin' for farmer's sand.

All the time we was workin', that farmer he's a-hangin' around, like a fly on a manure pile, buzzin' and settin', then buzzin' some more, givin' all the advice he could think of. Lefty, this other ol' boy on the crew, he said there wasn't nothin' worse than a sorry farmer that figgers he's about to get rich. But that farmer's wife she was nice. Ever' once and awhile she'd bring us out a pot of coffee. She knowed we wasn't eatin' too good, so she'd carry sandwiches or pieces of pie to us. Her and Brownie used to talk a little each time. She was real nice.

One mornin', just about the time we'd of been switchin' towers if we'd had any relief, that lady brought us out some coffee. Us guys had been fishin' out our bit again, and we was wore to a nub. We seen her comin' and ol' Lefty he said, "Damn, but I might could drank me a little coffee. Don't reckon she's poured any whiskey in it do ya?" We all laughed, but Brownie he said we'd earned us a little drank, and that he had some whiskey in his locker, then he walked over to this old trailer we used for a doghouse. Just about the time Brownie disappeared in the trailer, here come that farmer snortin' across the field from his barn. He hollered to his wife to stop. She was close to us, but she stopped, and her old man run up to her and commenced chewin' on her about how we was lazy and hadn't got him no oil and how he was fixin' to run us off and hire on this here rotary outfit he'd heard tell of. Well, she said she'd fixed the coffee for us because we'd worked all night. He slapped that coffeepot out of her hand and it spilled, then he socked her on one eye.

"Hold on!" I heard this voice holler. It was Clarence. Well, let me tell you, you don't wanta tangle with ol' Clarence. He's the stoutest ol' boy I ever seen in a oil patch. He never fought much, but when he did, boys, he's like a badger on a dog. Clarence stood right there on the edge of the floor with his big brown finger a-pointin' at that farmer, and he said: "Pick up that pot."

The farmer he glared at old Clarence. "Mind your own business, boy," he spit.

Oh, Lord! There goes our job, I figgered, so I just sort of leaned on the headache post to watch Clarence swarm the booger, but before ol' Clarence ever got to the farmer, here come Brownie from out of nowhere, a-snortin' like a gut-shot bear and wham! one-punch coldcocked the farmer, that bastard fallin' plop like a road apple.

All that time that farmer's wife hadn't moved. She just stood there holdin' her eye where he'd smacked her. Brownie turned to her, and Clarence he handed her the coffeepot. I could tell just lookin' at 'em that all three of 'em knowed we was through, and that Brownie'd probably lose his rig too. It was sad, but I felt kinda easy for some reason, like what the hell. Lefty he poked my ribs and hissed: "Ya know, I believe it's worth it." Then he sent a brown stream of tobacco juice into the big hole in the middle of the floor.

Whenever that farmer he come to, he commenced screamin' for us to take our rig and get our tails off his place or he'd have the sheriff after us. But he never got too close to Brownie, or Clarence either. And he never pushed his wife again. He just give her the evil eye, then stomped off.

Well, after Brownie'd made sure that farmer wasn't fixin' to beat his wife up, he come back to the rig, draggin' some from the night's work and from what he was a-thinkin'. He called us all together and he said, "Boys, I surely hate to tell you this, but there was show in the mud on that bit we just brought up. We're sittin' on a pool right now. What I figger is that it'll take that numb-nutted farmer an hour, or maybe two to fetch the sheriff. If we're lucky, we can have a strike by the time the sheriff gets here, which means we get our money no matter what. But we've gotta bust our butts if we're gonna finish before he gets back. Are you with me?"

"Let's make hole!" ol' Clarence he sang out, so we got hot after it.

About an hour later – us not more than inches from pay – here come that farmer with this here big old hayseed deputy trailin' along behind him. Lefty he stalked out to meet 'em because Brownie was a workin' on the long tail. They climbed up onto the floor, that farmer nosin' around while the sheriff he asked who was in charge. "I am," Brownie called, shuttin' the engine down and turnin' to the farmer. "I wouldn't get too close to that hole if I was you," he advised real quiet. "That's slicker'n snot, a real widder maker."

The farmer, feelin' real smart alecky with that deputy backin' him, just sneered: "I'll do what I damn well please." He stepped to the edge of the hole, turned around and kindly nodded his nose at Brownie, then he slipped.

Now the hole you dig with a cable tool rig is one hell of a lot bigger than what you dig with a rotary, but it ain't all that big either. A guy has to be pretty lame or unlucky to fall into one. That farmer he hit the rim of the casin', hung there a second, then slid into the hole. I seen his fingers grab at the edge, then just slide loose. We could hear some funny thunks and whacks while the booger fell, then nothin'.

Everbody, even the deputy, they run to the hole, but not too close; we all knew there wasn't no hope for the farmer. "Damn!" the deputy he said from where he stood just a little further back than the rest of us. "That's awful."

"Hardheaded," Brownie told him, shakin' his head. "He never would listen to nobody."

"What do we do now?" asked the deputy.

"You're the sheriff," Brownie told him. So the deputy he told us to stop diggin', and he hurried back to town.

The next day a man from the county attorney's office come out and talked to all of us, and had us sign these papers about how the farmer got killed. Then he talked to the widder woman. Brownie he went over too and explained how we was just ready to strike pay. It turned out that the farmer he was as broke as we was, and about to lose his place to boot. His widder never even had money to buy him a funeral. So Brownie he made her a proposition. A couple days later she got the go-ahead from the county attorney.

"We're cementin' it," Brownie told us.

"Hell," I said, "we don't need to stabilize it. We're right over the damned oil."

"That's part of the deal," he explained. "And that's gotta be done by noon."

"Why?" I asked.

"We're havin' a funeral."

Just after we pumped the cement down, me addin' some panther piss to make it set quicker, up drives this here fat preacher in a big black A model with three more cars a-followin'. Out of them cars pops a bunch of stringy ladies, and fellers with tan faces and white foreheads. Most of 'em was carryin' flowers. Directly, here come ol' Brownie out of the doghouse, all dolled up, with even a necktie, and joined them mourners up on the floor next to the hole right where we'd sprinkled sawdust, a real solemn look on his face like he was going to Sunday meetin'. Us boys we was standin' in our work clothes a little behind them church folks, figgerin' we'd watch the show, but ol' Brownie he turned around and hissed at us: "Get outa here."

At first we just stood there, confused, but ol' Brownie he glared at us, so we slipped on back of the long tail and watched the best we could. Well that tubby preacher he commenced jabberin' and I swear I figgered he'd never quit. He told how Brother what's-his-name was strong in the church and a good provider and kind to his wife (that widder kindly daubed her eyes whenever he said that; she had pancake makeup on the one her late lamented had blacked) and how he tithed whenever he could. Ol' Tubby he preached about the Kingdom of Heaven and Original Sin and how Jesus died for all Mankind, then he got going on Jews and how they not only crucified Our Lord, but how they kept decent folks poor with their banks and how Roosevelt was a Jew, and he was just getting started on the Pope of Rome whenever ol' Clarence he started the engine, and the rig took to shakin'.

Well that near scared the water out of them folks, so the preacher cut hisself off, and the funeral it ended with folks droppin' flowers down the hole. Just as they was leavin', I seen Brownie squeeze the widder woman's hand.

We never made but about a foot of hole through that farmer's carcass before we hit crude, a nice pool opener. And I knowed of a sudden that ol' Brownie'd found hisself a rich widder. The other boys knowed it too. Ol' Lefty he sang out, while we was finishin' Brownie's bottle after we'd capped the hole, "You know, Push, while I was a-pilin' sawdust on the floor for that funeral I noticed how it looked slicker'n usual, like some-body's poured top oil on it, and casin' looked like maybe some petroleum jelly might've been rubbed on it."

Brownie just looked at Lefty, the teensiest grin on his face, then he said, "Well, I hope you cleaned it up. I wouldn't want nobody to slip and fall."

ROAD KILL

. . . This is what I told her:

When I was a small child, my mother read to me from a book called Animals on Parade. *It was my favorite, with bears and elephants two by two, with leopards and camels, mice and ducks. For years thereafter, I would dream of animals parading, great highways of them. And I dreamed of marching along, one hand gripping the small fingers of a raccoon, the other clasping the ebony claws of a crow.*

As I grew older and studied biology, zoology, and evolutionary theory in college, my animal dream deepened. Soon great legions of rats, of bats, of gnats extended beyond vision or memory, toward prehistory; rows of buzzards and lizards and wizards, animals all, extending back to the dawn of time, to a primordial puddle where a mutual and schizophrenic ancestor somehow divided, actualizing its illusion of separate species. And in

my dream, that same single-celled maniac dwelled still within each of us,
constituted our shared biology.

I tried to explain it all to my wife that morning . . .

It's strange. You whiz along at fifteen, maybe twenty miles an hour, eyes squinting ahead, legs pumping, and you don't realize how much you're seeing until after you've seen it. That cat was no more than a sliver of vision, since I was really pumping – head down, butt up – at that point, just over the Copeland Creek bridge on a slight downhill. It might not have registered at all except that it had been knocked completely off the road and lay on the shoulder with its head protruding onto the blacktop bicycle lane, as though it was resting.

A couple of hundred meters down the road I knew it had been a tabby wearing a collar, and still intact. That last may sound like a cruel thing to say, I guess, but when you bicycle everywhere as I do, you get used to seeing road kills, sometimes dismembered by impact or repeated impacts, or flattened like furry Frisbees. When I began commuting on my bike, the sight of dead animals on the road initially shocked me. It was the only place I'd ever see the corpses of animals wild or domestic, and the whole deadly process seemed a terrible invasion of the animals' privacy, and of mine.

At the least, our own separate deaths – that final moment when our shared heritage is least deniable – should somehow remain private, even sacred. But people get used to things, or at least I did, and soon I would slip past the gray ruins of an opossum or the fragrant carcass of a skunk with only the slightest acknowledgment. Only unusual cadavers grasped my attention then: the slim form of a ferret, the askew feathers of a pheasant, the small smear of a skink – those I'd notice.

Aside from the oddly consistent remains of birds looking like feathered teardrops, opossums dominate road kills around here, grinning at eternity like they've played a joke on it. Skunks are second – you smell them a furlong away. Domestic cats are a close third. Gopher snakes, especially in spring, are common. There are a few deer dead on the road each year, and even a few dogs. Once I saw the small, dead, unmarred form of a rubber boa, and it caused me to stop my bike and gaze with unaccounted sorrow at an animal so rare that had lost the long gamble of existence, not to a predator who would use its flesh but to a car driven by a person who probably didn't know boas occurred. During certain times of the year, smashed salamanders and toads can turn bicycle lanes hereabouts into slalom courses.

And, driving to the store a couple of years ago with my little girl in the car, I hit a cat. It leaped from between two parked cars and the wet smack of the impact told me it was dead. In the rearview mirror I saw it thrash for several seconds, then lie still. I didn't want Denise to know what had happened, so I didn't stop – the cat was dead, believe me, I could tell. But I told myself that if it ever happened again, I'd stop.

So after passing that other tabby's body that Monday, I had thought of it for several seconds, registering clearly its unmarred face, its open eyes, and the repose of its body. There had been no dark halo of dried blood; no creamy intestines had lain exposed to the air. Then I returned to the personal problems I had been chewing on that morning and continued my ride to work. It was brisk and I remember thinking how good a cup of tea would feel when I reached the office.

I ride that route to work three times a week: Mondays, Wednesdays, and Fridays. On Tuesdays and Thursdays I travel an alternate course just to break the monotony, and I can't remember even thinking about that dead cat the next day, although I may have passed an opossum or two, their button eyes dull, on my alternate route. I don't give much attention to road kills. My life is so busy that I use the rides as a kind of medita- tion, almost consciously emptying my mind. Many days I've arrived at my office with no memory of having traveled there.

Wednesday I was pumping hard as usual, trying to cleanse myself of thought or worry as I sped north and zinged over the Copeland Creek bridge. That tabby had been completely out of my mind, and I was wheeling so close to the bike lane's margin that I had to swerve to avoid hitting its head and spilling. For a flash my attention captured that furry face as I maneuvered around it and its eyes stared back at me, or seemed to. I eased my tempo. The body had not moved, of that I was certain, but the cat's eyes in that instant had seemed not dull with death but sharp with the familiarity of one creature recognizing another. No, that was nonsense. It was just the way the head was positioned, as though resting, I told myself, but I nevertheless imagined I had even seen an appeal in those eyes. Still, the possibility . . .

A quarter mile down the road I stopped and looked back. There was the small, dark lump on dirt next to the bike lane just this side of the bridge. It was impossible, and I was late for work. The crazy things you think about. But what if it *was* alive, maybe paralyzed, what could I do? I asked myself as I continued toward my office.

Well, I could do nothing but kill it, put it out of its misery, and in so doing discomfort the hell out of myself. I could just picture myself kicking its head as cars whizzed by and drivers gawked. No, thank you. Nonetheless, the remote possibility that the cat might be alive ate at me all the way to work, but was quickly and mercifully forgotten once the day's business began.

You'd think that I would have at some point returned in memory to an event that had troubled me enough to stop my bicycle, but I didn't. In fact, I forgot entirely until Friday as I sped to work and once more was startled by the bright eyes of the motionless tabby. Immediately something lurched in me and I eased the rhythm of my legs. But, of course, if the cat had been dead on Wednesday – or even if it hadn't – it would certainly be dead today, so I squinted and pumped even harder than usual, seeking to submerge my doubt in the effort, but a question blossomed as I drove myself harder and harder, trying to concentrate only on my burning thighs: Why were there no flies?

After a pained instant, the answer comforted me. It was the morning chill. Flies don't appear that early in the morning during the fall – too cold. I accepted that notion, and whatever comfort it contained, until I arrived at work and was swept into my business world.

Each weekend, I take one long bicycle ride – something over fifty miles. My wife laughs and calls it my "postman's holiday," since I ride the bike to work all week, but I really enjoy the workout as well as the scenery of those journeys, which I vary considerably, often driving the car great distances so I can pedal through unfamiliar terrain. Sunday I did something unusual; I decided to pump out past the research institution where I work, then over the mountains east to the next canyon and loop home.

That afternoon, I swung onto the familiar course, riding easily to save my strength for the tough hills ahead. Again, my mind pleasantly empty, I crossed Copeland Creek bridge at a relaxed pace. Then I was alongside the cat, a little startled to see the animal still lying as it had been, and startled too that I had managed to forget it, for this time it was swollen and covered with flies. I stopped my bicycle, returned to the carcass and saw with piercing clarity that the head had moved or been moved slightly, as though something had released and allowed it to roll a degree or two to the side. Its eyes were closed.

For a moment I could only stand there, filling with a grief inchoate yet certain. Ahead the horizon seemed to spread and narrow like a squinting eye, into a final twilight, and my breath began to catch and surge. As I stood over the animal's body, a car slowed and a teenage driver called, "Gee, mister, did your cat get killed?"

"No," I choked, and he gazed at me a moment longer, then pulled away. I walked to the soft soil a few steps from the road and gouged a shallow hole with the heel of my shoe, then pulled the cat's body by its tail to the small grave. I covered it as best I could, then placed rocks over the mound. I did not add flowers, although some yellowish blossoms grew in a ditch nearby.

Instead I climbed back onto my bicycle and turned toward home, pumping harder and harder, trying to deflect questions that rumbled through me. Twice I veered in front of cars, nearly causing accidents, but even the squeal of their brakes didn't touch me. When I walked into the kitchen, my wife smiled over her shoulder and observed, "You're home early. Have trouble?"

I didn't reply.

After a second, she turned to examine me, then asked, "What's wrong?"

I tried to answer but could produce only raw sounds, like an animal drowning in its own blood. "The parade," I finally choked, then I told her . . .

ROMAIN PETTIBONE'S REVENGE

My older sister, Marie, always wanted to play doctor. She was the neighborhood's physician in back rooms and garages and lofts, behind pied bushes and fences and drawn curtains. As her little brother, I was often the patient, and her girlfriends were often attendants, as they poked and probed and squeezed my meager equipment.

Marie, the doctor, took great pleasure in making pronouncements like, "That's where Momma had the doctor cut his nozzle off. That's why it's so little. He can't even have babies when he grows up!"

"Oh, yes, I could!" I insisted.

"Cannot! Boys can't."

"Could too."

The other girls joined in: "Nuh uh! No you can't either."

"See, Romain," grinned Marie.

"I'm telling Mom . . ."

"You gotta be kidding!" interrupted the large lady named Flame. "You've *gotta* be kidding!"

Oh, man! I would get *her* mad at me.

Flame's thick arms, scrolled with tattoos, hung from a sleeveless leather jacket. She wore five rings in each ear, and another glimmered from a pierced nostril. "This is sexist shit!" she thundered. "Are you gonna let him *read* this sexist shit here?"

Having been so rudely halted while presenting my childhood memoir to the creative-writing class, I was stunned and waited for the professor to rescue me. That tweed man suddenly looked like a disoriented duck, so I sank into my seat.

"Well . . ." mumbled the gray-haired professor. He blinked several times and seemed to search the room for help.

The woman was so much bigger than me and so much angrier. "I won't have this *boy* definin' me. I won't be *aborted* by this *boy*." Even her fists were large.

I slunk lower.

No one responded for several moments while the tall, decorated woman glared at me, then a guy named Chad leaned forward and seemed to smile like a serpent as the gold ring he wore in his right ear glinted. He intoned: "Pettibone is like giving offense. He's like reflecting the *patriarchy*, offending Flame. He's like offending *me* too. He's like offending all *progressive* people. What're you going to do about it, Professor Litwack?" Chad tugged his sparse beard as he spoke.

"Ah . . . what exactly do you find offensive?" asked the teacher. He looked like he craved a drink.

"His sister examining him, hah! Who'd examine *him?*" demanded Flame.

Chuckling rippled through the class, but Flame halted it. "What's so funny? Inappropriate laughter gives offense too. What if he was insultin' an African American?"

"Yeah," added Chad. "What if the patriarchy like attacked our righteous black brothers and sisters!"

"Stay out of this," Flame snapped at him.

Zondra, the only black woman in class, agreed. "Flame's right. This is clearly a women's issue, Chad."

"Excuse me," ventured the professor, "but did you say 'Afro' American or 'African' American?" Was he trying to change the subject?

Flame did not laugh. "'Afro' is old," she said patiently. "Just like 'black' is." She glanced briefly at Chad.

"I was afraid of that," admitted the faculty member.

By then I was nearly out of my seat, not up but down, slumped to a mere puddle.

"What're you gonna *do*, Dr. Litwack?" demanded the tattooed woman, and by now Mary Alice, Fay, and Betty had joined Zondra and her. "Yeah, what? Who empowered this little patriarchal, gynophobic, phallocentric *boy* to write about women? Do you endorse this oppression?"

"I like don't," ventured Chad. "I *really* don't."

"Well," hesitated the professor, "I'm certain that Mr. Pettibone didn't mean . . ."

"I'm certain the dean'll be delighted to deal with this *boy!*" asserted Flame. "We've got a code here at San Francisco State to protect women and other ethnic groups from oppression."

Other *ethnic* groups? How did women get to be an ethnic group?

"What about the writing itself?" the professor tried to direct discussion back to the course's ostensible subject.

"Where'd you get that word 'pied,' Romain?" demanded Fay, the self-appointed expert on all technical matters.

"*Webster's Third International Dictionary,*" I snapped. She wasn't much bigger than me.

"Well, it's a dumb word and your writing sucks."

"Thank you for sharing," I replied.

"And you'll notice that this *boy* endorses the patriarchal notion of family that imposes the false notion of heterosexuality on the younger generation. What about that, Dr. Litwack?" demanded Flame.

There were only four men in the class: Chad, me, and two jocks – one black, the other white – who slouched at the back of the room wearing baseball caps backward and, as usual, saying nothing. Chad, the resident Sensitive Male, physically moved his desk away from mine. "Yeah, that stuff's like *real* hurtful, Romain," he said. "It sounds like the *patriarchy!*"

Finally I sat up and said, "Look, I just wrote the paper I was assigned.

All that stuff really happened. It's *you* women who're sexist. Reverse sexism is still sexism. You can write anything you like, but because I'm a guy, I can't!"

At first Flame's biceps bulged and I thought she'd punch me out for sure, but she turned to Zondra and sneered, "Sexist! Us! Hah! There isn't any such thing as 'reverse sexism,' *boy*, because sexism and racism were invented by white males, so *reverse* sexism and *reverse* racism can't exist. They're myths."

"Right on!" agreed Zondra.

Chad was rapidly nodding his scraggly beard. "Like straight shit, sisters," he cooed, "straight shit," and I at least had the pleasure of seeing Flame shoot him a dirty look. Chad blinked, then quickly added, "Especially colored women!"

Now Zondra's eyes snapped at him.

"I mean colored women of color! Women of color!" he quickly recovered. "That's what I *really* meant."

"Ah, perhaps, Pettibone . . ." the professor was saying, but I cut him off.

"This is bullshit! All I did was write what you assigned, an honest memoir. What about the First Amendment in this class?"

"The First Amendment only applies to *proper* perspectives, *boy!*" Flame explained. "We have a code to protect us from harassment and oppression now."

"Protect *you?*" I said.

As I left the Humanities Building that night, the black jock stopped me. "Hey, Pettiboner," he said, "how many feminists does it take to screw in a light bulb?"

I shrugged.

"The answer is 'That's not funny.' "

The two jocks laughed, but I didn't.

My interview with the dean was brief and to the point. "I've read the offending material, Mr. Pettibone," she said. "It doesn't appear to me that you necessarily intended to harass or give offense, but you have to learn to be more sensitive to the feelings of others. Understand that no matter what newspapers say, females and other Third World people still grow up in profoundly oppressive circumstances, so they naturally are sensitive when they feel themselves attacked."

I was genuinely grateful for her moderate tone. "I appreciate that, Dr. Hoover, but all I'm trying to say is that generalizations may or may not be true in individual cases. My sister's a lawyer. She can buy or sell me . . . as she reminds me regularly," I smiled. "She was student body president in high school . . ."

"That section of your essay . . . the part about your sister . . . was particularly disturbing, Mr. Pettibone."

I nodded. "It was troubling to me too, Dr. Hoover. That's why I wrote about it."

The dean stood, walked around her large desk, then leaned on it as she addressed me. "You're an intelligent young man, Mr. Pettibone, and you've got to understand that anecdotes like yours distort the weight of evidence and dilute the devastation that sexual harassment has caused and is causing women and other ethnic groups. It can lead to false consciousness."

False consciousness? I missed the point, I guess, so I said, "I'm not sure I understand why I shouldn't write what really happened."

Dr. Hoover sighed, then an edge entered her voice. "What I'm saying, Mr. Pettibone, is that your truth may not be true. It may be the product of false consciousness because it obscures the larger issue."

"Oh," I nodded. I was finally getting the message – nothing I said in my defense would be significant. Still, I tried one more time. "I'm really not trying to cause problems, Dr. Hoover, and I'm grateful for your patience, but it just seems to me that we're trampling on individual liberty for everyone when one group can create guilt just by claiming to be offended – the accusation becomes the guilty verdict – but members of another group can never be offended no matter what's said or done to them. I mean, it seems to me that the notion of individual liberty is sweeping the whole world right now – all over Eastern Europe, in China . . ."

"What's your point, Mr. Pettibone?" The edge in her voice grew sharper.

"How can anybody be free if others are oppressed – men or women, nonwhite or white?"

Once more, Dr. Hoover sighed. "Don't you recognize that the term 'individual' is racist and sexist? Who's *really* in charge under the guise of 'individual liberty'? White males. We're working toward a more humane, more compassionate collective consciousness here at the university." She walked back around her desk and scrawled something on a large yellow legal pad. "I was going to simply forget this incident, but it seems clear that you'll need to spend a little time in one of the sensitivity sessions mounted by the Women's Studies and Ethnic Studies departments."

Wow, I was thinking, I already feel like I've been mounted. All those 1960s radicals like my mom and her boyfriend couldn't win with Marxism in the streets or at the ballot box, but it sure seemed like they'd worked their way in here. I was lucky I wasn't paraded around campus in a dunce cap with slogans from Chairman Mao tied around my neck.

Well, I laid low for the next couple of weeks, but I did read some stuff in the library that I'd heard Flame and Zondra and the rest refer to in class. Was *that* ever an eye-opener. I really *was* lucky not to have been pilloried and paraded. Fortunately, Flame and Zondra lightened up on me almost right away. One of the jocks made the mistake of opening his mouth, and he said something about "disabled," so he became their focus: "differently abled" and "ableism" were tossed around, and "lookism" was added for good measure. Chad was smart enough not to join in this time because, I suspect, he knew the hulking jock would make *him* "differently abled" if he shot his mouth off.

But I didn't forget the Hitler Youth attack by Flame, Zondra, and the rest of the bigots. I had a plan.

My nemesis was due to present her childhood memories, I knew, and I'd overheard her talking to classmates. Flame was in the class primarily to make everyone else watch what they said . . . or wrote, not to do any writing herself, so she seemed to be trying to finagle a way out of doing the personal memoir assignment. I would help her. First I obtained Flame's telephone number from the student resource center, then I called.

As I had hoped, an answering machine replied: "Hello. Myra, Jane, Ashley, and Flame aren't in. After the long beep, leave your message and we'll get back to you." Beeeeeep!

Disguising my voice, I announced: "This is the English Department.

Professor Litwack's creative-writing class has been canceled this week. It will meet next week at the usual time. Thank you."

Stage two was to type up a brief memoir and put Flame's name on it.

My mother was short. My father was tall. He took advantage of her height to embarrass her. One day when I was little we were driving along Highway 99 and a song called 'As Time Goes By' came on the radio. He said it was his favorite one, and he pulled the car over to the side of the road, got out, and then opened Momma's door. He took her hands and pulled her out of the car and began dancing with her there on the side of the road while the radio played. Momma laughed and laughed, but I felt so sorry for her.

Drivers of cars passing by honked and waved, and Momma was laughing, but I could tell she was so humiliated. My sisters and me hid ourselves in the backseat until the song finally ended and they at last stopped dancing. We looked up and he was kissing her right there in front of everyone – imposed himself on her in a kind of public rape, and she was so intimidated that she smiled and kissed him back.

He was crazy. And mean too.

He could be real mean. If my sisters and me asked him to stop at one of the Big Oranges along the road, he'd say no, that he was going to make us each a pine float when we got home. Then, when we got there, he'd float a toothpick in a glass of water. That was the famous pine float.

One Easter he gave us pet bunnies. They were so cute. He barbecued them that Labor Day. That's how mean he was. Poor Momma. Poor us.

I attached a note, ostensibly from Flame, explaining that she was ill but would still like her paper critiqued by the class, then I put it in Professor Litwack's mailbox.

The following Tuesday, after we had read "Flame's" essay, no one seemed willing to speak up, so the professor finally observed, "That scene of the mother and father dancing alongside the road was delightful and original, don't you think? A little gem."

"I suppose the public humiliation of a woman might appeal to some men," said Zondra, and I thought I heard Dr. Litwack groan.

"What do you think, Mr. Torrelli?" asked the professor, clearly trying to avoid Zondra's path.

Chad looked around. He was a counterpuncher, not a leader, so this role was threatening to him. "Well . . . ah . . . I . . . ah . . . appreciate that she like reveals the . . . the *heightism* her family like suffered. I mean . . . ah . . . like her mother was real short."

Ah! My opening. As the shortest person in the class, I was ready. "Short!" I shouted. "Short! Don't you mean *vertically challenged*, Chad?"

"Yes," added Fay, none too lofty herself, "vertically challenged, Chad."

I heard the two jocks chuckle, and I added, "That's a *very* oppressive thing for you to say, Chad. And a hurtful thing for Flame to have written. Maybe the dean should be alerted to this."

Zondra, saying nothing, stared at me.

"Oppressive . . . ," stammered Chad. "Oppressive! I can't be oppressive. The patriarchy *is* oppression!" he declared and glanced around for support from the women.

"Wait a minute!" I demanded. "What's this patriarchy you're always talking about? Isn't it white males? You're a white guy, Chad, or had you forgotten?"

"Yeah . . . yeah . . . but I'm not the patriarchy because I'm . . . I'm in touch with the woman within!"

"I think you're in touch with the nitwit within," I snapped, and the whole class broke up, even nervous Professor Litwack.

"Nitwit!" Chad protested. "Nitwit!"

Everyone ignored him.

"Well, Mr. Pettibone . . ." said the prof, still chuckling.

"Flame can certainly say 'short,'" Betty interjected. "She's not trying to preserve the supremacy of tall white heterosexual males. They're the only ones who misuse language, who *can* misuse it."

Chad said nothing.

"As an ethnic group," I asserted, "we vertically challenged people are often ignored. It's a very hurtful form of harassment."

No one commented, but I thought Zondra's eyes were twinkling.

"She did say 'pet,' though, instead of 'animal companion,'" pointed out Mary Alice.

"Speciesism," I snapped.

Zondra was still staring at me. She knew. Oh, well, too late now.

"Flame *can't* be guilty of speciesism. She was just showing herself using the words back when they were imposed on her when she was little," suggested Betty. "She'd *never* say 'pet' today."

"Well . . . maybe so," agreed Mary Alice.

"What's a white male like you think, Chad?" I asked.

He squirmed, then sat straight. "Hey, I'm like an ethnic minority too. I'm like bisexual."

"Say, Romain," I heard Zondra's husky voice call. "What about the writing? Do you like the writing?"

"It's very effective." What else could I say without getting into trouble?

Fay had no reservations. "I think it's *real* good. Real revealing. It just shows that you have to suffer to write truth, that's why guys can't write good – the male power structure."

"I'm like bisexual," interjected Chad, his confidence rebuilding.

"She does use accusative pronouns in nominative positions," pointed out Professor Litwack.

"Perhaps from a white male perspective," snapped Fay. "Women're breaking that oppression, creating a new syntax of honesty."

"It still sounds like poor grammar to me," said the professor. "Not *gravely* poor, of course," he quickly added.

"Yes, it *would*, wouldn't it?" Fay responded.

Zondra still gazed at me. "What do you think, Romain?"

"I think Flame's in a whole 'nother space."

"For sure," agreed Zondra, grinning at last.

Then I added for the class to hear, "She sure devastates the patriarchal notion of family, doesn't she?"

"Oh, she *does*," agreed Mary Alice, "and that's the biggest rip-off of the whole male-imposed heterosexual conspiracy."

"I'm like bisexual," Chad said.

"We *heard* that before, chump," growled Zondra.

"Yeah, chump," I added.

Then the classroom door burst open, and Flame stood there for a moment, hands on her hips, decorated arms flexing. All eyes snapped toward her as she said, "Well."

My heart sank.

"We've just been discussing your essay, Ms. Leibowitz," explained Professor Litwack.

"You have?"

"Yes, and the consensus has been quite positive."

"It has?"

"I didn't know you were such a good writer," said Zondra.

"It's quite promising," Dr. Litwack smiled. He seemed relieved to have so positive a greeting for her.

"What exactly did I have to say?" Flame asked, her tone surprisingly moderate.

"I like the part about your father the best," Chad offered.

"My *father?*"

"What he did to your mother," Mary Alice added.

"What'd he do?"

Zondra began chuckling. "He was bad," she said, "a *bad* dude."

"Yeah, he was," agreed Flame. "He was pathetic, in fact."

Ah, the old Flame was back. For a moment, I thought she'd slipped into humanity. But I said nothing. This wasn't going the way I'd planned.

"His like heightism," offered Chad.

"He was a sawed-off little dude," said Flame.

"Vertically challenged?" asked Chad.

"Short as a toadstool, *boy.*"

"Oh . . ." choked Chad, "like short."

Professor Litwack glanced at his watch, then announced, "It's time for our break. May I see you for a moment, Ms. Leibowitz?"

The rest of us repaired to the hallway or rest rooms, the smokers wandering outside. Zondra called me as soon as I left the room. "Say, Romain!"

"What?"

"She's gonna find out."

I shrugged. "Find out what?"

"She's gonna find out and when she does, you're meat."

"Hey, Zondra, I don't know what you're talking about."

The black woman only smiled. "Okay," she said. "But she's still gonna find out."

I turned and slowly walked toward the men's room, hoping to reach it before Flame left the classroom. Just as I pushed the door open, I heard that voice: "Where's Romain?"

I didn't even pause to wash my hands but pushed open the far window and eased out. I walked rapidly across the large quad toward the parking lot on the west side of campus, glancing over my shoulder frequently. Just as I reached the student union I saw them, a mob of females pouring from the humanities building with a tall, sleeveless figure in the lead.

Oh, damn! I began to lope, passing the gym, the R.O.T.C. building, the crumbling education hall. But when I looked back, the mob was closer and there were more of them, enraged women seeming to emerge from each structure to join Flame's pursuit: fat and thin, tall and short, young and old, black and white, brown and yellow, red and . . . was that *the dean* I saw dashing from the administration building to join the vigilantes? Was that *the dean* who was carrying a rope?

I sprinted then – knees up, arms pumping – right past my car because I had no time to get in, start it, and drive away. Pulling hard, I circled back toward the football stadium, where I might be able to escape among the trees, but the feminists were closing on me as my legs thickened. I hit my afterburners and managed to accelerate once more, but I could sense Flame, huge as an eagle, swooping toward me.

I could feel . . . or almost feel . . . her breath, all their breaths, and I was getting in *real* close touch with the chicken within.

Helllllllllllllllllllllllllllllllllllllllllllllllllllllllllllp!

SCUFFLIN'

for Bob Young

'Mind me of a story: This Eye-talian, this Jew, and this colored boy, they killed in a wreck, you know, so they go up to Heaven and St. Pete he say, "You better *have* you some money to get in here. You better have you ten thousand dollars." Now them three they just scuffle to stay alive, you know, and they ain' got no bread. That Eye-talian he start cryin' and carryin' on, so St. Pete he let him in. Then the Jew he start barginin' – "Will you take seventy-five hundred?" – till he wear ol' St. Pete out, you know, and Pete he let him in, too. Finally, St. Pete he look around for the brothah but he can't see him nowheres, so he ax this angel, "Where that black boy go? Might as well let him in too." Angel he say, "You gon' have to find him you'self. He out lookin' fo' a co-signer."

Get it?

'Mind me of the time that little white hooker come in my liquor sto'. She park a bad Continental out front, you know, and she ax can she use my telephone. I know she gon' make a contact, that's why she ain' usin' no phone on the street, so I say, "Sho, baby, but I be a bu'iness man, you know, just scufflin' to get along. It gon' cost you." Now she a sweet-lookin' little thing, Jim. *Sweet.* When she say to me, "I'm a woman," and wiggle that tight little ass, I damn near gives in. But I say, "I *got* me a woman at home, and this be bu'iness, baby. We talkin' money."

Little who' she smile and say, "Doc, you the smartest man I met down here." She use my phone and, you know, after a while a cab come by and pick her up and she leave her bad hog at my place. When she come back, she give me fifty dollars cash money. And she keep comin' in, usin' my phone and pretty soon we gets tight and she give me the money *and* the booty. Get it? You take care of bu'iness, bu'iness take care of you.

Some dudes on the street, you know, they come in and borrow a little gamblin' money from me. I don' make no big loans – too easy to get caught doin' that – but I lets a cat have a dollar for a dollar-and-a-half, and they always pays me back. Folks know they got me if they needs some bread, no references. So they pay me soon as they can, you know. Not many problems when you take care of bu'iness. 'Mind me of the time this boy come in and say he need two hundred dollars. I say, "Man, you don' need no two hundred. That cost you too much: hundred skins a month. I don' hold no long paper."

He say, "Got to have it, Doc. Jew Baby gon' sell me a bad Bonneville for two hundred down and twenty a month."

"Twenty a month fo' *how* long?"

"Five years."

"*Five years!*" I say. "Man, that's a rip-off. Don' let no Jew Baby talk you into that."

"Hey, man," he say, "you *got* you a car. You got you a Caddy. I got to have me some wheels too, man. *Got to.* Jew Baby put me in some wheels for two hundred."

I say, "Looky here, Richard" – his name Richard – "looky here, when the dude give you one of those dollar-down-dollar-till-you-die deals, you got to *die*, man, to end it. Get it?"

"I needs my wheels, man," all the boy say. "I got me a family, man. Got to have my wheels."

Well, the boy never leave me sho't befo', and he be workin' steady, you know, so I goes against my judgment, but I tells him make sure the car cold – get it? – then see will Jew Baby take three bills cash. He come back and say Jew Baby take fo' hundred. I say, "The mothahfuckah take three-twenty or he better not show his white ass in this neighborhood no mo'." Richard laugh, then he go see will Jew Baby take three-twenty. Jew Baby, he ain' no fool. He take the three-twenty and Richard get a hog.

The mothahfuckah turn out to be hot. Jew Baby just change plates, he don' even file the serial number, so my man, Richard, you know, he drivin hot. Then I knows why Jew Baby give in so easy. "Richard," I say, "I tol' you the hog no good if it ain' cold."

"Jew Baby say it cold."

"The mothahfuckah *say* it cold?"

"That's what he say." Richard low, man, low as a snake's balls. He can't drive his hog, you know, and he in debt up to his ass.

I thinks for a minute, then I figure, what the fuck, man. Got to teach Jew Baby to treat people right, you know, if he want to work the 'hood. Hate to get into it, but I got to. "Where the mothahfuckah stay, man, that shootin' gallery on Fifth?"

"Yeah."

"And he still keep those two gray punks to guard him?"

"Yeah."

"All right, brothah," I say, "go home and get clean, clean like a mothah-fuckah, then come back here with yo' Bonneville. We gon' visit Mr. Jew Baby." I don' tell Richard, but he got to be clean, you know, so nobody get killed. You start some shit dressed all funky, dude kill you in a minute. You come on clean, dude got to think. Anytime I raise sand, I get clean. My five-hundred-dollar suit say you ain' dealin' with some street bloods, Jim, you dealin' with trouble. Get it? When you scuffle to live, you learns the edges.

I tells my clerk to watch the sto', then I calls in some tabs – these three big brothahs name Harold and Skeets and Tyrone, you know, they join me. They happy to pay off, so when Richard get back, I tell him to follow my Cadillac to the shootin' gallery. Now when you sees four black dudes in three-piece suits drivin' through this part of town in the middle of the day, man, ain' but two things they can be: cops or trouble. Lots of eyes follow us, you know, and they all happy when we slide on past 'em.

Like I figure, Jew Baby's punks don' give us no shit when we gets there. They back off and look at my mens and don' say shit. Good thing, too, cause I knows Tyrone carryin' – Tyrone *always* carryin' – and I believe Harold and Skeets carryin' too. I walks right up to Jew Baby and gets in his face. "Why you sell my man a hot car?" I ax.

J.B. he look, you know, real sleepy like always. "Nobody made the nigger buy it. He got what he wanted." I start to answer, but Jew Baby he cut me off: "You don' wanna mess in this, Doc. It ain't your business. People get hurt when they mess in other people's business."

"Looky here, Jew Baby," I say, "don' threaten me. Don' say shit to me. I *cut* yo' mothahfuckin' ass, mothahfuckah. And if you don' want yo' mothahfuckin' tongue on the flo', don' never call nobody nigger. Bloods decide who be a nigger. Don' need no offay punk to say shit." The cat, you know, he make me hot and I be fingerin' my steel. I keeps a .357 in my sto', but I carries a blade and I be cuttin' dudes before any Jew Baby born. He damn near in the 'mergency room, man, whether he know it or not. "Don' say 'nigger' to me never no mo'," I warns the mothahfuckah.

"I got friends downtown," Jew Baby say.

"Dead mens don' got no friends, mothahfuckah, 'cept the mothah-fuckin' undertaker," I tells him.

He stand there, not movin'. I know he carry a piece, but he know I can cut him and I got four dudes with me. He also know he fuck up when he call Richard nigger. From outside on the street I hear two mens holler at each other. Winos. "Well?" I say.

Jew Baby, he reach into his pocket and peel bills off his roll. He hand me three-twenty. "I want a receipt," he say.

"Give the mothahfuckah his keys," I tells Richard. He toss 'em to the white dude. "That yo' receipt," I say. "Now I gives you some advice. Number one, do not never make me come down here no mo'. Number two, do not never threaten me or my mens again. Number three, if you wants to work down here, you got to give somethin' back. You got to give people some respec', man, don' be callin' nobody no nigger and takin' they money. You can make you a buck-and-a-half on a buck if you gives somethin' back. Most these folks just scufflin', man. You still make money and you make friends. But if you sell hogs hot, you know, and tells lies and rips peoples off, you dead. I don' have to kill you, mothahfuckah, 'cause the street kill you. Get it?"

When we leave I takes the boys to Smokey's Bar-B-Que and buy some good hot links, and I tells Richard if he learn his lesson, he don' owe me no interest. Richard he say, "Doc, you the man. Next time I listen." Well, I likes that, you know. I likes a young man can learn. But this the last time. He got to pull himself out the shit if he get in it again. We feelin' loose so we get to jivin' and Skeets he say he hear Jew Baby a punk. "Don't surprise me none," I tell him. "He don' straighten his act out, he be a *dead* punk." And he were, just a year or so later, pigs find his body in the alley behind the shootin' gallery. Some dudes, you know, never learn.

'Minds me of ol' Happy. He a white cat stay down here in the lot next to my sto'. Dudes got some ol' couches, you know, and chairs there and they play a little whis', some coon can, some bones. Drink a little pluck. Hap the onliest gray dude stay there all these years. At first some young bloods, you know, rough him up, but Hap he fight back good for a dude without no legs. And when these kids steal his wheelchair, you know, I go gets it for him. I tell 'em, "Boys, the man got guts. Give him a chance. Don' make me come back no mo'." They young, but they smart. They leave Hap alone after that.

Well, Hap he ain' like no Jew Baby. He live on that lot, you know, and he sleep on cardboard boxes with the colored winos and he share his little short dogs and his big long dogs with 'em, drink from the same bottle. He scuffle down to the Union Mission every day for his vittles, then back he come to the lot. He never play no games – all the bread he snag go to wine – but he hang around, you know, and joke and give other dudes a taste. He never come in here axin' for nothin' free, but I slips him a taste from time to time, and I ain' lettin' him go a day without eatin'. If he broke and in bad shape, you know, I hires him to keep an eye on things a while. Last winter I give him a poncho that fit over his chair for when it rain so bad.

And Hap a heavy cat, too. He say some deep shit, man. He not like all those fools hang around talkin' to theyselves, lookin' through they eyebrows waitin' to kill somebody – mumblin', mumblin'. All them dudes they let outta nuthouses, you know, they too crazy to be afraid. When they jumps you, you got to kill 'em. Anyway, Hap he a stone wino, but heavy.

One day I tells him I don' drink and I don' force nobody to buy, but liquor, you know, my bu'iness. I been feelin' a little low that day, man, 'cause some cat call me a booze pusher and I don' dig no kind of pushers. Hap smile and he say, "You a friend to me, Doc. I know it's hard being friendly to drunks. We don't think sensible. I could be in a veterans' hospital right now, but they won't let me drink. I'm a alcoholic, out and out. I'd rather be on the street drunk than in the hospital dry. I want my freedom, and that means my freedom to drink. You never forced nothing on me."

"I never know you a vet, Hap. You lose you legs in the war?" I ax.

"No, I come home whole. But I got in this car crash right afterwards – I was drunk – and ended up like this. My own fault."

"How come you to stay here?"

"Don't take offense, Doc, but when you're crippled and an alcoholic, you feel comfortable with niggers. You know a little bit about all they been through."

I think about it a minute, you know, and decide he one white dude can say 'nigger' to me. I say, "I 'preciate that, Hap, but don' it get lonely, man?"

He look away and say, "Yeah, sometimes. Sometimes. But I ain't complaining. Life's *supposed* to be tough. Jesus could only redeem us *after* his suffering, right?"

"You right," I answer, marvelin' at what Hap just say. He heavy. "You sho' right. It's got to be sufferin' in this worl'," I say.

Life get tougher for ol' Hap d'rectly because two of those mumblin' mothahfuckahs kill him and steal his wheelchair. They take his coat, too, and his poncho, and they leave him behind one of the couches. I find him next mornin', you know, all cold, all alone, and he look real small, almost like a little baby child there without no legs. Pigs catch them two mumblers right away, and they put 'em back in the nuthouse where they belongs, but the mothahfuckahs out again now. They stays away from here, though, because somebody cut 'em if they come back. They crazy, not stupid. A good ol' dude, Hap, and heavy. Best white cat I ever know. Onliest one, you know, that understand what it all about.

'Mind me of a story ol' Moms Mabley tell. Moms say this white dude and this brothah arrested for killin' and sentenced to get hung. Well, come close to hangin' time and the white boy, you know, he cryin' and beggin' and carryin' on. Finally, the brothah he say, "Act like a man and stop all that bawlin'. Why don' you straighten up, man?" White dude he wipe his tears and answer real hot: "Easy for you to say. You *used* to it."

Get it?

HIS WAYS ARE MYSTER'OUS

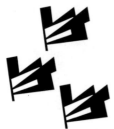

      Glendon was gazing toward the Tehachapi Mountains after having begun irrigating that morning when, with a sudden grip of recognition, he realized that it wasn't a sunrise he was watching at all, it was God Hisself revealed in His Golden Splendor just to him. "Thou art my Prophet," he heard a voice boom. "Preach my gospel. Convert sinners. Take wives unto thyself. I wilt send thou Signs." The young man's thin knees buckled, and he collapsed like a drunkard's dreams.

    When he came to, he found himself sprawled on a dirt bank next to the irrigation ditch, his shovel beside him, his billed cap knocked askew. The sun was over the mountains, and an unfamiliar lightness buoyed his body. "I cain't believe it," he whistled through his teeth as he straightened his cap. He had never been an especially religious person, although he had been marched to Sunday School throughout his childhood, so he could not understand why he had been Chose. His Ways Are Myster'ous, Glendon had often heard the preacher at the Free Will Gospel Church of God in Christ say, and it was true. It was surely true. Rising, he bathed his face in the clear water gurgling through the ditch, then turned toward the house. "I just cain't hardly believe it," he repeated.

In the bunkhouse kitchen that morning, he poured himself a cup of coffee and sat at the table, still trying to understand the Miracle that had occurred. The radio was blaring country music, but it now sounded profane, not entertaining, just as everything around him looked dull after the Grandeur he had witnessed. He said nothing, and finally Mrs. Watson, who was cooking, commented, "You're mighty quiet this mornin', Glendon."

How could he tell her? He sighed then announced, "I seen God a while ago."

"Sure you did, honey," replied the older woman without turning. "Want some grits with them eggs?"

"I really seen Him. I had me one a them revelation deals."

"Sure you did," agreed Mrs. Watson, plopping two fried eggs like the greasy eyes of a hanged man onto his plate.

Glendon stared at the eggs – were they a Sign? – then at the woman's broad back. "I'll take some a them grits, please," he said, having decided to disclose no more about his Mission, not right now at least. He had not been told to announce his prophecy yet, so he decided to wait for another Sign.

A moment later the other two irrigators, Manuel and J.R., strode into the room, poured themselves coffee, then scooted up to the table. "How they hangin', Glendon?" grinned J.R. The Prophet winced at the implied profanity, and J.R. seemed to interpret his expression as a greeting.

"Ola, Flaco," grinned Manuel.

"Say, Miz Watson, you sweet thang," called J.R., "when you gonna break down and step out with me?" He winked at Glendon and Manuel. He was a rough cob, J.R., and a womanizer, who seemed to take pleasure in pushing others. Glendon was always uncomfortable around him and his aggressive, mocking ways.

"When I get that desperate," the elderly woman parried without turning, "it'll be time to put me in one a them old folks' homes."

The irrigators laughed, but Glendon remained silent. What would be the next Sign, when would it come?

"Que paso, Flaco?" asked Manuel.

"Oh, nothin', but I'm gonna take some wives unto myself."

J.R.'s brows raised. "Say what? *Unto* yourself."

"Some *wives?*" asked Manuel, smiling.

Glendon nodded. Maybe he shouldn't have told them.

"Well, I hope they're better'n that warthog you took unto the dance last Saturday," grinned J.R., who always seemed to accompany the prettiest ladies.

No, he shouldn't have told them. They weren't ready. He'd wait for a Sign. Just as he finished eating, Mrs. Watson said, "When you're done, honey, I got a grocery list for you. Take the pickup into Arvin."

Becoming a Prophet had not lessened Glendon's appetite. He engulfed a second serving of biscuits laden with bacon gravy. "I swan," clucked Mrs. Watson, "if you don't eat for two, and slim as you are! If I's to eat like you, I'd weigh a ton."

"Instead of half a ton," whispered J.R., and Manuel nearly fell off his chair.

Not dignifying the remark with so much as a smile, Glendon stood. "Well, I gotta go get them groceries so's I can be back in time to change my water," he announced, letting J.R. know that he would have nothing to do with such comments. Taking the pickup's key from its hook, Glendon moved with detached dignity, his eyes scanning for a Sign.

"What's wrong with him?" he heard J.R. whisper to Manuel.

After a pause, Manuel replied, "Loco in the cabeza," and they both laughed.

"Leave the boy be!" hissed Mrs. Watson, and the two men quieted, still grinning at one another, while Glendon climbed – slowly and gracefully as a Prophet should – into the battered truck and clattered away toward town.

His market cart was loaded with supplies when he approached the checkstand and, as usual, picked up a copy of the *Enquirer* to scan while he waited for the clerk to check his groceries. The headline immediately leaped at him and he all but staggered; he didn't know what it meant, but it was clearly a Sign: "SIAMESE TWINS FACE FIRING SQUAD. One

Brother Guilty of Murder." It was like they were the only words on the page; all the other print could have been gibberish. His chest tightened and he gasped.

"You buyin' that paper or rentin' it?" asked the clerk.

"I'll take it," the Prophet replied huskily. Even his voice was changing, he sensed, deepening in response to his new role. "Did you read that deal about them two brothers that're stuck together and one's gonna get shot?"

"Huh?" the lady replied, not looking up.

"Well, they're just like me and you, stuck unto sin." The words came out of him without thought, as though some Greater Voice spoke through him.

"Thirty-seven eighty-eight," she said with a tired smile.

"Verily I say unto you . . ." the Voice spoke through him.

"There's other people waitin'." The woman's eyes narrowed and so did her tone.

"Oh," Glendon said. He paid quickly and carried the groceries out to the pickup, then hurried back to the ranch. He would teach them, all of them. He would spread the Word.

As soon as he had arrived and unloaded the groceries, Glendon hurried to his cabin, where he read and reread the mystical article, the Sign. Finally, remembering that he had to change the water on the sugar beets, he stood and headed for the door. On his way out, he spied something moving on the brass doorknob that the boss had installed when he had lived in this very cabin years before, and that Glendon kept polished. Squatting and squinting, he realized that it wasn't a bug as he suspected, but a curved reflection of his own angular form, yet there was more: next to him, attached like a swerved shadow, was a dim being, ominous and vaporous. He recoiled and swatted at it, but hit nothing; it was incorporeal and could not even be seen except in the polished brass.

Staring at the image once more, he noted that a tiny wizened face stared back at him, and that the thing itself was small, just the vestige of an evil twin – and that, Glendon realized, was why he had been Chose; he had his own evil twin under control, squeezed down to a nub. The evil face in the doorknob was surely the next Sign: folks're all stuck unto sin just like the mystical voice at the grocery store had said, and they gotta get shed of it to enter the Kingdom. He, Glendon Leroy Stone, had been Chose to spread the Message because His Ways Are Myster'ous, His Wonders to Behold. Glendon beheld himself and his pitifully shrunken evil twin once more in the knob, then hurried to the sugar beet field.

At lunch the Prophet kept his Message to himself because J.R. would make a joke out of anything. He realized that he should start converting the people nearest him before Spreading the Word, but couldn't figure how to avoid J.R.'s sharp and taunting tongue, so he sat tensely at the table, barely able to finish his second helping of chicken and dumplings, when J.R. suddenly jumped up and exclaimed: "Hell's bells! I forgot the water on the milo!" then sprinted out the door, leaving Glendon and Manuel alone at the table. His Ways Are Myster'ous.

The Prophet immediately faced the remaining irrigator and asked: "Do you believe on the Lord Jesus Christ?"

Manuel, whose mouth was full, mushed, "Humph?"

"Have you been washed in the Blood of the Sheep?"

"You mean the Lamb?" Manuel asked.

"The Lamb?"

"Hey," Manuel said, "I been baptized. I been confirmed. I go to Mass every Sunday. How 'bout you, ese, I never see you goin' to church."

Glendon did not dignify Manuel's smirk with a reply: He had been Chose and that was that. Then the Voice spoke through him: "Verily I say unto you, we are all born as twins, Good and Evil, stuck unto one another, and to enter unto the Kingdom, we gotta get rid of the Evil half."

"What?"

"The only guy born without this evil twin deal was Jesus Hisself!"

Manuel's brows knitted and he put his fork down. After a long pause, he asked, "What about the Blessed Virgin Mary?"

For a moment the table was silent, then Glendon responded: "She wasn't a guy."

Something in Manuel's eyes changed as he agreed, "That's right, she wasn't."

Glendon felt Manuel's gaze, felt it as he never had before. There was something new in it, something like respect. "Ain't you never felt the dark take you over, like whenever you're drinkin' beer or whenever you're with a woman? Ain't you never just been *took* unto sin?"

Manuel's gaze appeared troubled. "Maybe," he conceded.

"Well, that's whenever your bad twin's takin' over, and if your twin goes to hell, *you go too because you're attached.*"

"Where'd you hear all that?" Manuel's voice cracked, and within Glendon something swelled. The other man's eyes were troubled and, for the first time in his life, Glendon felt as though he had the power to influence someone else's mind: the Power of God Revealed.

The Prophet stood, feeling stronger than he ever had, carried his dishes to the sink, then strode to the door, calling over his shoulder, "Believe on the Lord."

"I do," he heard Manuel stammer. "Swear to God, I do."

If he did, J.R. didn't. "What's this religion deal ol' Manuel's tellin' me about?" he demanded at breakfast the following morning.

"Well, I'm fixin' to preach the gospel," Glendon stammered, not wanting to face the other man's disdainful eyes.

"You?"

"I been Called," Glendon mumbled.

"Oh, yeah," grinned J.R., and even Manuel smiled. It was clear that J.R.'s evil twin had took over.

For a moment, the table was silent except for the smack of meat being chewed, and Glendon felt their gaze heavy on his hot face. Finally he glanced up and, just as he did, J.R. stood with an odd expression on his face. He said nothing, but pointed at his gaping mouth, then dashed to the sink and tried without success to drink. He began hitting his own chest, his eyes all the while panning wildly around him.

"Hey, he's chokin'!" Manuel said, and he jumped up and began pounding the other man's back.

Mrs. Watson emerged from the pantry and asked, "What's wrong?"

J.R.'s face was darkening and he began swinging his arms like a man in a fight. Manuel ducked, calling, "Hey!"

Not knowing what else to do, the Prophet rose and, fearing that J.R. might accidentally hit Mrs. Watson, he moved behind the choking man and grabbed him, firmly pinning his arms. When he squeezed, J.R. made a coughing sound and a bullet of beef shot from his mouth. He collapsed in Glendon's grasp.

"Oh, God! Thanks, Glendon," J.R. finally gasped after being helped into a chair. "You saved my damn life! You saved my life!"

The Prophet stood there comforting the toughest guy he'd ever known, and through his head one message passed and passed again: His Ways Are Myster'ous.

"Don't thank me," he told the relieved man, "thank God. It was Him give me the Power." He had not only squeezed the chunk of beef from J.R., he had given the man's evil twin a good crushing too.

"I'll do it," J.R. assured him. "I'll surely do it."

Glendon noticed how the other man was looking at him, the obvious admiration, and he noticed that Manuel said nothing. He realized that he had brought into the Fold the two worst sinners he knew, maybe the two worst in Kern County. Why, the devil was easy to beat when you were Called; there was nothing to it. And he could tell that Mrs. Watson, a good Christian woman, now understood his Mission. She placed one hand on his arm and said, "That was a wonderful thing you done, honey. You'll have the highest seat in Heaven."

Well, maybe he *would*, Glendon realized, maybe he just would, but to earn it he would have to take his message to the World, show them his perfection as a kind of model deal. As he shoveled mud from rows that day, and patched up leaking ditches, he considered how he would begin spreading the Word. He had, of course, seen *Watchtower* sellers lining Arvin's corners on early mornings, all dressed up and grinning like street whores. They chose the right places, but they just *stood* there. Glendon would do them one better.

He dressed Sunday morning in his almost-new J. C. Penney suit. His boots were polished and he wore a necktie Mrs. Watson had given him for Christmas. He splashed on plenty of aftershave too. When he walked to the kitchen to fetch the key for the pickup, which he had permission to use, J.R. called, "This ol' boy smells like a French cathouse. Watch out, women!"

"You oughta be goin' to church with Manuel," the Prophet advised.

"Sure," grinned J.R.

No doubt about it, Glendon admitted, J.R.'s evil twin had took back over. He wouldn't be grinning if that meat was still stuck in his throat. Well, today the Prophet had other tasks, but he would save that sinner once and for all, and soon.

In town, Glendon stationed himself on the corner of Bear Mountain

Road and School Street, where most churchgoers would have to pass, as would the early-morning beer bar habitués. He stood quietly, hands clasped behind his back, waiting. Two small Mexican children, a boy and a girl holding hands, passed on their way to the Catholic church. "Do you believe on the Lord?" he asked with a smile. They glanced at him, then hurried on without replying.

Before the Prophet could become discouraged, a disheveled man approached walking in the opposite direction – heading, Glendon guessed, for that row of beer bars known locally as Tiger Town. Here was a sinner if ever he had seen one, the evil twin practically obliterating whatever remained of the good one. "Have you been washed in the Blood of the Lamb?" Glendon demanded. He could not mince words with sinners.

"Huh?" The thin man wore an old baseball cap at an askew angle with its bill pushed up so that he resembled in profile a duck with a broken neck.

"Have you been washed in the Blood of the Lamb?"

The man's rosy eyes seemed to throb as he examined the Prophet. "I ain't even had a shower. You can't loan a guy a buck for breakfast can you, pal?"

The old boy looked vaguely familiar; perhaps Glendon had once worked with him. In any case, he wasn't giving money away. In fact, he might just *collect* some like those TV preachers did, an idea he had been playing with. Feed the Hungry flashed into the Prophet's mind just as he started to say no. He realized that he was being Tested: His Ways Are Myster'ous. "You mean you haven't eat?"

"Not for days, pal."

"Well . . . here." He handed the man one of the trio of dollar bills he carried. "You *do* believe on the Lord, don't you?" he asked, but the man was already shuffling away.

"Sure thing," Glendon heard the unkempt man call over his shoulder, duck's bill bobbing toward Tiger Town.

Uncomfortably, the Prophet watched his dollar clutched in the man's hand disappear into the doorway of the Nogales Saloon. He wasn't certain they served breakfast there, unless the man favored pickled eggs and beer nuts, so Glendon continued staring at the distant doorway, half expecting the man to emerge in a halo of light and raise his hands toward Heaven in thanks for his meal. He knew this had to be a Sign, not one of those drunk-begging-money deals. All he saw, however, was two more men – one well dressed and wearing a vast white Stetson, the other bareheaded and tattered – slip inside the doorway. He was tempted to walk right down there and challenge those sinners, even if they were only eating breakfast, when he felt a tug at his sleeve.

He turned and faced a pale young woman – not much more than a girl – dressed in a green gown, who extended a rose wrapped in wax paper. "Peace, my brother," she murmured, smiling gently. "Won't you buy a flower for God's love?"

"A flower?" Maybe this was a Sign too.

"For God's love."

"Well, I been washed in the Blood of the Lamb."

"Won't you buy a flower?"

"How much?"

"God sets no price. Your love offering will suffice." She was a very pretty lady – her evil twin didn't show at all – and Glendon had not forgotten that he was to take wives unto hisself, so he withdrew a second dollar bill and handed it to her, then accepted the flower.

"Thank you, my brother." She touched his arm tenderly. "You are standing alone. Do you wish company and joy?"

"Well, I been washed . . ."

"Why don't you come with me to meet God on earth, the Bagwan Dawn Mahwa who has come to release life's love."

"Well, I been . . ."

Her grip on his arm tightened, and she pulled him. He noticed then other green gowns stalking the streets, several with people in tow. "Come my brother, to the earthly paradise where all is love and no needs go wanting."

Glendon jerked his arm free. "Hey," he said, "I don't think you believe on the Lord Jesus."

"He was a great teacher, like the Bagwan Dawn Mahwa who has succeeded him. Come to the new paradise. Join us. Join us." Again she gripped his arm.

"This ain't one a them *goo-roo* deals, is it?" he demanded.

Although the girl had given no visible signal, Glendon could see three other green gowns heading purposefully in his direction, and he sensed that they were reinforcements, so he hustled away after freeing himself from her grip, away toward Tiger Town where he thought she was not likely to follow. As he passed the Nogales Saloon, he heard harsh laughter and another girl in one of the green gowns fled, red-faced, out the door. "Where you goin', baby?" he heard a rough masculine voice call after her.

It's all different kind of sinners, he told himself as he stopped just beyond the saloon.

Glancing down the street, he noted that four green gowns were now heading in his direction, while one was scurrying the other way. Well, he knew a haven when he saw it, so he dashed into the Nogales's darkened interior and hurried to the bar's far end, then slid next to a guy – the same one with a crooked cap, the Prophet realized immediately – who was drinking his breakfast and, as it turned out, Glendon's dollar. Well, at least the old boy might keep them goo-roo deals away, the Prophet figured.

The red-eyed man turned and asked, "You ain't got a smoke, do you, pal?" He seemed unperturbed to find his benefactor seated next to him.

"I already *give* you a buck," Glendon pointed out indignantly. No doubt about it, he thought, this old boy is clean took over by his evil twin.

"No smokes, eh?" He sure looked like someone Glendon knew, but the Prophet couldn't name who.

Just as Glendon was about to snap a response that would shock this old sinner onto the Path of Righteousness, the thick-armed bartender said, "What'll it be?"

"Oh, gimme a beer," said the Prophet. He pulled his final dollar from his pocket.

"Comin' up."

"You wouldn't wanna buy me a refill, would you, pal?" asked the old drunk.

"I *already* give you a dollar," Glendon hissed.

No green gowns appeared, and the Prophet was drinking his draft with relief when he glanced at his image in the fancy mirror behind the cash register, a Man of God sitting next to a common drunk and slurping the devil's brew. His face warmed and reddened, his stomach suddenly churned, so he turned to the old boy and demanded: "How's come you to drink beer with that dollar I give you for breakfast, anyways?"

The red eyes faced him and he heard the man croak, "You *give* me the buck, so mind your own damn business!"

Glendon sensed that he had this sinner on the run. After he finished his beer – no sense wasting it – he really told him: "You got no business takin' folks' money that works hard for it. You're pullin' one a them beggar deals when you oughta be out workin' your ownself. Evil's flat took you is what's wrong and unless you wash in the Blood of the Lamb . . ."

For a second, Glendon didn't realize what had happened – the sudden shock – and by the time he did, the old boy had socked him a second time and was grappling with him, had him down in fact. He was strong for a skinny old weasel, or something was weakening Glendon, because the drunk – cap still firmly awry on his head – had the Prophet pinned to the floor while the saloon's other patrons laughed and shouted. Above him, Glendon registered only the flaring eyes and ghastly face of the man like sin itself.

It was humiliating because no matter how the Prophet bucked and surged, the old drunk stuck to him, and the laughter of those other drunkards burned his ears. Determined to teach this sinner a lesson, Glendon sucked in his breath for a decisive burst when, suddenly, he recognized the face snorting above his: it was the very one he had seen in his brass doorknob that first day, his own evil twin's, and that dark brother had him now as surely as Cain had Abel. Glendon Leroy Stone began to pray as he never had before.

THE GREAT NEW-AGE CAPER

Dunc he swaggered into the Tejon Club that afternoon a-wearin' this cap with "God, Guns, and Guts Made America Great" printed on the front.

Whenever I seen it, I said, "They give you the wrong hat there, Duncan."

"Wrong hat?" he said.

"Yeah, in your case, it oughta be 'God, Guns, and *Gut* . . .'"

That give the boys a laugh, but ol' Dunc he just grunted, "Eat shit."

The next thing you know, though, we was talkin' guns because Duncan claimed he'd bought him this fancy .30-06. He said he was gonna take it up to Greenhorn Mountain come huntin' season and bag him a buck. "I gotta get my deer, see," he said, quite the outdoorsman.

Well, he hadn't bagged nothin' but a six-pack at the Liquor Barn in years. I knew he wasn't no hunter, but he gets on these kicks and purty soon he takes to believin' his own bullshit. Around Oildale, ever' guy has to at least claim to be a deer hunter, seems like, or he ain't a real man.

Anyways, Big Dunc not only couldn't walk up a anthill without needin' oxygen, but he couldn't shoot worth a shit either, so I said, "I been out to the target range with you a time or two, Dunc, and the safest place to be is in front a the target. You couldn't hit a elephant with birdshot."

"Your ass!" he snorted. "Back in the Army I'uz a damn sharpshooter, see. The best in my damn outfit."

Bob Don that was slightly of the liberal persuasion like all your college types, he piped up, "What do you guys need with guns anyway? Insecure? Penis envy?"

"Huh?" said Dunc, a typical comeback. "What's that penis shit?"

"We need 'em because our forefathers told us to, Bundy," I responded. "It's in the Constitution, by the way!" I wasn't takin' no lip off of him.

"You need a musket, then, that's what our forefathers were talking about, not machine guns or automatic pistols or semiautomatic rifles. Those didn't even exist when they wrote the Bill of Rights."

"Oh, yeah," snapped Duncan. He was really on his toes.

"Why don't you guys knock it off?" urged Earl. He'd heard us on this subject before.

"They never said that, they said *firearms*," I pointed out.

"They said the right to bear arms, *period*, if you want to be technical, and arms in those days meant muzzle-loaders."

"Oh, balls!" I said. Your liberals won't talk reasonable.

"Well, I'm a-gonna get me my buck, see," groused Duncan into his beer. "And I'll carry all the damn guns I want."

Earl that run the joint, he slid out the pump .12-gauge shotgun he kept under the bar, then the .357 magnum he had in the slot by the cash drawer, and he said, "You guys shut the fuck up." He never did nothin' but show 'em to us, but he made his point. He was tryin' to watch the news on TV.

We shut up and Earl put his hardware away.

On the screen, some gal she was interviewin' this other gal that she was a ranger at this place where there was this big colony a barkin' seals – noisy as hell. Anyways, that ranger gal she grinned into the camera and said, "The bull elephant seals spend most of their waking hours trying to mate with the cows."

Big Dunc that was slurpin' a brew at the bar, he piped right up, "Just like me, see, them bulls, spend the whole damn day a-matin'."

Earl he couldn't resist: "Yeah, I seen some of the elephant seal cows you dated back in high school, Duncan. You and them bulls got more than double chins in common."

"Oh, yeah," snapped Dunc – his usual clever reply. Instead of arguin', he tried to divert attention away from his own pitiful teenage love life: "Oh, yeah! Well you shoulda seen the dogs ol' J.B. there usta take out, see."

He couldn't resist gettin' me into it, I guess, but I just ignored him. He's like talkin' to one a them elephant seals – all bark – so there ain't no point.

"Hey, Jerry Bill, guess who's back in town?" asked Bob Don Bundy, all pals again, and with this silly look on his face like a dog that found a fresh cat box.

I just shrugged. "Beats hell outta me," I answered. I mean, how do you answer a question like that?

"Earl?" asked Bob Don, tryin' to get somebody to give him a guess.

"How the hell do I know?" grunted Earl that runs the joint.

"Dunc?"

"Eat shit," grunted Big Dunc.

"Who?" I finally asked.

"Nedra Marie Dubarry Wilhite is who!"

"No lie!" I couldn't hardly believe it.

"Does Shoat know?" asked Earl. He was referrin' to ol' Nedra Marie's ex-husband that'd had her run outta town a few years back whenever he caught her and this young boyfriend dippin' into the till, among other things.

"She better hope not," I said. That's a fact because ol' Shoat's tough as a Mexican family – and that's *damn* tough.

Bob Don he's still grinnin'. "And guess what else I heard?"

Dunc cut the cheese.

"Is that your guess?" asked Bundy.

"That's the smartest thing you'll hear from him," I said.

"Eat shit, see," grunted Duncan.

"I heard she claims she's a *medium* now," said Bob Don with a grin.

"I'd a said she'uz a large," grunted Big Dunc. " 'Specially her tits, see."

"Duncan," said Bob Don Bundy that graduated Bakersfield Junior College and worked in a office so he's a smart sucker, "you've got a mind like a racehorse. It runs best on a dirt track."

"Eat shit," come back that silver-tongued Dunc.

Earl he scratched his head and munched a handful a beer nuts. "What the hell kinda *medium* you talkin' about?"

"Well, I saw this ad in a little throwaway paper that had her picture in it and it said she was a 'New-Age Healer and Psychic' visiting from Texas."

"No shit?" I said. Me, I'd read in the newspaper about that New-Age deal.

"Yeah," he went on, "it said she's gonna give a free lecture at the Veterans' Memorial Hall tonight and she's a-gonna talk about fire walking. A tickler, I'd guess, to draw people in. You guys wanta go?"

"That ain't her favorite kinda tickler, see," snorted Dunc, that can come up with a goodun ever' once in a while. I had to laugh.

That encouraged Duncan, so he snapped that paper outta ol' Bob Don's hands, stared at it and chewed on the words a minute, then asked, "What the hell's a 'physic'?"

"It's what you need," answered Bob Don, grabbin' back his newspaper. "Any of you guys want to go hear Nedra Marie talk about fire walking?" he asked.

The Tejon Club it ain't but a short mile from the Vets' Hall, so I said, "Why not?"

"I don't get it. What it is she's supposed to do," said Earl.

Since I'd read about that New-Age scheme in the paper, I knew the answer to that one. "It's this latest deal to make money that they come up with, kinda like the old tent preachers but for rich folks."

"I still don't get it," admitted Earl.

"It's just that people are willing to pay for almost anything," Bob Don explained, "even the illusion that they're getting better or younger or stronger or some such when they know they aren't. In fact, that's when they pay the most."

"Those Yuppie deals got more money than good sense," I said.

"What I mean is what do they *do?*"

"Play with each other, see," Dunc grumped. I knew he didn't have a clue, but he wasn't too far off that time.

"All kinda silly stuff," I said. "Pretend they're someone else, do this Chinese shit, beat drums, play like they're babies . . ."

"Play doctor," interjected Dunc – one-track mind – but I ignored him and kept explainin' to Earl.

". . . mess with crystals, walk on fire, even take these high colonic deals."

"What's that, them 'high-colonic deals'?" asked Wylie Hillis that he'd just walked in. "It sounds rank to me," he added.

"That's an enema," said Bob Don.

"A *enema!* No shit?"

"Lotsa shit," grinned Dunc. He's on a damn roll, just full a cute remarks.

"It sounds crazy as hell to me," Earl grunted.

Just then the telephone rang and Earl he shuffled over and answered it. He got this grin on his face, then said, "Hey, Dunc, it's the war department."

Big tough Duncan flinched like someone'd hit him, and he whispered, "Tell her I just left, see."

"He just left," Earl said into the phone.

Still grinning, Earl held that phone away from his ear for what seemed like a long time and we could all hear this midget voice buzzin', then he hung up. "She says the insurance man's at the place and you was s'posed to be home to talk to him and get your big ass home."

"Oh, yeah!" said Dunc, real defiant. But he was slidin' off his stool and suckin' down the last dregs of his draft. A second later he scooted out the door.

"By damn," grinned Wylie Hillis, "ol' Dunc's sure got that woman under control," and we all had a laugh.

"Gettin' back to that Nedra Marie Dubarry Wilhite deal, we oughta at least go see what's up," I suggested.

"Let's do it," grinned Earl.

When me and Earl and Bob Don we seen her onstage, she looked younger than a few years back. I believe she'd had ever'thing lifted that'd go up. "Gol dang," said Earl, "that ol' hide's lookin' prime!"

Well, there was this funny music playin' and the hall it was dim whenever ol' Nedra Marie she walked out in a semi-see-through gauze gown into these blue and red lights. The first thing she done was announce that her "eternal name," as she called it, was "the Very Right Reverend Doctor Ramadama" and that she was this "Ascended Master" deal and that she'd had these six past lives: she'd been a princess and a king and a wizard and a priestess and a queen and a Aztec virgin. "I figgered it'uz about that far back since she'uz a virgin," I said.

Bob Don sneered, "I wonder if she was homecoming queen too?"

Ol' Earl he whispered, "She never mentioned that she'd been a crook and stole that money from Shoat Wilhite."

"Nobody ever seems to remember being a hooker or a gravedigger or a day laborer," hissed Bob Don. "They were all kings and queens and high powers."

"Me too," I grinned.

"You're still a queen," Earl grinned real evil when he said that and I had to laugh.

Anyways, ol' Very Right Reverend Doctor Ramadama she give a long talk all about this "empowerment" deal and how a new age it was comin' and everyone was gettin' stronger and spirits they was fixin' to talk to us. She got me to laughin' whenever she flashed this slide on the screen a her standin' out in the country and there was this streak on the picture like her camera leaked light. "That," she pointed out, "is a wood nymph that led me to the trees. She's the fairy that dwells in my clan's power spot there and gives me strength to share my enlightenment with you."

Earl he'uz was laughin' too. "That streak it looks like the time we turned the lights out at the club and lit one of Dunc's farts," he pointed out.

It really did, and ol' Bob Don he said, "That's Dunc's power spot."

"Besides, we brung our own fairy with us," I said to Earl and we both poked Bob Don.

"Screw you guys," he grinned. This was better'n a damn vaudeville show. We got a lotta dirty looks for laughin', but it seemed like nobody wanted to tangle with us 'cause nobody said nothin'.

Pretty soon the Very Right Reverend, she advised the folks there, "You must activate your kundalini."

"Do what?" asked Earl.

"Activate your wienie," said Bob Don.

Earl grinned. "Hell, I could go that."

"That's exactly what ol' Earl's wife wants him to do," I added.

What ol' Ramadama – I like that name – never said was that she was workin' on gettin' rich. Her folks was peddlin' all kindsa shit in the lobby: crystal rocks and these funny cards with pictures on 'em and calendars and tapes and books – you name it.

Best of all, though, she said that the very next afternoon this young guy that never had but one name, OmAr (no shit, he really spelled it that way with two capitals – I seen it on a sign in the lobby), he'uz fixin' to walk on fire and show other folks how to do it and that they'd get real brave and real successful if they just done like he done. But, of course, it was gonna cost some hard cash.

See, it'uz like them ol' deals at the carnival that they let you in the tent to see the good-lookin' dancin' gals for a quarter, but if you wanted to see 'em buck naked, you had to shell out another four bits and go behind the curtain. When you did, it was their mother or grandmother that stood there, naked and ugly and bored.

Anyways, the audience it was fulla young, kinda rich-lookin' folks and it seemed like they all had stars in their eyes and drool on their chins. It'uz like goin' to the Assembly of God for a revival, seein' them glazed eyes, hearin' them shouts of "Yes! Yes!"

Whenever ol' Ramadama introduced OmAr, this expensive-lookin' young guy next to me, he said to the gal next to him, "OmAr was a Druid priest who advised King Arthur!" That gal she blinked her eyes, all thrilled, and she said, "I heard he was born at Stonehedge."

"No," interrupted this other gal that she overheard 'em, "I heard he just appeared on the summit of Mount Shasta and Ramadama transported him down with psychic energy."

"Ohhh," cooed the first gal.

"Oh, bullshit," said Earl. Then he added, "I recollect that he usta be a tentmaker back when I'uz in high school – usta activate my wienie most mornin's." Me and Bob Don broke up.

"If he *is* OmAr the Tentmaker, then I got to know him real good back in high school too," I chuckled.

"Who didn't?" agreed Bob Don. "This really is a goofy bunch of people, isn't it? It looks like they'll believe anything Nedra Marie tells them."

Well, dopey or gullible or whatever they was, them folks had filled the parkin' lot with all these big fancy German and Japanese cars. It looked like to me they had more money than good sense, and wasn't no one in cowboy boots but us three from the club. I guess we looked strange to them, what with the way some of 'em stared at us, then real quick averted their eyes if we caught 'em. We musta been hard-lookin' to them.

The next day I'uz in the club after work talkin' to Wylie Hillis. I told him about that fire-walkin' deal and how it'uz supposed to give folks power.

"Far walkin'," he spit, then shook his head. "Some folks don't have brains enough to pour piss outta a boot." He looked real disgusted for a minute, then he said, "I'll tell ya, J.B., I recollect one time at a tent meetin' back in Fayetteville I seen these ol' boys that was dancin' with *snakes* in their mouths. They said God give 'em *par*. In fact, they thought they was real parful, but this one ol' boy he got bit and died deader'n a turd. I b'lieve he'uz a tad less parful than the snake. Is that what that far-walking deal does?"

"We'll see. I think maybe you hit it on the head, though. This's just a way those Yuppie deals can act like Pentecostals without feelin' guilty."

"Ya reckon?" grinned Wylie.

That next evenin', there was another crowd at the auditorium for the fire walkin' and I couldn't resist. There'uz a goofy mix a folks wanderin' from the parkin' lot – heavy gals in mu-mus and skinny guys in them designer jeans, thin gals in these pants suits and fat guys in what looked like robes. Before I ever even got inside, though, I seen this one ol' boy maybe my age – no spring chicken – and he'uz dressed like one a them San Francisco hippies. Wellsir, he'uz a standing right in front a the door in one a them funny colored T-shirts and a bandana on his long hair; his eyes they looked like pinwheels and he'uz a-preachin' to whoever's dumb enough to listen, and I was. But just for a minute.

"Free the Oakland Five! We have to like legalize our sacramental LSD," he said. "LSD is like derived from living plants and it is like our brothers in the vegetable kingdom talking to us humans. It *must* be legalized! It like *must* be! All power to the people! Free the Oakland Five!"

He looked crazier'n a three-peckered goat to me, what with his little pointy beard and all. "Hey, pal," I said to him.

"What, man?"

"Free the Indianapolis Five Hundred!" I said, then I winked, made one a them V-for-victory deals with my fingers, and walked away.

"Right on!" he called after me.

Anyways, at the box office, I found out you could watch the fire walkin' for twenty bucks, but it cost another century note if'n you wanted to trot the coals. I said no thanks on that hundred-bucks part, and I damned near give up and went home before they got to the hot stuff because for a good two hours the Very Reverend Doctor Boobs and ol' OmAr they just talked and preached and cajoled a few more bills from the faithful, but finally ever'one paraded outside to the lawn behind the hall and there was this shallow pit, maybe ten or twelve foot long, and it was filled with what looked like charcoal briquettes. They looked damn hot to me. At the far end, somebody'd filled a kid's plastic wadin' pool with water.

First let me tell you that ol' OmAr, he had one a them A-rab towel deals wrapped around his head, and he was wearin' this gown that it looked like my wife Heddy's housecoat. When he had apprentice fire walkers all assembled at one end of the pit and was givin' 'em a pep talk, he swished his arms all around in that housecoat like a damn butterfly.

Me, I'uz with the spectators lined up along the side to watch folks hike them coals. And guess who I all of a sudden noticed in the big crowd with me: Shoat Wilhite. He seen me too, so we made our ways to each other, shook hands and exchanged howdies. He's a good ol' boy, Shoat, and I'uz really glad to see him. He had this other young guy in a suit and tie with him and he introduced him as Jim Fishman, his attorney.

"Jim and I intend to have a word or two with my ex-wife," he told me, and his eyes they went all hard and cold. "I warned her way back when never to come back here, but I guess she thought I was kiddin'. I wasn't." Me, I was glad I wasn't the one he'uz pissed at.

Just then all them apprentices they commenced chantin': "Cool, wet grass! Cool, wet grass!" and who should appear but the Very Right Reverend Ramadama herownself. She exchanged a few inspirational words with the suckers, then turned and announced to all of us, "I shall defy the great flames!"

There wasn't no flames but, like I said, them coals looked hot enough.

Ramadama she swirled around and begun callin', "Cool, wet grass! Cool, wet grass!" and she d'rectly stepped right onto the coals just as she noticed Shoat a-glarin' at her. She forgot the cool grass and hesitated on them hot coals, almost stumbled, then she said, "Ouuu! Owww! Eeee!" and hopped into that wadin' pool as quick as she could, her face suddenly lookin' old, like the one on that naked lady at the carnival all them years ago. Shoat and Jim they buttonholed her right now and marched her – she'uz limpin' some – back toward the hall.

A lotta the spectators they was laughin', and them apprentices they never looked quite so confident all of a sudden. In fact, maybe half of 'em commenced marchin' away despite ol' OmAr's protests: "Find your center! Don't surrender to fear. Empower yourself! Find your cool center!"

Apparently a bunch of 'em thought they'd find their centers somewheres else, because they departed.

OmAr he done the best he could to talk folks into crossin' them coals, walkin' across a couple a times real fast hisownself, but only a few turned their faces to stone and hurried across, sayin' "Cool, wet grass," then jumpin' into that wadin' pool. The others just drifted away into darkness. The edge had went from the evenin' and the big show it petered out d'rectly. Ol' OmAr he looked like he could use a tentmaker of his own.

Shoat come in the club that next long, hot afternoon and announced, "My ex-wife's gone and her fancy man's packin' up this afternoon. She won't be back . . . unless she wants to see the inside of the jailhouse."

"Have a brew, pard'," I said, and he accepted.

Not fifteen minutes later here come my boy Craig and his pal Junior and they'uz and laughin' to beat hell. "Hey, Dad," Craig called. "Me and

Junior went over to the auditorium after school to watch them close up that fire-walking pit and pack up." (I'd told him what I'd seen the night before and he'uz disappointed he never got to see the fire walkin'.) "Anyway, that Arab guy took his shoes off for some reason, so we took them and put them on the hood of a car in middle of that big parking lot. We wanted to see if he could walk barefoot across the hot blacktop like we do all the time." He grinned. "He couldn't."

Him and Junior commenced hoppin' on one foot then the other, callin', "Ouch! Eeek! Ohhh!" gigglin' and pokin' each other. Then ol' Craig he said, "Maybe he forgot to say, 'Cool, wet grass.' You know what? Me and Junior ought to start a pavement-walking class, sort of empower people to walk barefooted in Oildale during the summer the way all the kids do."

"You got it, son," I grinned, real proud. That boy was gonna be rich some day.

"Hey," said Bob Don real serious. "You guys shouldn't make fun of psychics like that. Look what they taught me," and he real quick showed us a crystal and popped it into his mouth and begun crunchin' it. Hell, I thought he'd went nuts – he was gonna break his damn teeth – then he grinned and showed us a plastic bag labeled Rock Candy. "Care for some?" he asked the boys.

While we'uz helpin' ourselves, Earl he got this real serious look on his puss and he turned to Craig and Junior. "Listen, you young bucks," he told 'em, "you better hope you never pissed off that A-rab. If there's anyone kids your age don't wanta piss off it's Omar the Tentmaker. Without him, your whole day might be ruined. Am I right, fellers?" he asked us old poops.

"Oh, yeah," we agreed.

Then I added, "All but 'cept Duncan. He might've had guns, God, and guts, but he only had him a little pup tent and the pup was usually asleep."

While ever'one else was laughin', that silver-tongued Big Dunc grunted, "Eat shit."

HOME TO AMERICA

Hideko hid. She had heard her brothers, Warren and Charles, talking the night before, heard them discuss the big policeman who was coming to get them, and the torture chamber to which they were being taken. She heard that little girls would be roasted and eaten, so Hideko hid, burying herself deep in the dirty clothes bin under soiled garments they could not take with them.

When the U.S. marshal arrived, Mother and Father searched frantically for her, their own sadness and rage rendering their efforts frenzied and random. "I think I know where she is," Charles finally volunteered, then he led them to the bin. Through the muffling laundry Hideko heard people approach, knowing only that it was the man who roasted little girls, and that he was near, near.

"What's wrong with her, Miz Takeda?" the marshal asked. He was a large, pale man with graying blond hair, who seemed vaguely uncertain about Hideko's closed-eyed terror. "I ain't gonna hurt you, honey," he soothed, trying to touch her, but she cringed.

Mother's own voice was tight and angry. "You're taking her, us, away from home, and you ask what's the matter. She's scared, that's what!" Then, to Hideko: "Poor baby. Poor, poor baby. Momma's with you. Momma's with you." Mother picked her up.

The pale-eyed man turned to Father. "Mr. Takeda, I don't like this either. I don't believe you folks're spies like they say, but I got my job to do. I really do."

Father, who was not much given to talk, nodded. "Yeah," he said.

The truck honked, causing the marshal to jump. "Sorry to rush you folks, but we got to get to town. Can I help you carry your things?"

"The order said we can take only what we can carry," Mother snapped, "so we'll carry it." Each of the boys lifted two bundles, and Warren wore his old Boy Scouts of America knapsack filled with sports magazines and books. Father carried four large bags – his and Mother's – and Mother carried Hideko and Hideko's own small bundle. Hideko, her eyes tightly shut, clasped only Raggedy Anne to her small breast.

Outside, in the yard, Mr. and Mrs. Epp, who owned the farm across the road, stood with Reverend Meyer, who'd just driven up. "Let me help," Mr. Epp volunteered, taking two of the bags from Father. Mrs. Epp put her arm around Mother, and both women immediately began weeping.

As they tossed the bags into the military truck, seeing two other families huddled in the darkness of the covered bed, Mr. Epp heard the pimply driver mutter something about "lousy Japs." He rushed to the cab and thrust his meaty arm through the window. "Son," he said with a low, quivering voice, his face flushed, "you use that word again and I'll break your goddamn neck!"

The marshal hurried to the cab, told the driver to keep his mouth shut, then eased Mr. Epp away.

They climbed into the truck, and Mr. Epp reached up to shake Father's hand. "Mas," he said, "we'll look after your place for you. Don't worry. Just take care of yourself and Lucy and the kids." Reverend Meyer advised them to have faith during these difficult times; "God hasn't forgotten you." Then they were bouncing out the country road toward town, sitting near the open, sunny end of the truck's bed.

"I wouldn't sit there," said a man from the depths of the truck. Father recognized him without knowing his name because the man displayed sheep every year at the county fair.

"Why not?" Father asked.

"They're throwing things in the truck. You wait, they'll do it again."

Father and Mother moved into the back with the other families, next to the cab. Warren and Charles stayed at the open end until Father spoke sharply to them, then they reluctantly joined everyone else. Hideko, curled on Mother's lap, clasped Raggedy and kept her eyes shut; she was trembling.

"Lucy?" It was Emily Kozasa. She had been crying, her eyes red and swollen. Next to her sat her aging, blind aunt who spoke no English, so Mother answered in Japanese. The men began talking too, speculating on where they were going, their voices quiet, yet harsh. Ed Kozasa said it looked like this was going to be a great growing year, but . . . The sheep man shrugged. "Or a great dying year," he muttered, and his wife poked him, nodding toward the children.

They could tell they were nearing town, for the farms they could see out the truck's back were smaller, and a few billboards sprouted along the road. The truck jolted to a halt at a crossroad, and there was a sudden hollow thunk! thunk! on its canvas sides; a clod flew through the open back and exploded on the floor. Warren and Charles sprinted to the open end just as high-pitched voices shouted: "Dirty Japs! Dirty shittin' Japs!"

"I see you, Arnie Presley!" Warren shouted. "I'll beat hell out of you when we get home!"

The truck jerked away from the stop sign, and Mother, her voice shocked, said, "Warren Ken Takeda! Who taught you to talk that way?"

"Do you know who that was?" Warren answered tightly. "It was that dumb Arnie Presley and his brothers. I'll kick his butt."

"Sit down," Father said, and the boys sat.

"I'll talk to you about this tonight, Warren," Mother continued, but Warren seemed not to hear her. He kept repeating to himself: "That stupid Arnie Presley."

"It really was Presley, Mom," Charles piped in. "I saw him too."

"That'll be enough from you, Charles. We'll talk about it at ho . . . we'll talk about it tonight." Mother bit her lip, and squeezed her silent, shut-eyed daughter.

Downtown, everyone climbed from the truck with their baggage. There were nearly twenty families, their belongings piled on the sidewalk next to a worn-looking bus. Around them crowded townspeople, neighbors, and a line of soldiers holding rifles with bayonets. The spectators were quiet mostly, talking among themselves: farmers, business people, many children among them. Seeing Hideko clinging to Mother, one older woman remarked to her husband, "You have to admit, they're cute when they're little."

A few younger men, cigarette packs rolled into the short sleeves of their T-shirts, explained to an older marshal why they should be allowed to hang "just one Jap" as an example. The marshal responded loudly, "I understand how you boys feel, but the rule of law has to be observed." With that, the leader of the young men flung a tattooed arm past the marshal and struck an old man who stood with his back to him. The old man's glasses and hat were knocked to the ground, his bundle bounced away, but he remained on his feet, while his tattooed assailant was restrained and led away by his friends, several of them shouting, "Remember Pearl Harbor!"

Another marshal, afraid of more incidents, quickly read the roster and urged people into the old bus.

Just as Warren tossed his bundles into the bus's baggage compartment, he felt a tap on his shoulder and, for a moment, expected a fist to smack his jaw. He turned and faced Coach Nizibian from the high school. "We're really gonna miss you this year, Scooter," the coach told him. "There goes our championship."

"Tell the guys I said so long," Warren rasped, his voice turning soft. "And tell that punk Arnie Presley I'm gonna pound the pud out of him when I get back."

"We're really gonna miss you," Coach said again, his handshake lingering, his own voice softening.

"Charley," Coach smiled, rumpling Charles's hair, "you let Scooter teach you a few moves. I'm gonna count on you in three or four years.

Mr. Takeda, these're fine boys." He shook Father's hand. "And I want you to know how sorry I am, and ashamed." Both men's eyes glistened.

Mother and Hideko were already in the bus when Father and the boys joined them. Just as they found seats and settled, they heard a rumpus outside. A large man in a business suit was arguing with the U.S. marshals. "I just wanta say a few words . . ." he urged, but the marshals said no. A man sitting behind the Takedas – Father recognized him as Mr. Takeuchi, who owned a small market in town – growled that the loud man was Harry Livingstone, president of the local chapter of the Native Sons of the Golden West. "He's a big windbag," Mr. Takeuchi added.

The bus was started and two soldiers who looked very young and frightened carried their rifles in and sat in front seats next to two marshals. From outside the bus, just as it began to move, Livingstone shouted: "We don't want you Nips back ever!" And many of the spectators who had seemed merely curious before were suddenly screaming and shouting, even throwing a few rocks and clods, their faces unrecognizable as the bus picked up speed. "Here we go," Mother sighed. Hideko, trembling on Mother's lap, did not open her eyes.

They arrived at the relocation camp late and were told they'd be processed the next day. It was dark, but they could clearly see the racetrack and the maze of stables behind it and the high wire fence around it, and they could smell the somehow comforting aroma of horse manure. Everyone stood as though stunned – eyes furtive and frightened – until soldiers marched them into a smaller, penned yard and building – "Holding Area One" the sergeant called it.

Mother carried Hideko, whose eyes remained tightly shut, into the barracks. It was empty and echoing, containing only metal cots without mattresses. Everyone was tired and hungry, but they bustled about, trying to make the best of things. One old man suddenly began shouting over and over that they were going to be shot, but he calmed quickly when friends comforted him. A soldier stood at the door of the building and announced that one member of each family could come to the mess to collect rations. For a moment no one moved. Was this the firing squad? Then slowly people began wandering toward the open door which framed the barbed-wire fence outside.

Sitting on the bare springs of a cot, Mother rocked Hideko, purred to her: "It's all right now, baby. It's all right," until finally Hideko stirred, sitting up though still leaning on Mother's chest and clasping Raggedy. She opened her bright brown eyes and looked down the hollow building and out the open doorway.

"Mommy," she asked quietly, "when are we going home . . . to America?"

Mother jolted, and her eyes at first seemed blank, then she focused on their surroundings. "Home," she said. "I'm not sure where that is anymore."

Charles glanced at his older brother, made a face, then grinned, but Warren poked him. He understood the gravity in his mother's voice, and it frightened him.

Father reached out and touched Mother's arm, saying only, "Hon' . . ."

Her chin was suddenly quivering, and she gazed stonily ahead. "No, I mean it! I wonder if we've ever *really* been home in America!"

Father's voice was certain when he replied, "This is our land, hon'. Ours. We were born here. Our folks helped make it what it is. We've got as much claim to it as anyone. Don't let those damned racists ruin it for you."

Her expression did not change. "Our land," she said, as she gazed down the long barracks toward barbs clustered like thorns on the wire enclosing them.

RISING ACTION

I am pushing a shopping cart through Safeway behind my mother when another, younger woman wearing white slacks strolls up the aisle ahead of us. Gazing at her slim flanks, I note VPL – the beguiling Visible Panty Line – and, while I am far from certain exactly what nestles within that outlined territory, my own Levi's are suddenly the scene of rising action. My pace slows and soon I cease walking at all.

Ahead, the VPL has stopped to inspect a product, so I can keep her flanks in view. Beneath those slacks, she wears white panties, and I can see her clad only in them, beckoning. Except for an occasional sloppy sitter at school, I've never seen any occupied underwear, although the silken empties at a women's lingerie display can send me breathless in search of a lockable door. My imagination, unlimited by knowledge, veers toward unspeakable realms.

I begin a slow friction-strut, tasting my own breath. My mother has continued her own measured stroll, unaware of the momentous event within my Levi's. "Ernest, will you *please* catch up!" Her voice sears me. I manage to ease beside her and she demands, "Why are you *walking* so funny and why were you *looking* so funny at that lady? Do you know her?"

My mouth opens, but no sound emerges. I try again, croaking, "Ahhh . . . no . . . I guess."

"Why are you *talking* so funny? I don't know what's wrong with you. Look how you're standing! I'm going to take you to Doctor Marconcini," she admonishes, and immediately I see my meager artillery lying limp and bloody on one table, me singing countertenor on another, while our family doctor stands nearby holding a red scalpel.

Mom turns to the VPL woman, who is passing, smiles, and shakes her head, "Boys!"

The white panties nod and smile back, then glance at me. Despite the scalpel scene, I am certain that I see interest in those knowing eyes, and I think of the bathroom and the lock on its door as I see her hips slide around the corner into another aisle. I am taking her there, rolling in the bathtub with her, wrestling in the clothes hamper, romping on the commode.

"Will you come *on*. And *stop* walking so funny. Did you hurt yourself at school?"

I struggle to keep up, prancing slowly like a crane on the hunt, a rapturous dance.

The next day after junior varsity football practice, Buzzer Gaona – proprietor of the ninth grade's only mustache – announces to Bobby Silva and me, "Hey, ladies that use those Kotex deals, they do it, man."

I have seen a Kotex box in our bathroom, so I demand, "Who told *you?*"

"Everybody knows that, don't they, Silva?"

Bobby is not certain. "I . . . guess," he stammers.

"I sneaked in the girls' bathroom at school and found some, man." Buzzer nods knowingly. "Some of the girls at school, they done it. If your mother uses 'em, she done it too, man."

"You better watch it," I warn.

"Everybody's mother done it at least once."

Silva looks troubled. "Maybe it was a mistake," he pleads. "Maybe mine didn't *know*."

"Some of 'em *like* it, man."

"You better watch it, Gaona," I growl, outrage pushing me toward recklessness.

He ignores me. "Mrs. Calloway done it, man. She gots two babies, don't she?" Mrs. Calloway is the women's P.E. teacher at the high school. Her tan legs have entwined me in dreams. Despite my lingering anger, there is rising action.

"Does she like it, do you think?" asks Silva.

"Heck, yeah, man. She gots them big jugs. They get those from doin' it all the time."

"No lie? You mean all the girls with big boobs do it?" asks Silva.

"Heck, yeah, man. They *like* it."

My mother is flat-chested, so I breathe more easily in spite of the rising action. I will not have to fight the formidable Gaona.

"Anyway, I was just kiddin' about your mothers, man," he adds with a tight laugh. "I got you guys pissed, huh?"

"No way," I insist.

A week later, I am leaning against the wall of the gym during lunch hour with Silva and Gaona. After a dull silence, Buzzer announces, "Brandy done it, man."

"Brandy did it?" I ask, a little stunned. Bedelia "Brandy" Vigil, a busty classmate, has been dating varsity football players. She is cute and the very chance that she might be doing it . . . well, action rises. In my mind I can suddenly see her soft brown body involved with mine. My breathing quickens. "I gotta go," I announce.

"This guy on the varsity, he told me he felt her up, man."

Action continues rising because, although I'm not exactly certain *how* it's done, I can see her doing it with the team, all of them, with the team manager, even with the bald-headed coach, and with me, rolling around the locker room among the towels. "See you guys," I choke.

These images are sinful, so next day I must go to confession. Guilt has lately burdened me. Brother Mario, our religion teacher, has been stressing what he calls evil thoughts, sins of self-abuse and inevitable damnation. "You are being tested," he warns, and his eyes always seem to meet mine. "Those who abuse their flesh in this world will have it *stripped* from them *eternally* in the next, *burned* and *twisted* and *torn*." He seems to relish each word like rare beef.

"When evil thoughts invade and you find yourself in the near occasion of sin," he advises, his eyes boring into me as though he can see the scene of Brandy and me that I am even then imagining, "a sincere Hail Mary will ease temptation."

But when evil thoughts encroach, I become the Shakespeare of eroticism and forget his advice entirely, then end up uttering a remorseful Act of Contrition instead of a prophylactic Hail Mary. As a result, each week I have been entering the confessional to cleanse myself – if only temporarily – of sin.

It is roulette with eternity, since I often manage only a few hours of sanctity before rising action sweeps me back toward flesh eternally burned and twisted and torn. I walk in fear of lightning bolts and runaway cars, of rabid dogs and wayward bullets, those dangers that might pluck me unconfessed at some capricious moment, full of sin and doomed. And that means I must regularly close a dark confessional door to earn a few minutes or hours of safety from Hell, then begin the cycle again – literally a spiritual rat on a treadmill to eternity.

This sacrament is vital, but there are necessary strategies. First of all, avoid certain priests: Father Riley, Father Perdue, Father Garcia, and Father Duggan – they are lecturers and they will expose you to a half-hour of purgatory at every opportunity. Seek priests reputed to be gentle, even somnolent, confessors – old Father Flaherty or Father Cronin or Father Dominguez; those three are famous among adolescent males because they rarely bother to admonish, only grunt, assign three Hail Marys, and offer absolution. Second, try not to engage any one priest too frequently so that he doesn't become familiar and recognize your habitual sins. Travel from parish to parish if necessary, even across town to St. Joseph's or Guadalupe or Perpetual Help in order to evade detection. Third, *never never never* confess to a missionary priest.

In search of Father Dominguez, I take a city bus all the way to Our Lady of Guadalupe Church for confession. The line of those waiting to unburden themselves is long and after nearly half an hour I realize that each individual seems to be spending considerable time in the booth. More ominous still, as I move closer I am hearing the dangerous rumbling of an unfamiliar voice from within those three darkened doors. I debate whether to leave and catch a bus to St. Joseph's in the hope of finding Father Cronin, but time is short; I could never make it. Well, I can leave – except that everyone else would notice my belated departure and someone would surely recognize me, perhaps tell my mother.

Quickly, I hatch a plan: I'll groan softly a few times, then more loudly, and grab my stomach. I'll double over slightly, then limp toward the bathroom in the vestibule. From there I can sprint to freedom. I have not avoided exposure for so long without resourcefulness, and this plan ranks with the best. I begin with a few short, soft moans, hurrying because I am only two people away from the now ominous confessional door. Immediately, I feel a strong tap on my shoulder and hear a familiar voice: "What's wrong, Ernest? Are you ill?" It is Dr. Marconcini who has, unnoticed, been in line behind me.

"No . . . no, sir," I improvise, "just gas."

"Do you want an antacid?"

"No, sir."

"You eat too fast," he adds, then returns to his place.

I am stuck now. I cannot flee. There is nothing left to do but quickly devise a plan for the confession itself, but just as my mind begins to churn, ashen-faced Billy Castro, an eighth grader I know slightly, emerges from the booth, rolls haggard eyes, and whispers the dreaded words, "A *missionary*, man!" He looks as though he has been burned and twisted and torn. Suddenly I really do feel sick, but it is too late. I am next and I must enter.

Kneeling in the darkness, I carefully plan my confession. I have become expert at hiding my most heinous offense. Employ unspecific terms to describe it and slip the explanations quickly into the midst of small sins. I line up the venial infractions, and decide where and how to obscure my great and repeated crime.

I am nervous but growing increasingly confident in my tested strategy – it has rarely failed me – when the small window slides open and finally I can get it over with. To begin, I acknowledge that I've had a nasty dream (the priest only grunts), that I've told a white lie to a friend (he grunts again), then I whisper quickly, slurring my words, "I have committed the sin of self-abuse, and I . . ."

"You have committed what?"

"I have committed the sin of self-abuse."

"What is this, this 'sin of self-abuse'? What sin is this?"

"Against the Sixth Commandment," I breathe.

"With yourself or others?" His tone has hardened.

Uh-oh! "Myself." I want to move on, so I add, "and I was late for mass once."

"What did you do?"

"I was just late."

"What did you do with *yourself?*" He is louder now, and I am afraid that those waiting outside can hear him, maybe even Dr. Marconcini.

"I played with myself," I gasp in a voice so faint that I am not certain that I hear it myself.

"Speak up!"

"Played with myself."

"Played with yourself? What does this mean?"

"Touched myself for pleasure," I mutter, using a term I learned in religion class.

"*Speak up!*"

I repeat so quickly that it sounds like one word. "Touchedmyselffor-pleasure."

"Touched yourself where?"

I gulp. "In the bathroom, mostly."

"Where on your *body?* And *speak up!*" I cringe at the sharpness of his tone.

I cannot immediately reply, so he adds, "Others are waiting."

"My private parts," I choke, wanting to flee, tensed for a sprint.

"Your *what?* You touch yourself *there* for pleasure, where God allows *only* procreation. Those are not *your* private parts, they are *God's* and you are abusing them! Do you spill your seed?"

Spill my seed? Oh, God . . .

"*Do you spill your seed?*" he demands.

"I guess."

"You *guess?* " His tone strips my flesh.

"Yes . . . I . . . do . . . spill . . . my . . . seed." My words are dead as clay.

"How old are you?" His voice has risen to a muted shout. Everyone is hearing this. Dr. Marconcini, I am certain, is scribbling notes.

"Fifteen," I whisper.

"Speak up!"

"Fifteen."

"And how often did you do this *terrible* thing?"

"Two times."

"Speak up!" His voice seems to echo through the church.

I have been in the confessional at least an hour – a world record – and I am despairing of ever escaping it. I will grow old here, that missionary shouting, *"Speak up!"* in my bruised ear, a great hoary beard caressing my knees, filling this small room until I suffocate. This is the anatomy of Hell. "Two times," I gasp.

"You did this *terrible* thing two times in just one week?"

"A day," I add as softly as human breath can escape.

"A *day!* A *DAY!* A *DAY!* You are a *ROTTEN* boy and you will *ROAST* in hell for your perversion!" People a block away are listening, I know, they are rushing from all directions to hear this, clustering in front of the church, a great grinning hoard, but I am so battered that by now I want only to accept what follows and escape.

I am willing to be castrated, to become a Trappist monk and to never speak again, to do *anything*. I will never again sin. I will never touch myself. I will never so much as *look* at a female, but please God, let me leave this booth. "I will give you absolution this time," fumes the priest, "but you had *better* turn your *rotten* life over to Our Lady or you will be cast into the flames where there is much moaning and gnashing of teeth!"

I am already moaning and gnashing my teeth, so when he assigns my penance and absolves me, I slink from the confessional, feeling the weight of eyes on my miserable, my doomed and utterly exposed form. I refuse to look up, for I am certain that spectators have now come in from the street to stare at me, that programs listing my various abuses are being sold at the door.

Eyes down, I slip into a pew and begin to say the rosary, my penance. I will not look up or around and, in the back of my mind, I have decided to remain in this pew until everyone else in the church has departed: I cannot face them, their sneers or their snickers.

"Hail Mary full of grace the Lord is with thee . . ." I am halfway through my third decade of prayers and beginning to calm somewhat when someone slips into the pew ahead of me. For a moment, I do not look up, then I do and realize that it is Brandy Vigil. She kneels and quietly prays. I lower my eyes, then lift them, my vision stopping just below her belt line where her sweet bottom lurks, an upside-down valentine in a tight red skirt, the near-occasion of sin placed there to tempt me, to ascertain whether this confession, this final chance at salvation, has been wasted, so I look down again, but in doing so I notice her slim brown ankles, one encircled by a golden chain. Something seems to pulse beneath that gold, and, just above it, the satin swelling of her calf twitches. Rising action.

I say three more rapid Hail Marys, but the passion does not abate. I add a Glory Be, yet the denim titillates and my breath shortens. I struggle through three more desperate Hail Marys. Then my eyes notice Brandy's VPL and I am seized by images of her lovely brown body with mine in a hammock, spinning, struggling together, slick with sweat.

When she stands and leaves, I remain kneeling, glazed with the knowledge that I am committing the gravest of all sins here in the gravest of all places, and that I must somehow return to that confessional if I am to avoid perdition. I squeeze my eyes closed, but all I can see is her anklet, her VPL. Finally, I stand and turn. The church is almost vacant. Near the entry loom those confessionals, three small doors, dark and apparently bare except for the middle one above which a small light is ignited, warning that the missionary lies in wait. Next to them, I behold the orange and red of an early sunset framed by the church's open front portal.

"ROTTEN!" still rings in my ears – that relentless judgment, that overwhelming force from which nothing is hidden, awaits my sin in the confessional, marshaling its prodigious power to finally refuse me absolution. I fear damnation, but I cannot this day return to that small dark box.

After a moment I swallow hard, then plunge out the door into the flaming world. I hesitate on the church's steps. It's not too late to return to the missionary, then I spy curvaceous Brandy Vigil standing across the street, perhaps waiting for a ride. She notices me and smiles, waves slightly. My breath catches and there is . . . there is gentle but undeniable rising action. I hesitate only a moment, then lift one hand and wave to her. "Hey, Brandy," I call with sudden abandon, "can I buy you a Coke?"

She smiles and nods, and without looking back I move from the church's portal toward the ruddy light of a larger world.

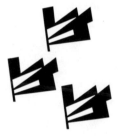

Driving with Gerry

I have never ridden in a pickup truck with Gerald W. Haslam while the busted speedometer glowed *o* and the radio twanged country music from a cracked speaker. But I can picture such a homely ride. The backdrop is a wheat-colored sun dipping down in the San Joaquin Valley. Road kills dot the littered highway, the paws of dogs and rabbits pointing toward heaven – a good sign. There are tumbleweeds snagged on fences, and in the furrowed fields, a tractor with its plume of black smoke. It's a good day for my spiffed-up friend, who is wearing a plaid cowboy shirt with imitation pearl snaps. A red kerchief around his neck flaps in the wind, and an ornate belt buckle with a silver dollar pressed in place winks in the sunlight. He smiles through his cologne – Brut or Aqua Velva – nothing fancy, but its sweetness enchants the valley. He turns to me and says, "*Amigo*, this is a hot-ass valley, and I love it!" He may or may not be sucking on a fresh piece of alfalfa. He will be nursing, though, a Pepsi, the sugary drink of all happy-go-lucky Okies.

Unfortunately, I haven't had the fortune of driving the San Joaquin Valley with Gerry. If I had, I might have heard a story – one completely fiction, or hearsay, or pulled from his childhood with his large bare feet planted in work and play. Perhaps we can soon drive south, down U.S. 99 with Bakersfield to our left and Taft and Oildale to the right, towns busting at their seams.

At a barbecue I once heard Gerry tell a story about playing football for Sacramento State, that is, warming the bench through a leafless fall. It was the late 1950s, and what better sight than young people crushing each other at the beginning of fall? The coach could have slapped his clipboard against his leg and shouted, "Haslam, get in there and do something! We're down by a hundred." But he didn't. Instead he asked for Gerry's jersey when a running back – a regular – tore his. So under the glare of stadium lights and ten thousand spectators, Gerry had to strip his jersey, his green and gold school pride, and hand it over to the coach.

Gerry Haslam is an essayist, regional historian, short story writer, and novelist. He is also a professor of English, a mystery to the local boys who grew up with him. Luckily we don't need a pickup truck on a valley highway to hear Gerry out. We have these pages, and the pages of his earlier books, to hear his stories of the valley. Gerry knows this place, in both its humanity and its geography, as he illustrated in his essays in *The Great Central Valley* – a book that at first appears to be coffee-table material but on closer reading is both thoughtful and scholarly. Better yet, he has explored this sun-brutal terrain first as a boy in Oildale and later as a man who has moved around the state of California and beyond. He has lived the valley through its people, from Mexican to Okie to Armenian to Portuguese to Yokut Indian – the wily crop of inhabitants who have assembled their lives and families in this valley. He knows the place, of this much I'm convinced, and his appreciation of valley life has deepened.

Haslam is a fine stylist and for many years I thought his prose had a literary kinship with that of Sherwood Anderson, a writer who lived what he wrote, with no qualms about being American – not European – in his stories. Both writers have scratched at new surfaces – Anderson at the flatness of Ohio and Haslam at the walled-in valley of central California. Both started humbly. Both served in the army, married, fathered children, and eked out a living first by labor and later by their wits. Finally, both felt tender about the experiences of everyday life. But while Anderson was primarily interested in the subliminal nature of his small-town characters, the understated and "grotesque" nature of manners, Haslam is drawn to portrayal of characters set in drama. Haslam is less interested in commentary than he is in a plain good story in which action precedes meaning. If we look at *Winesburg, Ohio*, we can see that Anderson was given over to large passages where the narrator describes the inner actions of his characters. He explained, truthfully, but seldom allowed the characters to speak for themselves. In turn, Haslam lets them speak in their valley drawl, even if what is mustered up by the characters, all poor and working class, some even drunk beyond memory, is outrageous gibberish. Haslam uses dialogue to his benefit. He lets them spit out their love, anger, craziness, and loneliness. This is the excitement of this new collection: talk that goes on and on while the characters with names like Haig, Flaco, Shorty, and Cleve tear up the world with life.

Haslam's voice can be reflective, wise, and delicately instructive. The opening story, "Condor Dreams," is a quiet tale of a father and son in an agricultural valley, the disappearance of nature, and a condor that serves as metaphor. It's about the passage of time: The father dies, pulled away by an unexpected flood in an arroyo. Years pass. The son becomes a boyish man who can't handle his father's farm. He still lives under the rule of memory and the prodding of his father's worker, Don Felipe, a half-Mexican, half-Yokuts Indian. The son is confused and full of vengeance that no weeping can resolve because the bank is taking over his farm. It's a telling reversal: A son finds self-knowledge and redemption through a sagacious worker, dusty with age.

In turn, Haslam can be whimsical and so funny that we may wonder whether what we are reading is from the same author. This is true of "Mal de Ojo," in which a boy sits at the feet of two Armenian brothers jabbing each other with offhand memories. The boy is mostly curious about Haig, the brother with an eye patch and crusty pronouncements of wisdom. Haig tells a story of one of the longest fistfights in small-town history: "We fought all the way up Van Ness Avenue to Blackstone, and then we fought for a mile down Blackstone. . . . The police stood back in awe to watch such a battle. Businesses closed. . . ." It's a confirmed yarn, though. The boy later realizes that Haig has been switching his patch from eye to eye, and that it's *he* – the boy – who is blind to trickery.

Haslam's stories are primarily the stories of men, some of them bright and courageous and some of them dim as twenty-watt bulbs. They drink a lot of beer and drive around, seldom getting anywhere. They sit in taverns, nursing beers, their lives used up in high school or early marriages. They hunker down on riverbanks where the cottonwoods hang over the water and muse over their lost youth. They speak about the ground-level advice that worked in the 1950s. Haslam has caught the pitch of these men – Okie or Mexican, farmer or farmworker, veteran or rowdy citizen – without parody. These are characters we know or have seen in passing, characters we make room for when they start to fight. In all their humor and craziness, in all their unexpected trials into manhood, there is a sadness that shadows our own lives, even if we're not from the valley and can't spit in a shallow river that pushes along on its own.

Gerry and I could jump into the cab of that pickup truck and take a wild ride through the valley. It would be early September, the almond trees letting loose their leaves and grape trays heavy with drying raisins. The sun is flush against the coastal mountains. A blackbird, big as a boot, sits on a wire and the Johnson grass has flattened from wind and the lack of rain. I look at the gauges: The speedometer won't flicker or the odometer roll to add up our miles. I turn to my friend and teasingly ask, "Gerry, what's this 'W' in your name mean when you write books?" He turns to me, imitation pearl snaps and all, and jokes, "Wily. Gerald 'Wily' Haslam."

Gary Soto
August 1993

ACKNOWLEDGMENTS

The author wishes to thank the editors of the following publications, where some of the stories originally appeared. All of the stories were copyrighted by the author in the year of original publication and are used here with his permission.

"The Killing Pen." *Tawte: A Journal of Texas Culture.* Summer 1975.
"Widder Maker." *Drilling.* December 1975.
"Home to America." *Sonoma Mandala.* Spring 1976.
"Medicine." *Scree.* Fall 1976.
"Return, Prodigal." *The Wages of Sin.* Duck Down Press, 1980.
"The Last Roundup." *Toward the Twenty-first Century.* Red Earth Press, 1981.
"Madstone." *Hawk Flights.* Seven Buffaloes Press, 1983.
"The Souvenir." *Cross Timbers Review.* Autumn 1984.
"Sojourner." *Unknown California.* Macmillan, 1985.
"The Condor." *Amapola.* 1986.
"Road Kill." AKA *Magazine.* Winter 1988.
"Rising Action." In *Eroticism: From Sublime to Grotesque.* California State University, Long Beach, 1989.
"It's Over." *Chiron Review.* Summer 1991.
"Romain Pettibone's Revenge." In *Contemporary American Satire II.* Exile Press, 1992.

WESTERN LITERATURE SERIES

Swimming Man Burning
by Terrence A. Kilpatrick

The Temptations of St. Ed and Brother S
by Frank Bergon

The Other California:
The Great Central Valley in Life and Letters
by Gerald W. Haslam

The Track of the Cat
by Walter Van Tilburg Clark

Condor Dreams and Other Fictions
by Gerald W. Haslam